Bantam Books by Patricia Sprinkle

Death of a Dunwoody Matron
A Mystery Bred in Buckhead
Deadly Secrets on the St. Johns

Deadly
Secrets
on the
St. Johns

Patricia Sprinkle

BANTAM BOOKS
New York Toronto London Sydney Auckland

DEADLY SECRETS ON THE ST. JOHNS

A Bantam Crime Line Book / September 1995

CRIME LINE and the portrayal of a boxed "cl" are trademarks of Bantam
Books, a division of Bantam Doubleday Dell Publishing Group, Inc.

ISBN 0-553-56857-4

Published simultaneously in the United States and Canada

Bantam Books are published by Bantam Books, a division of Bantam
Doubleday Dell Publishing Group, Inc. Its trademark, consisting of the
words "Bantam Books" and the portrayal of a rooster, is Registered in
U.S. Patent and Trademark Office and in other countries. Marca Reg-
istrada. Bantam Books, 1540 Broadway, New York, New York 10036.

PRINTED IN THE UNITED STATES OF AMERICA

OPM   0 9 8 7 6 5 4 3 2 1

Thanks

Writing a book about a place where you grew up is risky, especially when your family still lives there. They may need high walls and helicopter pads after this book comes out! But thanks Mama, Daddy, Priscilla and the other Apodacas, for the meals, memories, and bed you provided while I was researching this book.

Thanks to Dale Child, Marian Summerlin, Marjorie Beaufort, Allison King, and Jean Brinkman for talking about Jacksonville today, and to Ann Rose for helping me remember how it was—and for stories that led to Laura Grace. Thanks, Judi Howell and Margaret Parsons, for sharing the Park Lane. Thanks, Carol Harris and Arden Brugger in the Jacksonville Library's Florida and Genealogy Room, for helping me get the history right. Thanks, Dick Stratton, for describing the new Gator Bowl and suggesting a river chase. Thanks, Paula, Ann, Anne, Priscilla, and Daddy, for reading the manuscript. Thanks, mystery readers of Tallahassee, for the bugs! And thanks, Kate Miciak, for seeing the manuscript's holes and weaknesses and helping me fix them. What I got right is due to all of you. What I missed is my own fault.

Classmates and friends who look for yourselves and each other in this book: all these characters are fictional—and ten years younger than we are! But if you find someone who sounds familiar, perhaps I've captured, to a small degree, the delightful ambiance that is Jacksonville.

The Characters

THE L'ARKEN FAMILY:

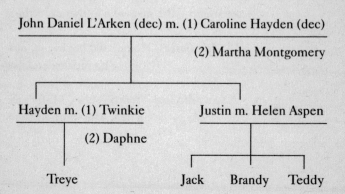

John Daniel L'Arken (dec) m. (1) Caroline Hayden (dec)

(2) Martha Montgomery

Hayden m. (1) Twinkie

(2) Daphne

Treye

Justin m. Helen Aspen

Jack   Brandy   Teddy

OTHER L'ARKEN RELATIVES:

Laura Grace Hayden – Caroline's sister who now lives with Martha

Charlotte Holmes Aspen – Helen's mother

LIFETIME FRIENDS AND ACQUAINTANCES:

Libba Weldon – a friend in need and a friend in deed

Sparrow Weldon – not only Libba's daughter, but Jack's girlfriend

Muffy Merriwether – a flirt with secrets, not all of them her own

Rob Wilmer – the man who knows everything

Tom Goren – Helen's old boyfriend, now a homicide detective

Lance McGrew – football hero, Muffy's ex, a man who wants answers

Deadly Secrets on
the St. Johns

From the *Florida News*, October 13, 1855

FOR SALE: The well known and very desirable plantation and residence of the late Henry R. Sadler, deced., situated upon the St. Johns River, about five miles above Jacksonville, called "Ortega." The plantation embraces about Four Thousand and Five Hundred acres, consisting of Pine and Hammock lands, well adapted to the culture of Corn, Sugar Cane, and Sea Island Cotton.

Prologue

"And now, my children, if you will gather around me, I will tell you the real true story of Ortega. There will be pirates in it, and Spanish gold.

". . . and there will be buried treasure—diamonds and rubies and pearls. And a haunted house with a chimney full of money. And a subterranean passage, and a mysterious well. And this well will have a ghost in it.

"Come out to our place some evening at sunset and I will show you the gold. It lies in the creek that is called McGirt, and it gives forth a mighty luster.

"But if any person from any land whatsoever remove this treasure or any portion thereof, may he never breathe the breath of the North wind. May he never smell the perfume of the orange blossom. May he never hear the song of the mockingbird."

From The Story of Ortega By One Who Lives There, *read before the Story Teller's League of Jacksonville, Florida, by Merrydelle Hoyt, 1923.*

Tuesday,
December 26

~~~~~~~~~~~~~~~~~~~~

The day of the murders began, as most Florida days begin, with a spectacular dawn.

Coral, magenta, and umber gently nudged away the last lingering stars as a man pushed past the river end of a ligustrum hedge separating two Ortega homes. It was the day after Christmas. The man could have been a tardy Santa Claus, except his scarlet jacket was stained, his beard scruffy and yellow. As a breeze lifted spikes of sun-bleached hair from his lumpy forehead, his own mother wouldn't have called him jolly. The scar from nose to jaw was no added attraction.

He didn't notice the sky. He was busy unsnagging his jacket from a twig. Freed, he nearly toppled into the choppy St. Johns three feet below. Grabbing a branch for support, he crawled out, then turned and spat into the offending bush.

He crawled along the concrete seawall, eyes on the gentle swell of the river. From time to time he peered over his shoulder. Though he saw no one, he crouched lower each time, until he scuttled like a crab.

This section of the seawall formed the butt end of a Bermuda grass lawn. By daylight it was winter brown, at dawn merely lighter gray than the river. A dock at the far end of the seawall, shared by two houses, had three boats moored at its end. The *Daphne Delight*, a thirty-eight-foot

cruiser, was splendid and new, with a creamy hull and
deep turquoise trim. The *Jack Three* was a twenty-footer,
black with silver trim. Between them, the *Ark*, a small flat-
bottomed johnboat, floated like an unlikely offspring.

The intruder narrowed faded blue eyes and considered the shadowy white bulk that was the L'Arken house
across the lawn. No lights gleamed yet in the windows,
but Dr. Hayden L'Arken would soon be up, preparing to
leave for early morning surgery. Crouching almost to his
knees, he half crept, half ran toward the boats at the pier.

He swung himself aboard one of them and searched
carefully. Suddenly he gave a quiet grunt of satisfaction
and, bending to reach behind a coil of line, retrieved a
gold-and-black lipstick case. His smile was pleased, but
definitely not pleasant.

Elated, and fairly certain it was still not light enough
for him to be observed, he vaulted off the boat, scuttled
back along the dock, and sprinted for the hedge.

Several miles away, Laura Grace Hayden pushed back an
airy white drape and raised bare arms toward the east.
"Come!"

A red ball tipped over the horizon, spilled liquid gold
down the wide black breast of the St. Johns, and slowly
silvered Jacksonville's skyline silhouette. Above the tallest
spires of Barnett Bank, Independent Life, and Southern
Bell, gulls wheeled and dipped in greeting across the coral
sky. Laura Grace's wrinkled face creased with delight.

She looked not unlike a gull: flat cheekbones, a long
straight nose, snapping black eyes. Her skin, however, was
mapped by age, framed by wiry gray hair, and dark with
years of exposure to the strong Florida sun. "A prune
draped in Spanish moss," her great-nephew Jack described
her. "She doesn't listen when doctors tell her about skin
cancer."

Laura Grace listened. She knew she could get cancer
and die. She just didn't care if she died. She hadn't cared
for many years. She'd already outlived her sister Cady and

all her friends except Martha L'Arken—who wasn't really her friend at all, but Cady's. It was only because of Cady that Martha had invited Laura Grace to share her condominium.

Laura Grace had accepted, but not because of Cady. Martha L'Arken lived in a big corner condominium in the old Park Lane, which sat like a sixteen-story wedding cake where the mighty St. Johns made a long, slow bend toward town. From her bedroom, Laura Grace could see a mile or more of water to the east. From the living room she could see ten miles of water to the south. If Martha had had a balcony, she could have even seen Ortega across three miles of water to the west. Laura Grace had grown up in Ortega, and would have liked to watch the sun set over its shore. However, she preferred the dawn.

On this pale winter morning the gulls swooped nearer and nearer. Laura Grace strained to see the cords they trailed behind them, weaving the pattern of the day. What colors did they bring? No two patterns were ever alike, and in them she sometimes could read what would happen before it did.

Others, who did not know the gulls' dawn mission and could not see their trailing cords, sought explanations for her prescience.

"Fey," said Nisbet, the Park Lane's old Scots janitor.

"Clairvoyant," declared Daphne, Laura Grace's chic niece by marriage.

"Magic!" insisted Teddy, who was ten.

Laura Grace, a good Episcopalian, was shocked. "It's nothing of the kind," she used to protest. "The gulls are messengers, and the patterns are there for anyone to read." People just shook their heads and thought her crazier than she was.

Laura Grace was crazy all right, but not crazy that way, so she stopped talking about the gulls and their cords. She just rose each dawn to summon them.

Today's pattern was especially complex, weaving silver for grace, gold for mercy, bright blue for change, and pale yellow for pleasant surprise. That would be Crispin coming, of course. Looking out her window, Laura gave a happy little bob of anticipation. But what was that final color? The gulls were too far away and heading downriver too swiftly for her to see.

She hurried to the living room. Padding barefoot across Martha's silky Persian rug, she tugged up the blind and peered out the front window to keep the birds in view.

"There's five this morning," she said over her shoulder. An assortment of faces gazed silently at her from silver frames on Martha's marble-topped table. Some of the frames held Martha's parents and her only brother with his family. Three, however, were very dear to Laura Grace. They held Cady's children—Martha's stepchildren and all the family Laura Grace had left. Her nephew Hayden L'Arken, who had inherited the Hayden family's dark features as well as the name, stood behind his first wife Twinkie and their son Treye. Hayden looked far happier, however, beside his second wife, Daphne, in a picture with a still-shiny frame. Slightly to the front of the table, Laura Grace's younger nephew Justin, as blond and beautiful as his father had been, sat flanked by his wife Helen and their three children, Jack, Brandy, and Teddy.

Laura Grace often talked to the pictures. Unlike their flesh and blood counterparts, they had the good manners never to disagree. "I still can't see the last cord!" Impatiently she shoved up the heavy sash and pressed her face to the screen, impervious to the chill damp breeze.

"What on earth are you doing?" Martha spoke sharply behind her. "December—and you without a stitch on! You'll die of pneumonia!"

Two strong hands clasped Laura Grace's shoulders and drew her back. The window descended with a thump.

Laura Grace scarcely noticed. She had seen the gulls' final cord. It was black. Danger? Or death?

———

By midmorning, Daphne L'Arken was mad as spit, and didn't care who knew it.

Daphne's moods were seldom tranquil. Pleased, she sparkled. Offended, she glittered. Furious, she raged. Hayden had been heard to boast indulgently, "Living with Daphne is like white water rafting. You never know what turbulence is around the bend."

Today she stormed into her peach-and-ivory kitchen, slammed a glass onto the countertop, filled it with ice, and splashed in two fingers of Scotch. Adding barely enough water to cover the ice, she stirred with one long freckled finger and drank it off without pausing for breath. Then she poured a second and glared at the broad rigid back of the maid bent over the sink washing new potatoes. "Don't look so high and mighty, Clarinda. You'd need a drink, too, if Muffy Merriwether'd just screwed up your party."

"Looks like you'll screw it up fine your own self." Clarinda spoke with the familiarity of an old family servant. She also made it clear from the way she shut a cabinet door that this was her kitchen and Daphne an unwelcome intruder.

Daphne's eyes narrowed. Really! Hayden simply had to get rid of Clarinda. No new wife ought to have to put up with a first wife's maid, even if she was a jewel who came any time she was needed. Just look at her! Squat as a toad, and old as the hills. Daphne wanted someone light and lithe who could wear a smart uniform at parties and serve drinks on a tray. Clarinda couldn't be let out of the kitchen. Her face would scare the guests.

But for twenty years Clarinda had cooked things the way Hayden liked them. Hayden might divorce good old Twinkie, allow Daphne to redecorate his riverfront home from overstuffed traditional to elegant modern, and trade in his black Cadillac for a silver Mercedes convertible. But he would not part with Clarinda. In an era when most Ortega families settled for a maid once or twice a week, Hayden still paid Clarinda to come every day.

Daphne's scarlet mouth set in a narrow line of resolution. No matter what Hayden said, as soon as tonight's party was over, Clarinda was out. If Hayden wouldn't fire her, Daphne would. After this evening, Hayden would let her do as she pleased. Tonight Daphne L'Arken was throwing the most elite party in Jacksonville. She was entertaining a past governor, a U.S. Senator, and the widow of a man once dubbed "The Lion of Far Eastern Diplomacy." And at the climax of the evening, Hayden's younger brother Justin would announce his own candidacy for Congress.

Unconsciously Daphne straightened and stood taller, a slender woman with soft dark hair floating around her head and eyes as green as emeralds. Twice a homecoming queen and one season's favorite debutante, Daphne L'Arken intended after tonight to once again reign in Ortega.

Muffy should *not* spoil it, dragging along Lance McGrew and Eddie Weare like this was some tacky Robert E. Lee Senior High reunion! She bit her lower lip and brooded over her drink.

"Who's been rufflin' your feathers, Stepma-ma?" She turned hotly toward the drawled greeting, accented on the last syllable. Then, hurriedly, she slid her drink behind her.

The youth in the doorway was as short and plain as his father, his black hair tousled and jowls unshaven. Yet even in bare feet, bathrobe, and boxer shorts, anybody could tell he was the son of the house. Daphne thought it a matter of breeding. Clarinda might privately call it something else, but Clarinda hadn't stayed where she was for twenty years by using that kind of language in white folks' kitchens.

"Are you finally up, Treye?" Daphne's nostrils flared in disdain.

He yawned before answering. "As you see, Stepma-ma. We grad students need all the sleep we can get, and it is, after all, my Christmas vacation." He scratched his bare chest and shook his head at Clarinda. "Don't feel like eggs this morning, Clarinda. How about just toast?"

Daphne snapped, "Clarinda can't spend all morning feeding you. She's busy. We've got nearly a hundred guests coming tonight!"

"I got time to make a bit of toast and pour coffee." Clarinda closed the refrigerator door and plodded toward the toaster. "Gonna turn cold tonight. You hear that, Treye? Low forties, they said." She reached into the pantry and brought out a loaf of white bread.

Daphne didn't care if it turned cold. In Jacksonville, winter often seesawed between the seventies and the low forties. She did care, however, that Treye get fed and out of the kitchen, so she could give Clarinda some last-minute instructions.

Treye sensed her impatience. "I'll pour my own coffee," he conceded. He opened a cabinet—then swore.

Clarinda jerked her head toward the other side of the kitchen. "The mugs is over there, since we re*deco*rated." She drew the final word out until Daphne's temper snapped.

"Here!" She took down a porcelain mug bright with peaches, and filled it with coffee—sloshing drops on the white tile floor as she thrust it at her stepson.

With elaborate care designed to annoy, Treye wiped up the spots with the dishtowel, then said, "Got any of Gammy's calamondin preserves, Clarinda?"

Clarinda hovered over the toaster like an eagle guarding its prey. "Your mama done took 'em all with her. They's some strawberry jam in the icebox, though. Store-bought."

Treye went to get it. His back to Daphne, he asked, "So what's eatin' you this mornin', Snow White?"

"I've told you not to call me that!" Daphne longed to slap them both—throwing out insults like she was deaf or stupid. Of course Twinkie had taken her mother's preserves! And yes, the kitchen was now peach and ivory instead of nautical blue and white. It was also a hundred times more modern. Hayden was happier, too, with a spring in his step Twinkie never put there—which Treye and Clarinda would admit if they'd stop mooning over how things used to be.

Without thinking, Daphne put her glass to her lips, then, horrified, took advantage of her stepson's back to pour the Scotch down the sink. She didn't care what Treye thought of her. As far as she was concerned, he was a mere inconvenience—an inconvenience with expensive tastes and a perennial shortage of funds. However, she didn't want him tattling to his daddy.

"Miz Merriwether's bringing two of they old high school chums to the party," Clarinda volunteered, handing Treye the toast on a white plate decorated with sailboats. Where the devil had she hidden that plate? Daphne had boxed those dishes for Goodwill with her own two hands, to free shelves for her own Royal Doulton.

"Some chums." Treye answered Clarinda with a smirk. "To get Snow White so riled up. If you aren't careful, Stepma-ma, I'll have to call you Rose Red."

Daphne started to retort, then caught her reflection in the beveled mirror over her kitchen desk. Treye was infuriating, but correct. Rage no longer heightened her fragility, made her sparkle. Nowadays anger mottled her skin, deepened the cobwebs around her eyes, brought out those damned freckles she worked so hard to cover. Taking deep breaths through her nose, she willed herself to stillness until her poise returned. Then, without a word, she strode toward the telephone to call her sister-in-law.

Tonight was going to be her greatest triumph in eight months of marriage. Nothing was going to spoil it. Not a sassy stepson, not plummeting thermometers, not an insolent maid, not Muffy Merriwether and her unwelcome guests. Not Judgment Day itself.

Half an hour later, Helen L'Arken stood by the sink in her own comfortable kitchen next door, watching Janie Lou polish a silver bowl, and arguing over the phone with her husband.

This kitchen hadn't changed much since Martha L'Arken moved into the Park Lane fifteen years ago and surrendered the family home to her younger stepson and his growing family. The yellow ceramic tile countertops, fruit wallpaper, tall pecan cabinets, and big center island with comfortable stools were the same. Helen's primary addition had been a cordless phone. She kept meaning to do the kitchen over, but somehow never did.

Helen hadn't changed much in those fifteen years, either. Tall and rangy in a green jogging suit, she had hair of a pleasant molasses brown—dark with golden highlights— that fell straight to cup her chin. High cheekbones provided a setting for unexpected amber eyes. Her loose, easy poise seldom faltered whether presiding over a charity fund-raiser, counseling troubled middle schoolers, or helping her youngest child unhook a flapping fish. Since Daphne's phone call, however, her brow had been furrowed with worry.

"Muffy should have asked Daphne!" she protested once more. "You know how picky she is about her parties, Justin. I know you and Eddie were best friends in high school, but this isn't a reunion. Besides, Lance used to be so rough, and Eddie ..." Helen took a deep breath and willed her words not to wobble. "Eddie's been gone for years. Who knows what he's like by now?"

"Who gives a hoot? Eddie was my friend!"

His words crackled in her ear like electric sparks, and pride surged through Helen's exasperation. Dear Justin, he truly was just. He was needed in Congress. Muffy and her little schemes must not spoil his chances.

Her gaze roamed through the kitchen windows to the moss-framed St. Johns. The sun had just come out from behind a cloud, and the river seemed to stretch out and purr.

*"Eternal Father, strong to save, whose arm doth bind the
restless wave . . ."*

The hymn flowed through her mind as the St. Johns
flowed past her home—reminding her that some things
endure even when life gets complicated.

Winging a quick prayer, she tried gentle reason.
"Daphne's not happy about it, and she's gone to a lot of
trouble for you," she told her husband.

At his blunt response, a brief smile flitted over her
lips. "Be nice, Justin! She thinks she's doing it all for you.
And don't forget that Crispin is bringing Sheila. She—"

He interrupted again, repeating his former arguments.
At that point, Helen gave up. Justin wasn't a Presbyterian
elder for nothing. Once he felt he had God and justice on
his side, nothing would budge him.

Instead of listening, she tried to conjure up a picture
of Eddie in high school. Instead, she saw him as she'd
seen him last, their sophomore year at the University of
Florida. In spite of the sunshine and her jogging suit, she
shivered. Were her foolish college skeletons buried deep
enough to protect them from avid media shovels during a
political campaign?

It was a short mental hop to Jack, spending a sullen
holiday with the family before returning to Florida for his
own fourth term. Was he burying a few skeletons, too—
skeletons that could hurt his daddy's chances for election?
She simply mustn't think about that right now!

Unable to stand still, she roamed the spacious downstairs, checking that it was ready for company. In the dining room, Janie Lou was spreading a snowy cloth over the
walnut table, scarred by years of homework and family
meals. The comfortable living room sofas and chairs had
been cleared of children's debris. All the rugs were straight
and freshly vacuumed to get up cat and dog hair. Everything was unusually tidy, except—

Craning her neck, Helen saw that sure enough, Jack's
tennis racket sat beside Teddy's fishing gear in the front
hall. If only those two could be as neat as their sister!

Carrying the phone back through the living room, she wrinkled her nose. Copernicus had been digging in the potted plants again, too. Disgusting cat! Helen drifted back to the kitchen and added a note to the already long list on the counter: *Scoop poop from palm.*

"Why can't you use the litter box like Newton and Gauss?" she muttered, then laughed in spite of herself. "No, darlin', not you. Copernicus. He's fertilized the areca again. Listen, I need to go. I'm still in running clothes, and Mama and Libba will be here soon. We're making Mama's special crab puffs. Then I need to take Jack and Brandy over to help Daphne move furniture before Crispin gets here. He said they'd arrive around four."

Justin spoke once more, his voice pleading.

Helen squared her shoulders and held her head high. "Okay, honey, if you want them to come, I'll alert Mama and Libba. We'll help Muffy entertain them." Her stomach might feel like a blender, and her knees like they'd been run through it, but she would support Justin in his bid for election if it killed her.

An hour later, Helen arranged flowers at the sink and listened inattentively while her mother poured complaints into Libba Weldon's patient ear. Charlotte Holmes Aspen adored Libba.

The feeling was mutual. As a plump little girl with a mother whose vagueness presaged early senility, Libba had been entranced by everything about Charlotte Holmes: the dark hair on her temples that draped to a loose knot at her neck, the crisp stylish clothes she wore even to the grocery store, the rich deep voice that rasped like a cultured sawmill, the dusky tan from well-oiled afternoons by the Yacht Club pool.

Helen, of course, had been no more impressed than a chick by its hen. No wonder Mama enjoyed Libba's visits all those growing-up years! The two of them drank pots of tea and talked by the hour. Gradually Libba had come to dress like Mama and even sound like Mama.

Mama had been heartbroken when Libba married a
boy from downstate her freshman year of college—and delighted when Libba came back after her divorce. And
while Libba had been devastated that Charlotte Holmes
had sold her lovely home on Pirate's Cove, these days she
visited Charlotte Holmes's new condominium almost as
often as Helen's.

Therefore, since Helen simply would not listen to reason this morning, naturally Charlotte Holmes turned to
Libba for support.

"Lance McGrew was a coarse, rude boy, precious, and
you know how he treated Muffy. Some people said he
beat her!" She mixed crabmeat, horseradish, cream
cheese, and onion with a fierceness that made Helen wonder if she'd rather be mashing Lance McGrew's brains.

"I wasn't living here then, Charho," Libba reminded
her, stripping crabmeat from another claw.

"No. Well, it didn't last very long. I'm surprised she'd
even consider seein' him again! He probably doesn't own
a tux. And while Eddie grew up in Ortega, we don't know
where he's been since college. He could be *anything* by
now!" Anxiety made her drawl as thick as aloe.

Forgetting that she had voiced much the same doubts
to Justin not long ago, Helen said drolly, "Simply anything, Mama. Dracula, Frankenstein, even a New York
banker."

Charho primmed her lips. "You weren't raised to talk
to your mother like that. In my day—"

Helen didn't listen to the rest. In Charho's day,
women grew up to please their mothers by becoming exactly like them. Her own generation loved their mothers,
but pleased themselves.

Libba gave Helen a swift, amused moue before replying, with just the proper shade of sympathy, "I don't think
you need to worry, Charho. Lance always behaved in public, and Eddie was a very nice boy."

Charlotte Holmes tasted a morsel of crab with a considering look in her eye, but it was not crab she was

considering. "You were crazy about Eddie back in high school, weren't you, dear? I wonder if he's ever married?" She let the query hang meaningfully.

Libba flushed. "Eighteen years of Greg Weldon was enough marriage to last me a lifetime, thank you! But it'll be good to see Eddie again. It's been a long time."

Finally, Helen got a swift mental picture of Eddie Weare in high school: a quarterback with sun-bleached hair, a shy, endearing grin, and eyes of heart-stopping blue. *Hold that thought*, she ordered herself.

Charho's sharp gaze missed little where her only child was concerned. Shoving the bowl away, she said with a trace of asperity, "It was still too bad of Muffy to invite him and Lance to this particular party. This is Justin's night, not a time to bring back old football heroes. And you have to admit, it's peculiar neither of them has been home for years."

"Lance got a job in Miami, and Eddie's parents moved during college," Helen pointed out. Dear God in heaven, how had she gotten cornered into defending those two?

Lifting the coffeepot, she quickly poured three mugs, distributed them, and slid onto a vacant stool at the island. Not until everybody had taken a much-needed sip did she deliver her ultimatum. "Muffy's invited Eddie and Lance, and Justin wants them there. That's all there is to it, Mama. You and Libba just help me entertain them. You hear me?"

"Of course, darlin'." Charlotte Holmes's large brown eyes widened with hurt. "You know we'll do anything we can to make this evenin' all you want it to be. But I've said it before, and I'll say it again: If those men haven't been doing somethin' they're ashamed of, why haven't they come home before?"

The noonday sun streamed onto I-75 with indecent brightness for the last days of a dying year. Sheila Travis narrowed her eyes, then pulled down the visor, wishing Jason hadn't polished the Cadillac's hood to such a silver sheen. A long lean woman nearing forty, she had short black curls and eyes so brown they were almost black. Today, however, they were red from the glare and the frustration of squinting down two lanes of sluggish RV's. And she was so hot! If the sun got warmer further south, she would surely swelter all week. Already her wool skirt lay on her thighs like an unneeded blanket. She shoved up her sweater sleeves and wished vanity hadn't made her wear Aunt Mary's taupe Christmas ensemble to meet Crispin's friends. A spring cotton would have been far more sensible. And why hadn't she remembered her sunglasses?

Because Atlanta was cold and drizzly when they left.

Thoroughly grumpy, she leaned over and punched buttons to lower the temperature on the car air conditioner. Air-conditioning, in December?

"You're sighing again." In the passenger seat, Crispin Montgomery bent to scratch his knee through warm-up pants. "What are you complaining about? I've got an anthill under this cast!"

Sheila gave him a quick smile of sympathy. Bless his heart, that was his first complaint in over an hour. When he gave her a lazy smile in return, happiness shot through her irritation like a sunbeam through clouds. Two years older than she and equally dark and lean, Crispin was the only man in two years of widowhood who made her consider, now and then, giving up her cherished independence. Today he looked particularly attractive in a black warm-up suit trimmed in white and aqua. Warm-up pants were the only kind he could easily pull over his cast.

He swiped a stubborn curl off his forehead and pointed to an upcoming sign. "Twelve miles to a Krystal." Sheila wrinkled her nose. She'd prefer something more substantial today than small hamburgers cooked with almost as much onion as meat. "You promised," he reminded her. "And while we're stopped, we'll get you some sunglasses. I don't want you meeting my friends looking like you've been on an all-night binge. Of course, if you'd rather borrow my wonderful mirrored glasses, the offer still stands."

"And arrive looking like I've joined the Mafia? No thanks. But I'll be glad to stop, even for a Krystal. Everybody in the world must be going to the Gator Bowl!" She swerved right to shoot past a red Toyota virtuously trundling down the fast lane.

He chuckled. "And half of them are Yankee Puritans who stick to the speed limit. This is probably good for your soul."

"Not for my vocabulary."

He shifted to ease his casted leg. "At least we travel in style. It was nice of your aunt to send her car back from St. Petersburg and give Jason a week off so we could borrow it."

"Just you try to ask Aunt Mary for Forbes before she's ready to let him go! The Cadillac isn't a loan—it's payment for your nephew."

Sheila's elderly aunt and Crispin's four-year-old ward were an unlikely but firmly bonded duo. Mary Beaufort, who had been lobbying to take Forbes to Florida even before their accident, definitely considered Crispin's injury just before Christmas divine intervention on her behalf.[1]

Crispin readjusted his lanky frame again, with a soft grunt of pain. "Don't tell her, but I'm grateful. I couldn't keep up with Forbes right now. By the way, have I thanked you for coming?"

"Twice. And I've told you, I wanted to come. You were determined to go to the Gator Bowl—"

"Damn tootin'! Justin's firm has a sky box on the forty-yard line. But we could have flown. I offered you a ticket."

As an Atlanta-based executive for a Japanese multina-

---

[1] *A Mystery Bred in Buckhead*

tional corporation, Sheila had enough frequent flier miles to take them both to Tokyo and back. However—"You'd have been miserable on a plane, Crispin, and I like to drive. Usually. I just hope you can produce your mythical Aunt Martha. Otherwise, you'll fly home, all right—as cargo."

In the six months they'd been dating, Crispin usually mentioned his Aunt Martha only in conjunction with a forlorn groom's cake in her freezer. "No longer mythical," he pointed out. "We're having dinner with her tonight."

"I'll believe her when I see her—and hope I can keep everybody else straight."

"It's not complicated. Look." He laid a finger on her thigh. She lightly smacked his hand, but he only moved down her leg. "Sensory imprintation, so you won't forget." He pressed a dot into her knee. "Aunt Martha, Daddy's sister, was best friends in college with Caroline Hayden, called Cady."

She raised her brows, incredulous. "Cady Hayden?"

He shrugged. "What can I say? Her mother must have thought it was cute. Anyway, Cady married a Jacksonville insurance tycoon, John Daniel L'Arken." He pressed another dot and drew a line. "Aunt Martha was maid of honor." The roving finger sketched a line and made two more dots. "Cady and John Daniel had two sons, Hayden and Justin."

"Which one's a doctor?"

"Hayden, and he's not merely 'a doctor,' he's a very prestigious plastic surgeon. He's also seven years older than Justin, who's my age and now runs the family insurance business." He was tracing circles on her knee. "Where was I?"

She stilled his hand with her own. "The boys just got born."

"Right. Well, when Justin was four, Cady died. Aunt Martha wrote John Daniel a sympathy letter, he wrote back, and within a year, Aunt Martha was the new

Mrs. L'Arken. I used to visit each July. Their house was wonderful—fishing dock, a tire swing, even a secret room off the landing where we had our pirates' base. Hayden, though, used to torment the dickens out of Justin and me. Still tries. To you I may be an esteemed landscape architect and nurseryman, Sheila, but Hayden calls me a gardener."

She widened her eyes in feigned innocence. "Aren't you? That's what you were calling yourself when I met you."[2]

"Don't tell Hayden. He and Daphne are thrilled you are coming to their party tonight, by the way. Daphne said to tell you she can't wait to hear about—quote—your excitin' years with the foreign service in Japan. End of quote."

"I wasn't in the foreign service. That was Tyler. I was just his not-very-exciting wife. Is Daphne obnoxious?"

"No, actually she's lots of fun. Witty, lively—she's been good for old Hayden since they got married last year. She's also gorgeous. Well, not exactly gorgeous. Dripping wet, she's quite ordinary. But she certainly knows how to work with what the good Lord gave her."

Sheila gave him a swift look. That was the kind of remark Tyler used to make just before suggesting she change her hair. Crispin, however, was bent over again, scratching his cast. "Drat!"

She braked before she ran up the tailpipe of a leisurely Winnebago. "We're staying at Justin's?"

"Right. Aunt Martha gave Justin and Helen the house several years ago, so they have the most room. But don't expect peace and quiet. They have three children, assorted cats and reptiles, and a basset hound named Einstein."

She glared at the Winnebago. "Move it, mister! I'll avoid the reptiles, Crispin, if you don't mind."

The Winnebago lumbered over. Crispin chuckled. "Atta woman! Hex them drivers!" He crossed his forefingers and held them up as the Cadillac pulled ahead, then laid his arm along the back of her seat and stroked her neck, sending pleasant sensations up and down her spine. "A piece of advice: Avoid Teddy, too. Jack's nineteen and all right. Brandy's sixteen and a doll—like her mother. But Teddy? Well, Teddy's ten, and a holy terror."

Contemplating nearly a week with a houseful of strangers, wildlife, and an incorrigible child, Sheila felt a surge of panic. "Couldn't we stay with your aunt—or go to a hotel?"

He pulled out his calendar. "Is this finally an affirmative to my repeated proposals? How about next weekend?"

She frowned. "You promised not to propose this week, Crispin, and here we are only three hours down the road. Seriously, your aunt really doesn't have room?"

"Sorry, but both her bedrooms are full. Laura Grace, Cady's sister, lives with her."

Sheila's head swiveled in astonishment. "Your Aunt Martha lives with her husband's first wife's sister?"

"Eyes on the road, woman! And think of it as her best friend's sister. Laura Grace was twelve years older than Cady and outlived her two sisters, so Aunt Martha took her in. We won't see much of her—I hope. All you need to really remember are Aunt Martha, Justin, Helen, Hayden, and Daphne. Jack and Brandy will be out a lot, and we'll ignore Teddy as best we can."

"I'll have to remember their names if I meet them in the hall. Write it down, Crispin. It helps to see things in print."

Half an hour later, while he plowed through four small burgers and a large bag of fries, she sipped coffee and peered at the chart he had obligingly scribbled on the end page of a paperback novel.

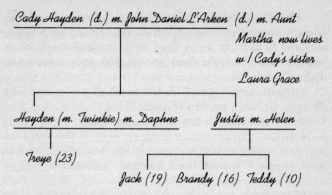

Cady Hayden (d.) m. John Daniel L'Arken (d.) m. Aunt Martha now lives w/ Cady's sister Laura Grace

Hayden (m. Twinkie) m. Daphne   Justin m. Helen

Treye (23)

Jack (19)   Brandy (16)   Teddy (10)

Her finger rested on an unfamiliar name. "Treye, Hayden's son. Will I need to remember him?"

"Not likely, although he may be at the party tonight."

"How much of Daphne and Hayden will we see after that?"

He finished his last fry. "They'll go with us to the game, and Daphne pops in and out a lot. She and Helen have known each other since elementary school, were both cheerleaders at Lee High, made their debuts together—" He flicked his hand. "You know."

Sheila did not know. She'd never lived anywhere long enough to have that kind of friend. Shoving aside the chart, she reached for her own burgers. "I'm surprised Daphne waited so long to marry Helen's brother-in-law."

Crispin leaned back against the wall of the booth and propped his casted leg along the bench. "Hayden got married before Daphne grew up, and Daphne married somebody from Baton Rouge and lived over there for twenty years, until her divorce. Jacksonville women tend to return to the roost eventually, with or without husbands. They stay around, too. Twinkie, Hayden's first wife, and Aunt Martha are still friends. If we meet her, just act civilized."

"I'll try." Sheila started her second burger. Anxiety was making her so hungry, she might eat three!

"It amazes me," Crispin continued, almost as if he were speaking to himself, "how after years away, those women picked up where they left off. Helen spends almost all her free time these days with Daphne, Muffy, and Libba."

"Muffy and Libba?" Bewildered, Sheila reached for the chart. "Who are Muffy and Libba?"

"Muffy Merriwether and Libba Weldon, two other friends."

Something about his tone made her glance at him quizzically. "What are their husbands' names?"

"Oh," he said, just a shade too casually, "they're both divorced. Libba, now, she and her daughter Sparrow came back to live with her parents a couple of years ago. She teaches biology or something at the local junior college. Helen said she's had a rough year. Her dad died last summer, then her mother's Alzheimer's got so bad, Libba had to put her in a home."

Sheila waited. When he didn't go on, she prompted, "What about Muffy? Has she had a rough year, too?"

He chuckled. "Not recently. After three ill-advised marriages, Muffy's currently living on charm and alimony. By the way, Jack's crazy about Sparrow. I think Helen hopes they'll marry one day."

Sheila forgot her manners and gaped at him. "This is beginning to sound suspiciously like one of those soap operas you got addicted to after the accident."

He shrugged. "Or a small town—which Jacksonville basically was, for years. Look." He swiftly drew a rough map below her chart. "The St. Johns River runs right through town. Flows north, by the way. It's miles wide, and until lately, people tended to stay on their own side. These three neighborhoods—" he lightly sketched a crescent along the western bank, "Ortega, Avondale, and Riverside—ran things. Naturally, folks who lived there married each other. That's who they knew."

Sheila pointed across the river. "What's over there?"

"Southside."

"Southside? Due east?"

"Not from downtown. The river curves and narrows there, so that's where the bridges are. Southside's south of downtown."

Clumsily, Crispin maneuvered himself out of his bench, and spoke with a trace of exasperation. "Look, Sheila, Jacksonville's a beautiful city. Sure it has a few quirks, and its drinking water tastes funny, but it's full of terrific people. And, unlike *your* childhood friends, none of the folks I know are likely to commit or get mixed up in murder."

Which just goes to show how wrong some people can be.

At two that afternoon, Jacksonville homicide detective Tom Goren scowled at his superior officer, Shep Talbott. "I've already got a full caseload. *Sir*," he added, with little respect.

"I'm shifting some of what you've been doing, Goren. Somebody's bringing that illegal abortion drug—what's it called?" Talbott checked a pad before him. "UR-four-oh-six. It's coming into the country in small regular shipments, and word is, it's coming through Ortega. If so, I want it stopped! Nobody knows for sure what that stuff does to women who use it!" The chief's ruddy face grew redder. Shep Talbott had five daughters and three grandchildren, and he had been in the forefront of Jacksonville's successful battle to shut down nude bars and adult bookstores. No type of criminal made him angrier than those who preyed on women and children. He cleared his throat and said testily, to make up for his previous show of emotion, "But we mustn't ruffle unnecessary feathers with this investigation. Somebody just needs to go out there and mingle." His voice softened into a rare personal tone. "You're my choice, Tom. You know Ortega."

Sure, Tom knew Ortega. He'd gone to Lee High with kids from Ortega, played football with them. Those kids grew up in big houses surrounded by moss-draped oaks, spent their afternoons playing tennis at the Yacht Club instead of bagging groceries at Winn-Dixie, grew up to become not second-string detectives, but officers in the brokerage firms, insurance companies, and banks their granddaddies founded. Among former teammates Goren could name two CEO's and a judge. All three men still lived in Ortega, took him out for beer after high school reunions, regularly sent him tickets to the Florida-Georgia game and the Gator Bowl. That didn't make him any happier about being assigned to this investigation.

Not that Ortega was crime-free. After the Revolutionary War, Pirate Dan McGirth used the island as his hideout. In the nineteen-thirties, Machine Gun Kelly was rumored to have holed up there from the FBI. During Prohibition, at least one man smuggled choice whiskey down East Coast channels and landed it on his Ortega dock, and not too long ago an enterprising businessman who called himself a "self-employed agronomist" was pulled in for growing marijuana in his Algonquin Avenue lawn. Many Ortegans preferred making laws for other people to keeping inconvenient ones themselves. What Tom was hearing now was credible. He just didn't want any part of it.

His chief was still talking. "All I'm asking you to do is spend time there, keep your eyes and ears open. But if anything unusual comes in from out that way, it's going straight to you. Understand?"

Tom glowered reluctant assent. He watched Talbott shuffle papers on his desk and produce a heavy ivory envelope with an embossed return address. "For a start, Hayden L'Arken is having a big shindig tonight. Rumor has it, Justin L'Arken's announcing plans to run for Congress. I don't think this has anything to do with that, but you never know. Maybe you ought to look in. What do you think?" He held out the envelope.

Tom totally missed the question—a clumsy attempt at mollification. "Hayden L'Arken?" It wasn't Hayden he was seeing. It was a pert minx with a cloud of dark hair and an inscrutable smile, grabbing him right after he'd assisted with the winning touchdown in the Thanksgiving game senior year. No other kiss ever tasted quite so sweet. He'd heard that Daphne had married Hayden L'Arken. The idea of that boring monkey and the gorgeous Daphne . . . it made him cringe. Not that he was any prettier—

"I've already got plans for tonight." That's what he meant to say. Instead he heard, in a voice remarkably like his own, a conceding growl. "I could look in for a bit, I suppose. Don't have a tux, though, and I won't be working."

His superior chuckled. "I laid a bet that that's what you would say. Just keep an eye on things, Tom, that's all. And don't look so downcast. You've been wanting a change. This ought to keep you away from homicides for a spell."

Police officers aren't always right, either.

High in a condominium overlooking the Ortega River, Muffy Merriwether fluffed her short red hair and critically examined her flawless skin in her bedroom mirror. "You're just jealous, Libba, but you can't have them—either one."

"I don't want either one." Libba was sitting on Muffy's bed, watching her. She would, however, have loved to have Muffy's new red dress, hanging on the closet door. Not for years had Libba been able to afford anything from an Avondale shop. She wondered who had paid for this one, just as she wondered who paid for the lovely condo. Libba would have given anything she possessed— except Sparrow—for Muffy's view of the river.

Her voice, however, was merely patient as she added, "Besides, I have to go early. I promised Daphne I'd supervise the caterers. But she's serious about not letting you spoil the party, Muff. Won't you call this off, at least for Helen?"

"It's for Helen I'm doin' it!" Muffy assured her airily. "I want Helen to see Eddie again, before she gets all caught up in that awful election. Remember what happened sophomore year?"

"I was married and gone by then," Libba reminded her.

Muffy spoke with a trace of genuine pity. "You missed a lot, sweetie. The exciting years of college—" Her lips curved in a gamine smile. "I just want to bring them back for one brief and shinin' moment."

Libba regarded her old classmate soberly. "Daphne asked me to tell you she'll have you thrown out if she has to. She means it, Muff."

Muffy turned. Her mouth still smiled, but her eyes were stormy and her voice sharp. "Daphne's been away too long, Libba. She doesn't know how things are these days."

Libba gave a short, mirthless laugh. "It's *you* who don't know how things are these days. Since Daphne got back, it's just like it used to be: whatever Daphne wants, Daphne gets."

Muffy raised one delicate brow. "Why Libba Weldon! That's the meanest-spirited thing I ever heard you say— and I love you for it!"

Libba colored.

Muffy pursued her advantage ruthlessly. "What's Daphne been getting lately that makes you mad?" Her brown eyes sparkled with sudden mischief. "Hayden? Surely you didn't—"

"No," Libba interrupted crossly. "I didn't want Hayden. But Twinkie did, and you saw how little that mattered once Daphne wanted him. Don't spoil her party, or you'll be sorry."

Muffy shook her head and turned back to her mirror. "We'll see who's sorry," she said airily, "if Daphne tries to throw me out."

"Be careful, Muffy. There's a lot ridin' on this party."

Muffy winked. "More than you know, hon."

Libba sighed as she stood. "Well, I promised to tell you. That's all I can do."

Muffy walked her to the door and watched until the elevator closed behind her. Then she called softly, "Okay. You can come out, now."

A man—big, ugly, with a lumpy forehead and a scar from nose to jaw—stepped from the den and encircled her with his arms. He spoke gruffly into her nape. "Tryin' to warn you off, Muffy, babe? Libba always did think she could get anything she wanted by being sweet."

Muffy agreed, but resented his criticism of her friend. "She believes the best of everybody." *Almost always,* she amended silently.

"Whereas I know the worst of some people." Lance's hands found her breasts.

She pulled away but made her voice playful. "Stop it, Lance. I told you, I'll take you to the party." Only when she stood a safe distance away did she add, "But that's all you get from me. Now or ever."

His laugh was unpleasant. "Baby, I can get anything I want from you whenever I want it. Look what I found this mornin', on one of the L'Arkens' boats." He reached into the pocket of his baggy jeans and pulled out a slim black-and-gold tube.

She caught a quick breath, but immediately regained her poise. With a sharp little laugh she asked, "Whose is it?"

He shook his head. "Don't play games with me, Muffikins. We both know whose it is, and when you dropped it. I know you're up to something, and I want in."

She continued to smile, but sidled nearer the kitchen. Five months of marriage to Lance ten years ago had taught her a great deal—like, don't talk to him without a weapon nearby. Her knives were right on the corner. If he came for her, she'd kill him, so help her God.

"I don't know what you're talkin' about, Lance. I borrowed one of the L'Arkens' boats Christmas Eve for a date. Maybe I dropped the lipstick then."

He laughed sourly. "Maybe you did, sugar. And maybe that's not all you dropped, hunh?"

To her surprise, however, he didn't wait for a reply. Instead, he turned toward the door. "I'll see you tonight."

Hating to detain him a second longer than necessary, she asked, "Shall I pick you up before or after I pick up Eddie?"

"I'm pickin' you up, baby. We'll get Eddie and I'll drop you off at Hayden's. I've got an errand to run before I party."

"You'll need an invitation to get in unless you're with me."

"Keep an eye out for me at the door, baby."

"You'll wear a tux?"

"Like a penguin."

"Why can't you just come in with us?"

"Because I have something to do first." He let himself out.

She hurried to her balcony to make sure he left. Her heart pounded as she saw him get in an old black Cadillac—pounded with relief, not desire. Those days were long over between them.

What did Lance have to do during the party? Whatever it was, she had no doubt of one thing: It would be unpleasant for somebody.

Just when Sheila thought they were almost there, they were stopped in the middle of a charming white bridge while a less than charming fishing boat churned through the drawspan. Tired, hot, and increasingly irritable, she complained, "You're wrong, Crispin. This river is nowhere near a mile wide."

It was gorgeous, however. Even she had to admit that. Beneath meringue-puff clouds dotting a sky of azure, the water rippled sinuously in the sunlight. Across the bridge, Spanish moss dripped from tall pines and wide-spreading oaks.

Crispin stretched and yawned. Any minute she expected to hear him purr. Instead, he explained, "This is just the Ortega River. It runs into the St. Johns out past Ortega Point." He pointed. Sure enough, out there, the water stretched forever toward smoky blue skyscrapers.

He lowered his window and took great whiffs of warm thick air. "Doesn't it smell great?" He laid his head back and closed his eyes.

Sheila heard a mosquito sing somewhere near her ear, and felt her hair begin to frizz. Sweat trickled down her back under her wool sweater. Unless it got cooler and less humid, she'd have to spend tomorrow morning shopping for clothes and would walk around looking like a tall dark bush.

"Is this an island?" He'd never said they were going to an island. She'd have known to bring bug spray and no-frizz conditioner.

"It used to be," said the traitorous male, "before they dammed Pirate's Cove. This was a plantation back in the late seventeen hundreds. Grew cotton, sugar cane—"

If it was this warm in December, what would a cotton field have been like in July? She was shuddering at the thought when he touched her arm. "The bridge is down. You can go now."

Once on the other side he said, "See the stucco house with the blue tile roof? That's where the gangster Machine Gun Kelly is supposed to have holed up back in the thirties. When the FBI arrived, he'd disappeared. Some people believe there's a tunnel from the house to the river. Follow the bend. You can't see the river from here for the houses, but Justin's got a terrific view."

Her bad humor dissipated in his excitement. She'd never seen him so boyish. What had those summer visits meant to an only child from a small south Georgia town?

On her left, houses towered nearly as tall as trees. Most had high walls, decorated with festive red Christmas bows. All were set well back from the street in deep lawns thickly planted with water oaks, magnolias, crepe myrtles, pines, and sprawling azaleas. They contrasted sharply with modest homes in neat yards across the street. Did people without riverfront lots resent the shrubbery that kept them from getting even a glimpse of the tantalizingly near water—or was it enough to live in the shadow of such greatness?

One small park broke the riverfront monopoly. Sheila noted it as a possible future retreat from children and reptiles.

Half a mile farther, Crispin jerked his head toward a brick wall topped by towering azaleas. "That's Hayden's." The high white house with dark green shutters was visible only through twin brick gateposts, but glimpsed down a curving drive dotted with blooming camellias, it gleamed like something out of *Southern Living*.

To one side of the lot, an ancient water oak waved Spanish moss in benediction. "That's a kneeling oak," Crispin told her. "I'll show you later why it's called that." He leaned forward as if to encourage the car. "The next drive is Justin's, where Aunt Martha used to live."

Sheila nosed the Cadillac through white brick posts, followed another curved drive, and stopped behind a ten-year-old Buick. "I guess Aunt Martha gave Janie Lou her car," Crispin murmured cryptically.

Sheila was admiring the house. White with green shutters, like Hayden L'Arken's residence, this was a sprawling homey place with a rope swing dangling from a thick branch, a tidy stack of firewood beside the garage, and a basset hound eyeing them from the wide, shady porch. In the three-car garage sat a green minivan sporting two bumper stickers: "Go Gators" and "Adoption, Not Abortion."

She bit her lip. It wasn't just the humidity and heat Crispin had failed to mention. She was prepared to sit through a football game for him, but she didn't want to spend a week tiptoeing through conversational minefields. She might be in for a lot of long solitary walks.

A small figure in jeans and a T-shirt launched itself from the porch and dashed toward them. The dog rose

and waddled after, a blob of dignity in the wake of streaming white braids and piercing shrieks that headed straight
for the driver's door.

"Crispin! Crispin!" When she saw her mistake, the little girl drew herself up to her full four foot ten and regarded Sheila somberly through wire-rimmed glasses. Her
eyes were blue, thickly ringed with long black lashes.
Their loveliness was startling in her plain freckled face. "I
am Theodosia L'Arken," she said, her poise not a whit im-
paired by two outsized front teeth. "You may call me
Teddy."

The dog squatted on his haunches like a long-tongued
sentinel. He remained where he was as the amazing child
dashed around the car, flung open the other door, and
cried, "Don't get out, Crispin. We have to go to Mamar's
right away! Ellgie's missing—probab'ly dead!"

"Teddy L'Arken, you stop that right now!"

A tiny soft-brown woman wearing a starched white
apron over her dove-gray dress hurried down the steps of
the big white house and scarcely skimmed the brick walk
in her haste to reach the child. Ignoring the guests, she
grabbed one thin shoulder and demanded fiercely, "What's
your mama told you?"

Teddy wrenched herself free, lips set in a stubborn
pucker. "Mama said wait for Crispin and—*Her*." She nodded in lieu of the name. "But now they're here, so we can
go help." Her lower lip trembled. "Ellgie could be hurt,
lying on a street bleedin' to death, with nobody who loves
her nearby to offer comfort. She's prob'ly—"

"She's probably already home," the maid interrupted
bluntly, "and nobody inside here listenin' for the phone
like they was told to."

"You can answer the old phone." Teddy danced in
desperation. "Please, Janie Lou, we gotta go. We just
gotta!" She turned, seeking an ally. "Don't we, Crispin?"

Crispin climbed out and fondled the long ears of the
dog, who had padded over to greet him. "Hiya, Einstein."

Then he hobbled to take the maid's hand. "Good to see you, Janie Lou. I want you to meet my friend, Sheila Travis. Sheila, this is Janie Lou Hartle, who keeps the family going."

Janie Lou leaned in the window and offered Sheila a thin brown hand. "Pleased to meet you. You all come right in and make yourselves to home. Miss Helen will be back shortly."

"But Janie Lou . . . !"

As the maid turned back to Teddy, Sheila frowned at Crispin. His list had omitted Helen's maid. He missed the look, asking, "What's going on?"

Janie Lou shook her head. "Miss Hayden's took it in her head to run off again. They's all out lookin' for her. Miss Helen went with Jack and Brandy. Mister Justin even lef' his office."

"We gotta go, too!" Teddy tugged Crispin's arm. "Right now! You can leave Her—" she jerked her braids in Sheila's direction "—here to answer the phone."

Crispin shook the girl loose. "Be gentle with the wounded, child! I'll go call Aunt Martha and see if she wants us to come."

His aunt accepted his offer. Teddy was jubilant, Sheila chagrined. She would have gladly accepted Teddy's suggestion that she stay here to answer the phone.

At the car, Teddy darted into the front seat between the adults. To Sheila, Crispin explained, "Laura Grace has been gone almost two hours. I've never heard Aunt Martha so rattled."

"Mamar feels responsible." Teddy joined the adult conversation without a qualm. "She went to the grocery store, and Ellgie left right after she did. The manager saw her go, but she thought Ellgie was just going to catch up with Mamar."

Over her head, Crispin translated. "Mamar is Mama Martha, and Ellgie is Laura Grace."

Sheila followed Crispin's directions back through Ortega and the equally lovely neighborhoods of Avondale and Riverside. As they drove, Teddy kept up a recital of the disappearance, concluding, "Mamar's terrified a mugger or rapist has got her!"

Crispin raised his brows. "I take it you've been listening in on the phone again?"

Teddy clamped her lips shut. She said nothing for at least half a minute, then heaved an enormous sigh. "Can't we drive any faster? I'm really worried about Ellgie."

"A woman after your own heart." Crispin grinned at Sheila over Teddy's pale hair. "The two of you could team up for the Daytona Five Hundred."

Sheila eased up slightly on the accelerator, but refused to give him the satisfaction of a reply. Instead, she asked Teddy, "Has—ah—Ellgie ever disappeared before?"

The straight bangs jounced. "Yeah, but she us'ly just goes to Memorial Park to talk to the gulls. Ellgie's nuts about gulls. But one time she wandered up to Five Points and once she went down Riverside Avenue. But they've looked all those places, and she's never been gone so long."

"But . . . but . . . but," Crispin teased, gently tugging on the nearest braid. "You always sound like somebody's disagreeing with you."

Teddy shrugged. "Somebody us'ly is."

A moment later she pointed across Crispin to a creamy tiered tower with a red tile roof, which rose above neighborhood homes. "That's where Mamar lives. Turn at the corner!"

Sheila obeyed, noting that a charming park with a black iron fence shared the riverfront with the condominium. As Crispin directed her into a parking lot behind the building, he murmured, "All I want to do here is calm Aunt Martha. Get her to tell you about the history of this building if you can."

"It was built back in the twenties, and was the third tallest building in Jacksonville," Teddy said promptly, "but who cares? I want to look for Ellgie!"

Martha L'Arken, too, was more concerned about her

missing friend than with history. She was waiting in the
lobby, and as soon as she saw them, she flung open the
door and ran to bury herself in Crispin's embrace. "Oh,
darlin'!" she cried in a drawl so deep it made Atlantans
sound like Yankee traders, "I'm sorry to bother you, but
Laura Grace's *never* been missin' this long! I'm so afraid
she's been—" Catching sight of Teddy, Martha fell abruptly silent and looked with deep embarrassment at Sheila.

Crispin detached himself, leaving one arm draped
around her. "Sheila, this is my aunt, Martha L'Arken."
Sheila would have known. Although she came only to his
shoulder, Martha had Crispin's black hair (hers lightly
streaked with gray) and his square jaw. She also had lovely
skin, but today her face was pink and shiny, her dark hair
mussed.

"Let's go inside," Crispin suggested, "and you can tell
us all about it."

Martha herded them toward the ancient elevator,
moving as lightly and gracefully as a much younger
woman. As worried as she was, she still paused to introduce them to the pleasant manager in her small office behind a double Dutch door.

But as the elevator crept upward, Martha's eyes filled
again. "We don't know where she could have gone! Everybody's out looking for her, but I just pray we find her before dark!" The way she said the last word, it sounded
like "dock."

"Maybe she'll come back on her own," Crispin
soothed.

"She never does, Crispin, and she's never been lost so
long." Martha's tears spilled over. "She knew you were
coming. She even got dressed!"

In the condominium, Sheila had time only for a swift
impression of airy rooms, big windows, Persian rugs, rosy
polished furniture, and gleaming mirrors before her hostess held out both hands and gripped her own. "I am so
glad you are here at last, Sheila, and dreadfully sorry to
have you see me in these tacky things I threw on to go to

the grocery store." She frowned down at her crisp red polo shirt and denim skirt. "And I'd planned such a lovely dinner for us all!" She cast a regretful glance toward the kitchen, then gasped in dismay, "Oh, Teddy, please get my chicken into the refrigerator! It's drippin' all over the floor!" Sure enough, a steady pink stream was running to the linoleum. Teddy trotted importantly away.

Martha dabbed her nose with a sodden handkerchief. "I honestly don't know whether to be terr'fied for Laura Grace or furious with her!" she hissed to the adults in a fierce whisper. "If she's merely gone off—but what if somethin' really has happened?"

Sheila and Crispin both stood several inches taller than the older woman. Over her dark head their gazes met. "What do you think, Sheilock?" he queried softly.

Sheila's past experience in solving crimes gave her no training in looking for a woman she'd never met in a city she didn't know. Only the despair in Martha's wet eyes made her ask, "Was there anything she talked about this morning that might give a clue about where she'd go?"

Martha considered, then shook her head. "No, most of the mornin' she talked about the banks closing."

Sheila looked down at her watch. "What time do they close?"

"Not closing for the day," Teddy called from the kitchen. Her scornful emphasis on the last word made the addition of "dummy" unnecessary. "Closing for good. You know, in 1929. She told me all about it Christmas Eve, Mamar, while you were at the midnight service." The child rejoined the grownups, wiping damp hands on the seat of her jeans. "We were up in my room, and she was fiddling with Jack's binoculars while I was doing a chemistry 'speriment."

Sheila repressed a shudder.

"Ellgie was looking out at the water," Teddy continued, " 'n' she started talking about pirates and buried treasure. Then she told me all about the banks closing and pro-bitchin' and Herbert Hoover and that damned Catholic Democrat, Alfred E. Smith."

"Theodosia Charlotte!" her grandmama exclaimed, momentarily distracted from worry.

"But, Mamar, *She* doesn't know about Ellgie—how she gets stuck on one subject for days and *days.*"

Crispin dropped a hand lightly to the girl's shoulder. "That's not what Mamar meant, Tiger, and you know it. How long's it been since you tasted a bar of soap?"

Teddy flushed and jerked away.

Sheila, herself once a child in a strict adult world, felt a flicker of sympathy. She returned to her original line of inquiry. "Could Laura Grace have possibly gone to the bank? Is it anywhere nearby?"

"No." Martha shook her head regretfully. "We bank at Barnett. You know the Barnetts, Crispin, from Ortega. Fine people. We've known 'em for ages. They sold the bank, of course, but it still has a local feel—"

Crispin deftly headed off that southern sidetrack into family history. "Sheila may have a point, Aunt Martha. Maybe Laura Grace went to the bank."

She considered the point doubtfully. "I don't think so, dear. I transact all our business. Why, I can't remember the last time Laura Grace went to a bank. She probably doesn't even know how to find the branch I use now'days."

"It's not the same one she used in 1929?" Sheila persisted.

Martha's headshake had become automatic. "Oh, no, dear. In '29 the Barnetts had just one bank. But the colored—" she caught Crispin's eye and amended hastily, "—blacks have taken over downtown. We never go there anymore. I wonder if Helen and Justin will think to look inside Riverside Presbyterian? Laura Grace wandered in there once."

Teddy quashed that idea. "Mama told Daddy on the phone to start there. Have you looked good under bushes in the park?"

Martha's flushed face drained of color. "Oh, honey, do you really think—?"

"We don't think anything," Crispin interjected firmly. "Does Laura Grace have a checkbook?"

Martha started to shake her head, then her hands flew to her hair. "She used to have a passbook. Let me see." She bustled away twittering to herself. In a moment she returned, looking hopeful. "It doesn't seem to be there. Perhaps she did go to the bank." Almost immediately, she plunged back into gloom. "But how on earth would she have gotten there?"

"By bus." Teddy hopped on one foot with excitement. "Ellgie loves to ride the bus, and I'll bet they'd let her ride free, she's so old. Come on!" She jerked Crispin so hard he stumbled. "She rode the bus to the bank downtown! I just know it! Come *on*!"

Crispin held her firmly by the nape of the neck and spoke to his aunt. "We'll go look, and I'll call you."

Martha started to nod, then froze. "Oh, Crispin!" Her face was pitiful to see. "The bank's not there any more! Not too long ago, they built a big new one behind the old one. She wouldn't know that. If Laura Grace got disoriented—"

Her terror spurred Sheila to action. "We'll go look at the new building, and around a few blocks. Then Crispin can call you." She forced herself to speak lightly. Privately, she was vowing that as soon as they'd cruised up and down a couple of downtown blocks, they would storm the police station. As much as she hated to admit it, a six-foot man was more likely to be taken seriously by the authorities than a plump dithery woman worried to distraction about her absentminded companion.

Laura Grace lay facedown on the floor, eyes closed, one cheek pressed to the carpet. With her arms spread out, she looked ready for crucifixion. She didn't care. She was waiting for justice. She had no doubt it would come. She just wished it would hurry.

People milled around her like leftovers from a live Nativity. Laura Grace kept her eyes opened a slit, watched them steal nervous, furtive glances in her direction. The security guard, a handsome man in his blue uniform, rested one knee on the floor near her head. Didn't seem to know how to kneel. Probably Baptist.

He bent so close she could smell mint Certs on his breath. "Please, ma'am," he said, "do get up. Please!" Good. He was finally begging.

Laura Grace, however, had no intention of getting up just because he begged. She wanted what she'd come for: two hundred and nineteen dollars and twelve cents. She waved her worn savings passbook in one outstretched hand.

"This isn't the bank anymore." A bald man in a navy suit used the same tone Martha used when asking her to put on some clothes before company arrived. "Barnett's is now the tall building around the block."

He'd said that before, ever since he got off the elevator and heard her explaining to the security guard what she wanted. He'd been saying it with tedious regularity ever since. Did she look like a woman who couldn't hear?

At least the bald man and the guard had shown her the respect due a lady. Laura Grace was glad she'd remembered Crispin was coming for dinner, and dressed up before she left home. She was a bit overdressed for an afternoon bank visit, of course, but Mama used to say a lady could get away with anything so long as she was genteel. Laura Grace was being genteel. Also firm. It looked like she'd have to go on being firm until these fool men got some sense in their heads.

"My money was placed in the safe in this very buildin'." She did not open her eyes, but she spoke slowly and clearly so they could not possibly misunderstand. "I asked for Mr. Barnett to put it there with his own two hands, and I never authorized him or anyone else to move it. You just run down and take a look. Perhaps it was mislaid. But hurry. I have dinner guests comin'."

A girl tittered. Laura Grace opened her eyes and shot her a baleful glare. Silly child, looked like a high schooler in spite of all that lipstick and bottle-red hair. And the young man who'd swallowed a derisive snort had terrible pimples. When did banks start hiring children too young to realize institutions could go under with people's money in them?

Laura Grace was old enough—and smart. She wanted her two hundred and nineteen dollars and twelve cents. She waved the passbook again.

The man in navy gave a nervous, shifty cough. "Ma'am, you could catch cold on that floor."

"If I do, I shall certainly sue." Laura Grace closed her eyes, again leaving just a slit so she could see how that sat with him.

The security guard peered from beneath bushy gray eyebrows and spoke softly. "Should I call the police, do you think? Everybody will be getting off work pretty soon."

The bald man looked helplessly around him. Laura Grace could read his mind on his face. He didn't like to call the police, but he didn't have a man or woman in his bank with enough gumption to throw her out. Everybody was awfully busy all of a sudden looking somewhere else.

A fine sweat broke out where his hairline used to be. "Please, ma'am!" He almost wept. "Please get up!"

Laura Grace was giving it serious consideration. Under this thin carpet, the floor was marble, and damnably hard. Did ancient Romans really lie around on marble couches? She'd begun to doubt her Latin book. She'd also begun to doubt her gulls. Pleasant surprises, indeed! Had they meant this stubborn banker who refused to give her what was lawfully hers?

Across the lobby, she saw six feet—a woman, a child, and a man with a limp—enter the large revolving door. Inspired, she warned, "Reporters will be here soon. If I tell them you are withholdin' my money, how will you show your face at the Seminole Club? Your days as a banker will be over, young man."

The boy with pimples snickered. "The Seminole

Club? That's been closed since—" Somebody shushed him. Laura Grace ignored him.

She was considering going home to call her lawyer, when help came from an unexpected source. Two small feet in scuffed white running shoes detached themselves from the other newcomers and almost flew across the marble floor.

"Ellgie? What have they done to you? Are you dead? Ellgie!" Whirling to confront the security guard, she shouted in flame-faced fury, "If you've killed my aunt, you'll be sorry! My daddy's going to Congress, and he'll have a law passed that—"

The old woman lifted her head and raised herself on one elbow. "I'm not dead, Teddy, dear. I'm just not lettin' these folks close their bank without givin' me back my money." She dropped back to the floor and shut her eyes.

The child knelt and gave her a shake. "Then you can get up, now, Ellgie. Crispin's here."

Sheila was touched by the joy that flooded the wizened face when the old woman heard Crispin's name. As he crossed toward her, Laura Grace immediately pushed herself up with her forearms and began the laborious process of getting to her feet, flapping aside all offers of assistance.

"I thought somebody'd come sooner or later," she told them with satisfaction. "Never imagined it'd be you, though."

Sheila, waiting unobtrusively near the door, thought Laura Grace had fainted and a small crowd of departing workers had stopped to help her. Observing their flabbergasted faces, however, she began to get a truer picture of what must have happened. This was certainly no longer a bank. The revolving door led now into a small lobby entrance for upstairs offices, guarded by a curved black security desk. To the left, an elegant brass grille from floor to ceiling blocked off a vast, dim, unoccupied space. Only the grille, a brass mailbox, brass elevator doors marked with a scrolled *B*, and a large brass directory remained of

Barnett Bank's former occupancy. These people had stopped on their way home simply to be nice to an odd old woman.

Laura Grace accepted their homage as a queen. Barely as tall as Teddy and twice as round, with wiry hair bristling like an elderly Medusa's, she waved something until Crispin took it. "Tell that young man to give me my money and let's get out of here."

She went to lean against the marble wall with a "whoosh!" of relief. Teddy sat down at her feet and immediately began an excited minute-by-minute account of their search.

The "young" man in question—balding and over fifty—turned toward Crispin. His face was flushed, his voice strained. "Is she related to you? She's been here nearly half an hour, and we didn't know whom to call. She doesn't seem to understand—"

Laura Grace touched Teddy lightly to still her for a moment. "*He's* the one who doesn't understand," she announced firmly. "I told Mr. Barnett to put my money in his safe himself, in 1928. It's probably slipped behind a shelf or somethin'. Now, Teddy, what were you sayin'?"

"This isn't a bank!" The bald man sounded close to tears. "Barnett moved to their new building years ago! But she kept insisting—" Lowering his voice, he spoke with many gestures. Once, Sheila observed, he pulled out a handkerchief and wiped his high brow.

Meanwhile, the others drifted out the door, furtively comparing the newcomers' stylish clothes with the little round crone's bright red blouse trimmed with lace and floor-length purple velvet skirt. A wide gold belt, gold evening flats, and a rope of pearls almost to her waist completed Laura Grace's striking ensemble.

"I thought she was a bag lady!" one woman exclaimed to another as the revolving door closed behind them.

Sheila smiled. Laura Grace's attire was certainly unorthodox, but a more experienced eye would have noticed

that the gold flats were expensive and the pearls exquisite.

"I'll be right back," Crispin told her and followed his
harried companion through a door in the brass grille. Ten
minutes later he limped back alone, carrying a slim wad of
money. "Two hundred and nineteen dollars and twelve
cents. Is that right, Laura Grace?"

Sheila and the security guard watched in disbelief as,
nodding, the old woman extended a claw, counted the cur-
rency carefully, then stuffed it into a tiny velvet evening
bag dangling from one wrist. "Just right. Did he mark my
passbook?"

"No, he kept it. You were closing out the account."

"Oh, yes. I forgot." She turned to Teddy and said in
a conspiratorial tone perfectly audible for thirty feet, "Always know where your money is, dear. Watch them put it
in the safe yourself and get the name of the person who
takes it. Don't let them cheat you!" She moved—
processed, Sheila thought wryly, would be more apt—
toward the door.

As Crispin limped over to Sheila, she cocked one eyebrow. "So, had her money fallen behind a shelf?"

He gave her a rueful smile and handed her the old
passbook. "Not exactly. Just thank God for teller machines
and put that in your purse for Aunt Martha while I thank
the guard."

In the past hour the wind had risen and the temperature
must have fallen fifteen degrees. Sheila was glad of her
sweater as they walked to the parking garage, and Teddy
was shivering by the time they reached the car.

"Can you drive, dear, with that cast?" Laura Grace inquired solicitously of Crispin.

"*She* drives," Teddy said, jerking her head in Sheila's
direction without actually deigning to look her way.

For the first time the elderly woman noticed Sheila.
"Who is She?" Like Teddy, she capitalized it.

Crispin took Sheila by the elbow and steered her forward. "This is Sheila Travis, my friend, who—" sternly, "—has spent her first afternoon in Jacksonville looking for you, Laura Grace."

Snapping black eyes peered up into Sheila's, then the wrinkled mouth split with a merry smile. "*You* must be the pleasant surprise my gulls promised this morning! Not Crispin at all!"

By avoiding Crispin's eye, Sheila managed to shake hands with a modicum of poise.

Meanwhile, Teddy smouldered at her elbow like a game warden who'd caught Sheila poaching not once but twice on her own preserve.

Crispin opened the back door with a flourish. "I've called Martha to say we found you, and she's rounding up the troops. With any luck, she'll have coffee made before we get there. Brrr! Let's get moving!"

"I don't want coffee," Laura Grace told him with the confidence of a woman who has accomplished a good deal and is now ready for her reward. "I want a fuzzy navel."

Crispin climbed in the front passenger side. Teddy stomped around the car and flung herself into the back with her great-aunt. Sheila started the engine and eased the big Cadillac into traffic.

Reaching to turn on some heat, she glanced in the rearview mirror, met Teddy's sullen gaze, and knew how she'd feel driving a tank with explosives inside.

After a few blocks, Teddy finally lowered the wattage of her glower; she turned to her great-aunt. "What else did the gulls say today, Ellgie?" she demanded.

Laura Grace puckered her brow. "Well, dear, there was grace, mercy, and the pleasant surprise. That was Crispin's guest, of course. And there was one more cord, a black one, that I thought meant danger or death . . . but perhaps it just meant that mule-headed young man at the bank."

"Maybe it did mean danger or death," Teddy said in

a considering voice. "For somebody. The day's not over yet."

In the mirror, she gave Sheila a meaningful glare.

"Well," Sheila told Crispin four hours later as they wended their way through twilit streets back to the L'Arkens', "if Teddy gets her wish and I do die tonight, at least it won't be from boredom."

From the Ortega River Bridge, the city skyline rested on the river's black breast like a diamond necklace scattered with sapphires and, here and there, a ruby. Lit by a nearly full moon, the river was whipped to whitecaps, and Sheila was glad she wasn't going boating tonight.

Crispin sighed. "Laura Grace gets crazier and crazier. I don't know what Aunt Martha's going to do with her. But at least, honey, she's not my blood relation."

"You ingrate! If it hadn't been for Laura Grace, you'd have had to introduce me to everybody and we'd have stood around making inane conversation. As it was—"

He laughed. "Did I *ever* introduce you to anybody?"

"Not that I remember. But I do like your friends. Very much."

They had arrived back at Martha's to find that she had, indeed, called in the troops and spread her mahogany dining table with coffee and drinks. She had also put a chicken on to fry, started rice, put on a rose shirtwaist, brushed her curls, and was halfway through making an apple pie while chatting with her family—who were massed in the central hall near the front door. Sheila suspected they were clustered there because it was easier to talk to Martha, but they looked like a welcome home party.

Laura Grace accepted it as such. Before Crispin could greet anyone or introduce his guest, the old woman waved aloft her evening bag and patted it with a satisfied smile. "Went down to the bank to get my money. May I have a fuzzy navel, Martha?"

"Justin will get you one. I'm in the middle of pie crust." Freed of worry, Martha was pretty and flushed, floured to the elbow, with damp tendrils curling around her face.

The tall blond man moved easily toward the impromptu bar. He had a broad face, eyes as blue as Teddy's, sensual lips, and a deep cleft in his firm chin. Worry had loosened his red tie and mussed his well-cut hair, but he looked calm and capable as he poured orange juice and peach schnapps over crushed ice.

Meanwhile, a loose-limbed woman with astonishing gold eyes spoke in gentle rebuke. "You had us worried, Ellgie! We didn't know what'd happened to you."

"Nothing happened to me, Helen. I just ran down to the bank."

A girl tearing lettuce in the kitchen giggled. "Just ran down to the bank? You scared us to *death*!"

A stocky young man with rough brown curls snarled. "It's not funny. We've all been hauling our asses—"

"Jack!" Justin said sternly. The young man subsided. Justin handed Laura Grace her drink and inquired, "May I mix you one, Sheila?" He gave her a rueful smile.

"You've certainly earned it," Helen added with a grateful smile.

Sheila smiled back, but shook her head. "I don't think—"

Laura Grace put a claw on her arm. "Taste mine. You're gonna love it."

The old woman might not be utterly crazy, Sheila decided. In spite of its name, the drink was delicious.

Justin brought Sheila's drink, then socked Crispin lightly on the bicep. "Thank God you thought of the bank, old man."

"It was me, Daddy! I knew right where to find Ellgie, right exactly, didn't I, Crispin?" Teddy bobbed between the two tall men like a nervous gnat.

"Shut up, brat," Jack growled, still smarting.

"Teddy, honey," Martha called, "I need you in here to help me peel apples. Crispin loves apple pie, and you are such a careful peeler." Teddy, visibly torn between being with Crispin and impressing him with her skill, slid reluctantly away.

While the others vied for Crispin's attention, caught up on family news, and made predictions for the upcoming football game, Sheila explored. The living room was decorated with what she suspected were Martha's favorite pieces: a dainty escritoire, mahogany piecrust table, and chairs and a sofa in tones that echoed the ivory, cherry-red, and empire-blue of an old Persian rug. Three enormous windows overlooked miles of river.

Sheila headed for a wing chair near the windows that was turned toward the view, then paused to examine a pair of photographs in silver frames. The old-fashioned elderly couple must be Martha's parents—Crispin's grandparents. Crispin had inherited the woman's chin and the man's unruly dark forelock. In the next frame were a gentle woman and a man with arrogant eyes. With a smile, Sheila gently touched the small boy between them. He looked a lot like Forbes.

She had just settled into the chair to enjoy the view when Laura Grace strode in and shoved up the middle window. "It's hot in here." She turned her back to it and hiked up her purple velvet skirt. The buttocks that met the brisk late afternoon breeze were brown and bare.

"Put down your skirt!" Jack snapped, from the doorway. His face flamed as he cast an embarrassed look toward the sofa. For the first time Sheila saw a pale young woman sitting there reading a magazine, idly stroking a fat gold cat beside her.

Laura Grace gave the offending garment one final flap, then lowered it. "Okay. I was just coolin' off a bit." Leaving up the window, she marched to the wing chair Sheila had chosen. "You've got my seat, dear. Take that one over there, please."

"Ellgie!" Jack bellowed, pulling down the window with a bang.

Sheila stood. "It's okay, I don't mind." She didn't. The

offered chair was in a dim corner beyond the sofa. With any luck, she could rest a bit while the others talked.

Jack flopped onto the sofa beside the young woman and muttered, "I don't care if she is old, she ought to have better manners."

"Shush." The young woman reached out to stroke his arm instead of the cat. She didn't raise her eyes from her magazine. Sheila leaned back and closed her own eyes.

Conversation flowed from the hall and kitchen in pleasing harmony. Unlike the twang of Tennessee, the slow drawl of lower Alabama, the rounded vowels of Charleston, or the witty sparkle of Atlanta, this accent was like warm honey, Sheila thought, wrapping you fondly in every word. . . .

Sheila must have dozed off, for she opened her eyes and found that Helen, Justin, and Crispin were talking to Laura Grace, and the young woman from the kitchen had joined the other two on the sofa and was regarding Sheila with frank interest.

Sheila smiled drowsily. "Are you Brandy?"

The young woman nodded, her hair falling in a cascade of russet curls. They framed a face lightly touched with coral lipstick, mascara, and brown eye shadow that made her eyes look like cinnamon. Her nails were polished in the same soft coral as her lipstick. Her denim jumper and forest-green turtleneck looked freshly pressed. In all, Brandy looked as if she had stepped from a shower a few minutes ago, and would retain the pleasant smell of soap all day.

"Yes, and I'm so glad to meet you. We could hardly *wait* to see what you—"

"Brandy!" Jack barked. For an arbiter of family manners, Sheila reflected, he could well start with his own. He jerked one thumb toward the other young woman, who was still reading. "This is Sparrow."

Sparrow looked up. Her eyes were the exact shade of a pair of aquamarine earrings Sheila had in her suitcase, and her hair was a crisp white wedge above sharp features.

Except for vivid red lipstick, two spots of blusher, and deep aqua eye shadow, she could have been carved from snow. As one ice-white hand—tipped with nails so deeply red they looked black—continued to stroke the cat, she seemed oddly contained for someone so young, as enclosed as a cloistered nun.

"Do you and Jack go to school together?" Sheila asked her.

It had been an idle, casual question, certainly not designed to pry. Yet Sparrow pressed her lips together and flared her nostrils. "No. I go to junior college here. Jack's down at Gainesville."

Laura Grace spoke abruptly. "A cat jumped off the ninth story once, Sparrow. Served it right. It was after a pigeon."

Sparrow's hand tightened on the cat's body, but before anyone else could speak, Martha called from the kitchen. "Dinner's about ready. Helen, are you sure you all won't just stay and eat? I've got plenty."

Helen fetched her coat and purse from a dining room chair. "No, Mamar, we have to get on home to dress, and Daphne's got enough food to feed an army. Crispin, be sure you all get to the party by nine."

"What's at nine?" he asked.

She gave him a friendly pat. "Wait and see. Just be there."

When they sat down to dinner, Martha held out her hands to her guests and smiled at Sheila. "I like to hold hands for the blessing." Sheila reached for Laura Grace, but the old woman hugged her fists to her chest.

With a faint moue of irritation, Martha bowed her head. "Dear Lord, we thank You for all the blessings You have bestowed upon us. This food, Crispin and Sheila's safe arrival. No, dear! We don't eat our napkin during the blessing."

Startled, Sheila opened her eyes. Laura Grace was cramming white damask into her mouth. She removed it long enough to explain, "I'm starved," then crammed it in again.

Martha resigned herself to the inevitable. "Amen."

During dinner, Sheila found herself growing sleepier and sleepier. She was content to let the others talk, paying little attention to what Martha was telling Crispin until she exclaimed, "Oh! Justin said he got your thyroid pills today, Laura Grace, but he forgot to leave them. Remind me to get them tonight."

Crispin smiled across the table and tried to bring Sheila into the conversation. "Aunt Martha was talking about Libba's mother, Sheila. I told you, she's got Alzheimer's—"

"We don't know that that's what it is, dear," Martha corrected him. "It could be hardening of the arteries. Bad hearts run in that family. Libba's dad—of course he wasn't in the same family—but both Maybelle's sister and their father, old Judge Covington—"

"Bad heart," Laura Grace repeated unexpectedly. "Old pirate had a bad heart and buried his treasure. The tree marks the spot."

"Yes, dear." Martha gave Sheila an apologetic smile. "Laura Grace wants you to know that Libba's grandfather's house, the one where Hayden and—and Daphne live," she corrected herself firmly, "has a kneeling tree, bent a special way, where the old pirate Dan McGirth is supposed to have buried treasure. The Ortega River was once called McGirt's Creek."

Laura Grace lifted her head and loudly began to recite: "Daniel McGirth was a soldier in the American Revolution. When his horse was stolen, Daniel McGirth turned to piracy. If English frigates chased him up the St. Johns, he put in at Pirate's Cove, where he was hidden by the Indian chief Ortega and his beautiful daughter Altamaha. Wherever he buried treasure, he bent a young oak to mark the spot."

Martha laughed indulgently. "Don't believe it, Sheila. Ortega's full of those trees, and nobody's found any trea-

sure yet. Especially," she added to Laura Grace, "old
Judge Covington. He lost everything he had before he
died."

Laura Grace reached for a piece of lettuce and began
spreading it with butter. In a voice that was rich and perfectly pitched, she crooned, "By the light—of the silvery
moon—I saw your spoon—must of been back in June. By
the light—"

"Here, dear," Martha interrupted, "have a biscuit and
stop thinking about pirates."

"Pirates land on the dock," Laura Grace persisted, her
black button eyes darting from Sheila to Crispin. "Dark
hats. Swarming out of boats. Carrying treasure."

Crispin spoke like one determined to keep sanity at
least within hailing distance. "I didn't realize Libba's
mother grew up in Ortega."

Martha helped her guests to more chicken. "She was
born there, but she grew up down this way. The
Covingtons were a distinguished family before the old
judge lost his money back in '29. Stock market, I believe.
He had a stroke right after that—Maybelle found him in
the yard one morning, utterly paralyzed. He stayed that
way nearly two years, poor man, until he died. Dear Mrs.
Covington—she was much younger than he—had to go to
work to raise those little girls. She did a fine job with
them. Fine!"

"The money's safe and sound," Laura Grace muttered.

"Yes, Laura Grace, now your money's safe and
sound."

Sheila was fascinated by how Martha could converse
in this Ping-Pong fashion between Laura Grace's fantasies
and her guests. Now, she turned back to Sheila to complete the story she'd begun. "The older Covington daughter never married. Maybelle married Ralph, a sweet man,
but after he left the Navy he never set the world on fire.
I hope he left Libba enough to pay her mother's bills."

At that point, Sheila suddenly discovered that her

head was too heavy for her neck and her upper lids were magnetized to the lower. She jerked her head up, prying her eyes open only by exercising great force.

"Honey?" Crispin asked from a great distance. "Do you need to rest a few minutes?"

Martha shoved back her chair. "You poor thing, you had to drive the whole way. Come lie down on my bed for a bit."

Five minutes later, Sheila drifted to sleep on Martha's pink perfumed comforter covered by a light blue blanket.

She woke some time later to Martha's distressed voice. ". . . gone for years! Why drag them along tonight? Helen is simply worried sick. I could just *kill* Muffy!"

Sheila lifted herself on one elbow and peered at the clock. Eight already? They needed to be going.

"Keeps her mouth shut," Laura Grace sounded like her own mouth was full. "That's what she said. Funny way to live. Hard to eat."

"Oh, pshaw!" Martha sounded like Sheila's Aunt Mary at her most exasperated.

That reminded Sheila—she still hadn't called Aunt Mary to say they'd arrived. She'd try to remember to call from Justin's, before the party. Swinging her long legs off the bed, she padded to the dining room.

Martha looked up with a concerned smile. "Feeling better?"

"Much," Sheila admitted gratefully, yawning.

Crispin pushed himself away from the table. "We'd better get on our way. It's going to take me a while to get in a tux."

Laura Grace also rose, clutched the seat of her skirt, and headed purposefully toward the living room. "It's hot in here again."

Crispin dragged Sheila out the door with indecent haste.

————

Again Teddy and Einstein met the car as if they had been waiting for it, but this time the child headed straight for Crispin's door. Her hair gleamed in white waves on the shoulders of a tailored navy velvet dress. Sheila gave Helen high marks for not putting this particular little girl in pink ruffles.

She followed Teddy and Crispin to the house, hampered by Einstein, who had constituted himself her waddling escort. At the steps, the child turned to Crispin and said loudly, "If you hadn't brought Her, we could of done all sorts of things. I've got a new fishing rod. Wanna go fishing with me in the morning before She gets up?"

He chuckled. "You'd better take *Her* before I get up, Teddy. She's a morning person. Besides, I don't like to fish. What happened to your pigtails?"

"They aren't pigtails, they are braids." Sheila could tell it was an old tease between them.

"Welcome!" Brandy, elegant in emerald velvet, held open a door of singularly beautiful beveled glass. How had the panes survived Jack and Teddy all these years, Sheila wondered.

Brandy beckoned them to the living room. "We've found the funniest pictures!"

They followed her, and found Jack and Sparrow huddled over a thick book. Jack, in a tux, still wore a look of stormy petulance. Sparrow, in a long white sheath slit to reveal one shapely thigh, absently stroked a long Maltese on the cushion beside her. Einstein abandoned Sheila and laid down at Sparrow's feet.

"Look at Mama!" Brandy exclaimed, claiming the book and holding it out. "Did you ever wear your hair like this, Mrs. Travis?"

Sheila scanned a black-and-white picture of a cheer-leading squad from the late sixties. The team had obviously had their hair done just for the picture. Those lacquered bubbles would never have survived a game. Helen was easy to recognize as the rangy captain in the center.

Since she was already identified with the aged and ridiculous, Sheila decided to contribute to their historical knowledge. "No, my hair's so curly, I ironed it."

They gaped. "Ironed it?" Sheila almost laughed. Her own adolescent horror had been that her hair wouldn't lie smooth. She had willingly laid her head on the ironing board every morning. Was that any worse, she wondered, than their own generation's sticking three or four holes through each earlobe, wearing two pairs of shorts when one would do, or pulling on a pair of tights and a bulky blouse and calling themselves well dressed?

Crispin took the annual. He pointed at the young faces in the photo. "Helen, Libba—" a well-rounded blonde on one end, more interested in something or someone to her right than in the photographer "—and Daphne, center stage, as always."

Daphne actually stood to Helen's left, a vibrant girl with a cloud of dark hair, but she smiled at the camera with the promise of a secret she'd be willing to share. Once you'd seen her, you had trouble looking anywhere else.

Sheila looked for one other name. So that was Muffy! Chin tilted and one hand on hip, she gave the photographer a come-hither smile far more provocative than those of her teammates.

"Look at Daddy," Teddy ordered, handing Crispin a group photo of young teens in shorts gathered outdoors around a wooden cross.

Crispin whooped with delight. "Church camp! I didn't know Justin still had that!" Sheila craned to look.

Justin had not yet filled out, but the square face and cleft chin were the same. His arms circled the necks of youths on each side of him, drawing them toward his chest. The blond boy was making a peace *V* at the camera. The gangly brunette ogled the photographer with crossed eyes; his tongue lolled out one side of his mouth.

"Good heavens!" Sheila looked from him to the well-built man beside her.

"What is it? Let me see!" Teddy tugged at the picture and studied it intently. "It's Crispin!" She pranced over to show her older brother and sister. "Look, it's Crispin!"

"Ug-ly," Jack complimented him. "Who's the other guy?"

"Eddie Weare," Crispin told him, "your dad's best friend. He was Lee's quarterback their senior year, when the team was number one in the state. His folks moved away during college."

"He may come to the party tonight," Teddy said importantly. "I guess that's why Mama let Daddy drag these down after she made us keep everything clean."

Sheila picked up a shot of three little boys standing on a dock with big smiles and one small fish—the same trio who would clown years later at church camp. "You have hidden talents," she teased Crispin.

He blew in her ear. "You don't know the half of them."

Teddy glared at Sheila and tugged Crispin's arm. "Let me see." She gave the picture a scornful stare, then blazed indignantly, "You said you don't like to fish!"

"That's why." Crispin let the picture drift to the coffee table. "We spent that whole blazing day on the dock, and that's all we caught. Aunt Martha wouldn't even cook it for us."

"I get better fish than that all the time!" Teddy marched upstairs in disdain. Sheila wondered if anyone else saw her smuggle the church camp picture behind her navy skirt.

Jack hauled himself to his feet and put out a hand for Sparrow. "We'd better get moving. Dump Copernicus and come on."

With obvious reluctance, Sparrow gave the Maltese one last pat and rose.

Brandy held out her hand to Sheila. "Come see your room."

At the landing newel post, Crispin paused. "Want to see the secret room?"

"No!" Teddy hollered down the stairs. "Don't you dare! Nobody goes in there without my permission!"

Brandy's room was as dainty and pretty as its mistress, with blue-and-white candy-striped paper, white ruffled curtains, tennis trophies lining the bookshelf, and pink satin ballet shoes hanging on one wall. Brandy crossed to a door in one corner, peered in, and gave a most undainty yell. "Teddy L'Arken, come get this iguana out of the bathtub right this minute!" Turning back, she added in more moderate tones, "You have to share a bath with Teddy and me." She indicated two tan-and-white cats dozing in the middle of her blue comforter. "If Newton and Gauss bother you, put them out."

One cat opened a large green eye and dared Sheila to try.

After Brandy left, Sheila dressed under their critical gaze, then surveyed herself in the mirror. Did she look like an emaciated eggplant? Should she have worn her black silk instead?

No, her new dress was lovely—a French crepe in soft aubergine, with a flared skirt, long sleeves, and self-embroidery on the cuffs. Aunt Mary had lent garnets to wear at her ears and throat. She fluffed her curls and went downstairs looking far more festive than she felt. In sixteen years as an embassy wife, she'd attended enough parties to last a lifetime. Experience didn't make her more eager to spend an evening with a hundred strangers.

Halfway downstairs, she paused to admire Crispin in his tux. He turned, saw her, and gave her a smile that nearly stopped her heart. *Tonight's party will be different*, Sheila reminded herself. *Crispin isn't taking you along to advance his career. He just likes being with you*. It was a satisfying thought.

At his elbow, Teddy glowered. "I don't see why I have to go to this old party anyway. All we do is stand in a row and look nerdy. Then Jack, Brandy, and Sparrow get to go to another party down at the Landing with their friends, but I have to stay in the kitchen with Clarinda until Mamar's ready to bring me home." She crossed her eyes and stuck out her tongue, then turned like a whirlwind. "But come on, we don't want to be late!"

The two girls slung coats over their shoulders and headed for the door. "We're to go by the road, so our shoes don't get messed up," Teddy informed them.

On the way over, Sheila pulled Crispin's arm so they'd lag behind. "What's got that puzzled look on your face?"

He fished in his pocket and held a photograph up to a dull orange streetlight. It was Eddie Weare at about sixteen, posed on the bow of a sailboat in his bathing suit. He looked like a young Neptune. "I can't figure out why Aunt Martha's in such a tizzy about Eddie coming home. She told me twice to stick near him."

Sheila took the photo and studied it. "If he's well-preserved after twenty-five years, I'll stick near him," she offered.

"Down, girl." Crispin pulled her to him and kissed her lightly. "I didn't bring you to Jacksonville to fall for Eddie Weare."

Brandy and Teddy slipped in what must be a kitchen door, but Crispin took Sheila up three brick steps to a door of polished oak. A short young man stepped back to let them into a gilt-and-ivory foyer with a green marble floor. His hair was black, his clean-shaven chin almost blue, and his face shaped like a monkey's. He gave Sheila a simian smile. "I'm Treye L'Arken, Hayden's son. What's a beautiful woman like you doin' with a turkey like Crispin?"

He might be homely, but Treye wore his tux like he wore it often. "Welcome to Daphne's Do: Do come in, do meet my impressive guests, do see my beautiful home. Also, don't miss the bar and buffet."

"Don't monopolize our most important guests, Treye," a slender woman admonished playfully. She wore a black mini slip dress that fell over her slender form so simply it whispered "Money!" Her only jewelry was small gold studs in her ears and a striking necklace of large gold coins. Sheila recognized her immediately. Daphne L'Arken would still be the center of any picture. Tonight she wore a French twist that would have made some women look old. On Daphne, it looked ready to receive a tiara.

She gave Crispin a hug, and Sheila a smile that immediately invited her into a circle of intimate friends. "We are so glad you were able to come. I once met your husband. A wonderful man!"

Sheila was trotting out her standard "Yes, wasn't he?" when two new guests arrived. One, a slight man, was striking rather than handsome. He had a Roman nose, rounded chin, and pouches beneath deep brown eyes. His rich, even tan was heightened by a rosy patch on each cheek like the rose on a peach. His hair fell from a side part like polished walnut. In spite of formal dress, he stood casually, left hand on hip, to greet Treye. When he let the hand drop, Sheila saw that his tux was artfully cut to minimize uneven shoulders. It could not conceal the curve of his spine.

The other, a big man with coppery hair and a pock-marked face, wore a gray suit and red tie. He kept jerking his head as if his shirt collar was too tight.

"Dang!" Daphne exclaimed softly with a rueful smile. "There's Rob Wilmer and—Tom Goren?" If she were puzzled, she swiftly regained her poise. Her smile apologized. "Just when I thought we could have a chat, Sheila. Please stick around later, so we can visit. Oh, Hayden, you found it!" She accepted a glass from a short dark man who had to be Treye's father. Daphne's emerald eyes thanked him as she sipped it gratefully. "I never can remember where I leave my drink. Sheila, this is Hayden L'Arken, my husband. Honey, this is Sheila, Tyler Travis's widow. How Crispin got so lucky I cannot imagine!" She winked at Crispin, then glided toward the newcomers.

A blunt hairy hand was thrust toward Sheila's, and a light baritone drawled, "Good to meet you, Mrs. Travis. How'd you get hooked up with this gardener? I was in Japan once, myself. Ever know that, Crispin?" He launched into a day-by-day account of a trip he'd taken to Tokyo a decade before.

As he droned on, Sheila tried to picture this hairy little man in surgical scrubs. Hayden had curly black hair everywhere except on top of his head—thick on the backs of his hands, curling from his nostrils, bristling above dark bulging eyes, even sprouting from his ears. He must look like a masked monkey! What kind of parents could produce one short, dark, hairy son and a Viking like Justin?

Speaking of sons, Sheila saw Treye start up the stairs at a slow trot just as Jack and Sparrow were coming down. As the cousins met, Treye smiled and Jack glowered— then turned deliberately sideways so they passed not shoulder to shoulder, but face to face. From the way Jack's hand dropped to Sparrow's shoulder and tightened, Sheila wondered if Treye was interested in her, too. If so, no wonder Jack acted like a dog circling for a fight.

Hayden was now on day eight of his Japanese itinerary. Sheila was switching her attention to the bright splashed colors of a modern painting on the far wall when a deep honeyed cry rang out. "Lord love you, Crispin Montgomery—more handsome than ever!"

A tall woman swept across the foyer and clasped both his hands in hers. As tall as Sheila's own five foot nine, her dark hair was the same rich gray as the dress that fell from her angular frame in graceful folds.

Without waiting for Crispin to introduce them, she proclaimed, "I am Charlotte Holmes Aspen, my dear, but please call me Charho. We are just delighted you could come for the game! If this man doesn't treat you right, you let me know."

Crispin bent and planted a kiss on the tanned cheek. "Hello, Charho. Sheila, this is Helen's mother."

Charho patted his arm. "Should have been his mother-in-law, if Helen hadn't foolishly fallen in love with Justin. Just broke my heart!" Her eyes twinkled roguishly.

"Broke both our hearts," Crispin agreed, smiling, "but your daughter never did have her mother's good sense."

"Her daughter has enough sense to break up this conversation before Sheila shoots you both." Helen's eyes sparkled like the rainbow sequins on her black bodice. "Isn't this fun?" She indicated the rooms full of people—men in tuxedos and women in gowns as delicate and lovely as butterflies.

"It would be more fun if we had something to drink," Crispin complained. "Hayden has monopolized Sheila since we got here."

"Not at all, not at all," Hayden rumbled, waving them away with one hairy hand. "You all go get some refreshments. We can finish our chat later, Mrs. Travis." He drifted off to the two men who'd arrived earlier, now standing alone.

A sugary voice behind Sheila asked, "Why, Crispin, honey, how on earth did you get that tux over your broken leg?"

A woman positioned herself to exclude Sheila while giving Crispin the best view down her strikingly white cleavage. With reckless disregard for those who dislike red on redheads, she wore a scarlet slip dress held up by the merest wisp of straps. A filmy stole shading from yellow to deep crimson looked like a flame around her milky shoulders. Even her evening flats were red.

"Have you met Muffy Merriwether, precious?" Charlotte Holmes asked Sheila. "Muffy's one of Helen's oldest friends."

"Not *that* old, Charho," Muffy said archly, "though I do remember Mr. Aspen." She still hadn't glanced in Sheila's direction.

Crispin gave the woman in scarlet a teasing grin. "Evenin', Muffy. How's your current love life? Any meaningful relationships?"

Muffy's red lips puckered peevishly. "You know single men in Jacksonville don't form relationships with women,

Crispin. They bond with V-8 engines and football teams."
She tucked a hand possessively through his arm.

He used the maneuver to turn her toward Sheila. "Let
me introduce you to somebody. This is Sheila Travis, who
came down with me from Atlanta."

"I'm *so* glad to meet you." Muffy would not win any
sincerity awards. She lifted her lashes toward Crispin.
"Teddy told me you were involved in a murder up in
Dunwoody last summer! I'm dyin' for you to tell me all
about it."

Did Muffy know it was Crispin's only sister who had
been killed?

Charho must, for she started to speak, but Crispin
beat her to it. "Ask me later, Muffy." He disengaged his
arm. "I want to introduce Sheila around and get something to eat."

"Sure. Be seein' you." She flashed a smile designed to
melt his bones, sketched the women a shadow of a wave,
and glided off to join Hayden's group.

As Charho, Crispin, and Helen began to discuss mutual friends, Sheila heard Muffy crow, "Tom! What a nice
surprise! And Rob! I haven't seen you since—oh, who can
remember? And Hayden! How's the world's greatest doctor? Tell Treye I loved usin' his boat Sunday."

The tall, ugly man was a raspy bass. "Didn't I hear
you were bringin' Lance and Eddie tonight, Muffy?
Where'd you stash 'em?"

"Eddie's around somewhere, Tom. Lance stood me
up." She gave a carefree laugh. "I guess you two'll have to
get me a drink instead." She linked arms with Tom and
Rob, and the trio moved off toward the bar, leaving waves
of Muffy's Chanel behind.

Charho leaned over confidentially. "Don't mind
Muffy, Sheila. Flirting's the only language she knows.
Helen, I'm going to take Crispin and Sheila back to see
Libba. Oh—and Martha and Laura Grace just arrived.
Find Justin and tell him to make his little announcement

real soon. Martha doesn't want to stay long, and Teddy's bored in the kitchen."

"Announcement?" Crispin raised one eyebrow. "What's Justin announcing?"

"It's a surprise." Helen was already seeking her husband with her eyes. "Get yourselves some food, then come to the livin' room. We're almost ready."

Tucking one arm through Sheila's and the other through Crispin's, Charho led them through the throng. When they reached an island of quiet, Charho demanded wickedly, "Dear boy, how *did* you manage to get those pants on?"

He grinned. "Had a seam split and fixed with snaps, like an infant suit. Couldn't disgrace Justin by coming in warmups, and that's all I can get on easily these days."

She threw back her head and laughed heartily. "Lord love you, honey, we'd have taken you in your birthday suit!"

Libba's blue eyes said the same thing as she moved swiftly across the dining room to give Crispin a warm hug. Sheila was glad Charho greeted her by name. This slim woman with stylish frosted hair and an electric blue dress brushing shapely calves had developed a poise far beyond that of the plump little cheerleader in the old photograph. Only the anxiety in her eyes was the same.

She greeted Sheila, then turned back to inquire about Crispin's accident. While they chatted, Sheila admired Daphne's lovely dining room. Deep peach silk draped over the windows through ornate brass rings. Lighter peach walls provided a backdrop for several fine paintings. Modern sculpture stood on pedestals, and the gleaming oak floor was covered with a pale Chinese rug. The effect was spacious, elegant, and restful, but as Sheila watched, Tom Goren stepped back and nearly toppled a small statue.

At her side, Charho twinkled and murmured, "Lovely room—if you like livin' in a museum." She put an arm around Libba's shoulders. "Libba's granddaddy built this house, but he died when his girls were still little, so it went out of the family. Hayden bought it about fifteen years ago."

"Granddaddy wouldn't recognize it." Libba's voice was light and breathless, and just a shade rushed. "From what Mama said, he was a cigars-and-bourbon man."

One of the caterers approached and murmured in her ear. "Excuse me," she apologized. "I need to tell Clarinda to put more crab puffs in the oven. They're goin' like hotcakes, Charho!" She hurried through a swinging door that must lead to the kitchen. Teddy sidled in on its next swing.

"Isn't it time *yet*?" she pled with her grandmother.

Charho held out her hand. "I think it's past time, honey. Let's go see if we can help them get a move on."

Sheila hadn't thought she was hungry, but Daphne's generous buffet quickly changed her mind. "Don't fill your plate with shrimp," Crispin admonished. "They've got crab legs, too." And prime rib, a cascade of fresh fruit, smoked salmon, a well-filled cheese board, a tray of crab puffs, and a heaping silver platter of caviar.

Sheila could just see the bar in a room of windows and lush plants next door, almost hidden beyond a crush of guests. To save Crispin the trouble of pushing through the crowd with his cast, she suggested that he carry their plates to the living room while she fetched drinks. He gratefully agreed.

There was a second door into the conservatory which she ought to be able to reach circuitously, avoiding most of the crowd.

She lost her way, however, and wound up in Daphne's peach-striped back hall contemplating several ivory doors and wondering which was the nearest route to the bar.

She never meant to eavesdrop, but the voice behind one of the doors spoke so suddenly and with such venom that, for a second, she could not move.

"Keep him out of sight, you hear me? He's disgustin'!" Could that be Daphne, without the honey in her voice?

"I told you, I didn't know." Muffy, exasperated. "He called to say hello, and he sounded so wistful when I told him the old gang was comin'—"

"Well, thank God Lance stood you up. The two of them together—" The next part was muffled.

Sheila backed away and bumped into a tall, hunched man who was shambling away from the powder room down the hall.

"Evenin'." He averted his face as he shuffled past. Sheila followed him with puzzled eyes. His dress was unusual enough to make her wonder if he could be a thief crashing the party to cart away some of Daphne's portable art. On the other hand, he could just be an eccentric guest who wore his tuxedo jacket with cuffed black cotton pants and brown loafers.

Libba stepped out into the hallway carrying a silver tray of crab puffs. She opened her mouth as if to call to the oddly dressed stranger, but said nothing. Sheila was relieved. If Libba let him go without challenge, he must be a guest.

She was about to ask Libba directions, but Libba turned abruptly and backed quickly through the doorway from which she'd just come.

"If you do, I'll wring your neck and tell Hayden to cancel your lease!" Daphne flung open the door, green eyes glittering, her chest mottled red beneath the gold coins.

Sheila was deeply embarrassed. She'd given enough parties in her day to know where guests had no business being.

Daphne quickly rearranged her features into a hostess smile. "Why, hello, Sheila. Were you looking for the little girls' room?"

"No, the bar." Sheila looked around as if newly lost. Daphne took her firmly by the elbow and steered her down the hall. "Right through here. Don't be too long, though. We're—"

"—looking for Lance McGrew and Eddie Weare. I heard they were comin' tonight." The big man named Tom wasn't really finishing Daphne's sentence. He was talking to a woman just inside the door.

The woman turned and her eyes met Daphne's. Daphne hissed between her teeth.

What was there about this woman to scare anybody? She was thick of waist, with a strong, plain face and a deep tan. She looked unashamedly fifty, and wore a sleeveless navy linen dress she could equally well have worn to church. Her arms were muscular. So were the calves above her navy pumps. Her honey brown hair, streaked with sun, was casually combed from a side part and held with a small gold barrette. The slight curl on its ends must be natural, for this woman did not look as if she wasted time curling her hair. Her face was bare except for a vivid smudge of lipstick.

Her eyes passed over Daphne, lingered briefly on Sheila, then returned to Tom with a disinterest in prettier women that was both arrogant and enviable.

Daphne swore under her breath and whirled back to the hall. "Muffy, wait a minute! I've got something I need you to do."

Sheila, abandoned, headed for the bar.

Out on the river, a frigid breeze sliced across the water. In his small boat, Lance McGrew shivered, hoping his tux wasn't getting damp under his orange raincoat. How miserable he was! How much longer would he have to wait? The wind was rising. Choppy waves flung his craft dangerously near the sea wall.

He was wondering for the umteenth time if he'd made a mistake, when he heard the distant *putt-putt* of a small engine. A bobbing light approached Sadler's Point. Would it stay on the St. Johns, or go up the Ortega?

Lance crowed with delight as it took a port bearing,

along the St. Johns. He waited until it was well past, then started his engine and pulled into its wake.

Through the gusty night the two boats crept along the Ortega shoreline toward the L'Arkens' dock, shrouded in dark.

Crispin, whose leg must surely be aching from so much standing, had secured two seats on a creamy brocade couch. Behind it, gauzy curtains framed floor-to-ceiling windows overlooking a terrace that sloped in well-lit beauty to the river.

Crispin was discussing football with the slight man named Rob. This close, she saw that his eyes were as dark as her own. Just beyond Rob sat the senator, whom she immediately recognized as an old enemy of Tyler's. When Sheila took her seat, the old man gave her a frosty nod, rose, and left.

"Sheila, this is Robert Wilmer. Rob, Sheila Travis."

Rob Wilmer's inky eyes twinkled. "Goodness, Mrs. Travis, you have the same effect as the wrath of God. At your approach, the sinners flee."

His roguish smile made her laugh. "I just wish I had that kind of clout."

"From what I hear, you've got the next best thing—a knack for seeing straight."

She turned to Crispin, surprised. He knew she preferred not to talk about her occasional past involvements with mysterious deaths. "Don't blame me," Crispin protested. "I didn't say a word. Rob has a reputation to maintain. He always knows everything there is to know in Jacksonville."

Wilmer's dark eyes held hers piercingly. "If we get any mysteries around here while you're down, we'll call you in, Sheila. Won't we, Tom?"

The last was addressed to the big man with copper hair, who had ambled up with two drinks. "This is Tom Goren," Rob Wilmer told Sheila. "He played football with

Justin, and now he's a homicide detective on the police force."

His last words fell into a lull in conversation. Several people looked around, and Sheila could tell the big man devoutly wished his friend hadn't been quite so forthcoming about his profession.

Sympathy warmed her smile. "How do you do, Mr. Goren?"

"Call me Tom, ma'am. And I do fine, thank you. Who you rootin' for on Saturday night, Crispin?"

From the Gator Bowl, they moved on to the Jacksonville Jaguars. Sheila, who knew even less about pro football than the college variety, sipped her drink and watched the guests.

There must have been a hundred, but by now a few faces were familiar. Daphne's prize senator stood with a man Sheila assumed to be the equally prized governor. Nearby Justin was shepherding his family into a rough semicircle by the fireplace. Libba hovered in one doorway. Martha and Laura Grace stood just behind Charho and Sparrow, to the right of the family circle. Martha looked slimmer in black. Laura Grace still wore her vivid red blouse and purple skirt. Sheila wondered if she donned underpants for formal occasions. Catching her eye, Laura Grace beamed across the room at her, held up two fingers in a circle of victory, and patted the little purse dangling from her arm.

Sparrow's attention was riveted on Jack, as if she'd like to straighten his tie and smooth away his glower. Beside him, Brandy beamed. Helen stood, poised but a trifle nervous, on her husband's right, one arm lightly circling Teddy.

"Look at that child's chin," Crispin said softly. "Are she and your Aunt Mary related?"

Sheila didn't reply. She had spotted Muffy Merriwether, a slender, scarlet flame in a far doorway. Beside her stood the plain woman in navy, and beyond them stood the man in tuxedo jacket and cuffed pants. He strained eagerly to see the family clustered by the fireplace.

"Friends—" Hayden stepped into the center of the room with the confidence of a frequent host. "We invited you here tonight for several reasons. First, I wanted to show off my beautiful wife. Daphne?" Daphne stepped forward, a pillar of black crepe and gold coins, to take a modest bow. A spattering of applause broke out like popcorn. "Second, we wanted to welcome some important people who have taken time from their busy lives to be with us tonight." Hayden introduced the male dignitaries, then looked around. "And Sheila Travis, widow of Tyler Travis. Sheila, where are you?"

Embarrassed, she half stood and nodded to another small patter of applause.

"Third," Hayden continued, "we wanted to provide sustenance to strengthen you for the contest Saturday night."

"Go *team*!" Daphne still had a cheerleader's voice, and even in slim black crepe and heels could stoop and jump, arms flung wide. The room erupted into cheers.

When the bedlam subsided, Hayden lifted one hand for silence. "Finally—and most important—my baby brother has something to say. Justin?"

Justin cleared his throat and stepped forward. A hush fell over the crowd.

"You folks are some of my dearest friends," Justin began, and there were murmurs of pleasure. "So I wanted you to be the first to know that I've decided to run for the U.S. Congress next fall. I covet your support, your checks—" he grinned as a chuckle ran around the room, "—and your prayers. Thank you."

The announcement was so brief that for a moment his audience waited for more. Then the applause was deafening.

"Way to go, Justin!" Tom Goren slapped big hands together in approval.

"L'Arken for Congress! L'Arken for Congress!" someone began to chant. The whole room took it up.

"Let's move to Florida and register!" Crispin shouted
to Sheila over the bedlam.

Sheila, however was watching Helen. Did she have an
inkling of the pressures to come? Was that why her eyes
were closed and her smile so resolute? Sheila suddenly
pitied the woman with all her heart.

As the crowd surged toward Justin to congratulate
him, a couple of previously alerted news photographers
pressed forward with cameras.

A voice rang out. "I propose a toast to my good friend,
Justin L'Arken! Justin, good buddy, how the hell are you?"

The man from Muffy's side stumbled through the
throng and enveloped Justin in an unsteady bear hug.
Sheila was certain that Justin, taken aback, hesitated for
just an instant before returning the embrace.

The news cameras rolled on.

The man backed away, held up a glass, and cried out
again, "A toast to Justin! Justin L'Arken!"

"Justin!" the guests replied, dutiful but a bit uncer-
tain.

Hayden had one hand up, as if wondering whether to
intervene. Charho looked around desperately. Helen
turned her face away. Muffy and the woman in navy had
disappeared.

Libba, flushed, hurried forward. She took the newcomer by the arm. "Remember me?"

His face lit with pleasure. "Course I 'member you,
Libba!" He enveloped her in a rough embrace. "Save me
a dance later, okay?" He looked around the room until he
found their hostess. "You, too, Daffy. Save me a dance,
okay?"

Daphne gave him a smile and a wisp of a nod, then
turned to speak to another guest as if the shabby intruder
were no longer there.

Tom Goren pushed his way through the crowd.
"Hello, old buddy," Sheila heard him say. "Let's get us

somethin' to eat." He and Libba escorted the man out. The other guests' sigh of relief was almost audible.

The damage was done, however. A news staff ravenous for the bizarre over the respectable would certainly not cut that awkward embrace and toast from their coverage of Justin's announcement.

Sheila could see Helen's dismay, Justin's frustration. She could not, however, catch Jack's reaction, for Jack had disappeared.

After the crowd thinned, Sheila and Crispin found Martha and Laura Grace in the dining room. Crispin joined Martha, chatting with friends. Laura Grace motioned for Sheila to join her at the dining room table, where she was piling a plate with Spanish peanuts. "I like peanuts," the old woman declared happily, adding another heaping spoonful to the mound. "Would you like to see where the treasure is buried, dear? I could show you."

Sheila hesitated. "Perhaps another time?"

The grizzled head bobbed in perfect accord. "It is a bit dark just now, and we wouldn't want to run into the pirates. It will keep. It's been there for years." She put one peanut between her teeth, bit it neatly in two, and swallowed the two parts whole.

"Was Dan McGirth a very wicked pirate?" Sheila asked.

The grizzled head swung from side to side. "Dan McGirth was just one of them, my dear. There are many pirates. They come up the river, you know." She stood on tiptoe and her breath brushed Sheila's ear: "Jacksonville thinks it's a white man's town, but the river is a black woman. She calls all the shots."

Abruptly she turned, carefully balanced another heap of peanuts on her pile, and said loudly, "Martha, it is time to go. I have enough peanuts."

She certainly did. The big silver bowl was empty.

———————

When Martha and Laura Grace departed, accompanied by a protesting Teddy, Sheila would have liked to go home, too. Instead, she followed Crispin from group to group, inhaling expensive colognes and nibbling Daphne's elegant tidbits. She spoke with Daphne's governor briefly—which was long enough—and successfully avoided further contact with the senator.

Gradually, she became aware that the living and dining rooms were almost empty of men. Crispin looked wistfully down the hall, whence came a shout of masculine laughter.

"Oh, go talk football," she told him, giving him a little nudge. "I can function at a party on my own. I've had years of practice."

He didn't, however, have to hobble away with such unflattering alacrity.

Outside, the security staff huddled in the shelter of the house, watching the front lawn and wishing the party would end. No one covered the river side. It was too cold for boating.

All the clouds had blown away, leaving the sky clear and bright with moonlight. At the end of the dock, the three L'Arken boats swung on their ropes. A fourth boat glided soundlessly in and tied up alongside.

Two dark shapes clambered onto the dock. Each carried a bulky load. On the dock, a man and a woman stood near one another as if indulging in a spot of romance. Their voices, hushed and anxious, floated across the lawn.

"Don't fall!" The first voice, the man.

"Loosen up! They're not gonna fall." The woman on the dock leaned forward, counting. Red hair glinted in the moonlight.

"If anybody should see—" The man's voice was nervous.

"Nobody's going to see. Who's going to be watchin' the water with all that partyin' goin' on?" Her voice was both reassuring and condescending.

"Easy for you to say. Just hurry! My teeth are chattering!"

"Okay, get them aboard." An imperious white hand waved toward one of the L'Arken boats and the two hefty sailors started carrying boxes aboard.

When the final box was safely stowed and the two sailors aboard their own boat, she asked her companion, "You know the drill?"

"Same as always. Now let's go back inside. I'm frozen."

When they had gone, another shape slid from the deep shadows and called gruffly, "Hold up. I'm coming along."

Strolling to the end of the dock, the newcomer first peered off into the darkness, then—wheeling abruptly—climbed into the fourth boat. "Cast off and head toward town."

Without a word, one of the sailors cast off the mooring line and the other picked up an oar. The boat glided backward, making scarcely a splash in the black water. Not until they were some distance away did they start a motor.

Ten minutes later another shadow moved down the dock. Slipped aboard the boat. Turned on a tiny flashlight to examine the boxes. Then, straining and panting, transferred them from one docked boat to another, fitting them neatly and covering them with a welter of orange lifejackets. The whole time, the noise of Daphne's party never reached the gently rolling St. Johns.

The first Lance McGrew knew he'd been spotted was when he saw the gleam of light on steel. Daphne's doors were securely closed against the chilly night. Nobody heard the shot.

Only one person saw two boats moving south along the St. Johns seawall, one towing the other.

In the front boat, three spoke in heated mutters.

"I say we take him out to the middle and dump him. Let him float out to sea!" said the first and biggest one.

"I say we turn his boat loose and let it drift where it will," said the second.

"No," said the last. "We take him up the Yacht Basin and dump him in Pirate's Cove. Then we let his boat drift to sea. Pirate's Cove is a fitting resting place, don't you think?"

It didn't matter what they thought. He was the boss.

Treye L'Arken lounged in a doorway, amused. "So there you are, Mama. I wondered if I'd find you here."

His mother had never been stylish, but she certainly had style. She stood like an aging hooker, one hand on the hip of her navy dress and the other waving a lit cigarette, uttering a stream of most proficient curses.

"Looking for an ashtray?" Treye asked. "Or plannin' to drop a lighted match and get the hell out?"

Twinkie's laugh was blunt and brutal. "I don't need your ideas. I've enough of my own." She put the cigarette to her lips, sucked it, then exhaled with the pent fury of a caved dragon. "This is the last straw, you know. The absolute last straw."

They stood in a cluttered room just off Daphne's kitchen. Libba's grandfather, an old man with a vivacious young wife, had designed the room as gentleman's retreat. He hadn't wanted a view of the river and he hadn't wanted a place to bring other people. He'd wanted a hideout paneled in downstate cypress, with a ceiling fan for hot evenings, a brick fireplace for chilly ones, a big leather chair that would shape itself to his dumpy contours, an ottoman for his short legs, and a secret closet for his prohibition supplies. He'd had enough money to get exactly what he wanted.

After a day on the bench, Judge Covington liked to settle into the chair, drink a glass of bourbon, and make dense clouds of smoke with expensive Cuban cigars while he read Zane Grey novels.

When Treye was a child and his mother had made the room her own retreat, he used to think he could still smell the old judge's cigars on damp days. By then, interim owners had installed steam heat, so Twinkie had filled the fireplace with a large wooden model of the *Shamrock*, a racing schooner her father sailed in his youth. The walls and shelves displayed sailing gear and charts, and Twinkie had dragged in a couple of chairs as old as the hills and almost as comfortable. In this room she pored over navigation charts and met with her crew to plot strategy for upcoming races. Her small son used to seek her here when he had something troubling to discuss. He'd sought her here tonight.

The past year had changed the room from a retreat into a storeroom. Surveying the jumble of boxes, furniture, and paintings merely propped against the wall, Treye curled his lips and said, in fair imitation of his stepmother, "This room has great potential, but we just haven't decided what to do with it, yet."

Twinkie snorted and took another greedy puff on her cigarette. "She'll probably paint the panelin', enlarge the windows, plant somethin' lovely outside, and put up flowered curtains."

"Probably," Treye agreed serenely. "But that's not what's botherin' you. Why did you come?"

"Because I wanted to be here for Justin's announcement. Because I *deserve* to be here, dammit! I've gotten him and Helen on more boards than they can name."

"You gonna vote for him?"

Twinkie's eyes sparked in the manner that had inspired her nickname. "Hopin' to get my mind off it, Treye?"

He shrugged. "Worth a try."

She turned and went to the window, stared out at the dark lawn beyond, and said with fierce emphasis on every syllable, "That doubloon necklace is *mine*!" In a calmer voice that did not deceive her son for an instant, she continued, "John Daniel gave it to me when Hayden and I got engaged. To me, not your father. The coins came from a Spanish galleon, and he'd had it made for Cady. After she died, John Daniel saved them for Hayden's bride." Her voice trembled on the last word. Treye pretended not to notice.

"How'd Daphne get it, then?"

She ground the cigarette out on the hearth. "My own stupidity. It was in a safety deposit box I forgot about, and your dear old dad still had one of the keys. I never wore it, and what with all the rest of the divorce stuff . . ." She waved one hand to dismiss that painful past. "Until I heard about this party, I frankly hadn't thought about those coins in years." Her laugh was bitter. "Then I remembered—and just knew Hayden would try to pull somethin' like this! So I went down to the bank. Sure enough, the rat had taken the doubloons."

"What else was in that box?"

"Nothin'! We'd rented it especially for the doubloon necklace. I flat out forgot about it until today."

"You never wore it," her son pointed out.

She shrugged and looked down at her plain navy dress. "I'm not a necklace kind of person. But it's mine, Treye. *Mine!*"

"Well, Mama, what are we gonna do about that?"

Crossing the foyer to join Libba and Charho, Sheila saw Helen tuck something beneath the thick wide magnolia leaves that formed the base of Daphne's dining table centerpiece. That was one way to get rid of unwanted trash, she supposed.

Charho was volubly expressing her feelings about what she called, "that disgraceful incident."

"I could paddle Muffy!" she declared in a voice that sounded as if she'd been weaned on whiskey sours and cigarettes. "There was no excuse for bringin' him in that state."

"He's changed a lot," Libba said sadly. "He never drank in high school. He even signed a pledge."

"Well, dear," Charlotte Holmes drew herself up, prepared to have the last word, "you never can tell what a man will do or become once he gets away from home—can you, Sheila?" She leaned close to confide. "We were speakin' of Eddie Weare. Used to be a fine young man, as Libba can tell you—used to sit with Justin on the front church pew every Sunday. And he used to be Libba's high school beau, didn't he, dear?"

Libba gave a slight puff of exasperation. "Charho, that's a long time ago. Now I need to make one more visit to the kitchen. Excuse me?" She hurried away, a spot of red on each cheekbone.

Charho's dark eyes followed her. "Oh, my dear! I seem to have offended Libba. Would you go see if she's all right? Ask for a glass of water, or somethin'."

As Sheila could have predicted, Daphne's kitchen looked like it belonged in *House Beautiful*—except for the squat ugly maid washing a silver tray at the sink.

Libba was leaning against a counter near a lovely floral arrangement. When she saw Sheila enter, she finished wiping her nose with a tissue and gave a self-conscious little laugh. "I'm all right. My allergies just started acting up."

Sheila smiled. "And I got thirsty for a plain glass of water."

"Of course! Clarinda, this is Sheila Travis, Crispin's friend. Would you get her some ice water, please?" While the maid filled a glass at the refrigerator, Libba washed her hands. "Don't mind Charho," she said without looking around. "She has a way of rememberin' what she wants to—like my datin' Eddie in high school—but forgettin' what's unpleasant—like he dropped me for Daphne. We broke up the same time Helen and Tom Goren did, right after the Homecomin' Dance senior year—which Charho has also conveniently forgotten. She never liked Tom very much." She shrugged and smiled. "Helen and I had a very soggy slumber party that next weekend, but it all seems like a hundred years ago now. Only Charho remembers that far back—right, Clarinda?"

The maid grunted. "They's sumpin' to be said for rememberin' the past when the present doan look so good."

Sheila finished her water, but still she stayed. She was not eager to go back and make trivial conversation. Gradually she became aware of voices in a room nearby. One of them, at least, sounded furious.

The maid shot Libba a warning look. "We got trouble," she said softly.

A volley of words was scorching. ". . . absolutely no right, legal or otherwise! Do you hear me?"

A man rumbled an interruption. Libba raised stricken eyes to the maid's. "Oh, dear! I was afraid of somethin' like this." She gave Sheila a swift, humiliated look.

Sheila did not recognize the voices. Setting the glass on the counter, she thanked the two women and exited as gracefully as possible.

An unseen woman's angry words pursued her. "Get me that necklace, or I'll get it myself!"

Sheila had had enough of strangers for a while. Spying a small empty room with a deep white sofa, mint green lamps, and softly playing Mozart, she decided to sit quietly, thumb through one of Daphne's expensive magazines and hope Crispin would soon be ready to leave.

She crossed to the window and looked toward the river. The sky was clear, stars as bright as downtown Jacksonville across the water. Not until she was seated did she notice the man in the corner near the door. It was the stranger in tux and cuffed pants, Justin's embracer, and he was going through old records with a forlorn air. Eddie Weare.

Seen close up, the golden boy of Lee High was now a hull of a man. The long straight nose had been broken and badly set. The skin was coarse and lined with veins, the once-blond hair colorless and lank. His hands trembled as he reached for a clear sparkling drink with an arm so emaciated it only half filled its sleeve. A line from Wordsworth came unbidden to her mind: *There hath passed away a glory from the earth.*

When he looked in Sheila's direction, his eyes were filled with abject apology, as if he knew how pitiful he looked, yet hungered for respect.

She realized that Eddie was not, as she had at first supposed, drunk. He was, rather, the remnant of a man who had been drunk far too often for too many years. Seeing her looking his way, he lifted his glass high. "Sprite. I'm sober six months now. Takin' pills to keep me that way, and I'm gonna make it this time. I surely am."

"I'm sure you are." She hoped it was true. But even if he did, Eddie would never regain his former luster.

Feeling a need to offer what comfort she could, she added, "I'm Sheila Travis, Crispin's friend from Atlanta. Are you Eddie Weare? He was telling me just this evening what a terrific quarterback you were at—was it Robert E. Lee Senior High?"

He moved eagerly across the room and stuck out a hand, still damp from his glass. He still wore, she noted, his high school ring. The blue stone gleamed in the lamplight.

"That's right, good old Robert E. Lee." Eddie's drawl was far in excess of north Florida accents, as if his words had to come from far away, but once begun, they poured out in a thick stream. "I played football with Justin 'n' Tom 'n' a coupl'a other guys, 'n' I went steady with almost every woman at this damn party, if you'll pardon my French. Libba, Muffy, Daphne—in college, we used to party 'til we couldn' party no more. And Helen, now— Helen—" He broke off, troubled at losing his train of thought.

"Have a seat," Sheila offered. "Isn't the river lovely?"

He shook his head. "Never liked the river, the whole time we lived here. Never learned to swim, didn't like boats. Everybody else liked boats. You 'n' Crispin like boats?"

"I like sailboats. I don't know if Crispin likes boats or not." Speaking automatically, she was surprised to realize it was true.

His haggard face lit with a smile, and he leaned so near she could smell crab dip on his breath. "Crispin's the smartest man I ever met. Not stuck-up, either. Got a great head for business. I got me a chance to buy a business. I surely do." He beamed at her with the eager intimacy of a lonely person who has found someone willing to listen.

"Oh, really?" Sheila moved toward the end of the couch. She didn't mind listening, if he just wouldn't breathe on her.

"Mind if I smoke?" She couldn't protest. He needed it too badly.

He lit a Marlboro and pulled a half-empty glass toward him on the end table. As he talked, he nervously flicked ash into the drink, creating a gray, nasty mess.

"Do I look all right?" He rubbed several cigarette burns in his trousers with nervous hands, then tugged down poorly ironed cuffs. "Muffy said I'd be okay, but do you think I look all right?"

"You look fine," she assured him. "Tell me about your business."

He was pouring out a rambling story about a small company for sale when Daphne appeared. She looked slightly puzzled. "Have you all seen a stray drink?" She peered around, absently touching her necklace and murmuring, "It's been a long time since you were home, hasn't it, Eddie?" Her mouth smiled. Her eyes did not. She extended a hand to Sheila like a sailor throwing out a lifeline. "Come talk with our former governor, Sheila. You all must have a lot in common, both bein' in politics and all. Excuse us, Eddie?"

Sheila had had enough politics to last her several lifetimes, and this particular governor was not one she would have voted for in any of them. She started to say she was quite content where she was at the moment when Eddie lunged to his feet. "You promised me a dance, Daphne. Let's have it now."

Daphne started to refuse, then shrugged. "Just a short one. Okay, Sheila?"

"It's fine with me." Sheila settled deeper into the cushions.

"All right, Eddie." Daphne smiled at him. "Just let me put on some music." She chose a compact disc.

"Not fast music, Daffy," Eddie begged when he heard her choice, "somethin' slow and dreamy." He headed for the player.

But Daphne grabbed his hand. "Dance, Eddie!" She kicked off her black-and-gold sandals and began to move absentmindedly to the beat. Eddie hesitated, then grabbed her hand and began to shake his whole body with enthusiasm.

"What on earth—?" Muffy lounged in the doorway, twirling one end of her scarlet stole.

"We're dancin', Muffy! Come dance!" Puffing with exertion, Eddie held out one elbow. After the slightest of hesitations, she kicked off her red flats to join them.

"Your hands are cold!" Eddie told her. "I'll warm you up." He grabbed her in a one-arm bear hug.

Muffy danced with a sensual, almost obscene abandonment. Daphne, at first restrained, seemed to catch her mood. Eddie had thrown himself into the music. Hand in hand but self-absorbed, the three danced as if they would never dance again.

Sheila closed her eyes. She couldn't doze with the music's relentless beat, but she was so weary her neck felt as if it wore a yoke, and her eyes were burning behind their lids. If there had been any graceful way to move through that bizarre tribal ritual to the door, she would have left.

One song slid into another. Muffy started singing along, then substituted the words to an old cheer. Eddie, panting heavily, took it up.

"Come on, Daphne, cheer!" Sheila heard Muffy command.

After a halfhearted beginning, Daphne's voice rose with the others in the final shout. "Lee High, that's—"

"Stop it!" The music ended midbeat.

Sheila's eyes flew open. Before her, Muffy and Daphne were frozen in the immortal cheerleader one-knee kneel, slim sheaths hiked almost to their hips. Eddie dragged his eyes with difficulty from exposed thighs and beckoned gaily. "Hello, Helen! Come dance with us!"

Helen L'Arken stood beside the stereo system, face white with anger, eyes like gold fire. Libba stood near her in the doorway, brows drawn down in distaste. Even Eddie was silenced while Muffy and Daphne climbed sheepishly to their feet.

"What on earth are you doing, Muffy?" Helen blazed. "You know better than that!"

Eddie gaped at her, slack-mouthed. Muffy leaned against him, flushed and damp. Daphne fumbled for her shoes, one hand at her chest. She gasped for air.

"Don't be a killjoy, Helen!" Muffy said gaily, breathing hard. She waved one end of her stole to fan herself.

"We were just dancin'," Eddie added petulantly. "Remember the Little Women dances, Daffy?" He spoke with desperate eagerness. Daphne was still too winded to reply.

"I remember the spring dance our senior year," Muffy answered instead, "when we cut out and went down behind the Garden Center." Her lips curved in a sly smile. "With a bottle of gin. Where'd you get it, Daphne?"

Daphne hid a giggle behind one slender hand. "From my daddy's bar. He thought Mama drank it."

"I remember!" Eddie crowed, obviously delighted that he could remember so much.

Muffy nuzzled his shoulder. "She shouldn't have made you drink, though, sweetie. Wasn't good for you."

"You made Eddie drink?" Libba asked from the door. "But he'd signed a pledge!" She looked from the two flushed women to the shell of a man between them.

Daphne waved one hand impatiently. "Oh, Libba, that was years ago!" Breathing hard, she fanned her flat freckled chest.

"Don't mind them, Libba." Helen made no effort to disguise her irritation.

Daphne took another deep breath and added, "Muffy's being terrible tonight."

"Muffy's being terrible tonight," Muffy mimicked. "Be careful, Daphne, babe, or you'll find out how terrible Muffy can be!" She lifted one slender arm as if to strike.

Eddie grabbed her wrist. "Don't you hit Daffy!"

"Ow!" Muffy recoiled in pain and fright.

Libba hurried across the room and took Eddie's arm. "Don't, Eddie. Daphne, the governor was asking for his coat. You'd better go."

"Oh, the governor!" Daphne tucked a few stray strands of dark hair into place and hurried from the room.

Muffy laughed, a brittle sound that chilled Sheila's blood. "What on earth would we do without you, Libba?"

Eddie reached for Helen's hand. "Dance with me, Helen."

"Yeah, Helen." Muffy shimmied. "Dance with Eddie. For old times' sake? Justin's not runnin' yet. He won't mind."

Helen yanked her hand away. "Take him home, Muffy. And you go, too. You know you shouldn't be dancin' like that with your heart."

"Whassa matter with her heart?" Eddie demanded.

Instead of replying, Helen looked at him in disgust. "Justin adored you. Now look at you!"

Eddie's gaunt cheeks turned scarlet. "Look at *me*? Whacha mean, look at me?" His words were becoming more and more slurred the angrier he became.

Helen shot Muffy a meaningful look. "Take him home. I'll talk to you tomorrow."

But Muffy shook her head. "I'm not ready to go. We'll both be good, won't we, Eddie? I'll bring you some more shrimp."

He glared at her, face still hot with anger. "Don't you ever hurt Daffy, Muffy. If you do, I'll—"

Libba once again interceded. Leading him to the couch, she said gently, "You're pretty winded, Eddie. Wait here until Muffy gets back." Her voice shook.

She must be exhausted, Sheila thought sympathetically, noting how pale and drawn Libba looked compared with those who had done nothing tonight but socialize.

As Eddie slumped to the cushions beside Sheila, Helen seemed to realize for the first time that her guest was in the room. She pressed one hand to her cheek in embarrassment. "Please forgive us, Sheila. We don't usually behave like this."

Before Sheila could reply, Muffy touched her gamine coiffure. "We were just lettin' down our hair," she said gaily. Her eyes dared them to object.

"Anybody seen Sheila?"

Crispin spoke from the hall. Helen moved aside to let him enter, and Sheila stood. "So there you are!" he exclaimed. "I wondered where you'd gone. Are you ready to go home?"

Eddie lunged up with a cry of welcome. "Crispin! I've been talking to your woman. She's prettier than a picture!" He pumped Crispin's arm with delight. "Old Daffy's pretty as ever, too. Hasn't changed a bit. Always was the prettiest woman at Lee."

"That's not kind, Eddie," Muffy chided him, but her mind was clearly on other things. "We've been dancin', Crispin. How about one, for old times' sake?" She tiptoed her fingertips up his chest.

"I've got a smashed knee," he reminded her, moving away.

She gave him an enticing smile. "I'll bet you could dance slow." She shimmied and arched her back.

"Not even like a lazy snail," he assured her evenly. "Come on, Sheila, I'm worn out. We'll see you folks later."

In the hall, however, he pulled her close. "Want to

take a stroll down to the dock before bedtime? The river's lovely in the moonlight."

Her heart gave a happy little flutter, but she said lightly, "What? With a man who can't dance?"

"I might manage to limp that far with the right prop." He draped one arm around her shoulder. She let her head rest briefly against him as he started steering her toward the back door.

Reluctantly she nudged him in another direction. "First we have to thank Daphne for her 'do.' "

The party was already wearing that sloppy face even the most well-bred party reveals at the end of a long evening. The bar was closed, the buffet table down to a few grapes, a few picked-over finger sandwiches, slices of browning beef, handfuls of boiled shrimp. The few guests who remained clustered around Justin near the door, giving final congratulations and promising their support.

As Sheila and Crispin entered the foyer, Daphne— once more the poised hostess—was saying good night to the governor. He exited with Rob Wilmer and Tom Goren. When Crispin began their own farewell speech, Daphne tucked an arm through Sheila's and said regretfully—as if Sheila had not witnessed the spectacle of ten minutes before—"I haven't had a minute with you all evenin'! Please come over tomorrow afternoon and let's have a chat."

"Make it Thursday," Crispin suggested. "Tomorrow I want to take her down to St. Augustine for the day."

"Oh!" Daphne clapped her hands in delight. "There's the most marvelous seafood restaurant you just have to try! It's a little hard to find, but I can tell you exactly how to get there." She started giving him detailed directions.

Sheila, only half listening, watched Muffy join Hayden in the dining room. He leaned against the table munching a sandwich while she filled a plate. Probably shrimp for Eddie. The pair seemed engrossed in conversation.

In the next room, Libba was collecting dirty glasses. The woman in navy was talking with Charho, Helen, and Treye.

Daphne's gaze followed Sheila's. "That Twinkie!" She touched her gold coin necklace, as if for reassurance. "She had no business comin' tonight!" She turned her exquisite back to finish her instructions.

Later, when it mattered, Sheila would struggle to remember what happened next. She knew Helen picked up a drink from the bar and handed it to Libba with a nod toward Daphne. As Libba passed the dining room table, did she set the glass down next to Hayden before she picked up a tray of glasses and headed for the kitchen? Or did she hand it to Hayden who, engrossed in his conversation with Muffy, set it down?

What Sheila knew for certain was that the glass was on the table while Hayden and Muffy finished their conversation. Then he nodded toward the drink and Muffy picked it up from the table and carried it to Daphne with one hand. She had a plate of shrimp in the other.

Daphne's smile of thanks was as dazzling as the gold coins at her throat. "How sweet, Muffy! Crispin and Sheila, to you!"

She lifted the glass and drained it. "What do you plan to see in St. Augustine?"

Crispin mentioned a few places. Daphne, Sheila noticed, became increasingly inattentive. When he paused, she nodded absently and murmured, "That's nice. You—"

She stopped. Her face was pink, her breaths short pants. Perspiration glowed on her glittering face. With a terrified look, she pressed her chest and slid to the floor.

There was a moment of shocked silence. Then Sheila knelt swiftly beside Daphne while Crispin propelled himself awkwardly across the hall bellowing, "Hayden! Hayden!"

Sheila could find only a reedy, irregular pulse. She gladly yielded her place as Dr. L'Arken dashed in and flung himself to his knees at his wife's side. Justin sprinted in from the hall and knelt at Daphne's other side.

"Call nine-one-one!" Hayden ordered.

Muffy stood frozen, her eyes wide with surprise. "Daphne?" Her voice was a startled little squeak. She bent at the waist and peered down at her friend.

By the time those in the Florida room realized anything was wrong, Sheila was already running to summon an ambulance.

In the kitchen, Libba was saying good night to the maid, who already had her coat on and was standing in the open door. Three caterers were putting away food at the far counter.

"Daphne's ill!" Sheila cried, looking around for a phone.

"What happened? Do we need paramedics?" Libba reached the phone before she did and was already dialing.

Clarinda hovered uncertainly in the doorway. "Do I need to stick around? I got company at home—"

"Go on." Libba flapped a hand in her direction. From the haste with which Clarinda departed, Sheila suspected there was little love lost between Daphne L'Arken and her maid.

Sheila relayed what information she could and Libba passed it on, along with the address, but she was so flustered she got the street number wrong twice. As soon as they were informed the ambulance was on its way, both women hurried back to the foyer.

Daphne still huddled on the floor, perspiring, pale, and moaning. Hayden bent over her, his face ashen. "It seems to be her heart," he said tonelessly.

Muffy knelt at Daphne's head, uttering sharp little cries of distress. To Sheila, they sounded affected and faked. On the other hand, she had to admit, coming from Muffy perhaps they could be real.

Eddie Weare stood at the dining room arch, tossing a drink down his throat. The others, stunned, drew slowly

near, staring at the slim form in black crepe that until five
minutes ago had been the life of the party.

Regally, Charho moved forward. "Give me her necklace, Hayden. I'll put it away. You won't want it at the hospital."

He took it off with great tenderness.

Hayden stayed by his wife until the ambulance arrived; once the ambulance doors closed, he and Justin followed by car. The paramedics had reported Daphne still
had a reedy pulse. The ambulance wailed away.

After that, the party was over. Charho took the necklace upstairs, then helped Helen bid farewell to the last
guests. Crispin handed guests the coats Treye brought
him. Libba and, surprisingly, Twinkie, assisted the caterers
in clearing up and storing food. Everyone moved in a
hushed silence broken only by an occasional voice.

"Let's throw that out. It won't keep."

"It was good of you to come. We'll let you know how
she is."

Sheila offered to help Libba clear the table, but was
waved away with an abstracted air. She went into the
kitchen, but Twinkie made it plain she was neither
wanted nor needed there. When she started picking up
glasses in the living room, one of the caterers said gruffly,
"Excuse me, ma'am, but that's my job." She retreated
hastily.

She felt as useless as Muffy, who sat slumped in a
chair by the dining room door holding a glass and a rapidly
disappearing bottle of scotch, tears making snail paths of
mascara down her cheeks.

Sheila went back to the living room and stood by the
window, looking at the river and arguing with herself.

Did you actually see *anybody put anything in that drink?
Of course you didn't!*

Nevertheless, she found herself moving casually toward the front hall to retrieve the fragments of the glass
Daphne had dropped.

It had already been swept up.

She went to the kitchen, hoping to find the glass shards in the trash, but they were not there. They probably lay buried deep in one of several fat white bags.

"Did somebody sweep up the glass?" she asked Libba.

Libba gave her a curt nod. "I think so, but thanks for offering. Twinkie, did you get those last glasses from the bar? I'll check upstairs, in case some were left there."

Feeling about as adept as Peter Sellers in *The Pink Panther*, Sheila went to the table and, under the pretext of admiring the centerpiece, felt under the thick magnolia leaves. Her exploring fingers touched something solid. With a napkin she retrieved a small brown plastic bottle of pills. The name on the label read "Laura Grace Hayden."

Sheila gnawed her lip in indecision. She ought to leave the bottle there. Thyroid pills couldn't have poisoned Daphne. But what if they were something else?

If they were something else, the police would seriously object to anyone removing them.

On the other hand, the little brown bottle could easily go the way of Daphne's glass before anyone was the wiser.

Choosing the lesser of two evils, she wrapped the plastic bottle in the napkin and slid it into her evening bag.

She paused in the doorway, murmuring to herself, "I wish I knew who mixed that drink."

With a hiccup, Muffy looked up. "I mixed it myself, smarty pants."

"Not yours, Muffy, the one you took to Daphne."

Muffy's eyes widened. "Oh, that drink! I'll tell you who mixed it." She pressed a hand to her mouth and shook her head. "Not right now. I gotta go to the bathroom!" She hurried out in stocking feet.

Sheila waited several minutes, but Muffy didn't return. Remembering that Daphne's drink had been sitting on the bar for several minutes before Helen sent it to her, Sheila went over to examine the bar—wondering even as she did so exactly what she expected to find. Libba and the caterers had already cleared away the bottles and glasses. All that remained was a bare counter with a spill on the carpet in front of it.

Feeling utterly foolish, Sheila dropped an earring and knelt to fumble for it, bending low enough to smell the spill. Nothing. She touched her finger to it and quickly tasted. Again nothing.

She clipped the earring back on her lobe and went to persuade Crispin to go to a hotel. Helen would no longer want guests this week.

To her astonishment, however, Crispin got huffy at the idea of leaving Justin's. "Don't be silly. I'm practically family, and you are with me. They will expect us to stay."

Helen came up behind them. "Of course you'll stay," she said—her mind obviously elsewhere.

The phone rang. Everyone in earshot froze. Muffy appeared in the foyer and went weaving toward it. Helen got there first.

Her hand hovered over the receiver for another ring before she picked it up. "Hello?"

She listened, then hung up. Her lips worked frantically, but no sound emerged. Finally she choked out two words. "She's dead."

Muffy burst into tears and fled upstairs. Helen ran up after her. That was the signal for the final exodus.

Treye went up to change, then drove to the hospital to join his father. Everyone else melted away.

Sheila followed Libba to the kitchen and picked up a dish towel. Libba shook her head and bit her lip to hold back tears. "Thanks, but I'd rather finish up alone," she said softly. Her cheeks had no color, and her blue eyes looked enormous in a face pinched with shock.

Admitting defeat, Sheila went to find Crispin. They took the shorter way home, across the lawn. He limped slowly on the uneven ground. Still annoyed with him, Sheila held his arm merely to steady him. He looked side-

ways at her. "Would you like that walk on the dock anyway, or is it too cold?"

He had to be kidding! Who could feel amorous right
now with Daphne newly dead?

Even if Daphne weren't dead, the moon now hid behind a mass of clouds and the breeze cut like a knife. In
addition, Sheila was extremely conscious of the little vial
in her evening bag. How could she say: "Hon, I may be
carrying evidence that one of your oldest friends murdered
our hostess"?

He was still waiting for an answer to his invitation.

"Not just now, Crispin. I want to go to a hotel. You
can stay if you like, but they don't need me here just
now."

"Forget it!" His tone made her flinch. "I need you
here, and they are glad to have you. Make yourself useful,
instead of wandering off."

"Wandering off?"

"Yeah. Like back there." He jerked his head toward
Hayden's. "Everybody else was working. You could have
found something to do."

Frustration and anger rushed through her. "Go to the
dock and fall off! You have the sensitivity of a fish!" She
stormed toward Helen and Justin's, leaving Crispin to
come as he might.

Martha looked up inquiringly as she entered. "Is the
party over, dear?" She reached for her bag and shook
Laura Grace, who was dozing on the couch. "Let's go,
Ellgie. The party's over."

Hearing Crispin coming in behind her, Sheila muttered a quick good night and hurried upstairs. It wasn't
her place to tell Martha that her new daughter-in-law was
dead.

Once in her room, however, she found herself too jit-
tery to go to bed. Miserable at her suspicions, furious with
Crispin, she wanted desperately to pack and go. On the
other hand, she knew all too well that she couldn't sum-

mon the energy she'd need to face the protestations she'd encounter between her room and the front door.

She undressed and went to shove up the wooden window. Like many old houses that are irregularly heated, this one was hot and stuffy. The window, however, wouldn't budge beyond an inch.

Frustrated almost to tears, she pulled a chair to the window and craned toward the crack, taking deep breaths and wondering how she and Crispin had come to quarrel. She hated quarrels. They made her sick at her stomach. Tyler had never quarreled. He had issued orders to his wife that she had almost invariably obeyed. This blazing anger from another person was a new experience.

Mildred, Aunt Mary's housekeeper, once said: "You only children don't build thick skin. Those of us with sisters and brothers learn to fight growing up. Fighting doesn't bother us any. We fight, then play again. You poor onlies never learn to fight and go on." Sheila sighed. Mildred was right. She didn't have the vaguest idea how to fight and go on.

She sat there in the darkness for nearly two hours. Wondering how she could sleep when she could scarcely breathe. Wishing she and Crispin had made up before she'd come up to bed. Wishing she had insisted on going somewhere else tonight. Wishing it weren't too late to call Aunt Mary. Wishing Daphne hadn't died.

She heard the motor of a solitary boat stutter and move farther and farther out on the river. It sounded as lonely as she felt.

A shower pelted her window and settled into a dreary downpour. She heard a car door slam. Then the front door. Feet climbed the stairs. They sounded so utterly exhausted that they, finally, made her weep.

Spent and exhausted, she headed into the bathroom to brush her teeth. An enormous black cockroach scuttled over the edge of the basin and disappeared through an infinitesimal crack. That was bad enough. Having to shove two unwilling cats off the comforter was worse. Putting her feet between the sheets and touching an iguana was the final straw.

The beady black eye stared at her, unblinking. Unwilling to pick up the creature—and having no idea what to do with it if she did—she tiptoed through the bathroom and woke Brandy in the next room.

Brandy roused Teddy with such wrath that the whole household appeared, with the exception of Jack. Sheila didn't know if he was still out with Sparrow or didn't rate an iguana in a guest's bed an emergency.

"Why did you put Iggy in Sheila's bed?" Justin demanded of Teddy—no longer a potential congressman, but merely a baffled parent.

Teddy slid Sheila a look that would have melted the Wicked Witch of the West. At her feet, loyal Einstein looked equally guilty. "I thought She'd like somebody to sleep with."

Brandy gave a small embarrassed squeak and, trying not to look at either Sheila or Crispin, managed to look at both. Her cheeks flamed.

Turning away so she wouldn't glare at Teddy, Sheila met Crispin's amused gaze instead. She glared at him. *If we'd gone to a hotel, none of this would have happened*, she signaled silently.

His lips twitched. She yearned to smack him.

Helen retied the belt of her robe, then knelt to rebuke Teddy. She wound up explaining about Daphne instead.

"I didn't know about Aunt Daphne," Teddy protested tearfully. With hair a golden stream down her blue flowered pajamas, the child looked small and helpless. Sheila felt wretched. What kind of a guest made such a big deal about a mere iguana on a night like this?

"I wouldn't have done it, Mama, if I'd known about Aunt Daphne," Teddy protested. "Daddy, why did she die?"

Justin wrapped his daughter in white terry cloth arms.

His handsome face was haggard. "We don't know, honey. Uncle Hayden thinks maybe she had a bad heart and didn't know it, and she'd been dancing too hard. You run along to bed—and take Iggy with you."

Teddy fetched the iguana and waved it aloft with studied nonchalance. "It's stuffed," she informed Sheila. "The cats would eat it otherwise." She headed down the hall, Einstein padding at her heels.

Sheila's face flamed with embarrassment. "I'm so sorry ... I didn't know ..."

"Of course you didn't," Helen assured her with a weary, rueful smile, "and it was a rotten thing to do."

Did no one but Sheila see that satisfied smirk as Teddy closed the bedroom door behind her?

Wednesday,
December 27

~~~~~~~~~~~~~~~~~

The room was white and cold. Refrigerator cold. The hands of the wall clock were straight up five A.M.

Tom Goren pulled back a sheet and contemplated a face that would never notice cold again. The features were ugly and scarred, and death had not succeeded in erasing a lick of cruelty. Yet Goren's big square hand trembled, and pity sat oddly on his craggy, pock-marked face. "Poor old Lance," he said heavily. "He got that scar in the Lee-Jackson game senior year. Last I heard, he was a collection agent for some firm down in Miami." His finger traced the ugly furrow from nostril to jaw.

"Cars," said Rob Wilmer. While his classmates played football, Rob—a lonely newcomer—had already been accumulating vast stores of information that would eventually make him indispensable in Jacksonville. "Call Rob Wilmer," people said these days. "He'll know."

Wilmer always knew. He'd known whom to call when he got home from Hayden's party last night, went for a stroll on his dock, and found a corpse floating beside the last piling. He knew now what Goren wanted to know. "Lance repossessed cars, but he gave that up a year ago. Nobody knows what he's been doing lately, but drugs are suspected. He seems to have plenty of money. Came back to Jacksonville just last week."

Goren sighed. "I wish the chief would give this to

somebody else." He'd always been a B-grade detective, the kind they sent out to bring in kids who shot convenience store clerks in front of five witnesses, or women who finally stabbed brutal husbands. "This thing feels bigger than what I'm used to handlin', Rob. I don't like either the responsibility or the press it's likely to get."

He reached for the sheet and covered the dead man's face. Wilmer meticulously straightened out a crooked fold. "I hear they aren't going to release any information about the death to the media for twenty-four hours." He didn't say how he'd heard. Rob seldom revealed his sources of information. "Any idea why?"

Tom shook his head. "I only heard it myself an hour ago, and you were there when I first saw the body. You know what I know so far."

"Why do you think he was found in Pirate's Cove, by my back door?"

"You think it was deliberate?" Goren's coppery brows rose above his cat tawny eyes. Mentally he pictured Pirate's Cove, at the end of the Yacht Club basin. On a map the basin looked like a duckhead, with the Cove for a beak. It used to go straight through to the Ortega River, or so he'd heard, but these days you had to want to go there to get there. Most of the houses were like Rob's, unpretentious but solid. Houses of people with money who didn't brag about it. Each had a dock. The body could have been dumped in the middle of the cove and drifted that far.

The slight man gave a delicate shrug, raising his elevated shoulder. "I don't know, Tom. If so, I sure want to know why."

"You and me both, buddy." Tom signaled the morgue attendant that they were finished.

In the hall, he took out a pack of spearmint gum. In spite of more than twenty years on the force, he felt slightly queasy. He kept seeing Lance charging down the Gator Bowl, dirt spurting from his cleats while Tom shoved aside Jackson bastards who tried to get in the way.

Thanksgiving, the last game of senior year, and they'd made the final touchdown, him and Lance, beating Lee's old rival 20-14 and guaranteeing the state championship. He'd never liked Lance McGrew, but that had been the proudest moment of Goren's entire life.

He offered Rob the gum pack, then shook out two sticks and rolled them before popping them in his mouth. "He could have been dumped at your neighbor's dock. Didn't have to be yours." He chewed hard, hoping the sweet saliva would keep him from vomiting.

Wilmer shrugged again. "Could have been. They aren't at home. Went to Colorado to ski for Christmas, and haven't gotten back. There's nothing to show where he was dumped, I suppose?"

Tom shook his head. He wadded the gum papers up and started to pocket them, then caught Wilmer's pained expression and tossed them into a trash can instead. "We can't all be as tidy as you, Rob," he said sourly. "Take the murderer, for instance. Maybe expected the body to float out on the tide. Didn't know enough about the currents in the Cove."

Wilmer's eyes were the dark rich black of cypress-filled waters. They held Goren's with the force of a magnet. "See why they've put you on this? They need somebody who knew Lance, knows Ortega—and what questions to ask. This may be *big*, Tom! Your chance of a lifetime!"

Goren shook his head. "It's too big for me, Rob. Don't try to make me out to be what I'm not."

Wilmer sighed as he fell into step, taking three steps to the other man's two. "I'm not, Tom," he insisted. "I'm just hoping you'll take this chance to become what you are."

Sheila's last thought had been that she would certainly sleep late to stay out of everybody's way. Habit, however, betrayed her. She woke before six and could not go back to sleep.

Finally she rose, pulled on jeans and a creamy fisherman's sweater, and headed for the dock. Maybe a cold wind and Old Man River would carry her troubles away.

She let herself quietly out the back door, surprised that Einstein didn't bark. Then she saw him, a brown heap beside a seated figure in jeans and a parka. At the end of the dock, almost shadows in a thick mist, three boats bobbed in the light swell.

Teddy looked her way, then deliberately shifted so her back was toward the house.

Sheila walked up the long drive to Ortega Boulevard, which had broad grassy verges instead of sidewalks. *No wonder my head aches*, she groused silently as she trudged through damp grass and dodged puddles like bright mirrors. *The child hates me, the others need us to leave, and who would have thought Crispin could be so pigheaded?*

What's really the matter with you is, you're used to getting your own way, common sense replied. It was true. In the process of breaking Tyler's dominion over her, she had gotten very comfortable with doing what she wanted. Was she ready to give that up—for anybody? She had a feeling this week would help answer that question.

She walked for nearly an hour, meeting nobody except a gray 'possum scuttling home after a night's prowl. Rambling up side streets away from the river, she tried to imagine Indian huts beneath the towering pines and oaks where suburban ranches now lined Algonquin, Apache, and Arapahoe avenues. Her imagination balked, however, on McGirts Boulevard. What kind of homes would pirates build?

Exercise gradually restored her good humor. She didn't mind the breeze, since its chill threatened nothing worse. This was a season she'd never experienced: a combination of fall and winter where roses bloomed beneath crepe myrtles as bare and knobby as bones, one tree glowed red, others stood leafless, while most—pines, oaks, magnolias—remained richly green. Hollies were bright with berries. Wispy moss fluttered like tattered gray banners high overhead. Fat balls of mistletoe dotted the oaks.

Birds chirped and trilled from wires and branches. A saucy mockingbird perched on a bush. It didn't move as she passed. She remembered something else Mildred once said. "Hunh! All those books say birds go south for the winter? What they do is go north for the summertime. They live down *here*."

As the sun rose higher and the mist dissolved, the air continued thick and humid, shimmering a faint green that turned the sky aqua and bronzed the lawns. She pulled her sweater away from her skin as she stopped to marvel at a clump of red poinsettias growing higher than a house.

Eventually, however, she had to think about the vial of pills in her suitcase. How long could Laura Grace go without her medicine? And what should she do about the vial itself?

If Daphne's death was definitely murder, she would turn it over to the police immediately. But what if she'd only died of a weak heart and too much dancing? Then, returning it would be extremely awkward.

Sheila retraced the route of that final drink. Several people might have put something in it, but had she really seen anything suspicious?

As she replayed the scene again and again, she always came up with more questions than answers. The little questions circled a much bigger one: Why would anybody kill Daphne L'Arken at her own party when surely they could do it far more safely—and less publicly—another time?

"You're as bad as Aunt Mary," she scolded herself, "needing a murder to put a little excitement in your life."

She checked her watch. Just past seven. Aunt Mary would sleep for another two hours, then need time for a cup of coffee.

Meanwhile, Sheila needed to remember that she was the guest of the woman who had tucked that vial under the magnolia leaves, and whose good friend had handed

Daphne the drink. The daughter of any southern mother knows what is due her hostess: courtesy, helpfulness, and a thank-you gift. Accusing her or her friends of murder is *not* on the list.

She ambled back toward Ortega Boulevard and came out near Stockton Park, that one public break in the string of waterfront homes.

The river drew her like a magnet. Growing up in a coastal town in northern Japan, the sea had always been a major part of her landscape. From here, the St. Johns looked like a small sea and made her realize how sadly landlocked she was in Atlanta. Wandering across a carpet of pine straw and rusty brown oak leaves, hands thrust deep in her pockets, she dropped onto a weathered bench beneath a magnolia as large as an oak. Lichen spotted its high gnarled roots. Finger roots crept over tan sand at her feet. How long had this dowager stood? Had she watched old Dan McGirth's pirate ship glide past?

Except for a saw whining in the distance, all Sheila could hear were the *whish* of blown leaves, a rustle of wind through the pines, and the soft slap of water on the seawall. Watching sunlight wink on water that today was a deep purply brown, and taking deep, cleansing breaths redolent with pine and salt, she felt more rested than she had when she'd awakened that morning.

A bend in the river hid downtown Jacksonville to her left. Far to her right she could see the L'Arken dock and the nearest boat, gently rocking. Straight ahead, halfway between her and the distant shore, a little boat making slow headway upriver reminded her of her father's favorite prayer: *Dear Lord, be good to me. The sea is so wide and my boat is so small.*

Several times Sheila told herself she ought to go, that the others might be getting up and wondering where she was. Dampness from the bench was soaking into her jeans. But something held her where she was. She felt as if she was waiting for something, or someone. What—a divine answer to all her questions?

When a rusty gray squirrel approached and scolded her noisily, she laughed aloud. "Sorry, God, I don't speak squirrel."

The bushy tail scuttled off, climbed a pine at least two feet thick, and chattered angrily down at her.

"Pretty view, isn't it? Of course you don't see the city from here."

Tom Goren rounded the bench and sat uninvited beside her. The big policeman looked far more comfortable this morning in a white polo shirt, windbreaker, khaki slacks, and scuffed Nikes. When he shoved up one sleeve, she was surprised to see he wore a Rolex. "Did I scare you?" he asked.

"No, I thought I'd suddenly learned to speak squirrel."

He took a minute to figure that out, then turned and peered up at their noisy neighbor. "He's certainly givin' you what for. Pesky things, think they own the parks."

"Why not? The people think they own the river."

He rubbed one big red ear. "Don't let anybody around here catch you sayin' that. These folks *do* own the river. You're up mighty early."

"So are you."

"Been up most of the night. You're on vacation." He let it sit between them like a question.

She bent down and flicked an ant off her sock. "I couldn't sleep. I kept thinking about what happened last night."

He shot her a swift look. "How'd you know what happened?"

She looked back, surprised. "I was right there beside Daphne when she fell."

Now *he* was puzzled. "What are you talkin' about?"

"Daphne L'Arken collapsed at the end of her party last night, and died soon after she got to the hospital."

He grew very still. "Daphne? Died?"

"Wasn't that what you were talking about?"

Without replying he pulled out a pack of spearmint gum and offered it to her. She took a stick and he took two, rolled them carefully, and popped them in his mouth like cylindrical pills.

Couldn't she think of anything but pills?

He wadded the foil and tucked it into his shirt pocket, and spoke around the gum. "What were you thinkin' about Daphne's dyin'?"

Now that the time had come, Sheila hesitated, and spoke cautiously, "How fast it happened, what a dreadful ending it was to a special evening."

His assent was a mere grunt, but his big pink hand covered with fuzzy red hair fisted on his thigh.

Sheila took a steadying breath and hazarded, "I was wondering if she could have been poisoned. They'll do an autopsy, won't they?"

Goren fished for the foil wrappers, spat his gum into one, wadded it up, and tossed it neatly into a nearby trash can. "Swish," he said softly. Then he shook out two more sticks, again offered her the pack, and tucked it away in his pocket when she declined. "What makes you think it was poison?" He popped the gum into his mouth.

She'd thought he'd forgotten her question. She'd almost forgotten it herself, and took a minute to reply. "Daphne's drink was handed from person to person before she got it. Someone could have dropped something in—"

His look stopped her. His eyes were like a cat's, gold on the outside and green near the iris. Above them, his eyebrows were bushy and light copper.

"Ma'am," he said. "I've forgotten your name, but I do remember what Rob Wilmer told me about you last night. You've built yourself a reputation in Atlanta for solvin' murders. Now I don't know how the Atlanta police feel about that, but I want to tell you straight off, so we don't have any misunderstandin', how I feel about it. I don't have anything against women detectives who are detectives, but I don't hold with amateurs, men or women. Ever since that nosy writer woman came on television, women all over America been thinkin' they could pop in and out of crime scenes givin' helpful advice. My advice to you is, enjoy your stay in Jacksonville, then go back where you came from. We don't need your help around here." He pushed himself to his feet. "Good talkin' to you." He lumbered off.

Sheila itched to pick up pine cones and pelt him. How dare he speak to her like that, as if she were pushing herself into his case?

She stomped toward the street, fuming with every step. She would take that little vial and shove it back under Daphne's magnolia leaf for the police to find—if they ever decided to look and nobody else got there first!

When she reached the small parking strip between the park and the street, Goren was waiting for her, leaning against the open door of an aqua-and-white fifty-seven Chevrolet.

"Nice car," she said, eyeing the huge fins.

"Yeah," he replied. "I'm headin' over to Dr. L'Arken's. Thought you might like a ride."

She shook her head. "I thought I'd walk down and see where Machine Gun Kelly used to live." Until she said it, the idea hadn't occurred to her. Now it seemed like a good reason to stay away from the house a bit longer.

"I'll show you. Get in." He slid into the driver's seat and started the engine.

A few minutes later he parked by the curb and opened his door. When she hesitated, he raised two brows questioningly. "Don't you want to see the tunnel?"

"Don't people live there?"

"Hey, it's too early for most people to be up. Come on."

He led her across the lawn and pointed into a small stucco addition to the house that looked like a fancy doghouse. "They say the tunnel went down there. If you look inside, you can see that the ground is a bit sunken. Of course, it could merely be where a dog once slept." She peered at him suspiciously. He was already moving toward the drive. "And if you look here, you'll see that while one side is perfectly smooth, the other is cracked, like the ground isn't solid underneath. It could be a tunnel—or just a Florida sinkhole. Satisfied?" He was already loping toward the car.

She went back to the kennel-like structure and examined the sunken ground again, then retraced her steps to the drive. He was right, of course. The cracks in one side of the drive *might* be due to uneven sand beneath it. But it was far more exciting to imagine a dark, disused tunnel leading to the nearby river. She could picture a desperate criminal and his wife, bent nearly double, shoving aside spiderwebs as they dashed underground, eluding baffled FBI agents who had just broken into an empty house.

"Find the tunnel?" Goren inquired around his gum as she joined him again.

"You have no soul," she informed him curtly. "It could very easily be a tunnel."

He bent to switch on the most elaborate car radio system she'd ever seen. "And Daphne's death might be murder." He pulled away from the curb. "But neither has anything to do with you."

She didn't reply aloud, but silently she vowed, *Okay, Tom Goren, I'll forget that drink, enjoy my visit, and go back where I came from. But I hope you* choke *on your chewing gum!*

They rode silently down Ortega Boulevard. At Hayden's drive, a red Alfa-Romeo turned in ahead of them. Treye climbed out. "Ooh, la, la," Tom murmured as he cut off the Chevy.

Treye climbed out and came back toward them. "Good mornin', Mr. Goren! Great car!" Seeing Sheila, he raised his hands in mock horror. "Oh, dear, I hope you aren't in trouble, Mrs. Travis?" He was homelier than ever in a faded navy blue sweatshirt, but he sounded as chipper as if he'd recently won a lottery, not lost a stepmother.

"Not yet. I went for a walk, and Tom was kind enough to give me a lift home."

Goren climbed heavily out and spoke over the Chevy's white top. "You're out early."

"Just doing my last hostly duty," Treye replied. "I found Eddie Weare asleep in the den when we got home last night. He'd tied one on, and I hated to disturb him, so I waited to wake him until morning. I just got back from taking him home."

"I heard what happened to your mother." Goren didn't bother to say how he heard, Sheila noted.

"Stepmother," Treye corrected him. The expression on his face hadn't changed.

"Stepmother," Tom agreed amiably. "Your dad around?"

Treye shook his head. "Dad"—he shook his head again, this time in disbelief—"Dad had surgery scheduled today, and by the time we got home, he decided it was too late to call his partners to cover for him. He's doing the first two, then he'll let them finish up. He left just after six. I ate breakfast with him, then woke Eddie and took him to where he's staying."

It was a long speech for a laconic young man. It also betrayed a new side of Treye: a son who must have set his alarm to get up early enough to share breakfast with his father; a young man kind enough to permit a drunk to finish the night out on the sofa before taking him home.

"Your dad's lucky to have you around," Sheila said impulsively.

His familiar grin flashed. "Yeah, isn't he?"

Not once, she noticed, had he mentioned Daphne.

Tom backed the Chevy out of the drive. Treye offered Sheila a friendly nod. "I was just goin' down to check my boat after the storm. Want to see her?"

"Sure." One more brief delay before going inside.

Teddy still sat on one side of the dock, legs dangling, fishing pole in hand. Beside her, Einstein dozed.

He opened one eye and thumped his tail when Sheila asked, "Catch anything?"

Shrugging, Teddy jerked her head toward a white plastic bucket full of water and two large fish.

"Way to go, Ted!" Treye grabbed the top of her head and shook it gently. Einstein gave a warning bark. Treye laughed as he went to the end of the dock, grabbed a line, and pulled the ski boat closer to the dock. He truly was in high spirits this morning.

"Jack Three?" Sheila asked, reading the name on the stern.

"Yeah. Jack and I share the boat." He leaped over the rail. "Come aboard, Sheila! You like boats?" His face was more monkeylike than ever as he squinted into the sun.

"Mostly sailboats," she admitted. She hoped Treye wasn't one of those motorboat enthusiasts who hate sailors.

He wasn't. "My mom's got the family sailboat. You'll have to ask her to take you out sometime. But at least come take a look."

Before she climbed aboard, however, he abruptly bellowed: "Teddy L'Arken, have you been messin' around in here?"

"Of course not!" Teddy sneered. "I don't go on your stupid boat without asking."

"There's a line uncoiled."

"I coil my lines." Teddy put her small nose into the air. Her end of the conversation was over. She rose and began to collect her gear.

Treye prowled his boat, eyes narrowed. "Has Jack taken her out this mornin'? Or let Muffy borrow her again?"

Teddy shrugged. "I dunno. Jack's still asleep."

He picked up the end of a dangling line and let it drop. "Well, somebody's been aboard. If I catch whoever it was—" He broke off and headed aft. "I think I'll take her out. Sheila, sure you don't want to go for a spin?"

"Not this morning. Maybe another time."

He seemed to have forgotten about her tour. She

didn't mind. She had no intention of ever driving a powerboat.

Strolling back toward Teddy, she asked, "You about ready for breakfast?"

Teddy pivoted on her heel. Her rod caught Sheila neatly between the ankles. The next thing Sheila knew, she was treading water in the chilly St. Johns.

Einstein bayed. Treye jumped onto the dock and hurled her a life preserver, but by then Sheila had swum to the ladder at the end of the dock. Her teeth chattered and the fisherman's sweater dragged her down like chain mail. Grimly she forced herself up the ladder and spat out a mouthful of bland, tasteless water. At least it wasn't salty. Retching, she lay on the sun-warmed boards. The wind felt cold through her drenched clothes.

Treye hurried back to his boat for a blanket. He flung it over her. She looked up to see Teddy's face, a study in dismay. Because she had dunked Sheila, or because she hadn't drowned her?

"Oh, Mrs. Travis!" she cried insincerely, "You'd better hurry inside before you get pneumonia! Come on, Einstein!" She wasn't in such a hurry that she forgot her bucket. She plowed up the yard with water sloshing over her shoes. "Mama? Mama! Mrs. Travis fell in the river!"

Treye helped Sheila to her feet and led her, shivering uncontrollably, to a back door.

Helen met them, thermal blanket in hand. Justin thrust a glass of brandy into Sheila's hand. She smiled her thanks, and tossed it down before wrapping the dry blanket around her. The brandy burned, but washed away the St. Johns. "Is the river polluted?" she managed to ask.

"We eat the fish," Teddy reminded her scornfully.

Sheila hurried upstairs, stripped off her sodden clothes, toweled vigorously, and decided a hot shower would feel terrific. She stood for minutes letting the hot water purge her of shock, anger at Crispin, frustration with Tom Goren, even fury at Teddy—although, as she shampooed, she *did* picture Teddy L'Arken tied to a stake on a fire-ant bed.

"You won't win him that way, sweetie," she told the child in absentia as she toweled dry.

Her bones were still cold, so she pulled on a wool skirt and cotton sweater and hugged herself for a minute or two, standing by the window.

From here, the river undulated smooth and inviting in the sunlight.

Going downstairs, she smelled bacon and was suddenly ravenous! Then her stomach clutched. Queasy, she stopped off in the powder room to spit out a mouthful of bile.

In the kitchen Brandy, her glorious hair halfway down a lilac peignoir, stood cooking pancakes on a long griddle. At the center island, Crispin and Justin, unshaven and still in their bathrobes, were shoveling in pancakes and bacon. "We're eatin' casual this mornin'," Justin drawled, waving his fork.

Helen was farther down the counter talking on the phone. Behind her hung a family calendar, so full it made Sheila dizzy to look at it. Justin caught her eye and gave a grunt. "Helen has a hard time sayin' no."

This morning, Helen's calf-length khaki skirt and yellow cotton sweater looked far more chipper than her face. Her nose was pink and her lashes damp. Sheila wondered if she'd slept.

Helen covered the mouthpiece of the phone. "Are you all right?" When Sheila nodded, she turned back to her conversation. "She says she's fine, Mama. Don't worry."

Teddy filled the dog's bowl at the sink in a virtuous silence, slid her eyes toward her mother, and sidled out of the room. Einstein padded behind her.

"That water's cold this time of year," Crispin said warily.

"Sure is," Sheila agreed. "I won't swim in it again. And I'm sorry to be so late."

"No problem." Brandy spoke over one shoulder. "You're in time for the women's shift."

Sheila looked at Crispin's plate, a sticky greasy mess, and had to sit down quickly. Was the river as safe as Teddy implied it was?

Helen said, in the patient tone of one repeating something for the third time, "Justin and Hayden are takin' care of *everything*, Mama. Don't *worry*!"

Justin, forking bacon onto his plate, gave his wife a sympathetic frown. "Tell her you have to go, hon. Brandy's got your breakfast ready."

Brandy deftly stacked pancakes onto three plates and moved toward a coffeepot. "Do you drink coffee, Sheila?"

"Do the Chinese eat rice?" Crispin asked over his own mug. "Sheila single-throatedly keeps one coffee-producing country in business."

Justin stopped chewing bacon long enough to muse, "Could be worse. Could be gin." He looked weary, but totally unflappable. Sheila wondered how he would look if someone he knew turned out to have murdered his sister-in-law.

To avoid facing that possibility—and to still her stomach—she took a grateful sip of hot black coffee. Crispin's eyes were on her. "You sure you're all right?" he asked.

He looked so—so blessedly *good* sitting there in his pajamas and bathrobe with his hair tousled! Sheila laughed. "Sure. I've even been up and dressed for hours. Dressed twice, in fact."

She hadn't realized how tense he'd been until she saw him relax. Had their quarrel scared him as much as it had scared her?

Brandy carried plates over and said bossily, "Teddy needs to apologize again for that iguana. Where on earth has she gone?"

"She's already got one mother," Justin reminded her mildly.

Brandy sighed and said earnestly, "Mama's too easy on Teddy, Daddy. That child needs a spanking!"

Sheila curled her fingers around her mug and said nothing. She would trust one of Teddy's apologies about as far as she could toss the source. With one hand.

Helen made a valiant attempt at being a good hostess, but breakfast was punctuated with long silences. They were still eating when Libba hailed them from the front hall. "May I put this in your freezer for a few minutes?" She came in holding up a plastic grocery bag.

"You went all the way to Winn Dixie?" Helen asked, surprised.

Libba shrugged and indicated her gray sweatshirt and jeans. "We were out of orange juice and a vegetable for dinner, and I couldn't go into Publix lookin' like this!" She shoved the bag in the freezer.

"Here, Aunt Libba, take my seat. I'm finished, and I need to go pack." Brandy slid off her stool and took her dishes to the sink. "Mama," she asked reluctantly, "do you really think it's all right if I go? I don't like to let them down, but—"

"What do you think, Justin?" Helen looked too weary to decide whether to lift her fork, much less anything more complicated.

Justin considered, then nodded. "I think you ought to go, honey. You've told them you would, and Uncle Hayden will understand. He's one of your sponsors, isn't he?"

Brandy nodded; her face crumpled. "So was Aunt Daphne."

"Where you goin'?" Libba inquired.

"Down to Homestead to work on Habitat houses with the church youth group," Brandy told her.

Libba took her hand. "Daphne loved service projects in high school. She'd want you to go. I know she would."

Persuaded, Brandy went to pack.

"Hope nobody has to weather a hurricane in a house Brandy helped build," Crispin commented, taking another piece of bacon.

"Hey!" Justin socked him lightly on the bicep. "I taught her everything she knows."

"Like I said," Crispin replied comfortably.

Libba fetched a mug and poured herself a cup of coffee. Her hands shook as she lifted the mug, and her face was white and drawn.

"You look worn out," Helen sympathized. "You did too much last night."

They looked wordlessly at one another. Suddenly, they flung themselves into one another's arms, sobbing. "I can't believe she went so fast!" Helen mourned. "I just can't believe it!"

Crispin shifted uneasily on his stool. Justin, more accustomed to weeping women, rose and held both in his huge embrace. "Go back to bed, honey. Get some sleep. You, too, Libba. You don't look like you got enough."

Helen sniffed. "You aren't going to aerobics this afternoon, are you?"

Libba shook her head. "I hadn't planned to do a thing today, but the nursing home called at seven. Mama was raising Cain again, and wouldn't quiet down unless I went. This year, it seems like things just get worse and worse."

Justin gave her a gentle shake. "Like I said, go home and take a nap. Things won't look so bad when you're rested."

She blew her nose on a paper napkin and gave him a watery smile. "Have you heard from Hayden yet today?"

Justin shook his head. "Not yet."

"I ran into Treye," Sheila volunteered. "He said his dad was taking his first two surgeries this morning."

"Good Lord!" Justin breathed. It sounded like a prayer for strength.

Helen went back to the stove, and in a moment set a

plate of pancakes before her friend. "Eat somethin', Libba. I'll bet you didn't get a bite last night, did you?"

"A nibble here and there," Libba admitted, cutting her pancakes into small bites. She did not, however, put any of the bites into her mouth.

Helen slid back onto her own stool. "Have you talked to Muffy? I've tried to call her, but she doesn't answer."

Libba poked at the pancakes with a fork. "Maybe she's turned off her phone."

"That's what I told her," Justin agreed.

Libba sighed. "She didn't look good when I saw her last. I offered to drive her, but she didn't want to wait for me. You don't reckon she had a wreck on her way home, do you?"

Helen's golden eyes echoed her worry. "Maybe we ought to go over and see. . . ."

Justin gave an exasperated snort. "Leave Muffy alone! She's got an ice pack on her head and is stayin' in bed with a colossal hangover."

He would have cause to regret those words.

Libba eventually departed—after returning from the front door to retrieve her frozen foods. Justin and Crispin went upstairs, giving no thought to the mountain of sticky plates they left behind. Helen stood and began loading dishes into the dishwasher.

As Sheila rose to help, Jack entered the kitchen, yawning and stretching above his terry cloth robe. Without a word he dragged down a bowl, filled it with Wheaties, spooned on sugar, poured on milk, and headed out to a glass-topped table in the Florida room, overlooking the river.

"Good morning, sunshine!" Helen called after him.

"Mmpghm," was all he replied.

Sheila collected plates from the island. "I appreciate Brandy giving up her room," she told Helen.

Helen filled a dishpan and swished her hands to make a mountain of bubbles. "She was glad to do it. Brandy is—

well, all the children are special, but Brandy is—Brandy."
She wiped the griddle on the stove. "They're all
adopted—did Crispin tell you?"

Sheila shook her head. Why was she surprised? None
of the children looked like their parents, and they were
certainly unlike one another.

Helen scrubbed at the immaculate counter. "I
couldn't have children, but we were blessed to get these
three."

Privately, Sheila thought they would have done better
to stop with two. Now she understood, however, Helen's
bumper sticker. A woman who has yearned for children
she cannot have might well feel about abortion like a hungry person watching crops plowed under.

Not certain what to say, she was glad to notice, out the
riverfront window, a sailboat approaching the dock.

"Look's like Twinkie's coming," Jack called from the
Florida room.

Helen peered out. "Treye's probably borrowed her
boat for some reason." She turned to explain to Sheila.
"Twinkie is Hayden's first wife, Treye's mother, and she
has a wonderful boat. She races up and down the whole
eastern seaboard." As the boat drew nearer, she added,
"Twinkie was there last night, but I didn't introduce you.
It was so awkward—" She scrubbed at an invisible spot on
the stove and sighed. "The whole situation is awkward."

The boat certainly wasn't awkward, Sheila thought,
watching the billowing sails drop at just the right instant
so that the boat glided precisely to the empty piling.
Sheila knew what skill that kind of apparent effortlessness
took.

A stocky figure leaped lightly onto the dock. "Merci-
ful heavens!" Helen tossed her dishrag in an untidy heap
on the counter. "What on earth—?" She, like Sheila, obviously expected Twinkie to head up the grassy lawn toward
them. Instead, the woman turned toward her old home.

Helen watched her go with a look of dismay. "I wonder what she's up to?" She went through to the dining

room and called upstairs, "Honey, Twinkie's just gone to Hayden's. Treye's out on his boat. Think I ought to go over, too?"

Sheila couldn't hear his reply, but Helen returned, plopped herself down on a stool, and took a swallow of coffee that surely must be cold. Sheila went for the pot and refilled both mugs.

Helen spoke almost as if to herself. "I could shoot myself for introducing Hayden to Daphne. Twinkie wasn't a perfect wife, but they weren't actually unhappy, and we all liked her. We *still* like her. I just wish—"

She stopped, then spoke rapidly as if glad to unburden herself to someone. "Daphne was so depressed when she came back. Her husband got custody of her two children, and she was sick at leaving them behind, so Libba and I started doing things with her—we went shopping, all joined an aerobics class, that sort of thing. Muffy had been in an aerobics class for heart patients—she's the one I was worried about last night." Helen hesitated, then plunged resolutely on. "But Muffy got better, and her doctors said she could join our class. We had a Saturday brunch here to celebrate. Twinkie was off sailing, so Hayden came, too. After that, he came over a lot when Daphne was here. I never imagined ..."

She shook her head and heaved an enormous sigh.

Sheila gave her a sympathetic smile. "It must have been awkward deciding who got the house."

Helen's laugh was humorless. "It was awkward, all right. It was in Hayden's name." She went to the window again and peered across the empty lawn, as if afraid she could be overheard. Twinkie, however, was nowhere to be seen.

Returning to her stool, Helen confided, "They'd both wanted it for a long time. I think Hayden wanted it all his life. He grew up in this house, you know, but it's not—" she reached for the right word "—not *showy* enough for Hayden. Anyway, when the one next door finally came on the market, Twinkie was racing up on the Chesapeake.

Hayden called to ask what he should do, and she said she couldn't come home to sign papers, so he should just go ahead and buy it. Nobody thought it mattered." Helen looked out at the sailboat. "Of course, when Hayden asked for the divorce, he gave her money to buy a house over in Ortega Forest, but ..." She set her mug down with an angry thump. "Sometimes we women are so dumb!"

Sheila was silent. She'd been that dumb herself. Tyler had bought stocks for years, putting them in his own name. He never offered to put her name on them, and she never asked. What did it matter? Until he died. Until she had to wait for the estate to be settled. Until she had to pay taxes on her "inheritance." And if he had ever decided to leave her? What would she have gotten then?

Crispin limped in wearing a royal-blue-and-gold nylon warm-up suit. He gave Helen a quick, brotherly hug. "We'll be gone until eight or so. I hope you'll take Justin's advice and get some rest."

Her smile was tremulous. "I'm gonna try, Crispin. It's been a tough twenty-four hours."

"Tell me something." He propped his good foot on the rung of one of the stools. "Aunt Martha said you were worried sick about Eddie Weare coming last night. Did you know what shape he was in?"

Helen shook her head so fast that her hair flicked her cheek. "No, I hadn't seen Eddie since college. Mamar must have been mistaken."

Down at his office, Tom Goren spoke into the telephone in disbelief. "Would you repeat that, please?"

The voice was crisp and irritated. "The preliminary findings indicate that Daphne L'Arken died of an overdose of Lanoxin, a heart medication."

"Horse droppings! She'd been cuttin' up with a couple of high school friends. If she had a bad heart and didn't know it, couldn't that have killed her?"

"It could have, Tom, but it didn't. When the lab report comes back, believe me—it's gonna show that that woman had enough Lanoxin in her system to kill even you."

As Sheila and Crispin drove back to Jacksonville after dinner, they journeyed toward a pewter sky painted with swaths of pearl-gray clouds. On each side of the interstate, sooty pines stood like sentinels. Against the darkness, one cloud of stunning whiteness towered over the road ahead.

This day, too, had been a dazzling brightness against the bleakness to which they must return. Sheila focused on the cloud, putting the encroaching darkness out of mind.

Crispin spoke drowsily. "If Moses had had a cloud like that, he wouldn't have needed a pillar of fire by night."

She reached for the temperature controls. "Speaking of fire, do you mind if I turn on a bit of heat?"

"Suit yourself—if you haven't worn out the controls."

She laughed. In the morning they'd needed heat to take the chill out of the air. By mid-morning she had switched to vent. At noon it was warm enough for air-conditioning. After dinner she'd gone back to vent. Now it was growing chilly again. What a crazy climate!

Crispin wriggled lower in his seat and started to softly whistle. He sounded as relaxed as Sheila felt. They had had a glorious day of sand dunes, sea oats, crisp blue sky, and old buildings.

At Ponte Vedra Beach, Crispin had risked getting sand in his cast so they could sit on Helen's beach blanket in a salty, slighty gritty breeze. They'd eaten ham sandwiches, yogurt, and fresh south Florida strawberries they'd picked up at a Publix deli. Later, they'd prowled the old streets of St. Augustine and wound up at the seafood restaurant Daphne had so painstakingly directed them to just before she died. They toasted her before they ate.

Over fried shrimp and scallops, Sheila had confessed, "Part of me keeps thinking we shouldn't be having so much fun the day after she died."

"I scarcely knew the woman," Crispin reminded her, "and you didn't know her at all. Save your mourning for folks you know."

She was willing to be convinced. That was the only time either of them mentioned the night before.

As she slowly negotiated construction on the Buckman Bridge, where the river was three miles wide, Sheila had plenty of time to wonder whether to tell him about the pills. She didn't want to spoil the day. She also didn't want to risk the truce they'd reached about the week: they'd stay this one more night with Justin and Helen, then drive over to St. Petersburg, Aunt Mary, and Forbes. If Justin still planned to go to Saturday night's Gator Bowl, Crispin would fly over Saturday afternoon for that.

She still hadn't decided to tell him when, just before Ortega, they overtook a passenger train running parallel to U.S. 17. "Miami to L.A.," Crispin informed her. "Passes right through Ortega every day, but passengers probably think they're going through a forest. Ortega does a good job of preserving its privacy."

The least she could do, Sheila decided, was to help preserve it, too. She wouldn't mention the pills unless she had to.

However, as she pulled into the L'Arkens' drive, she saw Tom Goren's Chevy fins parked next to a blue Buick. As she switched off the engine, Teddy dashed outside and headed directly for Sheila's door. "A policeman's inside," she announced—breathless, but with undisguised satisfaction. "He wants You."

For ten minutes, Tom Goren had been miserable, sitting stiffly in Helen L'Arken's living room trying not to look at her. Did she remember dating for a while, back when being a football player was enough to attract even a cheerleader from Ortega? Old Mrs. Aspen certainly remembered. Her nostrils flared, like something in the room stank. Helen, however, looked as at ease and pretty as she had at the senior Homecoming Dance. That was the last time they ever danced. Now he found himself remembering the arch of her back when he held her.

He shifted his weight, angry at his own sentimentality. Years ago Tom had opted for comfort, not sentiment. He'd never regretted that decision until now. He'd bought a small brick house on the outskirts of fashionable Avondale, a house that was old but not stylish, with a yard full of ivy that never needed to be mown. It didn't have much space—the whole shebang would probably fit into the three rooms from where he now sat—but it was plenty big for one, and he had it fixed up to his liking. He'd filled his living room with stereo equipment and a big-screen TV, his dining room with a pool table. Nobody cared where he ate, when he came home, what he did in his spare time, or if he filled his basement up with boxes of trash. If he'd married somebody like Helen, now. . . .

He tried to picture Helen perched on his worn recliner watching the big-screen TV, washing up in his kitchen, poking around in his basement. What a joke!

Then Helen turned, and lamplight touched the curve of her cheek. *Maybe*, Tom thought sourly, *it's me that's the joke*.

A Maltese cat tried to get in his lap. He pushed it away. With the perversity of its kind, the cat thrust its big head into his crotch and purred. Tom's scarred face blushed a fiery red.

"Copernicus, get down!" Unperturbed but firm, Helen lifted the mammoth animal and carried it to the front door.

Copernicus? He might have guessed her cat would have some damn fool name like that.

Justin came back from the kitchen carrying a black laquer tray with a gold company seal in the middle. "Here we are. Diet Coke for Helen, beer for me, Cokes for Tom and Charho." Served in chilled glasses, for heaven's sake. "Now, Tom, what can we do for you?"

Tom shifted uneasily. "We got the preliminary report

on Daphne—did Dr. L'Arken tell you?" He and Justin might have played football together, but Tom had never been on a first name basis with Justin's older brother.

"Yeah. They think she died of an overdose of some heart medication?" Justin obviously did not believe it.

Old lady Aspen leaned forward like a lean gray wolf. "That's simply nonsense! When could Daphne have taken it? She wasn't carrying it with her. That dress had no pockets. And she didn't go back upstairs after the party started. She was too busy for that. You must be mistaken."

"Did you have her in view at all times, Mrs. Aspen?"

"Well, except for a very brief time near the end—"

"That's when she was back in the den, dancing with Eddie," Helen contributed quickly.

"Poor old Eddie." Justin thrust his beer away as if he suddenly found it distasteful. "I didn't notice what happened to him after the party. I hope Muffy remembered to take him home."

"She didn't," Tom told him. "Dr. L'Arken's boy found him asleep in the den when they got back from the hospital. He let him sleep, then took him home this mornin'."

Justin sighed. "Poor devil. By the way, Tom, do you know where Muffy could be? Helen's been calling all day, but she doesn't answer."

Helen turned, contrite. "I'm sorry, honey, I didn't tell you. I called Libba again, and we went over and let ourselves in with her key. Muffy's big suitcase was gone, and a good many clothes. She must've gone out of town and just forgotten to tell us."

Before anyone could say more, they heard Sheila's car in the drive. A minute later, Crispin limped in, Teddy clinging to one arm and Sheila just behind.

When Justin started introductions, Sheila waved them away. "I met Detective Goren at the party last night, and again this morning, down by the river." She hoped they could get whatever this was out of the way quickly. She wanted to shower the salt and grit off her skin.

Tom's tone implied he was equally eager to finish and leave. "Mrs. Travis, this morning you asked me if I thought Daphne could have been poisoned. Why'd you ask that question?"

"Poisoned?" Teddy, who had plopped cross-legged at Crispin's feet with Einstein beside her, swiveled from the detective to Sheila. Behind her glasses, her eyes were enormous with curiosity.

Helen's eyes were as wide as her daughter's, but there was fear in them, not curiosity. Crispin made a noise somewhere between a grunt and a groan. Charho leaned forward, face grim.

Sheila wished she could think up a convincing lie, but habits of honesty are difficult to break. "I was standing by Daphne when she collapsed. She was a bit out of breath from dancing. But she showed no signs of distress until after she swallowed most of a drink someone brought her."

"Who?"

She'd only used the pronoun to postpone the inevitable. "Muffy." She added quickly, "But it had passed through several hands and sat on the table for several minutes."

"Who poured the drink?"

Sheila tried not to look at Helen. Helen, however, replied at once. "Daphne ordered it just before the bar closed, then got busy talking to some people and left it sitting there. She often forgot where she'd left her drink. When I noticed it, I asked Libba to take it to her. I thought she did."

"How'd you know it was Daphne's?"

Helen smiled. "From the lipstick on the rim. Nobody wore that shade but Daphne."

"But Libba only took the drink as far as the dining room table and left it with Hayden," Sheila emphasized. "It was on the table for several minutes before Muffy brought it over. Almost anybody could have slipped something in it."

"Anybody?" Charho objected. "My dear! There was

no one left at the party except Daphne's family and dearest friends."

Sheila nodded with a sigh. "I know. Perhaps she did just have a heart attack . . ."

Goren traced a circle on his massive thigh without looking at her. "Was that your only reason for thinking of poison—the fact that she died so suddenly?"

Was she going to have to trot it all out right here in front of everybody? He lifted his head and his eyes bored into hers. "No," she admitted, not bothering to hide her irritation at his indelicacy. "After they took Daphne to the hospital, I went to pick up the pieces of the glass she'd dropped. They were already gone. I even looked for them in the kitchen trash. They weren't there."

Charho made the kind of noise a well-bred lady makes when she needs to correct a guest. "Sheila had no way of knowin' that we recycle glass in Jacksonville, Tom. If you send a man to look in Hayden's blue bin, you will probably find remnants of several glasses. I personally saw two broken last night. Daphne's will no doubt be with them."

"I asked about the garbage this morning, and Dr. L'Arken said the caterers must have taken it with them. We're tracing it now." Goren jotted a note on a pad he carried. "So out of a broken glass and a sudden death you put together a deliberate poisoning, Mrs. Travis?"

This was the stickiest of all. "Could we speak on the porch?"

Justin sketched a broad, relaxed wave. "Don't worry about us, Sheila. Tell Tom what you know. We want to know, too."

She sighed. "I saw a vial of pills being hidden under Daphne's centerpiece earlier, and after Daphne died, I wondered about them."

Tom's eyes narrowed. "Daphne hid them? Or somebody else?"

"Somebody else."

Her tone must have reached him, for he abandoned

that line of questioning. "Were they heart pills? Did you take them out and look at them?"

"No, to both questions. But when I found that Daphne's glass had been removed—"

"Not removed, dear!" Charho protested. "Cleared away. You wouldn't want broken glass all over the floor!"

Sheila wouldn't have wanted Daphne dead, either, but nobody had asked her.

Tom Goren gave Charho a steady look. "Did you clear away the glass, Mrs. Aspen?"

"Of course not! I was takin' Daphne's necklace upstairs, then helpin' Helen see guests to the door. But surely one of the caterers, or Libba—"

"Right." Tom turned back to Sheila. "So what happened to the pills?"

"I took them, as a precaution, using a napkin to preserve fingerprints."

Teddy's expression changed to reluctant admiration, but Sheila avoided meeting her eyes. What if Sheila's evidence got Teddy's mother arrested?

"Whose prescription is it?" Tom asked brusquely, obviously wondering why she was so slow to talk tonight when she'd brought the subject up this morning without prodding.

Sheila bit her lower lip. "Laura Grace Hayden's."

Justin's jaw dropped. "Ellgie's thyroid pills? Who put them there? I took them with me last night to give to Mamar, and after the announcement, Helen, you said—" He stopped, too late.

Helen's face was white, but her voice perfectly composed. "I hid the pills, Tom. Mamar had already left when Justin gave them to me, and my dress had no pockets, so I tucked the bottle under a magnolia leaf, thinking I'd get it when we left. Frankly, this is the first I've thought of it since."

"Ellgie will need her pills!" Teddy seized on something she could comprehend.

Justin waved away her concern. "We can get her a refill, honey, or Uncle Hayden can write a new prescription."

Sheila appreciated his normal tone. Her own cheeks were stained with embarrassment. She wished she'd mentioned the pills to Helen before this. She wished she'd thought to look at them to see if they were, indeed, merely thyroid pills. She wished she'd left them where she'd found them.

From the look on Crispin's face, he was wishing all that, too. Or maybe he was just wishing he'd left her at home.

Tom Goren lumbered to his feet. "I'd appreciate it if you'd get the bottle, Mrs. Travis."

If Sheila had been Einstein, she would have gone upstairs with her tail tucked between her legs. Could things get any worse?

They could.

When she returned, Hayden was waiting at the foot of the stairs. Sheila wished she could run out to the dock and sail away on the river's silky blackness. Crispin, she saw, had hobbled out. Hearing water running in the kitchen, she presumed he'd gone for a drink. As soon as she handed over the bottle, she would make up a reason to join him—except she was not certain how welcome she would be.

"Let me see." Hayden reached for the plastic bottle as she held it out.

"Don't touch it!" Tom warned curtly, forestalling him.

"I just want to see what's in the bottle." Hayden sounded testy.

"That'll have to wait until I have the lab check it for prints. Do you have a sandwich bag, Helen?"

She rose and brought one back. Tom carefully sealed the bottle inside. "Now. You all agree that Muffy handed Daphne her drink?"

"Hell, I don't know!" Hayden growled, turning away. Sheila saw tears in his dark eyes.

"You can talk to Muffy when she gets back to town."

Helen addressed Tom, but her anxious eyes were on Justin.

"Where's Aunt Muffy gone?" Teddy piped up, surprised.

To Sheila, it was obvious the others had forgotten the child was there. Helen spoke in the tone a mother uses to answer one question and discourage more. "Just on a little trip, honey. We don't know where."

Justin had one idea. "Have you seen Lance McGrew, Tom? Muff said yesterday she was gonna bring him to the party last night, but apparently he stood her up. Maybe they—" The warning look his wife shot toward Teddy stopped him midsentence.

Tom Goren lifted one hand, as if about to say something, then dropped it as if he'd changed his mind. "I'll talk to Muffy when she gets back," he said heavily.

Einstein padded to the door and whined. "Oh, Teddy!" Helen exclaimed in dismay. "Didn't you take him to do his business?"

Teddy screwed up her face. "I was waitin' for Crispin."

Helen headed for the coat closet with a mother's martyred sigh. "You can't go out this late and your daddy's tired. Get me the leash."

"Let me do it," Sheila offered quickly. "I've been sitting all afternoon, and could use the exercise."

She didn't need exercise—she needed escape. Fingerprints, smingerprints, she'd sneaked a quick peek at the pills before she brought them down. They were small and white, exactly like Aunt Mary's Synthroid. How could she have read so much into the instinctive act of a woman stuck with something she didn't want to carry around for an entire evening?

When she left, Hayden was saying, ". . . Friday at ten, at Riverside."

"Yay, Sheila," she muttered angrily as Einstein tugged her down the drive toward Ortega Boulevard. "The man comes to tell his brother about his wife's funeral arrangements, and finds you accusing his sister-in-law of her murder." She was glad she and Crispin had already agreed to leave tomorrow. Maybe she'd never have to face the L'Arkens again. In that case, of course, she'd either have to give up Crispin, or not share the most important people in his life. Besides, darn it, she liked them!

The orange streetlights on the other side of the street gave the world a Halloween glow. The spooky atmosphere suited her mood. "You've let a few successes go to your head," she raged. "What were you trying to do, impress Crispin's friends that you're some hotshot detective? You're more of a busybody than Aunt Mary!"

She couldn't ever remember disliking her own company so much.

Fortunately, once he'd had a brief squat, Einstein left her little time for self-pity. His daytime waddle was all act. On his nighttime rounds he was Superdog, dashing along at an amazing clip.

Jogging behind, Sheila was soon out of breath. "What is this, penance?" she demanded as the dog hauled her around another corner.

When her lungs began to feel they would burst, she pulled back sharply on the leash. Einstein immediately sat, gently panting, and mocked her gasps with his eyes. "Okay, fellow, so I'm not in as good shape as Helen." Her side ached, and her heart pounded so hard she was surprised it didn't fall out on the street. She felt a tingling sensation on her left leg. It was a moment before she realized the tingle was not poor circulation, but something crawling. She had stopped right on top of an anthill.

Smacking and scratching, she pranced toward the street, startling a cat. It streaked up a nearby magnolia and Einstein lunged after it, baying frantically. Sheila tugged his leash—with no effect except to burn her palms on the leather. "Sit!" she finally shouted in Aunt Mary's most quelling tones.

To her astonishment, he did. "Okay, mister, let's try

walking for a while." She shook his leash. He stood and, having tested her mettle, proceeded to snuffle and waddle down the street at a dignified pace.

By this time Sheila was thoroughly lost. She hoped Einstein was brighter than he looked. Sure enough, at the next corner she saw a Chevron station down the block. This was Ortega Boulevard. The L'Arken houses were around a couple of bends to the right.

Overhead, the clouds had blown out to sea, leaving the sky clear and brittle. Stars peeped through the fuzzy arms of a massive oak. She dreaded going back to the warmly lit living room where kind and gentle people would try to pretend she hadn't made a colossal fool of herself.

Most of all, she dreaded facing Crispin.

However, she was getting cold and sleepy. Holding her watch to the streetlight, she saw it was nearly nine. Surely the guests would have left or be going soon. She permitted Einstein to lead her across the street to the side without streetlights, and along the grassy verge toward home. His long nose shifted from side to side, analyzing clues left by previous roamers. Just at Hayden's drive he lifted his head, took a deep whiff, and turned in.

"Wrong house, fellow." She jerked on the leash.

Einstein had his own ideas. "Rrowf!" He headed for a clump of azaleas that towered at least eight feet just inside the brick wall to the left of the drive.

"You've done your business!" Sheila reminded him, tugging on the leash.

His chest rumbling with a sound so deep it was more vibration than noise, the dog plopped down on his wide haunches and refused to move. His soulful eyes were on the azaleas.

Sheila tugged the leash again. "Come on! It's probably just a squirrel!"

"More likely a 'possum."

Sheila whirled. A fiery speck fell to the drive. Hayden, grinding out a cigarette with his toe. She was glad he couldn't see her face. He had already known she was a meddling fool. Now he also knew she was an incompetent dog-walker.

Since Einstein refused to budge, she let the leash go slack and pretended to be enjoying the scent of smoke mingled with pine, damp oak leaves, and a cloying sweetness she didn't recognize. Perhaps some night-blooming tropical shrub?

"Sorry to scare you. I was puttin' off going inside." As Hayden approached, Einstein minced toward the bushes, then backed up and sat quivering. The soft growl still rumbled in his chest. "I'm like Einstein. I keep hearin' things, and I think it's Daphne." He bent to fondle the dog's ears, then took the leash from Sheila and nudged Einstein with his foot. "What you got treed in there?"

Einstein growled like a small motor.

Hayden handed Sheila back the leash. "Let's just see . . ." He pushed back the nearest azalea branch and shook his head. "It's blacker than—"

He stopped, leaving the rest to her imagination.

Einstein quivered with excitement. "Wait here," Hayden commanded. "I've got a flashlight in my car. Won't be but a minute."

When he'd disappeared into the shadows, Sheila shivered. Overhead, Spanish moss wiggled like sinister fingers against the sky. Near the ground, not a glint of light penetrated the mammoth bushes. Of all her irrational fears, the worst was a fear of the dark. Tonight, anything could be lurking in those murky bushes, mesmerized by Einstein's growl.

How long would it remain mesmerized?

Didn't Florida still have panthers?

Did alligators crawl this far north?

She stepped closer to the quivering dog.

Hayden's bobbing light was a welcome sight. He also carried a garden rake. Pulling back a branch with the hand that held the light, he used the other to probe with the

rake handle. Sheila clung to Einstein's leash, poised for
flight.

A grunt from Hayden drew her closer. Then he exclaimed, "My God!" and fell to his knees.

Sheila knew he wasn't praying. She too saw what he'd
seen in the bright beam: a slender, stockinged foot.

Hayden pushed aside the largest branch and crawled into
the bushes.

Einstein raised his head and bawled like he'd raised a
bear. Sheila shared his sentiments, but felt she owed
Hayden some form of support. "Are you okay?" she called.

There was no reply. She moved closer. Einstein
jerked back, nearly pulling her arm out of its socket. She
tethered him to a handy dogwood, then, pushing aside a
branch, peered into the azalea ring.

At the center, the circle of bushes was hollow. Hayden
knelt in the flashlight's glow like a gnome in a child's leafy
domed playhouse.

It was no child who lay there, however. Hayden
played his light up a shapely leg, a black coat open to
show a brief red dress, and a filmy scarf blazing with the
colors of fire. The scarf looked too fragile to have done
such damage.

Daphne L'Arken's death might have been accidental.
Muffy Merriwether's certainly had not.

Distantly, she heard voices. "Good night!" A car door
slammed.

"Tom Goren!" Hayden said roughly. "Stop him!"

Without stopping to consider, Sheila sprinted up the
drive and into the boulevard. Einstein, left behind, yowled
his displeasure.

The old Chevy braked. Tom rolled down his window.
"What is it now, Mrs. Travis?"

"Muffy!" Sheila panted. "She's—oh, come see!"

She wouldn't have recognized her own voice.

His face peered questioningly up at her in the moonlight. What he saw must have convinced him, for when she backed onto the grassy verge, he swung the car into Hayden's drive and climbed out. Following, Sheila took time to clear her throat and wipe her sour mouth on her sweater sleeve. Then she explained, managing only basic sentences.

"Muffy's dead. In those bushes. Hayden's with her."

Tom gave her a grumpy, disbelieving look and strode across the grass. Einstein hunkered down by the dogwood, uttering deep little notes of distress. As if expecting Sheila to follow him like a ghoul, Tom held up one thick forearm. "Wait right there, ma'am. I'll take it from here."

She was delighted to obey. She would have been glad to just go on home. To Atlanta.

This was not the first body Sheila had ever found. The next few minutes were painfully predictable. Tom joined Hayden briefly, then the two men backed from the bushes, Hayden brushing leaf mold from his knees. Tom pulled out a cellular phone and began summoning the specialists who make their living from such situations.

Sheila and Hayden took Einstein a short way up the drive toward the streetlight, then stood shoulder to shoulder for comfort. When he lit another cigarette, her stomach turned over, but she did not move away.

Her mind was a jumble. One second she was swept with horror, the next, struck with a sense of the ridiculous: *How did I end up on a dark drive in Jacksonville, Florida, with two men I don't even know, standing guard over a corpse?*

She nearly giggled—and knew she was close to hysteria. Too little sleep, too much anxiety about meeting Crispin's friends, too much horror in twenty-four hours. She took a ragged breath.

Hayden touched her arm. "You're gonna be all right."

Incredibly, his words calmed her. She gave him a tremulous smile. "Do you doctors learn that tone of voice in medical school?"

He nodded absently. She could tell he had one ear

cocked toward Tom, who was saying into the cellular phone, "Yeah, it's the same address."

Hayden rubbed his hands together as if they were cold. Sheila wished she knew a tone of voice to make him feel better, too.

Tom called over to them, "No point in you all hangin' around here. Go on back over to Justin's. I'll come get your statements as soon as I can."

The navy Buick still sat in the drive. In down vests, Justin and Crispin shared the porch swing. "Waitin' for Charho to leave," Hayden muttered.

"Fine night!" Justin called as the trio appeared.

"How do you like that?" Crispin demanded. "I send her out with a dog and she brings home another man."

"Muffy's been murdered," Hayden said bluntly from the bottom step. "Sheila found her in my azaleas. You got any brandy?"

It was too dim for Sheila to clearly see the men's expressions, but she was certain that Justin went rigid at Hayden's curt announcement. "Murdered?" The word was a shocked murmur.

Justin glanced uneasily toward Sheila. Heavens! Did the man think she'd killed the woman?

Crispin, too, stared at her disbelievingly.

She shifted the correct blame to the appropriate shoulders. "Einstein found her."

Crispin pulled himself to his feet and limped toward the steps, but when Sheila reached the porch, he stepped back and opened the door without touching her. Justin remained glued to the stilled swing. Was he thinking about Muffy? His brother? Repercussions for his congressional race?

Einstein pressed himself against his master's leg. Justin scratched him absently. "Good boy," he murmured. "Good old dog."

"Brandy!" Hayden repeated, perhaps to spur his brother.

Even two snifters of brandy later, Sheila still felt guilty. They all knew she hadn't killed Muffy—at least, she presumed they did—but she was certain they couldn't quite forgive her for finding the body.

Not that anybody said so, of course. It was in the sidelong looks they gave her, the more-gracious-than-usual tone of voice in which they asked if she was all right, the way Charho kept saying to Helen, incredulously, "But Einstein nevah goes into Hayden's yard on his way back home. *Nevah!*"

As if Sheila had some built-in compass for corpses and had deliberately led the dog astray. As if anybody could lead that dog anywhere.

For the first time she understood why rulers in ancient times killed a messenger who brought bad news. The very sight of her reminded the L'Arkens of something they would rather not face, something which they would not have had to face this soon if she and Einstein hadn't gone poking about Hayden's azaleas.

Even Crispin, who sat beside her holding her hand, was visibly aware of the blow she'd dealt.

"Thank goodness Teddy's already in bed," Charho said eventually, turning to look out the window toward the river. Sheila heartily agreed. Whether stormily grieving or avidly curious, Teddy would have been hard to take.

Across the room, Hayden's face was a dull gray. Surely as a doctor he had seen worse sights. As if sensing her concern, he lifted his eyes from his clasped hands and gave her a quick look, but she could not read his expression.

"When did Muffy leave last night?" Justin asked.

Charho shook her head. "I didn't see her when I left. The last I clearly remember, she was sittin' in the dining room. That was when I went to take Daphne's necklace upstairs."

Hayden's head came up, alert. "I meant to ask you about that, Charho. Where did you put the necklace?"

"On her dresser, in that gray velvet jeweler's box. It was empty, so I assumed—didn't she keep it there?"

He shook his head. "The box wasn't there when I got home. I thought maybe you'd put it in a drawer somewhere, knowin' how valuable those old doubloons were."

Charlotte Holmes Aspen was too much of a lady to drop her jaw, but she said in disbelief, "Of course it was there! Right in the middle of the dresser. You must have overlooked it."

He shook his head. "I couldn't sleep, so I thought I'd put it in my study safe. The jeweler's box was not there."

"But I put it—"

Sheila didn't hear the rest of Charho's protest. She was vividly remembering two scenes: Muffy dashing up the stairs when she heard that Daphne was dead, and Twinkie L'Arken sailing up to Hayden's dock this morning. Tom Goren ought to know about both those things, but she would rather be drawn and quartered than mention them to Hayden right now—especially since she also remembered Twinkie vowing: "Get me that necklace or I'll get it myself!"

Helen spoke as if in a trance. "Muffy and I both went upstairs after you called last night to—" she couldn't complete the sentence that way, amended it to, "from the hospital. She was standin' in the upstairs hall, cryin'. I went into Treye's bathroom, and when I came out, she was gone. I assumed she'd gone home . . . You don't think . . ." Her voice trailed off into horror, and she whispered, "You don't reckon Lance . . ."

Justin said sharply. "Don't think anything, honey, until Tom gets here."

As if summoned by his words, Goren's heavy tread mounted the front steps. Justin opened the door before he could ring.

The detective had dirt stains on his trousers and a smudge on his cheek. He pulled out his notebook and sat on the sofa he'd vacated such a short time before. "Okay, folks. Tell me what happened."

Tom Goren made it clear he wanted only the facts of finding Muffy's body, not anybody's theories—especially Sheila's—about who might have murdered her.

And when Sheila tried to tell him about Eddie getting angry with Muffy the night before, Helen protested, "Eddie didn't mean anything!"

Tom was more interested in Hayden's missing necklace. "It's possible Muffy could have taken it after Mrs. Aspen left it on the dresser. Was it valuable enough to kill for?"

Hayden nodded. "To anybody who knew what it was."

Tom shut his notebook. "I'll send somebody by tomorrow for a full report and a picture, if you've got one."

Hayden nodded again, his face expressionless.

As Tom headed for the door, Sheila kept waiting for Helen to mention Twinkie L'Arken's morning visit to Hayden's.

But Helen had something else on her mind. "Lance was supposed to come last night. Do you think . . . ?"

"I'll look into it, Helen," Goren said brusquely. His tone—and the extra warning look he shot Sheila—said that this was his case. Their job was to answer questions, not ask them.

Sheila went to bed before eleven and fell asleep immediately, as if to shut out what was still happening next door. But she awakened an hour later. Mentally, she replayed the events of the past two evenings, trying to make sense of two apparently senseless murders. When no pattern emerged, she ordered herself to go back to sleep. She'd need her rest if she and Crispin were driving to Aunt Mary's in St. Petersburg in the morning. Leave crime and killers to Tom Goren and the police, she scolded herself. It's their business, not yours.

But sleep wouldn't come. Unanswered questions hovered over her bed like haunting spirits.

Had Twinkie crept upstairs last night to steal the

necklace while everyone else was distracted and stunned by Daphne's death?

Had Muffy seen her, and was she murdered to ensure silence?

If so, why on earth had Twinkie gone back to Hayden's this morning?

Had Muffy herself stolen the doubloons? Had she been killed for them before she reached her car?

Who could have known she had them?

Eddie, if he went to her car with her. How easy, to strangle Muffy and then bed down on Hayden's sofa as if he'd never left. But where was Muffy's car?

Or had Muffy put something in Daphne's drink, and gotten caught?

Caught by Daphne's husband, perhaps?

Was Hayden L'Arken pale and gray tonight not merely because his wife lay dead, but because he himself had mercilessly executed her killer?

There was one more possibility, one that made Sheila punch her pillow each time she thought it. Who was the most likely person to have seen Muffy take those doubloons? Also the most likely to have put something in Daphne's drink before it left the bar?

Helen L'Arken.

In the distance, a train wailed. Brandy's bedside clock said 2:10. Unable to bear her thoughts any longer, Sheila went to the window and looked across the river. Movement on the dock caught her eye. Two figures swayed, locked in each other's arms.

At first she thought it was Jack and Sparrow, or even Helen and Justin, enjoying a chilly bit of romance. Then one figure drew back and slammed a fist into the other's face.

The struck person staggered and sat down heavily on the rough boards, cradling what tomorrow would be a very sore face. The other turned and ran up the dock, a moving shadow that soon merged with the solid shadow of the house.

Disturbed, Sheila watched until the second figure got up and hobbled stiffly away. Were they prowlers? Should she alert Justin?

"Look, lady," she murmured aloud, "you've caused enough trouble. Justin has a perfectly good security system. Forget this whole mess. Get yourself to sleep. Tom Goren has everything under control."

Some of Hayden's doctor tone must have rubbed off, for she climbed into bed and slept instantly.

She woke only once, at the sound of a boat engine going up the river. Glad not to be out in the cold, she snuggled down and slept.

Thursday,
December 28

Sheila woke with the feeling she had forgotten something important. Not until she was folding garments into her suitcase did she remember: She had never even notified Aunt Mary they had arrived in Jacksonville, much less that they were coming her way.

She wasn't concerned about Aunt Mary's not having room. In addition to the bayfront condominium she kept for her own winters, the tiny plutocrat owned several furnished rentals nearby. She could always find bedrooms for special guests.

Aunt Mary would not, however, give houseroom to a couple who had turned their backs on a puzzle—especially a puzzle involving two murders. If she got a whiff of what was going on in Jacksonville, she'd insist that Sheila stay until the mystery was solved.

As she dialed, Sheila reminded herself, "Tell the truth . . . just not all of it."

"Of course you can come." Aunt Mary's gravelly voice paused while she deftly sorted out the family relationships with the skill of a born southerner. "It was Crispin's aunt's stepson's wife who died?"

"Yes. And with the funeral and everything, Crispin and I both feel—" Actually, Sheila didn't know what Crispin felt about anything at the moment. He'd scarcely spo-

ken to her last night after Tom and Hayden left. In the
upstairs hall, he'd looked from her to Helen with guarded
eyes. Even his good night kiss had been perfunctory
rather than passionate.

She drew her attention back as Aunt Mary was saying,
"I'll be glad to see you. Forbes has been wanting to go to
Busch Gardens and Disney World, and you know I can't
be running around with my heart."

Sheila wasted no pity. The aforementioned organ was
delicate only when Aunt Mary wanted to avoid exercise
more strenuous than reading a mystery or the latest stock
report. "We aren't coming down to run all over the state,
Aunt Mary. Crispin may even fly back up Saturday afternoon, for the Gator Bowl." If, of course, their hostess
hadn't been arrested for the murder of her two best
friends.

"When is the funeral, dear?"

"Tomorrow, I believe."

Aunt Mary's southern roots ran deep. "How fortunate.
It won't spoil the football game. Mildred's off today, but if
you can come by dinnertime, I'll whip up a little something."

A little something like a gourmet meal. Aunt Mary's
sole form of aerobics was opening and closing cookbooks.

Sheila hung up. She felt as if a boulder on her shoulder had turned into a hot-air balloon and floated away.

The boulder dropped back within the hour.

She, Helen, and Crispin were drinking post-breakfast
coffee in the sunny Florida room. Justin had gone to the
office for a couple of hours and Jack and Sparrow were out
in the *Jack Three*. Teddy, who had miraculously failed to
notice the dark circles under her mother's eyes, was playing a computer game across the room. Another time,
Sheila could have sat at the wicker glass-topped table,
drunk coffee, and enjoyed the view of the sparkling river
all day. Today, however, Crispin was odiously formal and

she herself full of guilt for the disloyal thoughts she harbored about her hostess.

If Helen suspected what Sheila was thinking, she gave no sign. Instead, she brought them all another cup of coffee with an apologetic smile. "I'm sorry you all are leaving so soon."

Teddy whirled from her game. "Leaving? You can't leave! You haven't even taken me to the Loop! And the zoo has all sorts of new exhibits. You *can't* leave, Crispin!"

"We have to, Tiger," he told her. "Something's come up." Only after he promised on his honor to do both the Loop and the zoo on his next visit did the child go grudgingly back to her game. Because of her presence, the adults avoided the topic of the previous night's grisly discovery.

Crispin and Helen were discussing the merits of ground eggshell and banana peel as a tomato fertilizer, and Sheila was thinking wistfully how nice Crispin looked in his red-and-black warm-up suit, when Charho swept into the room and sank breathlessly into a vacant chair. Helen rose to fetch another cup, but Charho waved her back. "I don't want anything to drink, honey, I want to talk to Sheila." Her dark brown eyes bored into Sheila's face. "I am so glad you haven't left! I started to call, but felt I could appeal to you so much better in person. Helen said this mornin' you plan to leave today, but precious, you simply cannot desert us in our hour of need!" She raised her clasped hands to her chest in mute, if theatrical, appeal.

Sheila looked back at her, bewildered.

Charho turned to Helen. "I believe I will take a cup of coffee. I didn't even finish my breakfast after Hetty called, and it's freezin' outside." She tugged the sleeves of her sweater over her tanned, bony wrists.

To Sheila, truly freezing weather required more than a white oxford cloth shirt, denim skirt, and bright hand-knit cardigan that looked like a souvenir from a trip to Scandinavia. At the moment, however, that wasn't why she fixed Charho with a wary eye. She only knew one Hetty—her fussy, ultraproper sister-in-law in Tupelo, Mississippi.

Sure enough, Charho added, in an offhand manner, "Hetty Stirling, now Travis. We're both Chi Omegas, you know."

They were also at least ten years apart in age, but what difference did that ever make to a Chi Omega? Sheila waited apprehensively for what was coming next.

"Last night I called a dear friend in Memphis." Charho accepted the steaming coffee with an "Ummm" of appreciation. "I just happened to mention that you and Crispin were our guests, then told her what happened to Daphne—and the dreadful aftermath for Muffy."

"What about Aunt Muffy?" Teddy's eyes never left the screen and her fingers still skillfully plied the mouse, but if ever ears looked perked, hers did.

"Teddy, honey, would you run out to my car and bring in the bag on my back seat?" her grandmother requested. "I brought your mother some South Carolina peaches from my freezer."

"What about Aunt Muffy?" Teddy persisted.

"*Theodosia!*" Charho warned.

"Yes, ma'am." Reluctantly the child left.

Charho waited until the door slammed behind her, then continued. "Clara wasn't a Chi Omega—she pledged Tri Delt to please her grandmother—but her younger sister Mitsy lives in Tupelo, and was a Chi Omega with Hetty Stirling at Ole Miss. Clara happened to call Mitsy this mornin' and told her what has occurred here. She also happened to mention you, Sheila."

Sheila hid a smile behind her coffee cup. She'd just remembered a bewildered Japanese friend asking her father after meeting a bevy of Southern women. "This word 'happen' has many meanings?"

"Oh, no," Sheila's father had replied. "Where we come from, it always means 'Don't blame me.'"

Charho continued. ". . . called Hetty later about the

Garden Club party, and asked if you were related. Why, Hetty was so surprised! When she heard about the murder, she immediately told Mitsy that you have some, ah, experience in—" she pronounced the next words as delicately as if they were an unfamiliar obscenity—"solvin' murders."

What Hetty had probably said was, "Oh, dear! I do hope Sheila won't get involved in *another* murder!" However, the damage had been done.

"Mitsy asked Hetty to call me," Charho said. "We hung up just a few minutes ago. It must have been the hand of God that sent you to us!"

To Sheila, it felt more like the bony finger of Chi Omega, stretching from Tennessee through Mississippi to tap her on the shoulder in Florida.

She could imagine what Hetty's husband Wyndham—Tyler's older brother—was saying just about now. "That woman can't stay out of trouble two weeks running! I've half a mind to run down to Jacksonville myself."

If she didn't head this off, the pompous lawyer would probably arrive accompanied by his only son, Amory. Amory had helped her solve a case in Dunwoody last summer, and Sheila had grudgingly come to enjoy his company, but she'd also had enough of Tyler's relatives to last at least another six months.

"Actually, Mrs. Aspen—"

"Charho, dear!"

"Charho. I've gotten involved with very few deaths, and only because I had some information about the people involved. I didn't know Muffy. I have no idea who could have wanted her dead."

Except any woman whose man Muffy had vamped . . .

Charho closed her eyes and pursed her lips, but she was a woman who refused to be defeated because she'd lost one skirmish. She took a breath to calm herself and brought out her big guns. "My dear, I *implore* you to help us. Justin will never get elected unless this is settled immediately."

"Mama! Nobody suspects Justin!" Helen looked to Crispin, seeking reassurance. "Justin didn't kill her!"

Crispin shook his head gently. "The media feeds on innuendo and what-if, Helen. Murder next door will keep them busy for days—or as long as it takes to find the killer. You need all the help you can get."

If the table hadn't had a glass top, Sheila would have kicked Crispin. Not only was he playing dirty to get her to stay, he was scaring poor Helen to death in the process.

"Honey, Justin didn't have to kill her." Charho sounded both impatient and infinitely sad. "His friends will vote for him anyway, of course, but somebody who doesn't know the candidates ...? Why, they'll look at Justin's name and remember just one word: 'Murder.' Then they'll vote for somebody else."

"But he didn't ... he wouldn't ..." Her face white with shock, Helen reached for Sheila's arm. "Please stay and help us. Please!" Her eyes glowed like topazes.

If her appeal wasn't genuine, the woman ought to be in Hollywood. But even if Helen hadn't committed the murders, most of the evidence still pointed that way. For the first time in her life, Sheila wished she really were trained as a private detective. Without credentials, prowling a strange town among strangers, what on earth could she hope to accomplish? "Helen, I wouldn't know where to start. I can't go all over Jacksonville asking people I don't know a lot of questions. They'd have no reason whatsoever to answer."

Charho swept one arm grandly over the table. "We'll tell you everything you need to know!"

Sheila gave her a small smile. "If you could do that, you could solve it yourself. Helen, Tom Goren seems very competent. I would love to help, but I don't know what I could do that he can't. And since my aunt is expecting us—"

The telephone rang. The sudden chill that swept the back of Sheila's neck was not a draft. She knew as clearly as if she were clairvoyant that telephone lines had been humming between Tupelo and St. Petersburg.

"You never said a word about *murder*!" Aunt Mary couldn't have sounded more offended if Sheila had gotten engaged to Ted Bundy and forgotten to mention it.

Sheila spoke low, so she couldn't be overheard in the Florida room. "We're just about packed, Aunt Mary. We'll be on our way in an hour or so, and ought to reach your place by midafternoon."

"Nonsense, dear! You can't just go off and leave those wonderful people when they need you."

"These wonderful people—whom, by the way, you have never met—are served by a fine specimen of Jacksonville's police force who grew up with them and knows them well. Furthermore, he made it very clear to me yesterday morning that he abhors the interference of amateur detectives."

"Who's a mature detective?"

Sheila whirled. Teddy leaned nonchalantly against the counter, slinging a plastic bag around in a way that promised pureed peaches on the menu.

Sheila bit her tongue. Drat! Not only had she attracted Teddy's curiosity, but she'd used two words Aunt Mary would worry like a dog. Sure enough . . . "Yesterday morning, dear?" The tone was both surprised and chiding. "But I thought Hetty said they just found the body last night."

Sheila moved toward the dining room, out of Teddy's earshot. "*I* found the body, Aunt Mary, and I did find it last night. Look, we'll see you in a few hours, and I'll tell you—"

"Sheila Marie!"

Any Southern-reared child knows what full names are for. Sheila, like Teddy earlier, automatically jerked to attention. She did manage, however, to clamp her lips together before she could blurt out the requisite "Yes, ma'am!" Instead, she lifted her chin stubbornly. "You can

Sheila Marie me until the cows come home, Aunt Mary, but I have no business rummaging around in this—" She stopped. Now Teddy hovered just at her elbow.

There was silence on the other end for thirty seconds. Then Aunt Mary said mildly, "At least tell me, dear, why the detective warned you *before* you found the body."

Sheila gave Teddy Aunt Mary's most frigid stare. The child reluctantly backed up a few steps. Sheila turned her back and lowered her voice. "Because I was wondering if Daphne L'Arken's death might not have been caused by a weak heart."

"You suspect murder in that case, too?"

"Suspec*ted*. Past tense. I'd found some pills and wondered if she'd been poisoned. Maybe she was, but not with those pills. They were the wrong kind. So see? I'm not half as effective as the detective assigned to the case. We'll see you about four."

"Oh, but we won't be here, dear! Your parents are meeting Forbes and me at Disney World for two days. We are all so excited! And Mildred and her sister are flying down to Jamaica to see a cousin while we're gone, so you and Crispin can't come just now. Perhaps it's for the best. You just stay up there and do what you can for that poor family. What I suggest is—"

"Disney World?" Sheila interrupted, astonished.

"*I'll* go to Disney World!" Teddy exclaimed.

Startled, Sheila missed Aunt Mary's next sentence. Fortunately, Helen had heard Teddy, too, and came to firmly haul her youngest child from the kitchen.

"That's rude!" Sheila heard her hiss. Teddy glowered, utterly unrepentant.

Meanwhile Aunt Mary concluded, "So I will call you when we get settled in, dear."

"I thought Daddy had tickets to the Sugar Bowl. And you weren't planning to go to Disney World when we spoke an hour ago."

"I told you, dear, I forgot." Although Aunt Mary spoke with the dignity of a duchess, Sheila suspected the whole trip had been planned since Hetty's intervening call.

"You mean to tell me that you are going to traipse all over Disney World with a four-year-old? With your bad heart?"

Aunt Mary's laugh was a silver peal over the wire. "Of course not, dear! Your father will take Forbes to Disney World. Dorah and I will be at the hotel when they get back each afternoon. On Saturday, Tom and Dorah will fly to New Orleans from there. Now I can't talk all morning. I still have to pack, close up the condominium, and get Forbes to the airport."

By which she meant she had to tell Mildred what to put in her suitcase, pull a door shut behind her, and show the child into a waiting limousine.

Sheila had to hand it to Aunt Mary. When it came to arranging other people's lives, she had no equal.

Sheila resumed her seat. "Aunt Mary has decided to go to Disney World, Crispin, so if Helen really wants us, we can stay for the rest of the week." She could at least keep Teddy occupied hatching nefarious plots.

"Disney World?" He cocked one eyebrow. "Call her back. Tell her I want a picture of her on Space Mountain."

Teddy had digested only the important fact. "Goody! We can go to the Loop today! And the zoo. You promised."

He stroked his jaw. "I'll make you a deal. If you'll go away for a while and let us grownups talk, I'll take you to the Loop for lunch. Since I can't walk very far, we'll save the zoo. And if I see you in yelling distance in the next sixty minutes, the whole deal is off."

"I'll go fishin'." She whirled and started for her pole, then turned back to ask, "Is She comin', too?"

"We need a driver," Crispin reminded her.

The child sighed her acceptance. "Come on, Einstein."

In less than a minute she and the dog rounded the

house and trotted to the end of the dock. When Teddy bent to pull in the *Ark*, Charho said to her daughter—for what was clearly not the first time—"I wish you wouldn't let the child go out in that boat by herself."

Helen's own eyes were anxious, but she immediately leaped to Teddy's defense. "She's been around boats all her life, Mama, and she's been handling that one since she was eight. She knows to stay right by the dock. We make her as safe as we can, but we can't tie her down." She watched Teddy haul up a bucket and carry it over to where Einstein was already dozing. "Besides, it looks like she's decided to fish from the dock today." She turned to Sheila. "I'm glad you're staying even if you can't solve Muffy's mur—" Her lips trembled. She pressed them together. Helplessly she shook her head. Tears streamed down her cheeks.

"Go lie down," Charho commanded. "You need a rest."

Helen hurried up the stairs. Crispin, Sheila noted, followed her with worried eyes.

When she was out of sight, Charho shook her head in exasperation and said crisply, "I'm sorry, dears. Helen's under a lot of strain just now with all this political hoopla. I don't know if she is strong enough to be a politician's wife. Sometimes I wish Justin would give up his notion to run."

"She's just lost two of her best friends," Sheila pointed out.

"Fiddlesticks! Muffy and Daphne weren't her best friends, they were just old acquaintances who needed somebody. Helen never could resist somebody who needed her."

Crispin, who had been growing increasingly jumpy the more Charho said, pulled himself to his feet. "I think I'll see how Teddy's doing." He limped outside and across the lawn. Sheila saw him speak to Teddy, then hobble to the far end of the dock and stand gazing across the water.

This seemed as good a time as any to begin this hopeless investigation. "What can you tell me about Muffy, Charho? Who might have wanted her dead?"

If she hadn't been so near, she would have missed the infinitesimal pause before the charming old woman declared, "Why, nobody, honey! Everybody just loved Muffy!" Her eyes were wide with conviction. "Muffy was as sweet as she could be. I knew that girl since she was a baby, and—oh, I hope you aren't thinkin' about the way she flirted. Nobody took her flirtin' seriously, least of all Muffy herself. It's just the way she was."

No matter how Sheila rephrased the question, Charho stuck to her story. Nobody, positively nobody, had any reason whatsoever to want Muffy Merriwether dead. On the other hand, Sheila noticed that Charlotte Holmes Aspen had no trouble remembering to speak of Muffy in the past tense.

As soon as Charho left, Sheila went to join Crispin. She had to speak his name twice before he turned, with the look of a man whose thoughts have been far away. "Crispin, can we go see your Aunt Martha?" she asked.

He shrugged. "Sure. But what do you think Aunt Martha can tell you?"

She shook her head. "Actually, it's Laura Grace I want to talk with. Alone."

"Offer to take her to the park," he suggested, already hobbling toward the car. "We'll be back by lunchtime, Tiger," he promised as they passed the girl and her faithful dog.

Sheila stood in Memorial Park half an hour later, shivering beside the concrete balustrade overlooking the choppy St. Johns. Now it was a sullen gray, and as the water pulsed and rushed toward the seawall, small white flicks rose on its surface like spurts of anger. A Navy fighter snarled overhead. On the far shore, trees looked blue with cold.

Sheila turned her back to the water and faced the large statue across the sidewalk. It was surrounded by a waist-high wall that probably used to enclose a fountain pool. The bronze figure was not, as she had thought, Mercury, but a winged young man standing atop a spherical sea in which others were drowning. She shuddered at the dying faces and turned away.

Laura Grace preferred looking out over the river. She seemed oblivious to the cold in a lightweight black cardigan and a calf-length orchid cotton skirt. Her scuffed white Reeboks and bright red socks made her look more like a bag lady than ever.

Not surprisingly, the park was deserted except for the two women and a flock of greedy gray-and-white gulls hovering to snatch whatever it was Laura Grace kept hurling at them from a red canvas carryall.

Since a childhood scare, Sheila had been nervous around pigeons. She found the raucous gulls, hovering to demand tribute, even more off-putting. They had sharper beaks and fiercer eyes. Backing away from a particularly avid beak, Sheila noticed a lone jogger enter the far corner of the park and trot toward them on the circular sidewalk. He or she wore a baggy dark sweat suit and a ski mask against the wind.

Sheila could have used a ski mask herself. Her head scarf was more ornamental than warm. She shivered, then was ashamed. Laura Grace's grizzled curls blew free.

Given the old woman's own bluntness, Sheila came straight to the point. Because of the wind, she spoke loudly. "Tuesday night, what did you mean when you said Muffy Merriwether lives by keeping her mouth shut?" She put it in the present tense. She didn't know if Laura Grace knew about Muffy's murder.

Laura Grace knew. "Muffy died," she shouted, flinging a handful of food in a wide circle. Squawking gulls swarmed from everywhere.

Sheila instinctively put one hand protectively on top of her head. "But what did you mean?"

Laura Grace flung another handful of food. "I didn't

mean anything. That's what Muffy said—'I live by keeping my mouth shut.' "

"Could she have meant that people paid her to keep their secrets?" Sheila bawled, surrounded by eavesdropping gulls.

Laura Grace gave Sheila a sly sideways look and came very close. In a normal voice, she said, "I know a secret. I know where the treasure is buried. I'll show *you*." The special emphasis on the last word was unmistakable.

Sheila nodded. "The pirate's treasure." Why had she ever thought she could get sense out of this old woman?

Laura Grace shook her head. "I don't know about the pirates," she said with regret. "Except Dan McGirth. Ask Jack. But nobody but me knows about the treasure." She hurled another handful of gull food and beamed up at Sheila. "I was waiting for you to come."

An elderly Snow White, waiting for her prince. But Sheila wasn't a prince. So far, she wasn't even a very good detective. She was just crazy like Laura Grace, standing on this windswept river balcony attacked by vicious gulls, babbling about pirates and treasure.

Nevertheless, she would persist for a few minutes longer, just in case there might be anything to be learned. "What do you think Muffy—"

Laura Grace bawled, "I'll show you, but not today. Today I have to feed the gulls." She skillfully tossed food directly down one bird's gullet and cackled in delight. "Gulls are God's special messengers, you know. They tell us what each day will bring."

Sheila doubted that. "What did the gulls say about yesterday?"

Laura Grace shook her head. "I forget. Bright lights, I think. Blue."

"Blue lights? Police lights?"

"I don't remember a day after it's gone. This is the only day that matters."

The old woman was right, of course, and her single-mindedness was enviable, but Sheila despaired of getting anything worth knowing out of this conversation. "What was today's pattern?"

"Secrets, surprise, and hope. I hope Martha's not fixin' squash for lunch."

The jogger came closer now, approaching a tall clump of azaleas and an ornamental concrete rail just beyond the fountain wall. Sheila hoped their bawled conversation wasn't carrying on the wind!

Remembering Laura's Tuesday prediction, she hazarded, "Was today's surprise another pleasant one?"

"Oh, no, dear! That was yellow. Today was orange. That's—"

Out of the corner of her eye, Sheila saw the jogger stop at the rail and lift a hand in what seemed at first a slow salute.

She shoved Laura Grace to the ground just as a gun fired.

Covering the old woman, Sheila scooted them both nearer the statue. They needed the day's whole quota of hope: She prayed the wall would shield them until help came.

If it came.

A second shot hit nearer, raising a spurt of concrete from the sidewalk. Any minute now the jogger would circle the statue, and a shot would surely find its mark. If they ran, one of them might get away. But Laura Grace could not run. Sheila had never felt so helpless.

Beneath her, Laura Grace squirmed and struggled. "Let me up! Let me up!" Sheila held her firmly, a compact bundle of rage and determination. "Let me up! I can't breathe!" With an incredible burst of strength the old woman elbowed Sheila away, scrambled to her feet, and flung a handful of gull food. "Go! Get him!"

Another shot rang out as Sheila grabbed her shoulders and pulled her back down behind the protective wall.

To her amazement, the only sound in the park was the raucous cries of the gulls. "They got him!" Laura Grace crowed exultantly.

Nothing happened. Almost anything was better than waiting to be crept up on. Cautiously Sheila looked over the wall. The dark-clad figure was tearing toward the corner gate, attacked by screeching gulls. One gull, a red stain on the white of its breast, lay near the fountain.

Laura Grace bobbed up beside her and uttered a cry of grief. "My pretty!" She scuttled to snatch up the dead gull and cradle it in her arms. Then she went to the balustrade and flung it into the river.

Sheila sat with her back to the wall, trembling too much to stand. Laura Grace came back and stood squarely on her Reeboks. "There was no death or danger today," she said grumpily. "I told you. Secrets, hope, and surprise. That must have been the surprise." She headed down the sidewalk, unbuttoning her sweater as she went. "I need to get home. These clothes are smotherin' me."

Sheila caught up with her at the Park Lane's front door. By the time they reached Martha's, the black sweater hung open to reveal withered breasts veined in blue. Martha stopped Laura Grace from disrobing entirely in the front hall. "You can't stay out here without your clothes," she told the old woman.

"Then I won't stay out at all. Besides, I have to mourn my gull." She slammed her own door.

Sheila leaned against the doorjamb and gulped great breaths of warm safety. Martha's radio was tuned to a station playing old dance tunes. Did people really shoot at one another in the same world where schmaltzy bands played "I'll Be Seeing You"?

Crispin came to the living room arch. "Are you frozen? You're as white as sheets used to be." He peered closer. "What on earth did she do to you?"

"Saved my life." Her knees buckled.

He more carried than led her to the sofa while Martha brought her a cup of coffee, and helped her hold it. One good thing out of all this, Sheila thought wryly. She had Crispin's attention again.

Finally she could control her voice enough to explain.

When she fell silent, Martha reached over and gave her a fond pat. "Oh, my dear, what a ghastly experience!"

Looking at Martha was restorative. She looked unusually pretty today in violet slacks and a matching sweatshirt painted with pansies. Even though she had not expected them, she'd already been powdered and lipsticked when they arrived. Did all Jacksonville matrons put on their faces before breakfast?

When Sheila had finished her coffee and stopped shaking, Martha asked anxiously, "Should we call the police?"

Sheila shook her head. "What could I tell them? I never saw a face. I'm not even sure if it was a man or a woman."

"If somebody is taking potshots in Memorial Park, it needs to be reported," Crispin insisted, limping to the phone.

Officer Yarborough came within a very few minutes, a man at least six feet tall with skin like burnished ebony and excellent diction. Sheila accompanied him back down to the park to show him what had happened.

He quickly found the second bullet, considered the nick where it had hit the sidewalk, then squatted beside two small spots of blood where the gull had lain. "And the perp was standing back there in the bushes?"

Sheila nodded. Although the park seemed deserted, she couldn't help glancing around uneasily, in case someone else might be lurking behind an azalea.

The tall policeman chewed one corner of his lower lip. "That's a mighty long shot for a handgun in this wind. And you're sure you can't say whether the shooter was a man or a woman?"

"No. I wasn't really looking, you see, and he—or she—was wearing baggy clothes and a ski mask."

"That didn't alert you that something was wrong?"

Sheila shrugged. "It's cold today."

The officer's face was inscrutable and his voice soft. "Ma'am, we don't get much snow skiing down here."

He left, promising to ask around and see if anybody else had seen the intruder. Sheila went back up to Martha's, doubting that he'd do more than file a report that somebody had been shooting gulls in the park. Maybe they were.

"Did you get anything from Laura Grace?" Crispin asked when she was once again settled on Martha's comfortable sofa with another cup of coffee and a plate of homemade Toll-House cookies.

Sheila shook her head. "Not really. When she said Muffy lived by keeping her mouth shut, she seems to have been just parroting something Muffy said. Who knows what Muffy might have meant?"

"Blackmail, for one." He reached for the pot to refill his own mug. "Could Muffy have been blackmailing anyone, Aunt Martha? She always seemed to have plenty of money. Where did she get it?"

Martha tucked one foot beneath her on the sofa and answered his last question, with obvious reluctance. "I don't really know. Muffy never could seem to settle to anything. She had a variety of jobs after college, but somethin' always seemed to happen."

Sheila smiled weakly. There was that *h* word again!

Martha reached for a cookie. "Muffy's dad was the same way. Don made a good bit of money, one way or another, but he went through every penny he ever made before he died. Muffy should have married somebody who could take care of her."

"It wasn't for lack of trying," Crispin pointed out.

Martha frowned at him reprovingly. "She chose poorly, dear. Her first husband was a charmin' rascal, but he never could keep a job. Her second was violent, even as a boy. He beat her, I heard. She left him after less than a year. Finally she married a man a good bit older than she, but he up and died within a few months and left everything to

his children by his first wife. Poor Muffy. And she does—
did so like nice things and parties."

Crispin set his cup down on the coffee table. "Aunt
Martha, is this your polite way of suggesting that yes,
Muffy may have blackmailed people?"

Martha sighed. "I honestly don't know, sweetie. I do
know that some of her bills were paid by friends. Hayden
let her live in a condo he'd bought in Charho's buildin',
for instance. And Justin and Helen took her a lot of
places—she was goin' with you all to the game. Maybe
other friends helped, too. But that's not blackmail." She
looked utterly bewildered. "When you've known people
all your life, what is there to blackmail them about?"

"She has a point," Sheila admitted as they walked back toward the car.

"So what now, Sheilock?"

"I don't suppose we could just drive on back to Atlanta and call to say we'd had an emergency?" She started
the engine, but did not put the car into reverse. "I keep
wondering if Daphne's coin necklace has anything to do
with this—and remembering bits of conversation I overheard at the party."

"Like what?"

"Like Daphne telling Muffy if she didn't do something or other, Daphne would—and I quote—'wring your
neck and tell Hayden to kick you out.'"

"That would give Daphne a motive to murder Muffy,
but Daphne died first."

"Right. I also heard Twinkie telling Treye to get that
necklace for her, or she'd get it herself."

"Whew! Sounds like maybe Twinkie is the next
stop." Crispin looked at his watch. "You ought to have
time for a short interview before we have to pick up
Teddy for lunch."

"Why should Twinkie talk to me?"

"She won't, but she'll talk to Aunt Martha. I am about

to make the supreme sacrifice of the day. I'll stay with Laura Grace. You be as quick as you can!"

Martha let herself into the passenger seat sooner than Sheila expected. All she'd done was brush her curls, put in gold love knot earrings, and slip on a pair of violet canvas shoes. "I didn't bother with a coat, since we won't be out," she explained breathlessly.

She wouldn't have needed a coat anyway. Now that the sun was back out, Sheila was ready to shed her blazer.

"This is awkward," she admitted as Martha directed her toward Roosevelt Boulevard and Ortega Forest. "I can't just ask Twinkie if she stole Daphne's necklace."

"Don't you worry about a thing." Martha leaned over and patted her hand on the wheel. "You're gonna do just fine. Look how smart you were about findin' Laura Grace. And Crispin is so proud of you!"

Comforting, if not exactly helpful.

Martha directed Sheila to a bridge she had not yet crossed, over the Ortega River on Roosevelt Boulevard. Just before the river, Martha indicated a brown building towering behind a mall. "That's where Charho and Muffy both live—lived." She cleared her throat. "It's much newer than the Park Lane, of course. I don't think it has quite the same charm, but the condominiums—especially those on the water—are gorgeous. Take the first right, just over the bridge."

But first they had to wait for a train. A very long train. Sheila counted four engines and ninety cars while traffic backed up behind her. Living in Ortega Forest, she thought, might have a few disadvantages.

On the other hand, Hayden L'Arken had not been shabby when he divorced Twinkie. Most people would find this neighborhood of sprawling homes on manicured lots more than adequate. Twinkie's was built of old brick, with black shutters and gray trim. Lovely—unless you compared it with what she had lost. Between the husband and the waterfront, which did she regret more?

As Sheila shut off the engine, Martha said brightly, "Well, let's go do our detectin'!"

Sheila caught her arm before she could open the car door. "Let's pretend you're just bringing me to meet her. Don't say anything about Muffy or the necklace unless it comes up naturally—and *please* don't mention that Charho wants me to play detective!"

Martha bent to retrieve her pocketbook from the floor. "Why, Twinkie already knows, dear. When Charho called this mornin' to say you and Crispin were comin' over, she'd just talked to Twinkie."

Sheila thought that over. "So when Laura Grace and I were in the park, Twinkie could have known I was there asking questions about Muffy's death?"

"Of course." Martha didn't find that odd. "Why shouldn't she? Charho is delighted you're willin' to get involved."

"Who else had she told?"

"I have no idea. Anyone she'd spoken with, I would guess. How can people help you unless they know what you want?"

Help? Sheila wondered as she climbed out of the car. Or shoot?

She was tempted to call Tom Goren and suggest he test everybody Charho knew to see if they had recently fired a gun. How long would it take to test half of Ortega—including Crispin's best friends?

If Twinkie had been taking potshots in Memorial Park earlier, she had changed her clothes. Now she wore a practical khaki skirt, pale blue oxford cloth shirt, and navy cardigan. She came to meet the car carrying two small potted poinsettias.

Holding them up, she said cheerfully in a raspy smoker's voice, "I saw these damn things on sale at Publix this mornin' and thought I'd stick 'em in the yard. Now I can't decide where to put 'em."

"Don't put 'em anywhere until March," Martha advised. "Bring 'em indoors and let 'em build up their roots until it gets a bit warmer. They'll have a better chance of survivin'."

"Good idea." Twinkie turned toward the front door. "Crispin called to say you were comin', but I haven't got the coffee made."

"Don't bother." Martha stood back to let Sheila precede her into the house. "We've had so much already today, I'm floatin'."

Twinkie's living room looked like it was never sat in. She led them, instead, to a large den at the back of the house where a low fire burned on a brick hearth. A brass barometer gleamed on a nearby wall. Three models of sailing ships sat on the mantel, and a navigation chart littered the overstuffed couch. It was the kind of room that made Sheila want to kick off her shoes, tuck up her feet, and talk sailing all morning—and made her devoutly hope Twinkie L'Arken hadn't killed Muffy Merriwether.

If so, she was a brazen murderess, for the first thing she said when they were all comfortable was, "Shame about Muffy, wasn't it?"

Martha, who had kicked off one shoe and was in the process of tucking her foot beneath her, asked, "Did Charho tell you?"

"No, Hayden. Called last night after he got home, all cut up. Said you and he found her?" She looked at Sheila.

Did Twinkie think she'd been romancing Hayden on his own drive the night after Daphne died? Sheila hurried to set the record straight. "Actually, Einstein found her while I was walking him. Hayden was coming home from Justin's about then, and brought a light to see what Einstein had found."

"I see." Twinkie turned back to Martha. "In a few days, Hayden will begin to feel relieved. Now he can sell that damned condo he's let Muffy have all these years."

Sheila was startled. She hadn't expected this to be so easy.

As she had hoped, Martha asked, "Why did he let Muffy have it, Twinkie? I don't think I ever knew."

When the woman's blue eyes twinkled, Sheila realized that before she got so stocky, Twinkie had not been plain. "Depends on who you ask. Muffy thought he gave it to her to keep her quiet. You may not know it, Martha, but Hayden cheated on one test back in med school. I don't know how Muffy found out about it—prob'ly got him drunk one night and vamped it out of him." She picked up a pack of cigarettes and shunted it back and forth in her hands like a deck of cards. "Whatever, she never saw him that she didn't imply he could be kicked out of the AMA if anybody else knew what she knew." She finally tapped a cigarette out of the pack and leaned her stocky body toward a lighter shaped like a sailboat on the end table. "Hell! Who'd care about that exam after all these years? I think Hayden gave her that condo because he felt sorry for her." Her lips curved in a sour smile. "He used to be a very kind man."

Sheila relaxed against the comfortable sofa cushions, remembering Muffy's greeting to Hayden at the party. "If Muffy—" she chose the next word carefully "—teased Hayden about that exam, I wonder if there were other people whose secrets she knew, too."

Twinkie gave her a sharp look. "More serious secrets?"

Personally, Sheila thought cheating on a med school exam was serious enough, but she nodded.

Twinkie and Martha looked at one another as if each hoped the other knew. Finally Twinkie shook her head. "Not that I know of. People did things for her, of course, gave her this and that, but it was no big deal. Like Justin and Helen gave her tickets to football games. His company buys them by the yard. Rob Wilmer's man did her taxes. A dress shop in Avondale gave her a dress now and then—sort of a walking advertisement—and her first husband's brother let her drive a Thunderbird. He's a

Ford dealer, probably wrote it off as company expense. But nobody gave her anything they couldn't easily afford."

Martha seconded her, in the tone of one pointing out the obvious. "Muffy grew up here. She was in the Junior League. What were people supposed to do—throw her out of the Yacht Club and let her starve?"

Sheila was still picturing that heartless scene when Twinkie snapped her fingers. "That reminds me! Charho paid Muffy's Yacht Club bills, I think. At least, once when we had lunch, she wrote a check to cover them for that month."

Sheila spoke thoughtfully. "When Charho introduced Muffy the other night as one of Helen's oldest friends, Muffy said something about Mr. Aspen. I wonder what that was all about?" She waited.

Martha looked into the fire. Twinkie considered her cigarette. Slowly, their gazes met. Abruptly, Twinkie tapped her cigarette over a nearly full ashtray. "Charho called me this mornin'."

Martha replied as if answering a question. "She's the one who urged Sheila to look into things."

Twinkie took a long drag on her cigarette and blew a cloud of smoke toward the fireplace. "Helen's dad was old enough to be her grandfather, Sheila. Charho, well—" This time she blew a smoke ring, and studied it as if she hoped to find words written inside.

Martha watched it fade. "Only once," she insisted gently, "and very briefly."

Sheila knew how to read between lines. "But how on earth would Muffy have known?"

Again Twinkie inhaled deeply, as if inhaling courage with nicotine and tar. "Once when Muffy's daddy was supposed to be out of town, Muffy took a boy down to her family's beach house. She found her daddy and Charho."

Sheila wondered why Charho hadn't choked Muffy years ago. "But it wasn't really a secret? Other people knew?"

Of course they did. Village tom-toms are not restricted

to jungles. In elite forests they are just played more discreetly.

Martha must have read her mind. "We've got long memories around here. There's a millionaire down the way from me. I remember when his daddy was a railroad conductor. His third wife would die if she knew her father-in-law'd been a railroad conductor." She laughed indulgently. "When you live in a town as long as we've lived in this one, Sheila, you know every blessed thing there is to know."

"I didn't," Twinkie said abruptly. "I didn't even suspect Hayden and Daphne were foolin' around—until it was too late."

"You were out of town a lot," Martha reminded her, "and we tried to warn you—"

Twinkie settled back and admitted defeat. "You're right. I didn't want to know."

Sheila had another question. "Why would Charho continue to pay after all these years?"

Twinkie stubbed out her cigarette, rose, and began pacing in front of the fireplace. All her movements had the large-muscled grace of a caged jungle cat, and the path she traced on the carpet was darker and slightly worn. Finally she admitted, "Charho thinks nobody but Muffy knew."

It hung between them like the sword of Damocles, with the same power to destroy.

Charho. An aging woman on a fixed income. Tired of paying for almost forgotten pleasures?

But why would Charho have killed Muffy last night? Sheila asked it another way. "Did anything happen between them at the party?"

Twinkie made an impatient gesture. "Of course nothin' happened at the damn party! All this is old stuff, Sheila. And people liked Muffy. She came on to the men, sure, but it didn't mean anything. Muffy was funny. She made us laugh. That was worth a condo to Hayden and me, worth a few club bills to Charho. If you think Muffy was killed because of somethin' she knew? Nothin' Muffy knew mattered—" she snapped her fingers again "—that much!"

"Except, perhaps, one thing," Sheila said soberly. "The secret of the person who killed her."

Martha glanced at her watch. "We need to be goin'."

"Stay for lunch," Twinkie offered, "if you don't mind funeral meats. Libba sent enough food home with me the other night to feed the Chinese army."

"We'd love to, but we can't this time." Martha gathered up her purse. If she'd had white gloves, she would have been pulling them on. "Sheila and Crispin have promised to take Teddy to the Loop for lunch, and besides," she hesitated, "it's almost time for my program."

Twinkie put back her head and gave a shout of laughter. "Martha's a closet Limbaugh fan, Sheila. Did you know that?"

"I just listen to him," Martha protested. "I don't believe everything he says."

Twinkie snorted. "I hope to God you don't. We've got so many turncoats rootin' for the Republican party and the Florida State Seminoles around here, us old Democrat Gator fans are scarcer than pigeon babies."

Sheila was wondering how to bring up the other delicate subject. "The necklace?" she murmured to Martha at the door.

Martha turned. "By the way, Twinkie, I noticed at the party that Daphne was wearin' the doubloon necklace. Didn't John Daniel give it to you, not Hayden?"

"Damn right he did, and I want it back. Tell that to Hayden next time you see him."

While Teddy chattered to Crispin on the way to lunch, Sheila considered the morning in her mind. Did Twinkie's parting remark mean she didn't have the necklace? Not necessarily, but either way, she'd have had scant reason to kill Muffy to get it—unless she'd killed Daphne first and Muffy saw her do it.

The same could probably be said of Charho, except Sheila couldn't think of a single reason why Charho would kill Daphne.

Probably, she reflected gloomily, the only valuable thing she would accomplish all day was getting Teddy out of Helen's hair.

Teddy directed her imperiously to a short strip mall of gray batten-board shops so carefully unpretentious they had to be exclusive. "Drive under the bridge," she instructed, pointing to a narrow walkway between facing buildings. Sure enough, around the corner, the building's end sported a plum script sign: "The Loop."

How could a restaurant so hard to find attract a clientele? Yet almost every parking space was filled. The food must be superb.

"I want a pizza," Teddy told Crispin on the way in. "With anchovies."

"Anchovies? Yuck! I don't know if I can eat at the same table with anchovies."

"They're great!" Teddy assured him.

"I like them, too," Sheila agreed. "I'll second Teddy's order." Teddy shot her a smoldering look and pranced inside.

The restaurant was an unlikely but attractive combination of plum and dark green, from wallpaper to tiny floor tiles. A woman in a business dress and a man in a three-piece navy suit sat near teenagers in jeans. Nearby, a two-year-old smeared pizza on his mouth while his grandfather tackled a Chicago-style hot dog piled high with toppings. Not exactly southern home cooking, but it looked and smelled delicious.

Sheila sat on a cushioned church pew and admired a massive oak sideboard while Crispin went to the counter to place their order.

Watching a man with a large gold hoop earring and skin the color of hot fudge finish off an Italian beef sandwich, Sheila was glad Laura Grace wasn't along. She'd probably think he was one of her famous pirates—especially since his red shirtsleeves were rolled over biceps large enough to easily carry treasure trunks.

Crispin hobbled over to hand her a tray of drinks. "Go snare us a table. Teddy's supervising the pizza."

Sheila found a plum vinyl booth overlooking a small cove of greenish-bronze water. As she slid in, she spotted Jack and Sparrow at a concrete-and-tile table on the outside deck.

In the past hour, the capricious north Florida wind had blown in more clouds, cumulus ones this time, with darker bottoms. They blocked the sun and threatened a storm to come. Even in matching teal-and-black Jaguar sweatshirts, Jack and Sparrow must be chilly. Why on earth would anybody eat outside today? Because they did not want to be overheard, of course.

Hunched forward, leaning on his elbows, Jack seemed to be trying to convince Sparrow of something. She shook her head, pressing one fist to her lips. Her nose was red and Sheila could see tears at the end of her lashes.

Sheila took the side of the booth with her back to them, hoping they wouldn't notice her.

"That's Fishweir Creek." Crispin slid in beside her.

"Part of the St. Johns," Teddy added importantly. Sure enough, beyond two spits of land that formed the creek's mouth, Sheila saw the ubiquitous river flowing wide and wind-tossed toward downtown.

Teddy sat at the outside end of her bench, facing Crispin, but not looking at him. Instead, she gave her whole attention to her pizza. Pepperoni, not anchovy, Sheila noted with amusement.

"So," Crispin said to Teddy in the tone of one concluding a conversation, "at best it's poor manners to brag what your daddy will do if he gets elected, and it can be downright dumb. He might not win."

Teddy's chin did look like Aunt Mary's when she tilted it like that. "He will win!" the child insisted. "He told Uncle Hayden he'll do whatever he needs to do to win. *Anything!*"

Sheila's imagination was vivid enough to picture Justin poisoning Daphne and strangling Muffy. She could even picture him framing Helen for the crime. She just could not imagine a single reason why he should.

The other two seemed to have reached a conversational impasse. "Is your pizza good?" Sheila asked Teddy, biting into her own. It was unusually salty, even for anchovies, and she caught Teddy watching her with a glint that had nothing to do with light off her spectacles. "Yum, salty!" she said, tilting her own chin. She'd finish that doctored pizza if it killed her.

"Did you know," Teddy asked her thoughtfully through a mouthful of cheese, "that a black hole is the opposite of nothing? It's matter squished so tight that its gravity gets powerfuller and powerfuller, so it just sucks everything in!" Her voice grew deep and mysterious. "There might be a black hole up there right now, just about to—" She gestured toward the window. As her gaze followed her hand, she gave a yelp of surprise. "Hey! There's Jack and Sparrow!" She slid over and rapped on the glass.

Crispin craned over Sheila. Jack glared at his sister and Sparrow gave her a small wave. Then they gathered up the remnants of their outdoor lunch and quickly departed.

Not before the trio inside had all seen something odd.

Teddy voiced the question. "Who gave Jack that big black eye?" she demanded.

About the same time of day, Tom Goren perched on the edge of Hayden's ivory brocade couch and rested his thick hands on thicker thighs. "Dr. L'Arken, I'm just telling you what they found. The pill bottle contained a full count of your aunt's thyroid medicine plus twelve Lanoxin tablets of roughly the same size and color. We're still waiting for the lab report to determine exactly what killed Daph—

your wife. Meanwhile, do you have any idea how those pills could have gotten in that bottle?"

Hayden regarded him steadily. "You'll have to ask my brother or his wife." His voice was sharp. "I never saw that bottle until Mrs. Travis handed it to me last night. And surely, Tom—" if Detective Goren was unwilling to admit they were more than police officer and victim, Hayden certainly wasn't—"surely you don't think I killed Daphne. I was crazy about her! Everybody knew that."

Tom nodded. Everybody he'd talked to said the same. Even, sourly, Hayden's first wife.

He stood. "I'll go next door and speak with Helen. By the way, have you heard from anybody about your missing necklace?"

Hayden nodded. "Two officers came by this morning. There wasn't much I could tell them, of course. Charho said she left it in a box on our dresser right after Daphne ... collapsed ... but neither it nor the box were here when I got back later that night."

"I'm sure they are questioning anyone involved."

The two officers were currently getting more questions than answers from Twinkie L'Arken. "When was that necklace stolen? What are you doing to find it? Those coins are hundreds of years old, and they belong to me! You'd better find them, and double-quick, or I'll sue Hayden's damn socks off!"

As a substitute for the zoo, Teddy begged to be taken by Boone Park on their way home. "You can sit on a bench and watch me swing," she pleaded.

Other days the bench would be sun-dappled beneath the soaring pines. Today it was gloomy and dark. Sheila didn't want to talk about the L'Arkens or murder, and Crispin seemed uninterested in discussing anything else. After a few abortive attempts at conversation, they said nothing.

This is how it would be in a few years if we got married,

she thought miserably. *Nothing to talk about, boring one another silly.*

Early in her marriage to Tyler she had started clamping down on her emotions. That hadn't been bad. She'd lived on a pretty even keel. These past few months with Crispin, he'd pried up the lid a bit. She'd learned to feel happiness, and tenderness. Now she knew it worked both ways. If you can feel joy, you can also feel pain. Was he worth it? Today, she wasn't sure.

It was after three before they returned to Ortega. The house smelled of chocolate, but no dessert was on the living room coffee table when they entered.

On the sofa, Helen was pale, her amber eyes worried. In a big chair nearby, Tom Goren's copper hair clashed with the dull puce of his face. Clearly he was a man doing a job he heartily despised. Even Teddy, who had been full of things to tell her mother, was silenced.

When the others entered, Tom stood with obvious relief. "Well, that about does it. I'll call if I have any more questions."

"Yes." Helen held up a hand to restrain him from leaving, her eyes on Teddy. "Don't leave your sweater on the floor, honey."

Heaving a sigh of martyrdom, Teddy slung the offending garment into a nearby closet.

"Now go see Aunt Libba in the kitchen. She's making brownies, and wants you to help. Tell her I'll be there in a little while."

Teddy hung back. "Scoot!" Helen commanded. Teddy scooted.

When the swinging kitchen door had closed behind her, Helen explained, "Libba's making food to take to Hayden's tomorrow after the funeral. There are some things left from the party, of course, but she thought—" She broke off, aware that she was rambling. "I didn't tell her, Tom, why you're here." She looked at Sheila. "They found extra pills in the bottle. The kind you thought might be there. I don't know when or how—"

"Of course you don't!" Crispin sat down beside her and put an arm around her shoulders with such an air of proprietorship that Sheila felt she had been hit between the eyes.

He hadn't been kidding when he said he would have married Helen if she hadn't chosen Justin instead! Had he carried a torch all these years? Had she herself always been merely second-best?

Confused—and shaken by a sudden anger that frightened her—she took the chair Tom had vacated. Looking at Crispin beside Helen on the sofa was like having an abcessed tooth all over her body, so she turned her attention instead to the stocky detective. His eyes, she noticed irrelevantly, were as tawny as Helen's.

"Tell me again about that bottle," Goren commanded. "Exactly when did you see Helen hide it?"

"Soon after Justin's announcement. Maybe half an hour?"

Helen murmured confirmation. "I'd looked for Mamar, but she'd already taken Teddy home." She was lovely, so pale with fright. No wonder Crispin cared for her. Sheila, however, was not sure how she could endure the rest of the week until she could go home.

"And then what?" Tom was still focused on the pill bottle.

"I never thought about it again," Helen admitted.

Tom rounded on Sheila and his tone accused rather than interrogated. "And you didn't touch it until after Daphne collapsed?"

"No. Then I stuck it in my purse. Did you check it for prints?"

"You must have wiped them off."

"I did not! I was very careful."

"Well, somebody did. Helen, do you know anybody who takes Lanoxin?"

Helen's hands clenched each other in her lap. She admitted, reluctantly, "Muffy did. And Mama, but she wouldn't—"

Crispin put a hand to her lips to still her. "Tom, are you accusing either Helen or her mother of anything?"

Tom shifted uneasily from one foot to the other. "No, not—No." Everyone knew what he hadn't said: "Not yet."

"What about that man who was supposed to bring Muffy to the party?" Sheila asked quickly. "The one who didn't come?"

"Lance McGrew," Helen said eagerly. "Try to find Lance, Tom. Maybe he knows something."

Tom heaved a sigh from the bottom of his big shoes. "I might as well tell you. It'll be in tomorrow's paper. Lance was found the morning after the party, floatin' beside Rob Wilmer's dock in Pirate's Cove. Forensics thinks he was shot before midnight."

They gaped at him. "You think it's all connected?" Crispin finally asked.

Tom shook his head. "I don't see how, but maybe."

"You said he was shot?" Helen's voice was scarcely a whisper.

Tom nodded. "That reminds me, ma'am. I heard a report about a shooting down in Memorial Park this morning. Was that you?"

"You shot someone?" Helen demanded, incredulous—then immediately got the real picture. "Somebody shot *at* you? God in heaven, what is happening to us?" She sagged against the cushions; tears streamed from behind her closed lids.

"Nothing is just happening," Sheila told her. "Somebody is deliberately doing these things. I saw the person who shot at me." Helen's eyes flew open with a question. Sheila shook her head. "Not to identify. He—or she, I suppose—wore a ski mask. But it could have been somebody from the party, somebody who killed Muffy and gave Daphne pills. Maybe," she shot a quick look up at Tom Goren to see if he were going to stop her, but he didn't, "maybe in that last drink. You picked it up from the bar, Helen, but did you notice anybody around it before that?"

As Helen puckered her brow in thought, Libba spoke apologetically from the swinging door to the kitchen. "Helen, I hate to bother you, but do you think three batches of brownies will be enough?"

In matching navy slacks and cotton sweater, she looked petite and pretty in spite of flour smeared on one cheek and weary shadows under her eyes. They closely matched Helen's.

If Libba noticed Helen's tears and the others' unease, she gave no sign. "Oh, hello, Tom! Teddy didn't tell me you were here, but I should have guessed. You always did have a nose for brownies. Sit down. I was about to bring warm ones in."

The detective gave her the first smile Sheila had ever seen on his face. "Man, Libba, that takes me back. Remember how you used to make brownies that summer Eddie and I used to drop by after preseason practice? Helen would bring over that tea punch stuff—"

"Tunch." Even Helen smiled wanly at the memory. "You and Eddie always emptied the pitcher."

"Sit down, Tom," Libba urged again. "Stay for a brownie."

He obediently perched on a big wing chair, asking soberly, "Sure is too bad about Eddie, isn't it?"

"What about Eddie?" The week's tension crept back into Libba's voice.

"Nothin' new. I just meant the way he looked the other night."

"Oh. I was afraid somethin' else had happened. . . ."

"No. He's pitiful enough as it is."

"He sure is," Helen agreed softly. "I wouldn't have known him if I'd met him on the street." She stood. "I haven't made tunch in years, but I can make coffee."

"I've already got it made," Libba told her.

While Helen and Libba were getting the food, the leaden clouds finally began to spit rain against the windows. Crispin jerked his head toward the fireplace. "I can't get down to light those logs with this knee, Tom, but a fire might cheer things up. Would you do the honors? And Sheila, come over here where we can watch him work." He patted the cushion beside him—the side where Helen had not been sitting.

Reluctantly Sheila took it. When Teddy entered a few minutes later, however, and pouted to find Sheila beside him, Sheila understood how she felt. She even moved away so the little girl could sit on the floor between them, leaning against Crispin's knee.

Tom left after one brownie and a quick cup of coffee. The others lingered, not saying much. Sated on warm brownies and hot coffee, nobody mentioned death. In the glow of one warm lamp, they could have posed for Old Friends Visiting in the Afternoon.

Except, Sheila thought somberly, watching the fire, *this group of old friends is quickly dying out.*

They heard a boat roar at the dock. A few minutes later Jack came in, dripping wet. "Where's Sparrow?" Libba asked, surprised.

"She went on home. We got soaked comin' back. It's pourin' out there." He ducked his head to hide his face as he swiped a brownie from the plate. He would have gone upstairs, but Libba spoke again, irritated.

"That's great. How am I supposed to get home—borrow a poncho and walk?" She heaved the sigh mothers reserve for their children's betrayals. "I'll just have to call and tell her to come back."

"Justin's coming home early, and he's stopping by the Panda House for Chinese food. Stay and eat," Helen suggested, "then go to the funeral home with us."

Libba indicated her slacks. "I need to change."

"Then Jack can run you home."

Jack, halfway to the stairs, was doing his dead-level best to keep anybody from seeing his black eye.

Crispin detached Teddy and stood. "We'll do it. I need some fresh air. Get your coat, Sheila." He started for the front door without looking back.

If he could have driven, she would have let him go without her. Instead, she offered, "I'll drive Libba. You stay here."

"No, I'll ride in back." He took a yellow-and-white golf umbrella from Helen and offered Libba his arm.

"I'll bring the car to the front steps." Sheila took another umbrella, a navy collapsible, and headed for the car. In the wind, the umbrella collapsed before she reached the drive. As she started the engine, she reflected that her soggy clothes exactly matched her mood.

The rain had brought an early dusk. Already the orange streetlights glowed through the downpour. As Crispin opened the door for Libba, rain hitting magnolia leaves sounded like a giant popcorn popper.

Having someone else do her a favor instead of the other way around seemed to make Libba nervy and anxious. To put her at ease, Sheila nodded toward the two fat purses on the seat between them. "You don't ever throw away anything, either?" she joked.

It took Libba a minute to figure out what she meant. Then she gave a breathless little laugh. "Not often." She added diffidently, "Charho says you're gonna find out who killed Muffy?"

Sheila sighed. "I doubt it. But tell me something. Tom Goren's not likely to let me into Muffy's apartment. When you were in there yesterday, did you notice anything odd? Out of place, perhaps, or—well, just odd?"

Libba did not answer right away. Perhaps she was mentally walking through Muffy's rooms. Orange shadows flickered across her face as she turned to ask, "Like what?"

Sheila, straining to see through a streaming windshield, admitted, "I honestly don't know. Anything out of place, maybe, or something that was there and shouldn't have been. Or something missing."

"No." Libba's voice was softer than usual, and a little mournful. "Everything seemed the same, I think—except a suitcase was missin', and some clothes." She caught a quick breath between her teeth. "You think whoever killed her went to her place afterwards and packed a bag to make it look like she'd gone away?"

Sheila nodded. "It's possible."

"That's monstrous!"

Crispin spoke from the back. "So was killing her. Who had a key to her place?"

"Why, I don't know. She could have given one to anybody, I suppose. She gave me one because she said she didn't want to die and lie there for days—" She came to an abrupt stop.

Nobody spoke, but they shared a single thought: Keys hadn't kept Muffy from lying for most of a day undiscovered.

As they rode in silence, Sheila heard the rain drumming one phrase over and over on the Cadillac roof: *Crispin loves Helen. Crispin loves Helen.*

She was so lost in unhappiness that she almost failed to hear Libba say softly, "Turn here."

Sheila's rambles had not taken her to this part of Ortega, the oldest part away from the water. Unlike the riverfront houses a few blocks away, these were simple bungalows constructed of brick or wood. Some were covered with asbestos siding to protect them from the harsh Florida sun and termites. This could be a modest neighborhood in any American town. Any Deep South town, Sheila amended, as the wind whipped Spanish moss and palms.

Libba's was a small brick house with faded brown eaves and shutters, guarded by a big magnolia on one side and a short bushy palm on the other. Sheila pulled in behind a middle-aged red Toyota and eyed the stream where Libba's front walk should have been.

Libba gave an apologetic little laugh. "I need to paint."

"Your hanging ferns look healthy," Crispin told her.

"Once a gardener, always a gardener." Sheila meant to

tease, but it came out shrewish. She wished she hadn't said anything.

"I could use a landscape architect," Libba said wistfully. "I can't get a thing to grow under that tree."

Sure enough, patches of grass straggled over stretches of bare sand. "Try sedum," Crispin suggested. "It grows almost anywhere."

"Have you lived here long?" Sheila asked, glad again for the convenience of her apartment instead of the cares of a house.

"Since I was nine. When Daddy retired from the Navy, Mother wanted to come home."

She ought to have guessed. Even a small house in Ortega would probably cost far more than Libba could now afford.

Libba pointed to a low-hanging branch. "When I was a girl, I used to climb up there with a pillow and dream that a prince would carry me away to his palace." She gave a forced laugh. "But some princes turn out to be frogs."

There is a corollary, Sheila thought. *Some princesses die young.*

On the way home, Crispin said brusquely, "Stop by the park."

"It's streaming rain," Sheila protested.

"And there's a distinct chill in the air," he agreed. "Especially in here. Drive around, if you like, but don't go back until you tell me what's bugging you."

"Bugging me?" Her laugh was as false as Libba's had been. "Why, what should be bugging me? Three people are dead and I got shot at this morning. Isn't that enough?" She would not demean herself by adding anything else.

"Not for you, Superwoman. I've seen you kick a gun out of the hands of a hardened criminal, and face a revolver at one and a half paces. Afterwards you were a bit shook, but you didn't glower as if you'd like to turn the gun on me. What on earth have I done?"

Brought me to meet the woman you love. She opened her mouth, but a sudden thickening of her throat kept her from saying it.

"Turn in at the park," he ordered.

Without thinking, she obeyed, and turned off the motor. Her chest was so tight her seat belt felt as if it would crush her. She unsnapped it and took a deep, ragged breath.

She knew they were facing the water, but she couldn't see a thing. Rain poured down the windshield, blurring her vision. Only when she licked her lip and tasted salt did she realize it wasn't the rain.

She heard Crispin grunt as he shifted in his seat, felt his long beautiful fingers gently massaging her shoulder. "Have I said something? Done something? What?"

She shook her head and tried to pretend she was scratching her cheek, not swiping away tears. She still couldn't speak.

He gave her a little shake. "Sheila? At least answer me! Don't do this to us!"

She shook off his arm and pressed her forehead against the steering wheel. "There isn't any us, Crispin. There's just you and me." She felt as if she were sinking in a swamp of misery. Any minute now, the ooze would smother her.

"The hell there isn't!" His voice was harsh.

She damped a small flicker of hope that rippled inside her and found the courage to speak—very carefully. "Crispin, you love Helen. I should have guessed sooner, but this afternoon—well, I saw the way you looked at her. I . . . I'm not willing to be second choice. It's better to find out now, before we get—too involved."

There! It had come out rather well. She took a deep breath. "There's nothing I can do to help here. I'm going back home tomorrow."

He didn't reply. Compelled by a need to make him feel better, she added hurriedly, "You can fly back after the game."

She heard the door open behind her. Startled, she turned in time to see him haul himself out of the back seat into the rain. The car shook as he slammed the door.

He passed her window and headed toward the water, hobbling but resolute. Rain pelted his red-and-black back. He wore no coat.

She opened her own door and leaned out, getting thoroughly wet. "Crispin! Come back! You'll get soaked!"

"What do you care?" he snarled, and stomped on.

She watched him go, feeling utterly helpless. Closing the door, she again rested her head on the steering wheel. "Dear God," she whimpered. She hadn't known she could hurt this much. She felt as if a cruel hand had reached into her innermost being and pulled out something fragile and precious by the roots. "Dear God. Dear God." Eventually the repetition soothed her. Her mind became a blank.

Did she sit for minutes, or hours? Time flexed like an accordian. Only hours ago they'd laughed on their way here to Florida. Days ago they dropped Libba off.

A gigantic clap split the air. Thunder? In December? Or had the wind cracked one of the park's huge pines? Her dad never would have a pine tree near his house. "Too brittle," he insisted. "You never know when they're coming down."

Sheila jerked up, suddenly anxious. Crispin was out there, with lightning and brittle pines. If they didn't harm him, he could catch cold without a coat, or the rain might soften his cast. She'd have to persuade him to come back.

She reached for the golf umbrella and opened the door. The wind was too strong to put up the umbrella, but she carried it anyway.

Halfway to the water she met him, limping back. His hair was plastered to his forehead, his suit clung to his body. "Are you all right?" he called, his voice wary.

"Yes. I brought you an umbrella." She held it out.

They stood, soaked, looking at one another over the closed umbrella. At the same moment, they began to laugh. Sheila laughed so hard, she didn't know if it was rain or tears streaming down her face. Then she was in his arms. She could feel his warmth through the damp clothes between them.

"You ninny!" he whispered into her ear. "You precious, beautiful, soaking wet ninny." He reached for the umbrella and formally raised it above their drenched heads. "Take me home before we both die of pneumonia."

"I need to tell you something before we go," he said as he climbed in the front seat, where he belonged.

She lifted a hand to stop him. Right now she didn't want to go back to all the questions.

But he reached out and took her hand. "No, this is important. That big noise a while back? It wasn't just thunder. It was me, having a shattering revelation. You were right—a bit. Ever since I met Helen, just before she and Justin got engaged, I have envied him. She's so sweet, and caring. And she looks beautiful surrounded by a houseful of kids. For years, I looked for somebody like her. I even tried to fall in love with a couple of women who reminded me of her—but it never took. When I met you," he lifted her hand and kissed it, "you were utterly different—delightful, whether you were climbing a tree or charging a loaded gun. It didn't occur to me until you said what you did a few minutes ago that I was trying to have my cake and eat it too—love both of you at the same time. But out there by the river, with water dripping down my neck, I realized I've been hanging onto a mirage. I'm not a suburban, minivan, kids-on-the-hearthrug type of guy. I like my woman puzzling over crimes and flying home exhausted from a big corporate meeting. I like my kid in measured doses, shared with Aunt Mary. You aren't my second choice, Sheila. You are my *only* choice. Okay?"

It was too precious a moment for speech. Sheila nodded, her throat tight.

Not until she heard his teeth chattering in time with her own did she start the car.

As she backed into Ortega Boulevard, he asked, "What's that smug grin on your face?"

She laughed aloud. "Do you realize you just called your archenemy 'Aunt Mary'?"

"Are you worn out?" he asked above the swish of tires on wet pavement. "Or are you up to a little more detecting? I'd like to invite Jack and Sparrow to join us someplace for dessert, and try to find out what's going on with him."

Now, it was fine with her to discuss the case. She didn't bother to analyze why. "Do you think he'd tell you?"

"Jack and I have been good buddies since he wore blue pajamas with feet in them. I read him thrilling sagas like *Peter Pan* and *Alice in Wonderland*. His favorite part used to be—"

She swerved to avoid an opossum gliding across the street. That reminded her of Einstein last night, and Muffy. Muffy had lain out Tuesday night in a storm like this. She could picture the pitiful body under the azaleas, plastered with rain.

"What do you think?" Crispin asked.

She shook her head. "I'm sorry. I completely missed what you were saying. I was remembering finding Muffy. Try again."

He sighed. "So there we will be at our wedding. The preacher will say, 'Will you, Sheila, take this man?' and the bride will reply, 'Pardon me, sir, what did you say? I was thinking about a corpse.' "

"And the groom will be thinking, 'You know, if they had put just a little more fertilizer on the bride's roses . . .' "

He tugged one of her curls. "What do you know about fertilizing roses?"

"Absolutely nothing. What were you saying?"

He didn't reply. Turning, she saw that the smug grin was now on his face.

"What's that all about?" she demanded.

He reached out and took her hand. "You just referred to our wedding in the future tense, instead of the conditional."

"Pure slip of the tongue," she assured him crisply. But she did not take away her hand.

Later that evening, as Sheila paused near Daphne's casket to speak to Hayden, she couldn't help remembering that last night they'd stood together beside another dead body. Her flippant side nearly quipped, "We've got to stop meeting like this."

With a quick murmur, she moved out into the hall and let Crispin linger in the viewing room with Hayden and Justin.

Treye hurried past, dapper in a gray suit and black tie, to join his father. A moment later, Eddie Weare shambled up and spied Sheila. He headed her way with an outstretched hand. "Hello. I don't remember your name, but you're Crispin's woman. Crispin's the smartest man I ever met!" Eddie looked even more disheveled than before. His blue suit didn't fit, his shirt collar was frayed, and his eyes were as pink as his tie.

A wave of stale alcohol and tobacco fumes flowed over her as he got near. He scrubbed at a cigarette burn on his jacket cuff, then gripped her hand, practically cutting off circulation in her fingers. She gently withdrew her hand as he continued mournfully, "We're certainly gonna miss Daffy. We surely are." His eyes filled with easy tears. "I just hate that I hadn't seen her all these years, then right after our dance, she died." He sniffed and rubbed his eye on his sleeve. "And then, did you hear? Muffy—Muffy—"

It was too good a chance to pass up. "What happened to Muffy, Eddie? Do you know?"

He shook his head and his lower lip hung slack. "She died. Just like Daphne. All the beautiful women are dyin'. Be careful you don't die too, ma'am."

"I'll try not to, Eddie. Do you know how Muffy died?"

He nodded. "It wasn't pretty. Muffy used to be pretty."

Before Sheila could ask him anything else, Libba took his elbow. "Eddie, have you spoken with Hayden yet?" Her suit was gray, becoming, and classic enough to last for years.

"I like your suit," Sheila told her impulsively. She felt a bit sorry for this woman who spent her life taking care of other people.

Libba gave the jacket a deprecatory little stroke. "I bought it last summer when Daddy died."

"Your daddy died?" Eddie exclaimed, distressed. "Mr. Ralph? I sure did like him. How'd he die, Libba?"

She shrugged. "He had a bad heart, Eddie. He'd been sick a long time." She gave Sheila an apologetic smile and tugged Eddie's arm gently. "Have you talked to Hayden yet?"

"No. I don't really know him, you see. I know Justin, though—" His head swiveled to peer around the hall.

"Justin's with Hayden. Come on."

As she led him into the viewing room, Sheila heard a voice behind her. It sounded far too cheerful for this place. "Good evening, Mrs. Travis! We meet again."

Rob Wilmer was a refreshing contrast to Eddie. His black tailor-made suit lay smooth over his uneven shoulders. A subdued paisley tie precisely centered a shirt so white it probably glowed in the dark. His eyes twinkled in a most unfunereal manner as he murmured confidentially, "I hear they've drafted you to solve all the Ortega murders."

This was the first time they had stood face to face. He was short enough that she had to smile down at him. "They say you know everything, Mr. Wilmer. Won't you save everybody a lot of trouble and just tell us who did it?"

He chuckled. "What? And spoil your fun? Not on your life. But be very careful, Mrs. Travis. Hunting murderers is dangerous work."

She nodded wryly. "Tell me about it. Somebody took a shot at me just this morning down in Memorial Park."

His eyes widened. "Now you've told me something I didn't know." He reached out to stop Tom Goren as he passed. "Tom, why hasn't anybody told me this beautiful woman is getting shot at?"

Tom paused reluctantly. "I don't joke about murder, Rob. And I don't hold with amateurs buttin' in." He walked heavily toward the casket, and Sheila was intrigued to see him brush away a tear.

"Poor thing," Rob murmured. "All the males in our class were in love with Daphne, you know. When she crooked her little finger, we'd all come running. At her first wedding, when the preacher asked 'Can anyone show just cause why this woman should not wed this man?' every woman in the church grabbed her date's elbow. I swear, it's true. So this is the end of an era. Guess I ought to go in and pay my respects, too." He strolled toward the viewing room with a quick, light grace, passing Crispin on his way out.

"Sheila, are you ready? Jack and Sparrow are waiting, and once I assured Jack I was paying, Sparrow suggested the Café Carmon."

Before she left, Sheila heard Tom Goren say to Treye, "I am so sorry about your loss. You have my deepest sympathy."

She turned to catch Treye's reaction. He looked temporarily disconcerted, but recovered enough to give Tom a pallid smile.

The rain had stopped, but many streets were flooded and the air was thick with fog.

Sheila carefully followed Jack's red Jeep onto I-95. Even at that hour, traffic was brisk on the Fuller Warren Bridge. "Until they took the tolls off, going to the southside was a big deal," Crispin marveled. "Now people go back and forth for dessert."

"How much was the toll?"

"A quarter. Each way."

He directed her to park in a square of 1930's stores built around a fountain to resemble a Spanish village. On the sidewalk, Sheila paused to browse in the enticing windows of White's Bookstore. "Later." He tugged her arm. "They're waiting next door."

Café Carmon was both charming and chic. Eight black tables with black-and-white chairs. Black-and-white wicker stools at a black bar with a white formica top. Black-and-white tiles on the floor. Even the menu was black and white. A copper-and-brass samovar and a floral arrangement on the counter were all the color that management supplied.

Not a table was empty. Viewing the array of desserts in a glass case near the door, Sheila saw why.

The young couple had secured a table near the back. Sheila smiled down at Sparrow's white slacks, black sweater, and the black-and-white striped cats dangling from her ears. "No wonder you wanted to come here. You look like an advertisement for the place."

Sparrow stopped drumming her long red nails on the table and gave Sheila's taupe suit and dark green blouse a shy appraisal. "I have some jade earrings that would match your blouse."

Sheila laughed. She was so happy to be with Crispin that she felt like laughing at everything tonight. "We ought to swap. The first time I saw you, I thought of some aquamarines I have that would match your eyes."

Crispin sat down across from Jack and said in a falsetto, "My dear, you really should have chosen a different tie. Purple, to match your shiner." In a normal voice, he added, "It's a beaut, by the way. Should we pity the other fellow?"

Jack ducked his head. "I ran into a door."

Crispin gave him a skeptical look. " 'The time has come, the walrus said, to speak of many things'—like whether pigs have wings."

"Look!" Jack barked. "If you plan to harp all night,

we'll go somewhere else." He half rose. Several customers glanced around curiously. Sparrow looked down. Her face and neck flamed.

Sheila felt as sorry for her as she had for her mother an hour before. Ignoring Jack, she said to Sparrow, "I don't see anything to compete with white chocolate mousse drizzled with raspberry sauce. How about you?"

The smile Sparrow gave her was both grateful and apologetic. Sheila wondered what she'd be like away from Jack. "I always have their carrot cake. It has pecan cream between the layers, and coconut on top."

The men both ordered peanut butter pie. "And bring lots of coffee," Crispin told their waitress. "This woman doesn't look like an addict, but she needs coffee like the rest of us need air."

Jack rose abruptly. "I need to use the bathroom."

"By a curious coincidence, so do I." Crispin pushed back his chair. Sparrow's eyes were full of worry as she watched them leave.

"Are you all right?" Sheila asked cautiously.

Sparrow's eyes filled with tears. She squeezed them shut and pressed her lips tight together, breathing deeply. "I'm sorry," she finally whispered with an attempt at a smile. "I guess it's just . . . everything. Muffy, Daphne—"

"And Jack?"

Sparrow's hand clenched so tightly she'd have nailmarks on her palm, but she said nothing.

Coffee was put before them.

"That smells too good to wait for the men." Sheila took a sip. "Delicious! And piping hot." She studied Sparrow over the rim of her cup, but said nothing. Years as an embassy wife and one in a school of graduate students had taught her how encouraging silence can be to the young.

She'd drunk half her coffee before Sparrow finally spoke. "He won't tell me what's wrong, but he's been rotten all week. Jumpy, and mean. Then he got that black eye . . ." She picked up her napkin and dabbed her cheeks, and her voice was full of bewilderment, "He won't tell me a thing!"

Sheila raised an eyebrow. "He's not always so—ah—grumpy?"

Sparrow managed a watery smile. "You mean obnoxious? No, usually he's real sweet." She sniffed and bent to fumble in a jumbled shoulder bag for a tissue. "I can't expect you to believe that, though. Not after the way he's actin' this week."

"Maybe he didn't want Crispin and me to come."

Sparrow shook her head so hard her earrings knocked against her slender neck. "Crispin's like his favorite uncle or somethin'."

"Crispin's Teddy's favorite uncle too, but that didn't make her delighted to welcome me."

Sheila hadn't meant to say it aloud, but she was glad she had. Sparrow laughed in spite of herself. "I heard about the iguana. Poor Teddy. She thought Crispin was waitin' for her to grow up and marry him."

Sheila shrugged. "Who knows? Maybe he will."

Sparrow blinked. "But aren't you . . . ? I mean . . ."

"We're thinking about it, but we haven't come to any decision. I've been on my own for two years, and you can get awfully used to doing what you want when you want. Ask your mother."

"Oh, no." Sparrow shook her white wedge, setting the cats dancing again. "Mama would love to be married. Growin' up, all *she* ever wanted to be was a wife and mother." She spoke sarcastically, as if repeating the other side of a familiar argument.

Sheila chose what she thought was a safe reply. "Like Helen?"

"Helen?" Sparrow was puzzled. "Helen's a middle-school guidance counselor. In the inner city. She hates cookin' and housework!"

Sheila felt a spurt of annoyance. Crispin had told her what Hayden and Justin did—why not Helen? *Why didn't you ask?* the voice in her head reminded her. *You just as-*

sumed her life revolved around volunteer work, parties, and family. How on earth did Helen juggle that busy calendar after a day with middle-schoolers and their problems?

She tuned in as Sparrow said ". . . when Mama got married, she and Daddy just weren't compatible. They fought all the time, and he spent all the money. So she got her master's and went to work." Her voice showed no emotion whatsoever, and her face was like marble.

The young woman's frantic worry over Jack was more normal, it seemed to Sheila, than this calm acceptance of what must have been a childhood of considerable pain. No wonder Sparrow contained herself. If you cut her spirit, it might bleed sorrow.

However, this wasn't supposed to be a therapy session for Sparrow. Ruthlessly, Sheila dragged the conversation back to Jack. She couldn't imagine why he would kill either Daphne or Muffy, but couldn't leave his curious behavior unexplored.

"When did Jack change? Did it have anything to do with Tuesday's party?"

Sparrow considered the question dubiously. "I don't know. It may have. I was at Daddy's for Christmas, and didn't get back until that afternoon. We all went over to help Daphne get ready for the party, and that's the first time I'd seen Jack since Thanksgivin'. He was already different then." She sipped her coffee for the first time, wrinkled her nose, and put it down.

"Is it cold?' Sheila asked.

Sparrow shook her head in some confusion. "No, I—I don't really like coffee. I usually drink tea."

"Why didn't you say so?" Sheila signaled the waitress. While they waited for a cup of tea for Sparrow and a refill on her own coffee, she gave the young woman a gentle lecture on asking for what she wanted when men tried to order something else. She suspected Sparrow didn't hear a word.

When the tea was sugared, lemoned, and gratefully sipped, Sparrow continued as if there had been no interruption. "That afternoon, Jack wasn't mean, but he was, like, on another planet. The first time he was rude was when we had to go look for his aunt. I thought at first he wanted to be with me, but ..." She broke off and shook her head.

"He seemed all right that evening, when you were looking at the pictures," Sheila remembered.

Sparrow nodded. "Then at the party, he got all jumpy. After his daddy's announcement, he said he had a headache, and told me to drive Brandy down to the Landin' for a party we were all supposed to go to. He said he'd try to come later, but—" her aquamarine eyes filled with more tears "—he never did. Ever since, he's gotten worse and worse!" She finished in a desperate whisper.

"Could he be upset because his dad's running for office?"

"Oh, no! Jack's real proud of that—at least he was. I don't know how he feels about anything right now." She set down her tea and sighed. "Even me."

"The men are coming back. Do you want to repair your damages?"

Sparrow fled to the women's room.

Crispin and Jack resumed their seats with the air of men who have reached a grudging detente. Sheila tried to read Crispin's expression. He gave her a slight shrug and reached for his coffee.

As soon as Sparrow returned, the observant waitress whisked desserts to each place.

"That's a mighty slender slice of mousse," Crispin observed. "Is it any good?"

"Even better than it sounded," Sheila assured him. "And extremely rich. Swap a bite?"

Their attempts to lighten the atmosphere fell flat. Jack attacked his peanut butter pie without a word.

Again trying to break the ice barrier, Sheila said lightly, "Jack, this morning I was talking to Laura Grace, and she said I ought to ask you about the pirates. Are you the pirate expert in the family?"

He slammed his fist so hard on the tabletop, the coffee spoons rattled. "Keep out of our family's business! Do you hear me? I don't care what Charho and Mama asked you to do—"

"Steady, fellow!" Crispin grabbed his shoulder.

Before he could say more, a cheerful voice called from the restaurant door. "Hiya, Crispin, Sheila, Jack, Sparrow!" Treye approached them on the balls of his feet with a hopeful smile, as if unsure of his welcome. "This is Nellie. Mind if we join you?"

The redhead on his arm must spend her life in salons and tanning beds. Sheila wondered what she'd look like without the red hair coloring, black stockings, thick matte makeup, artificial lashes, and three-inch heels. Nellie could have put some of her money to better use for remedial education and an extension on her skirt.

Jack shoved back his chair. "Come on, Sparrow. We're finished."

Treye grabbed his arm. "Don't you take that boat out again without askin'. You hear me, cuz?"

Jack jerked away and, without a backward look, stomped out.

Sparrow looked uncertainly from the door to Crispin. "Go ahead," he told her. "We'll come later."

She gave him a quick, frightened smile, then thanked him and ran after Jack, cat earrings swinging from side to side.

Treye called to the waitress, "Could you clear two of these places, please? We'll both have truffle cake."

"I don't think I like truffles," his date objected. She swept tousled red curls out of one eye and swung her knee suggestively close to Crispin's. "Don't pigs eat them?"

"You'll like it," Crispin assured her. Then, as the waitress set down the truffle cakes and offered coffee refills, he turned to peer into Sheila's eyes. "Okay. It's only up to her eyeballs."

Treye's date gave him an uncomprehending smile and

turned her attention to her plate. Sheila noticed, uncharitably, that Nellie could manage to do two things at once. She was also swinging one toe nearer and nearer Crispin's calf.

He shoved his chair away from the table and turned sideways to better accommodate his cast. "From the way the temperature dropped when you got here, do I deduce you gave Jack that shiner?"

Treye grinned and flexed his fingers. His hands were very white, and as covered with thick black hair as his father's, but his knuckles were scraped and purple. "Sure did. His daddy runnin' for Congress seems to have gone to his head, so I took him down a peg or two."

His date's eyes widened, as brown as the chocolate crumb in the corner of her sticky red lips. "His daddy's runnin' for Congress?"

"Down, Nellie." Treye slapped her hand lightly. He glanced over his shoulder, then leaned forward to ask, confidentially, "What's really eatin' Jack? He's been a real f—" he caught Crispin's eye "—a real fool during this holiday. Leaves lines uncoiled on the boat. Takes it out without askin'. We're supposed to share that boat, but Jack's been actin' like it's his private property. What's eatin' him, man?"

Crispin raised one eyebrow. "Don't you know?"

Treye looked at him without speaking for a long minute, then nodded. "Yeah. I'm afraid I do. But I hope to God I'm wrong. What do you think we should do?"

"What do you suggest?" Crispin asked.

"Damned if I know. Do you think Sparrow's supplyin' him? She's in pharmacy school—Damn shame, too."

"Why?" Sheila asked sharply. Was Treye a throwback to a generation of men who believed women belonged only at home?

He shrugged. "Sparrow always wanted to be a vet. She's crazy about animals. But Libba couldn't afford to send her away—if we can believe anything the beautiful Daphne had to say."

His date laid one talon on his lips. "Shhh, Treye. Don't speak ill of the dead."

His laugh was bitter. "She can't haunt me any worse dead than she did alive. Less. I'll have a better chance of getting steady funds from Dad. Daphne was one expensive woman." He gave Nellie a playful slap. "Like someone else I could name." she wrinkled her nose at him and bent forward for a kiss, but he turned back to Crispin, his eyes concerned. "What do you think all this—the deaths, I mean—will do to Uncle Justin's chances of goin' to Congress?"

"Hard to tell," Crispin replied. "Sure won't help him any. The best bet would be to get it cleared up as soon as possible. Did you know that Sheila has a bit of experience with this sort of thing?"

"Yeah. Daddy said Mrs. Aspen and Helen asked her to help." Treye didn't sound any more impressed than Tom Goren.

Nellie was, however. "Oooh! You're in Congress?"

"No." Without enlightening her further, Sheila asked, "Treye, you were standing near the bar before Helen sent Daphne's drink over to her. Did you notice anybody put anything in it?"

His smile was sardonic. "Or did I put anything in it myself? No, Mrs. Travis, to both questions."

"Well, did you see Muffy after she went upstairs?"

He started to shake his head, then stopped and snapped his fingers—just like his mother. "Sure! I went up to change before goin' to the hospital, and she was on Daddy and Daphne's bed, bawlin' her eyes out."

"You didn't happen to notice the doubloon necklace on Daphne's dresser, did you?"

"Daddy's already asked me that. I did notice, and it wasn't there." He rubbed his blue-black chin. "That's why I went into their room in the first place. I knew Mrs. Aspen had taken it up, and Mama'd been mad as hell about that necklace earlier. She claims it's hers. Anyway, I decided to put it where she couldn't find it until Daddy got back." His mouth curved in a wry smile, but his eyes were bleak. "I try to help them fight fair whenever possible. As it turned out, though, neither the necklace nor the jeweler's box was on the dresser. I figured Mrs. Aspen had put them in a drawer somewhere. And since Muffy was in there, I didn't like to rummage through the drawers."

"Could Muffy have had it?" Sheila pressed. "Maybe under her on the bed? Or tucked down somewhere?"

He considered, then shook his head. "She turned over and sort of twisted up when I came in, and that dress she had on left nothing to the imagination. She didn't have the necklace. I'm certain."

As they walked toward the car, Crispin asked, "Well, did we get more from this evening than a ton of calories?"

"You sure did—smoldering looks from Treye's date. I thought for a while she was going to climb in your lap."

"You noticed, yet did nothing to protect me?"

"I didn't like to spoil your fun."

"That wasn't fun, that was dynamite. I needed all the protection I could get." They laughed, but neither of them really felt like joking.

They walked hand in hand across the empty street. "Crispin, do you think Treye's right? Is Jack on drugs? If so, Sparrow's not supplying him. That girl's worried sick. What happened when you went off together?"

"Not much. I asked what was the matter and if I could help. Jack basically said, 'Buzz off, old man, I can handle it.' I hope he can. But I don't think it's drugs—I think something's eating him alive. Maybe some scrape he's gotten into at school, and is afraid to tell his folks."

She stopped under a streetlight and withdrew her hand to rummage for her keys. "I think you're right. For one thing, aren't drug addicts supposed to be euphoric at least some of the time?"

That, finally, drew a chuckle from him. "You don't think our Jack is euphoric?"

"He's one of the most consistently obnoxious young men I've ever been privileged to meet."

A lone car was now coming down the street. At the rear of the Cadillac, by chance or Providence, she dropped the keys just as Crispin bent to scratch his cast.

That's why the bullet went over both their heads.

By the time they knew it had been fired, it had hit a lamppost and ricocheted back to transform the Cadillac's passenger window into a crazed glass honeycomb.

A car roared out of the square.

Sheila and Crispin straightened cautiously. The sidewalks were deserted. Only when Crispin hobbled over to examine the window did a few people creep out of doorways and sidle toward the Cadillac, speaking in hushed voices that soon swelled to a shrill roar.

They had all seen the car, but agreed on only two things: it was black, and driven by a white man in black.

Treye hurried out of Café Carmon, his pale face green under the orange streetlights. "Are you all right? Somebody yelled there'd been a shootin'—"

Crispin pointed to the window. "Behold the victim. The next shooting will occur when we return this automobile to Sheila's aunt. That corpse will be mine."

He wasn't feeling as funny as he was trying to sound. Sheila saw that his hands were shaking. Oddly enough, Treye was shaking, too. She was touched by his concern.

She herself was feeling better since she'd examined the lamppost. "Crispin, look. The bullet hit way up there. Either he was a dreadful shot, or he was trying to scare us, not hit us. Quick, get in the back seat!"

As blue lights and a siren's wail split the air, she backed out, sped down a street, and rounded a corner.

"What are you doing?" he demanded, hanging onto the back of her seat. "We need to give evidence."

"I don't want to have to answer questions. We could be there all night, and what did we see? Nothing." She turned left, then right at the next corner. "Can you get us home from here?"

"Not if you keep this up. All I know about the Southside is that no two streets run parallel. Are we being followed?"

"No, I overreacted. What should I do now?"

He laughed. "Look for a policeman. Failing that, try to find a main street leading to a bridge."

It took half an hour, but eventually they found a bridge. "Not the same bridge, but it'll do," he told her. "Now could you slow down? That wind is ruining my coiffure."

It was also chilling the air. Sheila turned up the heat and asked over her shoulder, "Do you think that sort of thing is common in Jacksonville, or was he really gunning for us?"

"I got the idea he was after us. There were other people on the sidewalks, and now that I think about it, wasn't he parked down the block when we came out?"

Sheila couldn't remember, but it was a thought more chilling than the unwelcome breeze through the shattered window.

They arrived home to find Rob Wilmer seated with Hayden and Charho in the younger L'Arkens' living room. Helen opened the door with anxious eyes. "Treye called. He said you'd been shot at?" She looked from one to the other for denial.

Crispin let Sheila answer. "We were just in the wrong place at the right time," she decided to say.

"This is dreadful!" Helen turned. "Justin, this is the second time today Sheila's been shot at."

Charho gasped. Hayden looked startled. Justin tilted his large face toward his guest. "Is that right?"

Sheila nodded ruefully. "This morning, though, the person with the gun could see clearly. Tonight may have been just a random drive-by shooting."

"So much more comforting," Rob Wilmer murmured.

Helen turned to him angrily. "It's not funny, Rob. What's happenin' to this town? Crispin, maybe you all ought to go on home tomorrow!"

Was that what someone hoped? Sheila eyed them all warily. Hayden, in a chair by the fire, looked drained but not malevolent. Justin looked big, calm, and unflappable. From one end of the sofa, near a vase of lovely yellow long-stemmed roses, Rob Wilmer gave Sheila a rueful, apologetic smile.

"Can't leave the house." Crispin lowered himself into a nearby chair. "Sheila dragged me away from the scene of the crime. Police ought to be looking for her any minute."

Sheila frowned in his direction, but he didn't see. He'd leaned back and closed his eyes.

Charlotte Holmes Aspen, her dark eyes troubled and her voice deep with worry, patted the couch cushion between herself and Rob. "Come sit down, precious, and tell us what happened."

Sheila was glad to obey the invitation. Her knees were suddenly wobbly. She described what had occurred, concluding, "But whoever it was is either a dreadful shot or was only trying to scare us, and there wasn't a single thing we could tell the police. We're fine, except I sure could do with a cup of hot coffee." She didn't feel cold, but she must be. Her teeth were chattering.

Charho spoke urgently. "Coffee for two, Helen, laced with sugar and brandy!"

Crispin's eyes opened long enough to follow Helen with a slightly bemused look. He looked at Sheila, smiled, and shook his head. She grew warm all over. What she thought he meant—what she hoped he meant—was that he was not only cured, but astonished he hadn't been cured long ago.

Helen returned almost at once, with two steaming cups. Sheila took a sip and nearly gagged. Helen must have filled the cup with sugar and brandy before adding a drop or two of coffee. Crispin's eyes met hers again; he lifted his cup in wry salute. Sheila took a deep breath and forced the coffee down.

Rob Wilmer's black eyes missed nothing. "Jacksonville's giving you a rough time, isn' it?" His smile was full of double meaning. "I'm sorry you've had such an unfortunate welcome, Mrs. Travis. You'll have to shake our dust from your sandals at the city gates." He set his own cup down with a clink. "I'll go and let you all get to bed. Shock can be so wearing, and I've got several hours' work ahead."

Helen rose to see him out. "Thank you, Rob, for the roses. They are lovely."

He touched her arm lightly. "Not all the mourners are next door, my dear."

As his engine started, Sheila remembered, "Oh! There's something I wanted to ask him!" As she got to the porch, however, his taillights were turning at the gate.

"What was it, love?" Charho asked as Sheila returned. "Perhaps we know the answer."

"Nothing important." She resumed her seat and reached for her coffee. "I can ask him another time."

The face Justin turned to her was tired and drawn, and she suspected he wished her and her futile investigation at the bottom of the St. Johns. However, his voice was courteous as he suggested, "Call him. He'll be home in a few minutes. Shall I get his number?"

"No, it really can wait." She wanted to ask Rob why his man did Muffy's taxes—and she wanted to watch him as he answered. He was suave enough to give her a plausible answer, but she was certain she could tell if he lied.

"Go see him tomorrow," Hayden suggested. "Rob never goes to the office until ten—unlike us poor old surgeons."

He reached for a magazine, tore off the back cover, and drew a rough map. "He lives just down on Pirate's Cove Road. It's only a few blocks."

Sheila stuck the map in her pocket and the conversation moved to transportation arrangements for tomorrow's funeral. When Charho and Hayden left a few minutes later, everybody was glad to head up to bed.

Sheila sat at Brandy's dressing table brushing her hair, basking in some memories from the day and trying to make sense of others. "Leave the alarm off until Jack gets in," she heard Helen call down to Justin.

Sheila knew she ought to get up and put on her pajamas, but the brandy and sugar (surely not all that coffee!) had stoked her furnace. She couldn't sleep, and the question nagged like a throbbing tooth: Why *did* Rob Wilmer's man do Muffy's taxes?

She knew she wouldn't sleep until she had at least asked.

She changed into jeans and her fisherman's sweater—freshly back from the cleaners after its swim—and tiptoed downstairs. Hayden's map showed Pirate's Cove Road very near. Rob said he'd be up for hours. If his lights were out, she could always come home.

Because of the smashed window, the car was cold and the windshield cloudy. Busy trying to find Aunt Mary's defroster, she had to swerve to miss an oncoming car. She misjudged, went off the pavement, bumped across the grass, and had to swerve again to avoid a brick wall. "Steady!" she said aloud, gritting her teeth. "You'll get picked up for drunk driving." Wouldn't Tom Goren love to get that report?

Sheila herself would have loved fluorescent house numbers on Pirate's Cove Road. Even curbside mailboxes would have been nice, she thought, but Ortega still got doorstep mail delivery.

The large gracious houses dozed in their landscaped waterfront lawns. Only three were still lit.

A scrap of yellow police barrier tape fluttering from a bush caught her eye. She remembered that Tom Goren had said—heavens! was it just this past afternoon?—that a body was found yesterday morning by Rob Wilmer's dock. This must be the place.

A light still burned in the hall. Sheila saw its glow through small panes of glass set high in the door, and found herself drawn as a needle to a magnet. She enjoyed Rob's kind of repartee. Whether she found a secret here or not, the conversation ought to be fun.

As she got out, her common sense reminded her to be careful. *Ultimately, you're looking for a secret worth killing for,* she reminded herself.

Rob's house was not ostentatious, but it had the look of durability and comfort that takes wealth to achieve. Sheila smelled boxwood as she mounted two shallow steps and pressed the bell.

No one answered.

She rose to her tiptoes and, with mental apologies to Aunt Mary, peered inside. She saw no one, but could hear a television or radio somewhere in the back. Since she had come so far . . .

She pressed the bell again. Again, no reply.

A concrete walk led around the house to the left. With a quick hope that he didn't keep dogs, she followed the walk to the back.

She thought at first she'd stumbled into a zoo. Beneath the sickle moon, a tiger crouched by the corner of the house. An elephant cast a huge shadow. A six-foot rabbit—

Rabbit? She peered closer. They were clever topiaries, standing on beds of white marble chips that sloped from a terrace to the seawall. No one would guess from the formal front of Rob's brick house that all this whimsy lurked out back.

Heartened, she headed for a glass sliding door off the terrace, through which a narrow shaft of light streamed.

A bright light shone in her face. She ought to have expected movement sensor lights on the waterfront side of the house. Rob was as vulnerable from the water as the street. Perhaps more.

Shielding her face, she rapped on the glass. "Rob? Are you still up? It's Sheila Travis."

Years later when she remembered that night, her face would still flame and her stomach lurch. It took several seconds for her mind to process what took less than one to imprint through a two-inch crack in the drape: the silk-robed body on the sofa, the despicable instruments lying on the coffee table, what was happening to the woman in the video at the end of the room.

By then, however, she had already knocked. Rob had jumped to his feet and was hurrying across the room. When his eyes met hers through the crack in the drape, his widened with shock.

He bent to remove the burglar rod, slid the door open. The air that poured out was warm, close. She took one step back and would have turned to go, but his jet-black eyes held her as rooted as the boxwood rabbit.

"Mrs. Travis! What a surprise! If you had called, I would have dressed." His face creased into a parody of his usual self-assured smile. Still his eyes held hers. To keep hers from roaming? She had no intention of letting them roam. She wished she could also shut out the screams of the woman being whipped in the video.

Her thoughts must have showed on her face, for he backed toward the coffee table—still keeping his eyes locked with hers—and fumbled behind him through several revolting things that were not remote controls until he found the one that was. The television fell silent.

He came back to the door, belting his black robe tighter. When she said nothing, he lifted his high shoulder even higher. "We cannot always judge by outward appearances, Mrs. Travis. I am sure you understand that."

She shook her head, disgust mixed with a deep compassion. "We all choose what we do with what we are,

Rob. It looks like you've made some spectacularly bad choices."

Instantly, he seemed to coil like a snake. "What did you come for?"

She took another step back. "To ask you a question."

His brows rose. "It must have been an important question."

She shrugged. "It will keep. I can call you tomorrow." She could, but she wouldn't. She knew his secret.

"What was the question?" he persisted.

A night bird rustled in one of the bushes. Sheila willed herself to stillness, hoping to keep her voice from reflecting the revulsion that still churned her stomach. "Someone said today that your man did Muffy Merri-wether's taxes. Is that true?"

His lips twisted in a smile of genuine amusement but his eyes were still a flickering blackness. Snake's eyes. "You came out at this hour to ask about taxes? Are you looking for an accountant, Mrs. Travis?" He gripped her arm.

His insistent use of her formal name began to grate. "No, Mr. Wilmer, I came to ask *why* you would pay some-one to do Muffy's taxes." Daring to tiptoe on the very edge of a chasm, she asked, "Did Muffy know about—" She nodded toward the television and the array of articles on the coffee table.

"I'm afraid so. We bumped into one another on the sidewalk and I dropped a parcel. She drew her own con-clusions. A few days later, she came to my office and pret-tily asked if I knew anybody who did taxes at a reasonable rate. As a favor, I asked my man to do them for her. I did not, however, kill her—not that that matters now."

"Of course it matters! That's what I really wanted to know."

His laugh was low and humorless. "You should have called, Mrs. Travis. Your coming to ask was singularly unfortunate—for both of us. Come in where it's warm while I do some furious thinking—although I am not so much furious as perplexed." He stepped back and waved toward the warm bright den. "Please come in. It's cold out here and I am not, ah, dressed for the occasion."

"No, please, I need to get back." She took a step back. "Crispin—"

"Would never have let you come alone if he'd known you were coming." His voice was silky, but there was nothing silky about his sudden grip on her wrist. She would have bruises tomorrow. "You did sneak out after the others went to bed, didn't you? Now please come in."

The quiet determination beneath his words licked her like a flame. She had no intention of entering that house. However, at the moment she felt distaste but no fear. She had studied karate for years.

To put him off his guard, she pointed to the elephant. "Your leafy pets are charming. Do you do them yourself, or have a man to clip them for you?"

"I have men to do many things."

She braced herself to throw him.

At once, like a viper, he struck. She gasped as her arm was twisted painfully behind her. "I understand you study karate, Mrs. Travis. I, too, have some training. Now, let us go inside."

She started, reluctantly and in agony, for his door.

"Hands up!" An unfamiliar voice rang from behind the foliage tiger. "I've got you covered!"

Wilmer swung Sheila around between him and the invisible assailant. The momentary distraction was enough. She got a foot between his legs, threw him to the ground, and ran. For the moment she had surprised both Rob and the unknown gunman. But who was he? And what did he want? Hearing swift footsteps behind her, she discovered she had no desire to find out. Gasping for breath, she sprinted across the lawn toward the Cadillac, tensed to hear a shot from behind. Flinging herself inside, she started the engine and roared down the street.

Heart racing, she twisted and turned, watching to be

sure she was not being followed. Ortega is not known for square blocks or straight streets. It took her a quarter of an hour to find Justin's house. In that time, she cursed herself for a fool. "Why didn't you just circle the house, dear, and go back to see what happened?"

Then she realized that the question was not her own. She was hearing it in familiar husky tones.

She muttered an answer aloud, between clenched teeth. "Because, Aunt Mary, I'm not a real detective. I'm a sucker who ought to be in St. Petersburg. And I've had all I can take for one day."

Her hands were sweaty on the wheel in spite of the shattered window. She paused at the gate and looked warily to be sure there were no unfamiliar cars before she pulled in and parked. When she'd turned off the engine, she faced another problem. Jack's Jeep was there. He would have put on the alarm when he went to bed. How could she get in? And would Rob Wilmer follow her here as soon as he got dressed? Was he *that* desperate to keep his vile secret?

Climbing out of her car, she scanned the upstairs windows. Which room was Crispin's? If she tossed a handful of pebbles, could she waken him without waking the entire household, too? Probably not. And how was she to find pebbles in the dark, or aim them at this distance?

"What took you so long? Are you okay?"

She whirled. A shadow detached itself from the hood of Jack's car and came toward her. She poised for flight, but the figure held up one hand. "It's just me, and I don't really have a gun. It was a stick."

Jack faced her in the moonlight. She could have hugged him. Instead of petulant, he looked proud of himself—and well he might! "You fooled me. More importantly, you fooled Rob. How on earth did you get there?"

He laughed, the first pleasant laugh she'd heard him utter since looking at his mother's high school picture. "When I was comin' home, you nearly ran me off the road. I thought I recognized the car, and—well, it looked like whoever was driving shouldn't be. So I followed you." He came so near she could see the whites of his eyes shining in the moonlight. "I heard a little bit. You think Mr. Wilmer killed Muffy, in spite of what he said?"

She shook her head. "I don't know. Did he recognize you?"

"I don't think so. I left as soon as you got away, before he even got to his feet. Was he trying to put the make on you? I'd never have thought Mr. Wilmer would use strong-arm tactics on a woman. Besides, he knows you came with Crispin."

"He got confused, I guess." She put her arm through his, relieved. He hadn't seen everything, then. "Thanks, Jack. I can't remember being so glad to see anybody in my life."

He walked her in, then turned. "I've got something to see about down at the dock." From the stairs, she noticed he set the security alarm before he hurried out the door.

While she was dressing, she heard a boat motor give a cough, then catch. Hurrying to the window she saw the *Jack Three* heading downriver.

~~~~~~~~~~~~~~~~~~~~~~~~~

Sheila waked late, trying not to remember the several other times she had waked shuddering, again seeing Rob Wilmer's eyes in the moonlight. As she put on her taupe suit with a fresh, creamy blouse, she flexed her wrist. It was bruised, and sore.

At the foot of the stairs, she met Jack, natty in a navy blazer and red tie. "Don't worry about Mr. Wilmer," he said huskily. "He must have been drunk last night. And look, why don't you and Crispin use my car? I've got to ride with my folks." He held out his keys.

She took them with a grateful smile. She knew what Aunt Mary would say about her driving to a funeral in a red Jeep, and Sheila herself might wish Treye had offered his Alfa-Romeo instead, but Jack's chivalry was too touching to refuse.

This day—Daphne's funeral day—was gentle and humid, with a sky of brilliant blue. Fleecy clouds floated over the river, which rippled like a belly dancer showing her skill. The only reminder of yesterday's downpour were large puddles, bright and reflective as mirrors.

Daphne was buried out of Riverside Presbyterian, where Hayden, Justin, and Helen had been elders for years, so the soaring Gothic sanctuary was comfortably full. Sheila and Crispin were escorted down what seemed like a mile of red carpet and shown into a long mahogany pew behind the immediate family. Libba, Sparrow, Charho, and Teddy were already there. Teddy scowled when Sheila took the seat beside her to let Crispin have the aisle for his cast.

Teddy's scowl only reflected what Sheila was already sensing. She'd attended funerals of state without personally knowing the deceased, but this was the first time she had felt like an interloper or, worse, an imposter. She pictured her title in a playbill: The Stranger, Posing as Family Mourner.

Soon, however, she was tapped for another minor role: Keeper of Laura Grace. Martha preceded the old woman down the aisle. Crispin let them in between him and Sheila. Laura Grace shoved and pointed until Martha obligingly switched places so she could sit beside Sheila. As soon as she was comfortable, Laura Grace beamed and thrust out a pack of cherry Life Savers. When Sheila mouthed "No thanks," Laura Grace tucked them back into her lumpy purse, pulled out a black Episcopal prayer book, and held it for Sheila to share.

Sheila obligingly held her side of the volume while Laura Grace bent her head piously and began reading in a papery whisper. Sheila glanced down at the pages expecting one of the rites for burial of the dead. Instead, Laura Grace was reading Psalm 111, which began, *Halleluia! I will give thanks to the Lord with my whole heart, in the assembly of the upright, in the congregation.*

She had reached verse seven, *The works of His hands are faithfulness and justice*, when the minister rose.

Laura Grace put away her prayer book and fumbled with something at her chest. Then she popped in another Life Saver and nudged Sheila in the ribs. Sheila looked, and pressed her lips together to keep from smiling. The old woman's irrepressible spirit had once again triumphed over respectability. Pinned to the proper black dress Martha surely had chosen for her was a fuzzy caterpillar in rainbow hues. His head was attached by a spring, and it bobbed cheerily as Laura Grace sucked her candy and gently nodded to inner music only she could hear.

No matter how Sheila shifted up and down the small space between Teddy and Laura Grace, Hayden's ravaged face was between her and the pulpit. Trying to ignore Laura Grace's sassy caterpillar and unable to stand such an intimate view of Hayden struggling to contain his grief, Sheila concentrated on the church's lovely dark wood reredos and an arched window in jewel reds and blues above.

The service was brief, but moving. The minister had taken the trouble to gather anecdotes about Daphne from people who remembered her as a child, teenager, and charming adult. While pointing to the hope of resurrection, he nevertheless made it clear that even the Almighty was grieved at this vibrant life cut short. Sheila felt tears prick behind her own lids by the time the service was over.

The only discordant note came when Treye and Jack rose as honorary pallbearers. Jack waited to see where Treye would stand, then deliberately crossed to the other side. Treye balled his right fist and raised it slightly, then turned with a glower.

On her way out, Sheila saw Eddie Weare, blubbering like a baby. In the back row, his hair subdued by the dimness, Tom Goren watched all who left the church. Beside him, Rob Wilmer gave a small forefinger salute as she passed.

Crispin asked softly, "Do you think Rob had a thing for Daphne? He looks positively wretched." No more wretched than Sheila had felt, avoiding his eyes.

Martha planned to take Teddy and Laura Grace home after the service. "Let me do it," Sheila offered. "You drive Crispin to the cemetery instead."

"We were goin' out to eat," Teddy objected.

"We'll go out to eat," Sheila promised. She would have promised the child anything to get out of going to the graveside service and avoid Rob Wilmer.

Teddy chose the place to eat, seconded by Laura

Grace. Sheila scarcely noticed where it was, nor what she ordered. The other two were perfectly happy to keep up a running conversation between them. Sheila's food tasted like sawdust.

She took the pair back to Martha's and sat down with a stack of magazines while they disappeared into Laura Grace's room. From the sounds emanating from it, they were watching a soap opera. She suspected Helen would not approve, but decided not to interfere.

She couldn't concentrate on the magazines. Her mind kept returning to various people who might have killed Muffy Merriwether. And/or Daphne L'Arken.

Rob Wilmer certainly had reason to buy Muffy off, if Muffy knew the kinkiness he was into, but was that worth killing her for? Would this town's good old boys ostracize a single man with a crooked back for watching pornographic videos? Not on their own, perhaps, but if their wives heard about it. . . . However, when would Rob have murdered her? Sheila distinctly remembered him leaving Daphne's party with Tom. Of course, he could have slipped something in Daphne's drink before he left, and come back to meet Muffy later. But why should he kill Daphne?

Twinkie had a far better motive for that—and for Muffy's death, too, if she'd caught Muffy purloining the doubloon necklace. But when had she had the opportunity?

How about Hayden? He might have murdered Muffy, but Daphne? She could still see his small simian face, contorted with grief.

She went over the party one more time. Helen hiding the pills. Helen giving Libba the drink. Helen going upstairs after learning that Daphne was dead. Justin going with Hayden to the hospital. Helen going to bed alone.

The phone rang. Teddy called, "It's for you."

It was Crispin, saying if she didn't mind, he and Justin needed to spend some time at Justin's office, going over Martha L'Arken's finances. Sheila didn't mind. She would go home and take a nap. If she could sleep, she could postpone thinking about the person with the best opportunity to commit two murders: Helen L'Arken.

A loud voice downstairs, male and furious, woke her. "You could have told me! Nobody ever told me!"

Brandy's clock said 3:29. Sheila lay, half-waking, half-dreaming, and waited for another angry shout. Instead, after a time (she did not know whether short or long), a door slammed and feet climbed the stairs. Dragging feet, as if the body were too heavy to bear. The steps passed Sheila's door. Down the hall, a door closed. Then, Sheila heard the sound of muffled weeping.

It had to be Helen. She considered offering help. But whatever grief Helen was venting, she would not welcome intrusion just now. The best Sheila could offer was privacy. Pulling the bed's extra pillow over her ears, she drifted back to sleep.

In her dreams she heard someone calling for help. She could not reach them, no matter how hard she tried, for her feet were handcuffed to her bed while someone flailed her with a whip. Around her were scattered those dreadful instruments she had seen on Rob's coffee table the night before.

She woke with the sheet wound around her ankles, feeling hot and cobwebby. Her head ached. Maybe a river breeze would help. She'd go sit on the dock. Later, maybe she'd go find Eddie Weare.

Pulling on her jeans and a burgundy silk shell—too fancy for the jeans, but the coolest top she'd brought—she tiptoed downstairs and out the back door. On the dock, she lowered herself to the sun-warmed boards and clasped her arms around her knees, listening to the water slap against the pilings and admiring the *Daphne Delight*. It was as elegant as its mistress had been. Would Hayden keep the boat? Would he keep its painful name? The *Jack Three* was gone. Sheila wondered which of the stormy cousins had taken it out.

Overhead, three gulls dipped and whirled between her and Ortega Point. She saw no cords attached to them. Perhaps Laura Grace had cataracts that skewed her vision.

The gulls swooped nearer. One landed on the dock and pranced near her. "You got it right yesterday," Sheila said aloud. "Plenty of secrets and unpleasant surprises. What else was it Laura Grace said you promised?"

He cocked his head and stared at her. She remembered.

Hope.

"You got that one wrong, buddy!" What was the hope for Rob Wilmer? Not much, unless he decided to make better choices. *Choose this day whom you will serve.* That verse had been on her father's office wall all her life. Whom was Rob Wilmer serving? He probably thought he served nobody, when instead he was utterly enslaved.

She shoved her fingers roughly through her hair, unwilling to spend any more of this lovely day brooding about Rob.

She thought of Crispin instead, and her spirit warmed at the memory of their twilight reconciliation. Yes, yesterday had moments of hope.

Two gulls swooped near the end of the dock, screaming and darting toward the water, then off again. The one on the dock turned and waddled toward the two boats bobbing gently on the tide.

"Damn! Has Jack taken that boat out without askin' again?"

She jumped, startled. It was Treye, in black Bermuda shorts, a white windbreaker, and a yachting cap. He came down the dock, swinging a small duffel bag, and paused beside her. "You didn't see him, did you?" he demanded.

She shook her head. "I took Teddy and Laura Grace back to Martha's. Jack was gone when I got back."

Treye dropped the duffel bag and pounded one fist into the other palm. He glared toward the river, as if it had been partner to Jack's perfidy, then he shrugged. "Well, as long as he brings it back before tonight. I've got a date."

He looked toward his house, then at his father's boat. "I think I'll take Daddy's boat out for a short spin. He's not going to be usin' it today. Want to come along?"

"Not now, Treye. I'm feeling lazy. Don't even want to make the effort to climb over a rail. Has everybody left your house?"

"Almost. Libba and Clarinda are finishin' up in the kitchen. And Dad's still there, of course, lookin' more like a ghost than our Daphne." He shook his head in derision. "I'd never have thought the love bug could bite somebody his age so hard."

"You rude boy!" Sheila retorted. "Your father's not ten years older than I am!"

His bushy eyebrows gave an appreciative wiggle. "Ah, but you are wrong. Beautiful women are ageless." Then he touched his cap and walked toward the end of the dock with a jaunty swagger.

She watched him go. Saw him stop, peer into the water, and stiffen. He turned, his face ashen. "My God, there's another one! Somebody's drowned by the dock!"

"Don't look," Treye pleaded, holding her back.

She shook him off and knelt on the boards. It was a man. The water rippled his blue coat and pants. Heavy black shoes dragged his feet slightly under the water. Floating blond hair made his head resemble an enlarged anemone. On his right hand she caught the gleam of a ring. A large high school ring. She had seen that ring Tuesday night.

"It's Eddie Weare! Get a line!" She pulled off her shoes, headed for the ladder, and climbed quickly down. The water was freezing. She tried to reach him from the ladder, but he floated just out of reach.

"Here!" Treye handed her a boat hook.

Hooking Eddie by the jacket, she tugged him toward her. When she knelt and tried to get a line around him, however, the angle was too awkward. Eddie started to float back out.

"Help me!" she cried, grabbing for his belt.

Treye hurried down the ladder, but he slipped and kicked her in the small of the back. The next moment, she sprawled on top of Eddie!

She struggled off in horror. Sank. Surfaced, and gasped with shock. Began to tread water.

"Push him over here," Treye called, reaching for her from the ladder's bottom rung.

Between them they managed to haul Eddie to the ladder and get the line around him. His vacant eyes chilled Sheila almost as much as the cold waters of the St. Johns.

An hour later she sat on the end of the sofa nearest a roaring fire, wearing a fleecy yellow warm-up suit Helen had loaned her. As she sipped hot coffee liberally laced with sugar and brandy, she reflected that she owed the L'Arkens at least one bottle of Gran Duque d'Alba.

On the other end of the sofa, Helen mutely stared into the fire. She'd been asleep when Sheila stumbled into the house, but by the time Sheila had put on dry clothes, Helen was downstairs wearing a denim skirt and oxford cloth shirt, with her hair freshly brushed. She had shown the ambulance attendants where to go, made coffee, and poured in brandy. She had lit a fire. But she had forgotten to clean her face. Mascara lined her lower lids and her eyes were puffy with sleep or weeping.

Treye, in a black sweatsuit, shivered in a chair drawn close to the fire. Hayden perched on the edge of a straight chair he'd set close to Treye's. Their faces were identically bleak.

"If only we had found him sooner," Treye kept repeating. "If only we could have saved him."

"Nobody could have saved him," Tom Goren told them bluntly. "He was dead long before you fished him out." He peered through the blind at the forensic team busy on the dock. "How long were you sittin' out there, Mrs. Travis?"

Sheila had been staring at the roses on the coffee table. How pretty she'd thought them last night! Now the blossoms reminded her of things she'd rather not remember. One of the heads had broken off. Not the only broken thing around Ortega today.

"Half an hour?" she replied. "Maybe a little less? Then after Treye came, we chatted for maybe five minutes."

Treye nodded. "About that."

Hayden roused to ask Sheila, "But you didn't notice Eddie in all that time?"

She shrugged. "I didn't go to the end of the dock. I was watching gulls."

Tom shot her a suspicious look, implying that nobody in their right mind would sit for half an hour watching gulls. Sheila heartily agreed. If he asked, she'd promise to never do it again.

He switched his attention to Hayden. "Eddie came to your place after the funeral, didn't he? I saw him in the den."

Hayden nodded. "I guess so. I remember shaking his hand, but I don't know if that was at the house or the . . . the cemetery." The word seemed wrung from him.

"Did he come over here, Helen?" Sheila noticed that Tom's voice was gruff but gentler when he spoke to her.

Helen lifted her eyes to his. "What?"

"Did you see Eddie after the party?"

She hesitated, then shook her head. "No, I came home and went up to nap."

Sheila, warmed by the fire, grew cold again. The voice that wakened her. It had been Eddie Weare. Why should Helen lie?

The others finally left. Hayden and Treye went home, and Tom wandered out to the dock where the forensic team still worked. His unofficial verdict was that Eddie had gotten drunk and wandered off the dock.

"I wish we could reach Justin and Crispin," Helen

said in a lifeless voice. "But once those two get together they drive all over town, rememberin' old times."

Sheila spoke gently. "Helen, before Crispin and Justin come, I need to tell you something. I woke up once this afternoon, and heard somebody shouting down here. It was Eddie, wasn't it?"

Helen shrank against the cushions. She started to shake her head, then buried it in her slender hands. "Yes, Eddie was here. Yes, we quarreled. And yes, he probably threw himself off the dock afterwards." She lifted a white face to Sheila. "Dear God in heaven, what am I going to do?"

"You'll have to tell Tom," Sheila replied evenly. "That will help pinpoint the time of death. I looked at the clock. You were quarreling at three-thirty."

"I can't tell Tom," Helen protested. "Not everything. I can't even tell Justin. But I've got to tell someone, Sheila. I can't stand it if I don't."

Sheila braced herself. Was she about to hear a confession of murder?

"In college—I went to Florida, you know. Justin went up to Citadel, but Daphne, Libba, Muffy, Eddie, and I all went to Florida. Well . . . Daphne and Eddie dated for two years, but he got worse and worse. His drinking, I mean. He was on a football scholarship, and by the end of the season our sophomore year he could scarcely play. They cut him from the team. Daphne dropped him about then, too. She didn't call it that—she said they'd grown apart. But Muffy said Daphne didn't want to come home at Christmas for all the deb parties with Eddie around her neck. Muffy could be cruel, but she could also be right." Helen stopped, reached for a tissue from a box she'd put on the coffee table, and dabbed her eyes. "When Daphne dropped him, Muffy thought Eddie was going crazy. He'd call her all hours, drunk and crying, asking her to make Daphne take him back.

"He got so bad, he didn't study. Finally he flunked out. But in those days, if you weren't in college, you got sent to Vietnam. He showed up in my room one Saturday with his draft notice, cryin'. Said his life was hell, he didn't care if he died, he didn't have one good memory to take away with him.

"Muffy was gone for the weekend, and I felt sorry for him. We started drinkin' together. I didn't usually drink, but he'd brought several bottles and there wasn't anybody else around. We—well, we drank too much, and I let him spend the night."

Sheila feared what was coming next, and wished she didn't have to listen. Helen, however, was a snowball rolling downhill. Nothing could stop her until she crashed.

"He left the next mornin', and I was never so disgusted with myself. Never! Until I found out six weeks later . . ."

Helen took a deep, ragged breath and clutched a small round pillow to her abdomen. In the darkness it gave her a pregnant silhouette. "You've met Mama. You can imagine what she would have said if I'd come home pregnant that summer, especially with the baby of a drunk. I couldn't face that. So I asked Muffy to help me. We, we—" She stopped and lifted both hands in the air imploringly. "You know. We *stopped* it."

She reached for her coffee cup and took a swallow of liquid that must be stone cold. Then she asked, "How do you feel about abortion, Sheila?"

Sheila spoke cautiously, but honestly. "I really don't know, Helen. I've never had to face the issue personally, so I've never taken time to think it through. I do believe it's far more complicated than people on both sides make it sound, and while I'm usually strong on people making choices, I'm also strong on the sanctity of human life. And the current numbers scare me."

Helen shook her head. Her eyes shone like a cat's in the firelight. "I didn't make a choice. I made an uninformed, terrified request. I wasn't told anything I needed to know to make an intelligent choice. They covered up all the nasty parts—I guess so I wouldn't be more scared than I already was."

Tears streamed down her cheeks and dripped onto her trembling hands. "Nobody told me how many nights I'd wake up cryin', wonderin' what my baby would have looked like, and whether it would have been a boy or a girl. Nobody said I'd find myself countin' years and watchin' children the age my child would have been. Nobody said that some days I'd be sure I did the right thing and other days, out of a clear blue sky, I'd start cryin' and wonder if I'd made a dreadful mistake. Nobody told me how much someday I'd want a baby—and that I might never be able to have one." Her voice dropped to a whisper. "At the time I thought my choice was between a quick operation and facin' Mama. Nobody told me the stakes were far higher than that. Damnation!"

She slammed her fist into the small pillow so hard she left a dent, then gave Sheila a tremulous smile. "Sorry. But you see, I'm close to this all the time. I work with middle-schoolers in a dreadful neighborhood. A lot of those children sleep around. Not because they want to, I think, but because they honestly don't know they can say no. Some of them get pregnant, and most of them have already made at least one poor choice—dating the wrong boy, being in a vulnerable place alone, seeking love through sex, believing in a miracle to keep them from getting pregnant instead of using protection. How equipped are they to make a wise choice about abortion—especially without all the facts? But when I suggest that they need more facts, I get lumped with people who yell a lot about being pro-life, then vote down any program to alleviate the squalor and pain in those kids' lives. Some days I just want to *scream*!"

She reached for another tissue, blew her nose, and shuddered. "End of soapbox oration. Sorry I got carried away. I'm going to be a terrible politician's wife."

Sheila smiled. "At least you know what a wise

politican has to know: that both sides have only half the truth."

She liked Helen even more now that she understood her pain. However, hers was a secret that could certainly ruin her reputation—and blow Justin's chances for election out of the water.

"Eddie never knew?" Sheila hazarded, remembering his furious words earlier.

"Nobody knew, except Muffy. And I never meant to tell Eddie. But this afternoon . . ." She stopped.

Now that Helen had started, she needed to tell the whole story, but she obviously did not know how to begin. Experience had taught Sheila that silence often encouraged people to pour out their hearts. She waited.

Helen spoke into the silence. "Muffy told Eddie the other night I'd never forgotten him. He took it the wrong way."

Probably, Sheila thought uncharitably, *exactly the way Muffy meant him to take it.*

"So this afternoon he wandered over here from Hayden's. He tried . . ." At the memory, Helen shuddered again. "When I pushed him away, he got furious. Finally, without meaning to, I flung the whole story at him, and told him I'd already done more for him than he ever deserved." She pressed her fingers to her flaming cheeks. "How could I have said such a thing?"

Sheila wasn't concerned with what Helen had said. She was worried about what Helen might have done. Only Eddie and Muffy had known Helen's secret. And now, Eddie and Muffy were dead.

They sat in silence while the fire burned low and darkness gathered. Helen went to the door when Tom came to say they were finished on the dock and leaving. Sheila added another log to the fire. Neither of the women felt like turning on a light.

The doorbell rang and Libba put her head in, hesitantly. "Anybody home?"

There was enough light to see that her hair was wind-blown and her suit a bit rumpled. Libba looked—as usual—tired and a bit anxious, and her voice was more breathless than usual. "Why are you all sittin' in the dark? Are you all right?"

"Eddie drowned at the end of our dock, Libba." Helen's voice was dreary. "Sometime after he left Hayden's."

"Eddie?" Libba sank into the nearest chair. "Had he been drinkin'?"

Helen nodded. "He must have started before the funeral. When I saw him later, he was scarcely coherent."

"I saw him at Hayden's," Libba said thoughtfully, "but I didn't have time to talk. Poor dear! But maybe it's for the best. What kind of life would he have had?" After a moment, she added, "Who found him?"

"Sheila and Treye." Before they could tell her more, however, they heard a car door slam. A minute later Crispin limped in.

He flicked on a light and echoed Libba. "Has the power been cut off? Why are you all sitting in the dark?"

Justin followed him in and, without looking into the living room, went to the hall closet to hang up his suit coat. He then gave the kitchen a puzzled glance. "I take it that dinner is our old family favorite, take-out food? I know you're on vacation, honey, but Sheila's gonna think you don't know how to cook. What happened to that turkey you were gonna smoke?"

When Helen didn't immediately answer, the men noticed for the first time how quiet the women were. When Helen lifted her eyes to her husband's, he saw her face. "Honey?" He went over and touched the mascara smudge beneath one eye. "What's the matter?"

Helen pointed toward the window; tears streamed down her cheeks. Libba reached into the box and handed her another tissue. She blew her nose and added it to the crumpled pile beside her. Then she said, in a choked voice, "It's Eddie, Justin. He fell off our dock and drowned. Right here!" She sniffed and rubbed her cheeks as if they were cold. "Tom came."

Justin and Crispin sank into chairs. Sheila told them what had happened.

"I can't understand it," Justin said, when she had finished. "One death right after another. What's goin' on?"

Crispin gave him a considering look. "Think somebody doesn't want you elected?"

"Nah, that's not it. But I sure won't have a chicken's chance in a foxhole of *gettin'* elected unless Tom can clear all this up."

Sheila's eyes met Crispin's. He jerked his head toward the kitchen. She rose, picked up her cup and Helen's, and followed him.

In the kitchen, Crispin gathered her into his arms and kissed her thoroughly. "You looked like you could use that. New clothes?"

"Helen's. Mine got wet when I jumped in after Eddie."

"You went swimming again? Woman, it's December. Only New Yorkers swim in Florida in December!" He pulled her toward him again and held her close. "You must be frozen."

"Half, anyway," she agreed. "That's the last swim—"

The phone rang. Crispin answered. "I don't know, Tom," he said after a moment. "Ask Sheila."

Tom Goren's bass rasped through the wires. He sounded greatly disturbed. "Sheila, did I notice some roses on Helen's coffee table this afternoon?"

"Yes, Tom. Rob Wilmer brought them last evening." She managed to say Wilmer's name without a single tremor.

"They've just brought me the contents of Eddie's pockets. In with his change and keys, he had one yellow rosebud. I've called Hayden, and he doesn't have any yellow roses at his house. Tell Helen—" He stopped and cleared his throat. "Tell Justin and Helen that nobody's to go anywhere until I get there."

In the end, Helen confessed. Admitted that Eddie had come by. Admitted that they had quarreled. She skimmed over the meat of the quarrel, and Sheila saw no reason to enlarge her story.

Tom's face was puce and his forehead beaded with sweat. "Helen, if there's anything else you aren't tellin' me ..."

Brown hair brushed her cheeks as she shook her head. Her amber eyes were wide and frightened. "I didn't kill him, Tom. I didn't push him in the water. I didn't even go with him out to the dock. He left, and I went upstairs to take a nap."

"Did you hear her come up, Sheila? You say you were napping."

"Don't make it sound like a crime, Tom. Naps are very beneficial. They—" Sheila fell silent. His face was getting too red to be healthy. "Yes, I heard him shouting, and yes, I heard Helen come upstairs after the door slammed downstairs."

"Mind telling me why you didn't tell me any of this before?"

"I wasn't really awake, so I wasn't sure if I heard it or dreamed it."

"You could have dreamed it?"

"Tom," Crispin clasped his hands between his knees, "you saw Eddie at the party Tuesday night. He had a thing for Daphne, left over from college. If Helen told him that the roses were for Daphne—"

"I did." She nodded. "He said they were pretty, and I said Rob brought them in Daphne's memory. I didn't see him take one, though." She fingered the incriminating empty stem.

Justin caught on to what Crispin was suggesting. "But he did. So maybe after takin' one of Daphne's roses, he went for a walk on Daphne's dock—to think about her. He was unsteady on his feet, to say the least. So he fell in."

"He couldn't swim," Sheila contributed. They all looked at her, startled. She was startled, too. She was no more certain than Tom Goren that Helen hadn't walked Eddie out to the dock, pushed him in, then returned to slam the door and run upstairs to weep. So why was she helping this team effort? Nevertheless, she persisted. "Tuesday night, Eddie told me when he lived here, he always hated the water, because he couldn't swim."

Justin nodded happily. "That's right. He couldn't! He—"

They heard cars in the yard. Several cars. Libba rose and went to a window. "It's reporters. Even a television mobile unit."

"I'm not ready to make a statement," Tom growled.

"I . . ." Justin made a move to get up, but he looked like a man heading to a firing squad.

Sheila caught Crispin's eye. *Do something,* he seemed to plead.

"Introduce me, Tom, and let me talk to them," she offered impulsively. "After all, I found the body."

She went outside and shamelessly used Tyler's name. His prestige was still strong enough to make a good story. She described finding the body. She made it clear that Helen was asleep and Justin at his office at the time. She praised the beauty of the city and the graciousness of the people she'd met. She finally sent them away with enough to chew on for a day or two.

But she was grim as she watched Tom Goren drive out after them. He and she both knew that if he and Justin hadn't played football together at Lee, if he hadn't gone steady with Helen in high school, Helen would be on her way downtown right now for serious questioning.

Saturday,
December 30

Of Sheila's days in Jacksonville, Saturday started out to be the most peaceful.

She went for a walk without finding a single dead body.

She did not fall in the river.

No one shot at her.

And she spent most of the day without having to endure either Teddy's glowers or Jack's sulks.

She returned from her walk to find the breakfast table set in the pretty dining room. "Adults only," Helen told her with a valiant attempt at a normal smile. "Jack took his boat out early, and Teddy's gone to a friend's."

At the beginning of the meal, the phone rang constantly with friends and campaign supporters wanting a personal account of Eddie's drowning. Finally Justin put on the answering machine and came back to consume three eggs with bacon, melon, and two pieces of toast.

Sheila was glad there was little conversation. She was trying to think of anybody she could interview about the recent deaths. Eddie's drowning had put a sizable hole in her suspect list.

While Helen started another pot of coffee, Justin called a Cadillac dealer he knew. "Sorry, Sheila," he reported afterwards. "They're off until Tuesday. I forgot about New Year's."

So had she. "We'll just get the window fixed in Atlanta. Thanks."

In a few minutes, Helen fetched the fresh coffee with the announcement, "Hayden's going to tinker again. I saw him trudging down the dock carrying his red toolbox."

Justin gave a brotherly grunt. "He doesn't like taking that boat out half as much as he likes taking her apart. Sometimes I think he became a plastic surgeon so he could work with his hands."

Helen frowned. "I just hope he gets everything back together in time to leave." She added, for Sheila's benefit, "We'll leave about three for the Gator Bowl."

"Tonight? By boat?" Sheila was confused.

"It's a tradition," Justin told her. "We dock at Metropolitan Park, next door to the Gator Bowl. Some people have been there all week, on boats or in their RVs. The game is just one part of a weekend-long party. After the game, there'll be fireworks and more partyin'. We'll spend tonight on the boat and come home tomorrow afternoon."

Sheila turned to Crispin quizzically. "Can you get on and off a boat?"

He gave her a lazy smile and tapped his cast with his knuckle. "We'll find out, won't we?"

The only jarring incident came a few minutes later when the kitchen door slammed: In stormed a very angry Treye.

"Uncle Justin, what's goin' on with Jack? He's had that boat the whole blessed week. He's even been takin' it out at night! And somebody's messed up Daddy's engine, too. It won't start. You tell Jack we're supposed to *share* that boat, dammit!"

Justin waved his nephew toward a vacant chair, then signaled for Helen to bring him a cup. "I'd noticed, actually. We've scarcely seen him all week. Any idea what he's up to?"

Treye's eyes slid to Crispin's and back. "I haven't talked to him since Christmas. But if you see him, tell him I want that boat tonight and I want it tomorrow. He and

Sparrow can go with you folks and Daddy—if Daddy gets his up and runnin'." Waving away Helen's proffered coffee, he stomped off.

Justin chuckled. "And you worried, Helen, that our son wouldn't have a brother to grow up with? Those two fight more than Hayden and I ever did."

Helen watched Treye cross the lawn to his own house, and sighed. "Yes, but Treye is right to be worried. Jack is up to somethin', honey, and I'm worried sick."

Later that morning, Helen left to shop for groceries and Justin to stock up on drinks for the weekend. Both turned down offers of assistance, so Crispin and Sheila wandered out to the dock to encourage Hayden.

"What's the matter with the boat?" Sheila asked him.

Up to his elbow in grease, Hayden spoke without lifting his head. "Somebody messed with the engine. I'll get it right this mornin' if I don't get too many interruptions."

"We know when we aren't wanted," Crispin admonished him.

"What do gardeners know about boat engines?" Hayden reached for a wrench. "Just a little adjustment here—" He turned something and looked over his shoulder. "Now if you have experience layin' ghosts, Mrs. Travis, I could use your help. I think we've got one next door. I keep findin' things out of place, but nothin' missin'. Know anything about that?"

Did he seriously think he had a ghost? Or did he think she'd been snooping when he wasn't there? Suspecting Twinkie was still hunting her necklace, Sheila responded lightly, "Don't know a thing about ghosts, Doctor. Sorry."

"Know anything about boat engines?"

"No, I'm a sailor. Sorry again."

"Oh." He returned to his repairs without another word.

Crispin took her arm. "Come on, Sheila. Leave the gnome alone. We can work on the jigsaw."

She was glad to leave the dock. She kept looking into the water, expecting to see Eddie's corpse. However, she wasn't particularly anxious to work a jigsaw, either.

The puzzle sat on a game table near the Florida room windows. Crispin had explained when they'd arrived on Tuesday that the family always started one Christmas Day and kept at it until it was completed.

"That map of Scotland I gave you took until March, didn't it?" Crispin had teased Helen later.

"This one may take 'til June," Helen replied. "Justin bought it in an art museum store, and it's a killer." Sheila had glanced at the picture—Russian knights on horseback watching serfs dig out buried treasure beneath a night sky alive with fireworks. The puzzle, she deduced, could well be the basis for Laura Grace's current 'obsession with pirates.

Every day, Crispin had put in a few pieces, but Sheila had not been even tempted. She hadn't done a jigsaw since she was a child, and considered them a waste of time. This morning, she began looking for pieces merely to pass time with Crispin.

Gradually, a gold horse with mane and tail of flowing golden curliques engrossed her. So many pieces that looked like gold horse weren't!

They worked steadily and quietly. The house was unusually peaceful.

Then they heard a door slam. Jack strolled toward the kitchen without a word.

"Hey!" Crispin called.

Jack came to the Florida room door, brows raised.

Crispin's tone was light, but his eyes were stern, as befitted one who had read stories to the young man when he wore blue-footed pajamas. "Your folks would like to see you occasionally, and know where you're staying. And your cousin wants some time on the boat."

Jack shrugged. "I'll bring it back by tomorrow." He loped to the kitchen and called back, "What have you people been eatin'? There's not a single decent leftover!"

With that dismal pronouncement, he left. Outside, Sheila and Crispin heard a car door slam, and voices.

Jack returned in Justin's grip, protesting. "Aw, Dad, I've got some stuff I really need to do!"

His father steered him firmly toward the kitchen. "You've had that boat long enough, son. It's your cousin's turn. And Charho called. She needs you to come over and do a few jobs around her place. It's time you made yourself useful, for a change. Now call Treye and tell him the *Jack Three* is his for the next two days."

Jack protested, Justin insisted, and eventually, with a smoldering scowl, Jack complied. Justin hadn't finished putting away whatever he'd carried in with him before they heard the front door slam again and the Jeep roar away.

Sheila wailed. "How are you finding so many more pieces than I am?" Crispin had built almost the entire corner of serfs digging out the treasure chest, while her horse still lacked two legs, a rump, and most of its tail.

"Organization, milady. I found the pieces with my colors on them before I started. The whole thing would be easier if we sorted all the pieces into piles by color."

"That's cheatin'!" Justin called from the kitchen.

Sheila was already busily amassing a pile of pieces with gold on them. "Let's do it," she whispered. "We can mix back up all the ones we don't use. Like Eddie said, you're the smartest man in the world."

She separated out two pieces that were more mustard than gold. In a few minutes she had begun piles not only of gold and mustard, but lemon and chartreuse, as well. She looked at them and sighed. "I wish this week could be sorted like this. The pieces would all fit, if we could just get them in order."

A movement on the water drew their eyes. Twinkie L'Arken's sailboat was gliding up to Hayden's dock. He came on deck and greeted her. She tied up and climbed aboard the cruiser.

Crispin swiped the curl off his forehead, his eyes on the pair on the dock. "That piece, for instance? You could try a hundred years and never get it to fit."

"You don't think they'll get back together and live happily ever after?"

Justin joined them in time to overhear. He shook his head. "They didn't live happily ever before. And look—"

With a wave of his hand, Hayden was ordering Twinkie off his boat. Face flushed with anger, she climbed back aboard her own. She jerked the line off the mooring cleat.

"Too bad it's not a horse, so she could ride off in a cloud of dust," Sheila said with regret. Instead, Twinkie hoisted sail and headed downriver.

Almost at once, Einstein whined at the door. Sheila stretched and stood. "You finish this blasted horse, Justin. All these curliques are beginning to look alike. I think I'll take Einstein for a waddle. But don't finish the whole puzzle while I'm gone!"

Crispin gave her a rueful smile. "Wish I could go with you. I haven't been much company for you on this trip."

She bent and kissed his curls. "I've seen far more of you—" She stopped. She'd been about to say "—than I ever saw of Tyler." She needed to get out of that habit of constant comparison, even if Crispin invariably won.

The men were both still waiting for her to finish the sentence.

She grinned. "—than Helen's seen of Justin. And you know I like to walk alone. Come on, Einstein." She bent to fasten his leash.

She hadn't been smart. She knew that half a mile from home, as soon as she heard a car approach from behind and slow down.

Rob Wilmer hung up the phone in his silver BMW convertible and smiled over the door. "So, Mrs. Travis, they said at the house you were out walking the dog. You've got a nice day for it."

Her blood had turned to ice water. Not a soul was in

sight. She nodded warily. "Yes, the weather's been nice for a couple of days now."

"And will you be going with Justin to the Gator Bowl?" His eyes were narrowed, but perhaps the sun was in them.

When she didn't reply, he smiled. "Of course you will. I already asked. I'll see you tonight, in the sky box." With a wave, he drove off, leaving her trembling and a bit sick.

He hadn't said a single unpleasant word, so why did she feel so threatened? "What was that all about?" she asked Einstein.

His brilliance didn't extend to understanding humans.

On the walk home, Sheila realized she had never talked to Crispin about Rob and Thursday night. The day before had been taken up with the funeral and Eddie's death. Today, she had frankly put it out of her mind—until now. Maybe it wasn't the kind of thing she wanted to talk about, anyway.

She got home to find the family down by the dock, in an uproar. Both Jack and Teddy had returned, and Teddy was throwing a fit. "You promised! You promised!" she shrilled.

"I promised you could pull it behind Jack's boat," her father replied—obviously not for the first time, "but Treye needs the *Jack Three* this weekend."

"Yeah," Jack snarled. "Sparrow and I've got to *drive* down later."

"And Uncle Hayden doesn't want to be bothered with a johnboat, honey," Helen added. "Wouldn't you rather spend the night at Charho's like we planned? You don't like football."

"I do! I do!" Teddy jumped up and down. "I *love* football!"

"That's a switch," Jack said sourly. "You always hated it before."

"Well, I don't hate it now. I want to go to the game!"

Hayden, who had been stowing food below, came on

deck. "It's no trouble to tow the thing. I just don't know what she plans to do with it."

"You can't take it out without an adult," Justin reminded Teddy. "There'll be too many other boats around."

"I can sit in it and watch the fireworks," Teddy insisted. "And you promised."

Hayden moved down the dock and untied the johnboat. "Can't start breakin' promises until *after* you get elected, Justin."

Justin gave in, with reluctance. "Teddy, do you absolutely promise not to untie this boat without an adult?"

"I promise." Her look of triumph went straight to Sheila.

The ride to town on the river was lovely, even if Teddy did claim the seat next to Crispin. Sheila enjoyed getting a view of the city from the water. She was amused to watch Libba helping Hayden with the boat. Of course, Libba seemed to be a helper by nature, but Sheila remembered how helpful she had been both at the funeral home Thursday evening and at Hayden's after the service. She also remembered one of Aunt Mary's maxims: "If you want to marry a widower, wear your best hat to his wife's funeral." In trim navy slacks and a bright sweater, Libba looked like she might be following that advice!

Or had she actually made a widower out of him? That was a new thought. Sheila replayed the path of that fatal drink once more. No, Libba had held the drink the briefest time of all, and she—Sheila—had watched her the whole time.

They passed under a third large bridge, and Crispin called, "We are now heading due east. Remember?" Sure enough, the river looked about half a mile wide here. Suddenly Sheila caught a whiff of something delicious. "What's that glorious smell like roast coffee?" she called to Helen.

Helen laughed. "Roast coffee. The Maxwell House plant is right over there. And here's Metropolitan Park."

Sheila quickly caught the mood of celebration sweeping down the rows of food tents, bands, and boats. Her heart lightened. This could be fun!

Gator Bowl Night,
December 30

That evening, Sheila peered down a mountainside of bleachers at two football teams savagely butting heads on a brightly lit field. Where, she wondered, did the people of Jacksonville get their stamina? They had partied all day and were now yelling themselves hoarse.

To Sheila, the players looked like toy action figures from this height. Why on earth should sky boxes cost more than seats nearer the action?

She felt grumpy, and attributed it to so little sleep all week.

She hated to admit it could be football.

She hadn't confessed to anyone that this was her first live football game since she was in college. When she had agreed to come, she'd persuaded herself that she would have no more trouble pretending to like football than an opera novice would have pretending to enjoy *Aida*.

For those new to opera, however, something interesting is usually going on onstage. And opera aficionados are, by and large, reserved in their enthusiasm. Football looked like a series of reruns: two lines of men rushing at one another, falling down in clumps, getting up as whistles blew, then lining up to begin again. And the fans—

"Hey, Sheila! This is the life, right?" Hayden raised his beer in a toast. His face was flushed and beaded with sweat. Nobody would guess that he had buried his wife two days before, unless they asked someone why he was partying with such deadly earnestness.

She smiled and lifted her cup of coffee, wishing she could do something to ease the pain in his eyes.

He and the rest of the men—Crispin, Justin, and a series of wandering friends—divided their attention between the field and a television showing close-ups of the game. Why couldn't they have just enjoyed the game at home?

Teddy certainly could have. The child had spent most of the time popping in and out of the box with friends, asking, "How much longer 'til halftime?"

Sheila could share that sentiment.

Helen, Libba, and visiting women friends seemed delighted to be perched high above a football field, ignored by the men. They even seemed genuinely interested in the outcome of the game. Helen kept binoculars trained on every play. She was rooting for a different team than her big blond husband, and they kept up an affectionate rivalry with each new score.

Beyond Helen, Libba squinted slightly as she leaned forward in her seat, wholly engrossed in cheering on her team to make up three points. She hadn't unclasped her fist for the entire quarter.

Now the players stood idle. Sheila looked from her watch to the large lit board at the end of the field. The game had started well over an hour ago, yet the clock said they still had four minutes left to play in the second quarter. "Why aren't they playing?" she asked Helen. "Is someone hurt?"

Helen pointed to a pudgy man in white standing on the twenty yard line with his arms folded. "Time out for TV commercials." She got up and passed around a sandwich tray.

Sheila bit into crabmeat salad and silently fumed. She was giving up hunks of her life for television commercials? Her hosts, who had paid a small fortune for this box, found nothing strange about being forced to wait while some sponsor advertised beer? Why would intelligent people permit themselves to be so exploited?

In a perfect world, she mused, sponsors would give away tickets to produce a crowd, or the game would run uninterrupted and commercials be inserted into a televised version.

The teams faced off again. Not remembering which team was which—and frankly, not caring—Sheila scanned the crowd. Many in the bleachers were bundled into coats, sleeping bags, and quilts. At noon the temperature had climbed to seventy, but since sunset it had plunged. Thirty-five degrees was predicted for tonight. Thank goodness the sky box was warm. She had put on a black wool pantsuit, but had long since removed the jacket. A cotton blouse was enough. She suspected these enthusiastic fans would have kept the box warm enough even if it weren't so well heated!

She also appreciated something else. Rob Wilmer had never showed up.

Neither had Jack. Almost as if reading Sheila's mind, Helen put down her binoculars and asked, "Libba, tell me again about Jack. Sparrow said he wasn't home?"

"He didn't answer the door," Libba repeated for the fourth or fifth time. "Sparrow rang and rang, but he never answered. She decided to stay at home and keep tryin' to get him."

Helen gnawed her lip. "With Treye not here either, I'm afraid—"

"Will you two stop worryin'?" Justin called from across the box. "Those boys are big enough to take care of themselves."

Sheila leaned forward and pretended to be avidly interested in whether the ball made it ten yards or not. She actually had no idea who was carrying the ball. Anybody who could see a football at that distance was either an eagle or a liar.

She was worried about Jack, too. She couldn't help remembering his face the night before, and Treye's at the breakfast table. Something was going on between those two, and she didn't share Justin's confidence that they could handle it.

Without warning, the players suddenly straggled off the field. Crispin laid a hand on her shoulder. "Halftime, hon. Having fun?"

She stood and stretched. "I could use a cup of coffee."

Helen also stood. "Swap places for a while, Crispin. I want to sit with Justin so I can brag."

"Tacky!" Libba chided her, rising to join the rush to the food. "Stay right here, Sheila. I'll bring you both some coffee. Black, right?" She hurried off.

Crispin limped around to Helen's vacated seat and pointed at the sky. "Look!"

A small plane droned over the Bowl, disgorging three sky divers with flares on their heels. They drifted into the stadium and landed precisely on the field. When they departed, a brunette queen processed to the center of the field with her court. "She looks like Daphne," Hayden said sadly as bands marched onto the field in a skirl of brass and a swirl of colorful flags to join her.

Sheila sipped fresh coffee and held Crispin's hand. His leg pressed against hers. By the time the teams returned to the field, she was enjoying the Gator Bowl.

In an Ortega bedroom, a man twisted and turned, trying to loose his bonds. What a fool he'd been—in several ways!

But there was another who was an even greater fool. Dammit, he had to get out of here, or—

Again he jerked against the bonds. But it was futile. They'd been tied by an expert.

After the game, the *Daphne Delight* was crammed. Sheila pressed against Crispin in one corner of the cabin, trying not to get stepped on by people waving food and drink. Helen and her fellow fans were jubilant. Justin and *his* fellow fans were disgusted. Happy or not, all were loud.

"Think we'd freeze if we went on deck?" Crispin murmured into her hair.

"I'll risk it if you will." Nevertheless, she fetched a raincoat and scarf to supplement her light wool blazer.

They climbed the ladder and headed for the stern, facing the river. Standing with Crispin's arm around her, Sheila didn't mind the stiff December breeze. Treye must have arrived during the party, for the *Jack Three* was moored alongside. A solitary figure moved inside the small unlit cabin.

"Ahoy there!" Crispin shouted.

In the darkness, the figure turned away.

Sheila saw, to her surprise, that beyond the *Jack Three*, Twinkie's sailboat floated, brightly lit and crowded. Twinkie, stylish in a tweed pantsuit, weaved on deck with the grace of a drunk but practiced sailor.

Teddy pranced up, eyes shining. "Time for fireworks, Crispin!" she cried. As adults began to throng up from below, she crowded in on his other side—ignoring her little *Ark* bobbing astern.

Reflected on the water, the fireworks seemed doubly brilliant. Sheila pointed to the lights of several boats moving back and forth on the river. "Are they safe with the fireworks?"

She had asked Crispin, but Little Bigmouth replied. "Of *course*. That's the Coast Guard. *They* know what they're doing."

"So now you know," Crispin whispered into Sheila's ear. Chills ran up her spine that had nothing to do with the breeze. "Thanks for coming," he murmured under cover of the explosions.

"I've loved it," she replied softly, and meant it.

"Yuck," Teddy muttered.

The other adults watched for a few minutes, then began to drift back below deck for refills and a further rehash of the game. Soon only Crispin, Sheila, and Teddy remained on deck.

"Crispin," Justin called up the ladder from below. "Stop smoochin' your woman long enough to come pay what you owe my wife."

"Owe her?" Crispin yelled back. "You owe us both!" He stood. "How about a cup of coffee, Sheila?"

"Don't try to bring it up with your bum leg," she told him. "I'll come get some in a few minutes." As chilly as it was topside, she preferred the wind to the noisy crush below.

Thus it was that Sheila and Teddy were sitting alone beside the starboard railing when three young men glided up in a small, sleek speedboat, tied up to the far side of the *Jack Three*, and climbed aboard. Fraternity buddies, come to watch the fireworks, Sheila supposed. She paid them little mind. She was enjoying the fireworks as much as her young companion.

When the wind freshened, however, she bent to address the uneven part in Teddy's hair. "Why don't we go below with the others, and watch through the portholes?"

"You can't see anything from there!" the little girl replied disdainfully. "Look! A green one!" Sure enough, the white chrysanthemum spreading itself against the black sky fell like a shower of emeralds onto the river.

After an especially loud explosion, Sheila looked upward in anticipation of the finale. Only a smattering of pink and blue lit the sky and fizzled down. "Sounded better than it was. I guess—"

She stopped, astonished. Teddy had given a shout. Now she was throwing one leg over the rail.

"They've got Jack!" Teddy toppled into the *Ark*.

Sheila saw the speedboat that had been moored by the *Jack Three* backing steadily away.

"Wait!" she called to Teddy. "Let me get your dad!"

"No time!" Teddy was already reaching toward her engine. "They'll *kill* him!"

Sheila would later wonder what propelled her over the rail.

"Teddy's guardian angel," Helen would assure her with grateful eyes.

"Common sense," Martha would insist. "You couldn't let that child go off alone."

Crispin was probably right. "Aunt Mary," he told her. "It's in your genes."

Whatever, Sheila landed in the flat metal bottom of the johnboat just as Teddy gunned the engine. The entire exchange had taken less than a minute. Not one soul among the L'Arkens' guests noticed their unexpected embarkation.

The other boat was now a white wake and stern light in the darkness.

The wind was pushing in a bank of storm clouds that hovered just beyond the other shore, about half a mile away. Sheila clutched her jacket around her and wondered how to convince Teddy she couldn't and shouldn't take a small boat onto the river with a storm brewing. Too late. Teddy had already cast off and was expertly backing the *Ark* away from its larger host.

"Keep your eye on their light!" Teddy shouted above the engine's roar. "I dropped my glasses in the river."

Oh, great, Sheila thought as she strained to distinguish that particular bobbing white light among the lights of the Coast Guard cutters. *Not only is the river wide and my boat small, but my captain is half blind.* "Dear Lord, be good to us," she muttered fervently between chattering teeth.

Over her shoulder, she called, "Their boat is far more powerful than this. Let's alert the Coast Guard." She pointed to the lights of the nearest cutter.

Instead, however, Teddy revved her engine. The tiny boat slapped water as it sped across the rolling river in pursuit of the speedboat.

"Maybe they're just Jack's friends!" Sheila yelled. How could she persuade this child to turn around?

"They shot him!" Teddy's next words blew away in the wind. The rest were muffled by the engine's roar.

". . . he ran . . . jumped in their boat . . . they caught him!
Come on, *Ark*!" She pounded her hull encouragingly.

Sheila doubted that Teddy saw what she thought she
saw. Why would anyone shoot Jack? Why shoot *anybody* on
a boat in a party crowd when they could shoot him more
simply—and less publicly—another time?

*Because fireworks mask the sound of a shot and they knew
he'd be alone,* replied a voice in her head. *If Teddy hadn't seen
him, he might not have been found until morning. And if they'd
left the gun, we might all have thought he'd committed suicide.*
The way Jack had been acting all week, even his parents
might have believed it.

Once he'd reached the intruders' boat and Teddy had
shouted, though, they couldn't dump him in the water.
Not there. Not yet.

Sheila still didn't really believe it. Jack and his friends
had probably been playing, and Teddy's fertile imagination had filled in the rest. However, if the men *had* shot
Jack—and if he *was* still alive—what were she and Teddy
supposed to do even if they did catch up with them?

She resolutely pushed down that thought. This johnboat could never keep up with a speedboat.

On the other hand, Teddy would have to be outrun
before she would turn back. The other boat headed upriver, only to be waved away by a Coast Guard cutter. Of
course! Nobody would be permitted to travel through the
hail of fireworks debris.

Sheila blew on her hands, wishing she had brought
gloves. Just then, the white stern light ahead was joined
by two more lights. The speedboat had turned. Boat lights
are designed to give more than illumination. Red means
port, green means starboard.

"Hard to port!" she called to Teddy. The johnboat
turned, too, toward the lights of a fourth downtown bridge.

Down the slick black breast of the St. Johns the two
boats churned, leaving two silver wakes behind. Overhead,
the moon slipped in and out of clouds. If the speedboat
would only roar ahead and disappear into darkness, Sheila

could insist that Teddy turn and go for help. Instead, the lead boat kept a leisurely pace—like a family going home early from the celebration to avoid the rush. For the first time, Sheila admitted that Teddy could be right. For a speedboat, it was unusually reluctant to call attention to itself.

Hopefully, it also had no notion it was being followed. She had to admire Teddy for keeping carefully astern and closer to shore, as if merely following a parallel route. After they passed beneath the bridge, the river curved sharply north toward a fifth bridge. The river had widened again. A small island lay directly beneath the bridge. Beyond that, there was only darkness.

"Let's go back," Sheila called. "We'll never catch them now."

Teddy shook her head. As they passed under the bridge, there was enough light to see her jutting lower lip.

For what seemed hours—and was probably closer to twenty minutes—the little boat bucked the water. Sheila eyed the clouds warily. How long before the storm broke? Already the river was lapped with whitecaps and running hard.

She also wondered how much gas the *Ark* had. Enough to get home? Enough even to land near a phone?

Again the light ahead became three. Red again. She called over her shoulder to Teddy. "They're turning hard to port!"

"Up the Trout River," Teddy called back, jubilant. She shoved the tiller so hard a wave filled Sheila's lap.

She shivered, fruitlessly trying to brush off the water before it soaked through her pants. "Never," she vowed through clenched teeth, "will I ever enter a motorboat again."

She was relieved that Teddy at least knew where they were. The river had made a *Y* with roughly equal arms, and Sheila could not have distinguished which was the St. Johns.

"Fall back a bit," Sheila called as the lead boat

slowed. "Don't try to catch them. Let's see where they go."

Teddy nodded willingly. Maybe she, too, had begun to wonder what they would do with three strong men if they caught them.

Another bridge loomed overhead. As they passed under, Sheila could see in the distance the silhouette of a second, larger bridge. From the way it was lit, it must be I-95 heading north. Between the two bridges, the lead boat showed its green light and headed toward what seemed a deserted shore. "Starboard," Sheila called more softly. Teddy turned after them.

They heard the first boat cut back its throttle. Teddy did the same. The moon glided out to bathe the water with its pale, faint light; from the boat, a large bulky object toppled into the water.

"Jack!"

Teddy's scream rang out across the water.

The other boat turned, quivered. A large white cloud drifted into the moon's path, flooding the river with sudden brightness. Sheila could clearly see three shapes leaning intently in their direction. A flash of yellow erupted just behind the forward light.

"Duck!" Sheila screamed as a spurt of water rose to port. "They're firing at us!" She fell forward into the bottom of the boat.

Instead of following suit, Teddy shoved the tiller sharply to port, then back to starboard. "Shoot them back!" she yelled. "I'll get us close enough. Shoot them now!"

"Teddy!" Sheila crouched beneath the bowline and scrabbled to climb over the seat, trying to reach the child without exposing more of herself than necessary. Teddy had created a rapidly moving target approaching, rather than retreating from, the enemy. "I don't have a gun!"

The little boat wavered. Another spurt of water shot starboard as the distance between the two boats closed.

"You have to have a gun!" Teddy screamed hysteri-

cally. "Detectives *always* carry guns!" Their boat plowed
steadily ahead.

As if it could bear to watch no longer, the moon slid
behind a towering thunderhead. The river was cloaked in
blackness.

Sheila flung herself astern. Pushing Teddy into the johnboat's flat bottom, she seized the tiller and fumbled to cut
off the running lights. When the boat was in total darkness, she shoved the tiller hard alee. As soon as they
turned and churned away from where they had been, she
ordered curtly, "Cut that motor!"

For a wonder, Teddy obeyed without question.

They drifted silently, invisible as long as the moon
stayed withdrawn—unless the other boat had spotlights.
Sheila's heart sank.

"Please, God," Sheila whispered. Teddy was shaking
so hard, she rocked the little boat.

Masculine voices floated across the water. An engine
roared. Then, as Teddy put out her hand for their own ig-
nition, the first boat sped downriver and disappeared.

Sheila drew deep, gasping breaths of relief. Pressing
one hand to her mouth, she felt as limp as if she had been
thrown over a clothesline and beaten with a baseball bat.

Beside her, Teddy sobbed into the silence. The moon
slid back out for a better look, and Sheila saw great tears
rolling down the child's freckled cheeks. Reproach filled
the myopic blue eyes.

"You were s'posed to have a gun." She sniffed and
wiped her nose with the back of one hand. "Why didn't
you have a gun?"

"I don't own a gun." Sheila brushed tears from her
own cheeks. For a minute or two they wept together in
the night.

She was afraid to restart the engine, but they were
drifting downstream at an alarming rate. The other boat
might have tried her own trick and be waiting nearby to

hear them start up. They'd have to risk it. Another few
minutes and they could crash into the bridge supports.

"Start the engine," she said more briskly than she felt,
moving aside to give Teddy the tiller. "Let's go see what
they threw overboard." She was afraid she knew.

Again, the moon was helpful. It stayed in a large patch of
clear sky while Teddy trolled carefully through the water.
Kneeling in the hull, Sheila peered at the heaving water.

She didn't know which she dreaded more: that they
would never find Jack, or that they'd find him dead. If
Teddy was right (and Sheila was reluctantly beginning to
accept that possibility), he had been shot at close range. If
he'd also been thrown overboard, he'd been in the water
at least ten minutes.

"There he is!" Even with blurred vision, Teddy saw
him first, a lump darker than the water. She skillfully maneuvered in beside him.

"Jack!" Teddy cried, then slapped her mouth with
one hand and peered in terror around them. "Jack," she
called again, softly. "We came to get you."

The figure in the water moaned. They could see he
was keeping himself afloat with one arm.

Teddy jerked her head toward Sheila. "Get him in."

That was easier said than done. The young man's
clothing was sodden, and he was so dazed that he was no
help at all. With a sigh, Sheila accepted the inevitable.

Crouching in the bow, she stripped to her underwear
and, without permitting herself time to think about what
was coming next, plunged off the boat. The cold took her
breath away, but, resolutely treading water, she clutched
the back of Jack's coat and called, "Come about!"

As the child and the woman struggled to get him over
the rail, the storm finally broke. Driving rain pelted from
above. It was even colder than the river beneath. In her
arms, Jack groaned.

The next few minutes were a panicked blur. Sheila
pushed from behind while Teddy tugged from above. The

boat wobbled under the uneven weight, and once a strong current nearly dragged Jack away. Sheila clung to the side of the boat with one arm and pushed with the other, certain that one or the other would soon be jerked from its socket. Her teeth beat a tap dance rhythm. Her shoulders and calves cramped with cold.

At last, with one final burst of strength, Teddy hauled her limp brother aboard.

Sheila pulled herself into the boat while Teddy spread Sheila's raincoat over Jack's body to shelter him from the rain. He had fainted, which was just as well.

"He's breathin'," Teddy said urgently, "but I don't know how bad he's hurt."

"You head back." Sheila spoke through chattering teeth. "I'll see what I can find out." Rain snaked down her nearly naked body as she gently probed the motionless young man. "He was hit in the shoulder," she finally informed the worried little skipper. "With any luck, the cold water stopped his bleeding, but he'll need help soon."

With her teeth, she quickly tore her favorite blouse into strips. With no idea whether she was doing the right thing or not, she pressed them against where the wound seemed to be. The first-aid course she'd taken years ago had not been given in the dark on a rainy night.

By now, it was well past midnight. People had drunk their New Year's eggnog and gone to bed. No lights shone through the slanting sheets of rain between them and shore. Awkwardly she pulled on her soaking clothes.

"The river's not so wide near the bridge," Sheila told Teddy, hugging herself for warmth. "Head in there. Maybe there'll be a convenience store or something where we can call for help."

The engine sparked to life and the johnboat growled downriver.

Slap, slap, slap! The boat fought the waves. Jarred by the thud of the bow against the water and unnerved by the engine, Sheila thought wistfully of the peace and quiet of traveling under sail. With tonight's wind, and in this current, they could have made good time—

She suddenly became aware that this was no ordinary current. It ran hard, and seemed to get ever stronger. She had forgotten how close they were to the sea. In only a few miles, the river would widen and run into the Atlantic. No wonder they were moving at such a clip! The johnboat was being inexorably sucked down the Trout River toward the St. Johns.

Teddy's next words confirmed her fears. "The tide's going out! I can't steer!"

Sheila felt a momentary letup in the storm as the bridge passed overhead.

"The next bridge is the Dames Point Bridge!" Teddy's face was white, her eyes huge with terror, as she battled the rudder. She, too, had recognized their peril. "If we go past it, we'll go all the way to the ocean!"

The starboard shore was close, but it was also across the tide. Gingerly, Sheila climbed over Jack and made her way astern. She grabbed the tiller with Teddy's determined fingers beneath her stronger ones. Together they shoved with all their strength. The boat bucked, resisted, and continued to sweep onward with the tide.

"Dear God!" Sheila groaned. Breathing deeply, she shoved with all the force she could muster. For an eternity, the rudder didn't budge. Then, miraculously, the bow of the little boat nosed slightly starboard.

Another wave crashed over the starboard side, dousing them. Sheila was too wet and cold to mind, but she could hear Teddy's whimper above the motor's roar. She could also smell salt on the wind. The ocean was near.

"Let me take it," she yelled to Teddy, releasing her grip enough for Teddy to let go. Teddy's fingers seemed glued to the wood. Sheila clawed them away, then pressed her body against the tiller.

She had heard of women lifting enormous weights in desperate situations. Later, when she could think again, she would know that somehow she had found that kind of strength for just long enough.

The boat hesitated, then swung across the tide.

Rocking and stuttering, the little craft plowed toward shore. "We're gonna make it. We're gonna make it!" Teddy sobbed.

Sheila's heart tightened in relief. She saw something she'd feared she would never see again: a lighted house.

The house had a dock, with a gently rocking day sailer. Sheila nosed the johnboat toward a wooden ladder at one side of the dock, and Teddy quickly tied up. The rain slanted down cruelly. "I'll go ask for help," Sheila told her. "You stay here with Jack. Here's my coat. Try to keep him dry."

She climbed the dock ladder with hands so cold she could scarcely cling to the rungs. Unsteadily, she staggered toward glass doors just beyond the riverside deck.

As at Rob Wilmer's, motion sensor lights flooded the area at her approach. Through open drapes, she could have been looking in on heaven. A brown leather couch and recliner. Soft dry carpet. A gentle fire. A steaming cup on a table by the couch. A short woman with brown hair wearing a navy robe and slippers. As the outdoor lights flicked on, the woman rose from the cushions, put down her book, and peered uncertainly toward the glass.

"Help, please!" Sheila cried, pounding on the door with her palms. "Call a doctor! We have a wounded man in our boat! He's been shot!"

She was not surprised when the woman hurried from the room. No one ought to let in a stranger, hair plastered to her head and eyes frantic, without reinforcements.

She was relieved, however, when the woman quickly returned. A man was with her, yawning and squinting. Fuzzy white hair stood up around his pink scalp and his plaid bathrobe was belted over a round little belly, giving him the look of a middle-aged cherub.

The woman had donned a raincoat and carried what looked like a medical bag. As soon as she opened the door she asked, "Did you say you have an injured man aboard?"

"On our boat." Sheila gestured, then sagged against the door frame. She felt as limp as pampas grass.

The woman hurried swiftly toward the dock.

"She's a doctor," the man told Sheila unnecessarily. "Won't you come in out of the rain?"

"There's a child—" Sheila turned back toward the water.

He put a gentle hand on her arm. "Katherine will send the child along. Come on inside." He steered her firmly toward the fire. A detective novel lay open on a table beside a steaming cup of cocoa. "I'm Stephen Roberts. My wife is Katherine. Let me get you somethin' hot to drink and a blanket to wrap up in." He bustled away without asking for Sheila's name.

By the time the man returned with two mugs of cocoa and soft blankets, Teddy had dashed into the house with a message from "Dr. Katherine" to call 911.

Their host made the call while the child huddled near the fire. Her forehead was plastered with wet wisps of hair that had escaped her braids, and her clothes clung to her thin body.

Sheila wrapped her tightly in a warm blanket. "We also need to call your parents, Teddy. Is there a phone on Hayden's boat?"

Teddy accepted a cup of steaming cocoa and took a gulp before replying around melted marshmallow, "I don't know the number. I'll call Mamar." She poked one arm out of the blanket to dial.

"Hey, Mamar, it's me," she said inelegantly when the ringing stopped. "Sheila and I had to follow some people who shot Jack, and then we nearly got swept out to sea. We're at Dr. Katherine's house, but I don't know where it is. Can you come get us?"

She listened for a minute, then held out the receiver. "She needs to talk to you."

Sheila had suspected she might.

When Sheila reached Helen and Justin, they were horrified—as she had known they would be. They were also grateful that Sheila had gone with Teddy. "Have the ambulance take Jack to St. Vincent's Hospital," Justin told her after she tersely outlined the night's dramatic events. "Helen and I will meet them at the emergency room. We'll find a car for Libba to bring Crispin out to get you, but it will take a while. Traffic's dreadful, and it's farther by land than . . ." He broke off to listen to someone at his shoulder. "Oh, Sheila? Tom Goren's here. He wants to talk to you."

"What's going on?" Goren rumbled over the phone. She could picture his tawny cat eyes glaring across the watery miles.

"Three men boarded the *Jack Three* in the slip next to Hayden's during the fireworks, and shot and abducted Jack. Teddy saw them, and took out after them." She didn't bother to say why she had come. She still wasn't sure herself.

"Did they get away?" Tom demanded.

"Yes, but we got Jack. He was shot in the shoulder. We're waiting for the ambulance now." She concluded, with a practicality he probably didn't appreciate, "You might check the *Jack Three* for prints before anybody else goes aboard."

"Yeah," he said morosely. "I'll see you later."

It sounded more like a threat than a promise.

As soon as Sheila had hung up, Teddy darted for the door to the deck. "I have to go be with Jack!"

Sheila was feeling the same urgency. It seemed callous to leave him outside in the storm while they got warm and dry.

Just as they reached the door, however, the doctor returned, streaming wet, and stopped Teddy with a tone of rebuke. "I told you to get dry clothes on, child! Run up to the blue bedroom at the top of the stairs and look in the dresser. Our granddaughter keeps jeans and sweatshirts there."

"But I want to go to Jack!" Teddy insisted, pulling away. "He *needs* me!"

"Jack is fine." The doctor wiped raindrops off her cheeks. "He has lost a lot of blood, but I think he'll recover. We'd never get him up from the boat, though. We'll just have to shelter him from the storm until the paramedics arrive. Perhaps a tarp, Stephen? Then *you*," she turned to Sheila, "can wait with Jack for the paramedics. You, Teddy, skedaddle!" Her tone brooked no defiance.

Teddy glowered, but she skedaddled. Sheila remembered how Hayden's tone had reassured her before. Medical schools really must include elocution in their curriculum!

Stephen hurried to the garage and returned with not one but two orange tarps. On their way down the dock, above the wind and rain, he outlined a plan. "Let's push the boat under the dock and make it fast, then cover the boy with one tarp and spread the other over the dock above."

He hadn't taken enough thought for himself to change from his pajamas and slippers, and he must be past sixty. It was logical for Sheila to go down the ladder and make the boat fast. But as she peered at the swaying boat and remembered the chilly water, she thought wistfully that she would almost exchange women's suffrage to get excused from this exercise in equality.

The next few minutes were something she never wanted to repeat. Jack was too groggy to know who she was as she wrapped the tarp as closely as she could around him. Chilling rain snaked down her neck while she maneuvered the boat under the dock. The boat bucked and swayed, making it difficult to secure. The pilings were slick with rain, her shoulders sore, and her fingers so numb with cold that she could scarcely tie a knot. All the while, rain dripped between the planks above.

While she worked below, Stephen laid the tarp and fought to secure it with chairs from the deck. As the wind snatched unattached corners, he swore above while Sheila swore below.

When Stephen had the upper tarp arranged to his satisfaction, he called down, "Will you be all right, my dear? They ought to be along soon."

Sheila—climbing under the tarp beside Jack and pulling it over them both—reflected that "all right" and "soon" are relative terms.

After a short eternity, heavy feet clumped down the dock. A hearty voice called, "Hey, down there! You can come up now."

Climbing around a wet ladder from a rocking boat wasn't as easy as he made it sound. Twice her feet slid off the slick rungs, and she wondered if she were about to get yet one more baptism in the St. Johns.

In short order, Jack was raised to the dock and sent to the hospital in a wail of sirens.

Afterwards, Katherine—who had changed into a purple fleece jumpsuit—held out a towel and a pile of clothes, including a bright turquoise jogging suit. "This will be short on you, but at least it's dry. Shower and put it on." Sheila wanted to clutch its warm fuzziness to her wet, cold chest.

Crispin had never looked so good. Sheila went into his arms and fought back tears. "It was awful," she murmured.

She turned to make introductions and found Libba and the doctor chatting like old friends. "I think Jack will be fine," Dr. Katherine assured them once more as they prepared to leave. "He was fortunate that the water was so cold. Tell Helen to just drop the clothes off at Sissy's when she has time."

"What nice people!" Sheila murmured sleepily on the

way home, her head on Crispin's shoulder. "I didn't even get their address or phone number."

"It's okay," Libba replied above the noise of the rain. "Kathy's sister went to school with Helen and me, and still lives down the road from Helen."

"What did I tell you, hon?" Crispin asked softly, hugging Sheila close. "Jacksonville's like a small town full of very nice people."

"Not all of them," she reminded him. "Somebody shot Jack."

Sheila awoke to Crispin shaking her gently. "I'm sorry, Sheila, but Tom Goren insisted you stop by the hospital before we go home."

She opened her eyes and tried to remember where she was. Where did she get this soft sweat suit, and why was it too small? Crispin shook her again. She saw he was at the back door of an unfamiliar car. Outside, the first pale shades of dawn lit the sky.

"I'll take Teddy on home and stay with her," Libba murmured from the front seat. "Helen and Justin can bring you all home later."

Yawning, Sheila climbed out and stumbled after Crispin down interminable corridors. Finally they reached a room where Jack lay high on a hospital bed. His shoulder was bandaged, his face as white as his pillowcase. His eyes looked warily toward the door when they entered, and even with a roomful of protectors, he looked frightened. Sheila didn't blame him. Who could promise that his attackers would not return to finish their botched job? When he saw who it was, however, he gave a weak smile.

Helen and Justin, faces drawn with anxiety, stood close by him. Tom Goren stood beyond the bed.

To Sheila's chagrin, Rob Wilmer sat in a chair by the window. Like Jack's, his eyes were wary. But they defied her to give him away, and he spoke with determined insouciance. "Good morning, Mrs. Travis! I'm Tom's designated driver tonight. You've had quite an evening!"

"Are you all right?" Helen came forward swiftly and enfolded Sheila's hands in her own. "We don't know how to thank you. If you hadn't gone with Teddy—"

Justin put an arm around each woman and hugged both. "We'd have lost two children, Sheila. We owe you a debt we can never repay."

Sheila smiled at the young man on the bed. "How *are* you, Jack?"

He smiled weakly. "Better, now, thanks." His voice was hoarse. He clasped her hand gratefully.

Tom Goren stepped forward, holding a notebook. "While it's still fresh on your minds, I want you both to tell me everything you remember. Mrs. Travis, you first. Tell me exactly what you saw down at the dock tonight, and what happened afterwards."

"But sit down first," Justin urged. "You must be exhausted."

Thankfully, Sheila sank into the chair he pushed forward for her. "I didn't see anything," she admitted, "except three men board the *Jack Three*. I thought—"

"I don't need to know what you thought," Goren interrupted. "Just what you saw or heard."

Irritated at his brusqueness, she replied tartly. "Then you'd do better to ask Teddy. She was the one who was watching when Jack was shot. I didn't see or hear a thing until she shouted and scrambled over the rail." Then, ashamed of her flare of temper before the others, she succinctly described the chase, the *Ark*'s brief encounter with the speedboat, and Jack's rescue.

Tom Goren wrote it all down, then turned to Jack. "Now you, son. What's going on?"

Jack hitched himself up on his pillows. "Daddy?" he asked uncertainly.

Justin rested a hand on his son's shoulder. "Tell him everything, Jack. Just the way it happened."

The young man hesitated, then said, "Yeah." It

sounded like a sigh of relief. "Shall I start at the beginnin'?" he asked Goren.

"Might as well." Goren poised his pen over the notebook.

"Well, Christmas morning, I woke up 'way before anybody else, and took the *Jack Three* for a dawn spin. Comin' back, I remembered a six-pack of root beer hidden in the bulkhead where I hoped Treye wouldn't find it. Instead, I found eight boxes, all alike."

Tom gave an involuntary grunt. "Word's out somebody's bringing drugs through Ortega."

Helen gasped. "Surely not!"

"We don't know it was drugs," Rob reminded them both. Tom turned back to Jack. "How big were the boxes, son?"

Jack tried to hold his hands up, winced, and gave up. "About eighteen inches square."

"Did you open one to see what was inside?"

"No. They were taped shut, and both Treye and Muffy had been using the boat all week. I figured they might be Christmas presents. Whatever they were, they were none of my business." He stopped and motioned. His mother held a glass of water to his mouth and he rinsed his mouth and spat into a plastic basin. "I must have swallowed half the damn river." He shuddered, then continued. "That night, I couldn't sleep again, so I went downstairs to get a glass of milk. I heard the *Jack Three*'s motor start."

"How'd you know it was yours?" Goren demanded.

"It has a little cough it always makes, as if it isn't going to start. I watched it go out, figuring Treye had a late date. I even wondered if Muffy was using the boat again. But most of all I hoped nobody was stealing it. I decided I'd wait a while and see if it came back. So I got a book and read downstairs, waiting."

"Did it come back?"

"Yeah. A little before four. I couldn't see who got off, but they went toward Uncle Hayden's, so I figured it was

Treye. I went down and checked to be sure everything was okay, and it was—but the boxes were gone."

"Did you ask Treye about it?"

Jack shook his head. "The next time I saw him was when we went over to help Daphne move furniture for the party. I went upstairs to store an extra end table in her bedroom, and he was in there talking on the phone. That was odd, because he'd told me once he couldn't stand to go in that room after his daddy married Daphne. But there he was, talking real soft. When I went in, he turned and looked at me like—I dunno—like I was trespassing or something. And he was mad. He said something quick, like, 'Look, I gotta go, there's somebody here,' and hung up."

Helen's eyes were troubled. "Did you ask Treye who it was, honey?"

"No, he hurried out before I could. Then, before I could ask him later, stupid Ellgie got lost . . ." He made a quick gesture of impatience, and winced again.

"Why didn't you tell me, son?" Justin demanded. "I could—"

"You couldn't have done a damn thing, Daddy," Jack interrupted irritably. "There wasn't anything *to* do. But I decided I'd watch Treye at the party. Sparrow, Brandy, and I were supposed to go down to a party at the Landing right after your campaign announcement, but I told them I had a headache. Sparrow drove Brandy, and I said I'd come later if I felt better. Instead, I hung around and watched what Treye did."

"Did you see any suspicious behavior?" Tom's face was grim.

"Yeah, I did. Soon after nine, he went out the back door, toward the river. I followed him and watched from bushes near the house. Somebody else was already on the dock."

Tom's pencil was poised. "Could you see who it was?"

Jack hesitated. "I—I think it was Muffy. The light wasn't real good, but it was a woman with red hair."

Goren prompted, "What happened next?"

"A boat came to the dock and two men unloaded something onto the *Jack Three.*"

"Would you know these men?"

Jack laughed brusquely. "I sure did tonight, when they boarded the *Jack Three* at the Gator Bowl. They thought I was Treye, and—"

"Let's tell it in order, son. First, the night of the party, they loaded boxes onto your boat. Then what?"

"When they left, Treye and Muffy—if it was Muffy—went back to the party. Then a man came out of some bushes on the other side of the dock. Nearly scared me sh—" he glanced at his mother "to death."

"Could you see who that was?" Even Rob Wilmer had abandoned his I'm-only-here-to-drive-Tom pose. He leaned forward with real interest.

Jack looked his way and seemed to be thinking, then said, "No. I couldn't see his face. He went away with the two goons in their boat."

"Then you went inside?" Goren asked.

"No, I waited until the two boats were out of sight, then I boarded the *Jack Three.* Sure enough, the bulkhead was full of more boxes. I transferred them to the *Ark*, Teddy's johnboat, and hid them."

"*Two* boats?" Rob repeated.

"Yeah," Jack said thoughtfully. "The other one must have been waitin' at another dock, because I saw it pull out and head downriver behind the first one. I watched until I was sure they couldn't see me before I went aboard the *Jack Three.*" His forehead wrinkled. "Funny thing, though. Just as I was about ready to go in, the two boats came back, and one was towing the other. At least I thought it was the same two. I remember thinking maybe they didn't want Treye to know which way they really went."

Goren wanted clarification. "And this time they headed upriver?"

"Yeah, toward the Yacht Club and Pirate's Cove."

Goren gave Rob a quick look. Rob nodded. "Could have been," he said softly.

Goren tapped his pencil thoughtfully on his pad. "Did you open *those* boxes, Jack?"

"No. By then I was pretty sure it was drugs inside. I didn't want to risk spilling any, in case drug-sniffing dogs ever came aboard."

"Smart thinking, son," Justin said approvingly.

"And then?" Goren prodded.

"I went back to my room and watched the dock until the party was over, in case Treye took the boat out. He didn't, though."

"He came down to the hospital to be with Hayden," Helen explained.

Jack signaled for more water. By the way he touched his mother's hand as she held the glass, Sheila knew the young man merely wanted her near. "Later," he continued, "after I heard you all come in and go to bed, I took the *Ark* out toward the middle of the river and dumped the stuff." Sheila remembered the lonely motor she had heard in the night.

"Brave boy!" Wilmer congratulated him. "But didn't you worry that somebody might get mad if the packages disappeared?"

Jack started to shrug, grimaced with pain, and said defiantly, "I'm not scared of Treye!"

"Not Treye, the people Treye was supposed to deliver the stuff to—and those he was delivering for. Didn't you wonder what would happen when he arrived at his drop-off without the merchandise?" Rob leaned forward in his seat, obviously worried about both youths.

Sheila felt a twinge of remorse. So what if the poor man had his faults? He was single, lonely, disfigured, and he kept his peccadillos to himself.

No evil exists in isolation, said a voice in her head.

But he's a good friend of Helen and Justin, she told the voice, *and I'm likely to see a good bit of him anytime I come to Jacksonville with Crispin. Maybe I'd better stop playing judge and jury and let the poor man live his own life. Who gets hurt by it?* But then a memory of the woman she had seen on his television screen flitted across her brain. She shuddered in revulsion and turned away to cough so no one could see the conflict in her face.

All those thoughts took less time than it took for Jack to answer Rob's question: "All I was thinking about was Daddy's campaign, and what would happen if people thought the family was selling drugs."

"Thanks, Jack." Justin's voice was gruff.

Jack sighed. "I wanted to tell you, Daddy, but I hated to get Treye in hot water, so I just decided to disable Uncle Hayden's boat and keep the *Jack Three* out a lot. Wednesday night I even took my sleeping bag down and slept on deck. But about two, Treye came aboard, and when he found me there, he went crazy! Accused me of messing up the lines, dirtying the boat without cleaning it, all sorts of dumb stuff. Said if I couldn't take better care of it, I could jolly well stay off it for the rest of Christmas vacation."

"What did you say?"

"I told him I'd found his dumb packages and dumped them. He told me I'd gotten him in a lot of trouble. I said that was nothing compared to the trouble he'd be in if anybody found out he was selling drugs."

"What did he say to that?" Wilmer asked.

Jack's voice broke and his eyes reddened. "He said it was none of my damn business, but if I told, he'd tell the papers Daddy got him involved in the first place. I yelled that that wasn't true and—" Jack's voice quavered at the memory "—an' he laughed! Said it'd ruin Daddy's chances of getting elected! That's when I hit him."

"Looked to me like he hit you," Crispin commented casually. It was the first time he'd spoken since they came in.

Jack grinned and admitted huskily, "He did black my eye. He's better at that than I am."

Goren regarded him somberly. "I don't suppose you

kept one of those boxes, did you, Jack? We need some evidence before we can pick him up."

Jack shook his head. "You won't have to pick him up. He's tied up in my bedroom." At their astonishment, he grinned again, weakly. "This afternoon I—"

"Don't get ahead of yourself," Goren admonished. "You were telling us about Wednesday night, when Treye hit you."

"Okay. Well, there's nothing more to say about that." He gingerly touched his cheek, which was still faintly yellow. "I took the boat out all day Thursday, to make sure Treye couldn't use it. I didn't know what else to do. Sparrow went with me, and she was freezing, so we stopped by the Loop for lunch, but Sparrow was so scared and crying, she wouldn't go inside."

"What about Thursday night?" Sheila asked.

"The night I followed you?"

She shot him a warning look, but too late.

"Followed us where?" Crispin demanded.

Sheila carefully avoided Rob's eye. "It doesn't matter, Crispin. What happened next, Jack?"

"I took the boat down to Charho's condo and tied up in an empty slip. I needed a good night's sleep, and figured Treye wouldn't think to look there. Sparrow came and got me and took me home so I could sleep in my own bed. The next morning I went back and took the *Jack Three* out before anybody was up. That worked so well I did it again Friday night. I meant to keep doing it, but yesterday Daddy made me leave the *Jack Three* for my poor cousin Treye." He glanced up at his father with some of his former truculence.

"You should have told me," Justin admonished.

"He's getting tired," Helen warned, bending over her son and smoothing his hair. "Can we cut this short and finish tomorrow?"

Rob Wilmer yawned. "If we don't, I'll need a pallet on the floor."

"Okay, Jack," Goren conceded. "Tell us about tonight

and we'll all leave. I'm putting a man outside the door, so you can rest easy."

Jack yawned, too. "Okay. Well, when Treye insisted on taking the *Jack Three* tonight, I knew something was up, so I told Sparrow I had a headache and didn't want to go until time for the game. About five-thirty, a boat arrived at our dock. Treye went out and they loaded boxes onto the *Jack Three*."

Helen gasped. "In broad daylight?"

Jack nodded. "Yeah. They thought we were all gone. I didn't know what to do. I thought about calling the police, but what if it was something harmless? Besides . . ." he cast an imploring look at his father, "what about the election? I wished we had a gun so I could go down and stop them, but all I knew to do was watch. I didn't even have the *Ark* so I could follow Treye."

"We're all glad you didn't," Crispin reminded him. "If Teddy hadn't taken it along—"

Jack gave a flicker of a smile. "Yeah. I'll have to thank her for that." He adjusted himself on his pillows and yawned again. "Anyway, Treye went back to the house for something', so I dashed down and got one box and took it to the house. Then I rigged up a booby trap like we used to when we played pirates, 'n' when he started for the dock I held up the box and yelled that I had his stuff. He came, madder'n a hornet, 'n' he tripped the trap. I knocked him out, 'n' carried him up to my room and tied him up—I was doing that when Sparrow came, and she left before I could get to the door. I carried all the boxes to our garage and covered 'em up, then I tried to call Sparrow, but she wasn't home . . ." His eyes closed. He opened them and fought to keep them open, but failed.

"Finish it, son," Goren begged. "Just another minute or two. What happened last night?"

Jack spoke without opening his eyes. "I took the boat to the Gator Bowl 'n waited for somebody to show up."

Helen gasped. "You could have been killed!"

"Why didn't you call the police?" Rob Wilmer demanded.

"Th'election—r'porters—" Jack's words slurred.

Justin bent low over the bed and spoke softly. Jack smiled sleepily. "I know, Daddy. I love you, too." Then he turned his face into his pillow and slept.

"I'll call for somebody to guard the door," Goren reached for the phone, "and I'll order a squad car to pick me up. Rob, you don't need to wait around. Go on home."

"Nonsense." Rob stood and pulled down his cuffs. "I'll drop you at Justin's on my way home, Tom. Have your driver meet you there. I'll bring my car around while you're calling."

He bid the others farewell, then gave Sheila a tentative smile. "Mrs. Travis, you do have some of the most interesting nighttime adventures!"

Goren stepped out into the hall and used his cellular phone to call the department. Meanwhile, Crispin insisted on staying with Jack until the guard arrived. "I'll be home before breakfast," he promised. "I've had all the hospital food I want for a while."

When Helen, Justin, and Sheila got to the hospital lobby, Sheila exclaimed, "Oh! I left my purse in Jack's room! I'll be right back." Waving away Justin's offer to fetch it, she hurried off. She joined a few minutes later, breathless, to confess, "Sorry. I forgot—I didn't have a purse with me. Teddy and I left Hayden's boat rather quickly."

Justin chuckled as he led them to an unfamiliar white Cherokee someone must have loaned him. "It's okay, Sheila. You don't have to make excuses. We all know why you went back."

It was strange to ride through the city so early on that last morning of the year. The sun was up, and birds flew overhead, but the streets were virtually deserted. Most people were still sleeping after the previous night's celebrations. The few who were out drove slowly and cautiously, in case the others might still be drunk.

As Justin drove home, he told Helen, "Twinkie's gonna be madder'n a wet hen if they arrest her son at our house."

"It's her own fault," Helen said angrily. "Hers and Hayden's. Neither one of them has paid Treye a speck of attention since the divorce, nor given him much money, either. It's like they each expected the other—"

Justin patted her hand, and she subsided. But she muttered softly, "I feel so sorry for that boy."

They pulled into the drive behind a squad car. Rob met them on the porch, his face dismayed. "Someone got here first." Behind him, the front door stood open, and there was only a gaping hole where there had once been beveled glass. "Tom's looking around inside."

Tom stood amid chaos. Chairs and tables lay on their sides. Dishes were smashed. Magazines were flung on the carpet.

"Teddy!" Helen shrieked. "Libba said she'd bring her here!" She ran toward the stairs.

But Tom held her back. "It's messy, Helen, but there's nobody up there. Whoever got here must have taken everybody."

Helen's face grew ashen. She sagged against Justin. He led her to the sofa, and sat beside her, holding her close. Goren went to call the specialists. The Jacksonville police department would do well, Sheila thought, to set up a L'Arken division.

Rob perched on the edge of a chair he had righted. "Helen, Justin, if there's anything I can do—"

Helen shook her head. "Go on home, Rob. We'll call you if—when—"

"As soon as you hear *anything*," he finished for her. He stood. "Good night, all. I don't expect to see you at church?" He made a question of it."

Helen shook her head. "Not today, Rob."

When Rob had gone, Sheila went to the kitchen where Goren was just finishing on the phone. "Do you and Rob spend a lot of time together?" she asked. Did Tom share his friend's kinky tastes?

"No, I hadn't seen much of him since high school, until we ran into each other going into Hayden's the other night. Then Rob called me when he found Lance floatin' by his dock. It spooked him, as you might imagine."

She smiled. "I've got another sort of spook for you. Come in the living room."

He reached for the phone again. "Look, Mrs. Travis, if you don't mind—"

"It won't take but a minute, Detective Goren. Please."

His face made it clear that this was a waste of his precious time, but he followed her.

"Justin," she asked, "can you still open the secret room?"

Justin look up at her, puzzled. "How'd you know about that?"

"Crispin told me. He said you and he used to play in there when you were kids."

Justin nodded. "These days it sort of belongs to . . ."

"Teddy. I know. Will you open the room, please?"

He rose unwillingly, went to the staircase, and pressed something on the newel post. Tom grunted in amazement as, on the landing above, a narrow door slid open silently in the paneling.

A familiar voice rang out. "I thought you'd never get here! What took you so long?"

Teddy came through the door. Behind her waddled Einstein, muzzled with a scarf. Libba followed, brushing her slacks. She wrinkled her nose and called down the steps, "I'd recommend a good sweepin', Helen."

"Treye?" Sheila asked.

"He's in there," Teddy replied carelessly. "Libba

wanted to take out his gag, but I didn't. I was afraid he'd yell or somethin'.'"

Helen gaped up at her youngest child as if she were a ghost. "Why on earth did you go in there? And where are your glasses?"

Teddy chose to answer the first question. "Sheila called and told me to." She ran down the stairs and danced excitedly in front of Sheila. "You were right! Bad men did come! They made terrible noises." She looked around at the chaos and her eyes widened. "Wow! If you hadn't told us to hide—" She turned and explained to her astonished parents, "Sheila told me to try to get Treye in the closet, but if he wouldn't go, we were to get in ourselves and not open the door to anyone. She said Daddy or Crispin would open it when they got here." She ran to fling her arms around her mother's waist. "Libba wanted to come out when we heard you talkin', but I wouldn't show her how to open the door."

Sheila smiled. She'd never thought she'd be so glad to see this particular child. "You did just right, Teddy."

Goren looked from Teddy to Sheila. "How'd you know anybody would be coming, Mrs. Travis?"

She met his eyes over Teddy's head and shook her head slightly. "Right now, Detective Goren, Treye may be glad to see even you."

Goren mounted the steps two at a time. He peered into the small door and looked back at Justin with delight. "What is it—a card room? I've seen one of these over in Avondale, but I didn't know there were any in Ortega. Built during Prohibition, I guess?"

Justin nodded. "Probably by my sainted grandfather. He's the one who put on the garage, and the room's built over it. Can you get Treye out, or do you need some help?"

"I can get him," Goren said grimly. "Come on, fellow. Easy, now."

Treye lurched out. His hands were tied behind his back and his feet were tied together. A bandanna filled his mouth. He was soiled and disheveled, and he refused to meet the eyes of any of his family.

While Goren untied him, Justin headed downstairs again. "I'll call your daddy, boy. But he's still down on the boat. I'll go down to the station with you until he gets there."

Treye nodded shamefacedly.

Helen put out her arms, and Teddy ran into them. "Can I sleep with you tonight—I mean *today*, Mama?"

Helen hugged her younger daughter tight. "If you promise not to hog the covers," she said happily.

What seemed to Sheila like half the Jacksonville police department arrived while Libba, yawning so broadly she could scarcely stand, was declining Helen's offer of a bed. Goren briefed his officers while Libba drove herself home and Helen took Teddy upstairs. Those left in the front hall heard Teddy exclaim, "Look at Jack's room! His computer's ruined!"

Justin spoke seriously. "Treye, I want you to cooperate with Tom fully so we can catch the men who did this. Do you hear me?"

"I don't know who did it, Uncle Justin! Honest! Teddy hustled me into that room, and we didn't see them."

Justin regarded him with impatience. "Jack's talked, Treye. And somebody took a shot at him last night—a shot we suspect was meant for you. Now tell us what you know, boy!"

Goren returned in time to hear him. "You know who you were workin' for, don't you, Treye?" His golden eyes were like a tiger's sighting its prey.

Treye hung his head. "I didn't know anybody but Muffy," he mumbled, "and Muffy's dead."

"Let's go down to the station and have a little talk." Goren took the young man by the arm. "You coming with us, Justin?" Justin nodded. Goren turned to Sheila. "You get yourself some sleep."

She gave him an incredulous look. "We can't *all* go to

bed, Detective Goren, unless somebody guards the house. At the moment, as you may recall, we have no front door."

"Hank," Goren bellowed. A police officer stuck his head in from the porch. "Stay here until Mr. L'Arken gets back home. We don't want anybody coming in this house except members of the force. *Nobody*. You got that?"

"I got it." Hank went back to the porch.

Justin escorted Treye outside. Tom Goren started after them, then turned at the door. "Looks like we all owe you some thanks again, Mrs. Travis." His tone, however, said clearer than words, *But we don't need any more of your meddlin'*.

Sheila woke to feel a weight on the other side of the bed. She had put the cats out of the room before she got into bed. Had they somehow opened the door and joined her? She opened one eye and met a myopic blue gaze. Teddy was full-length on the other side of the bed, legs crossed and one cheek cradled in her palm. "I thought you weren't ever gonna wake up. Me 'n Mama've been up for ages and ages."

Sheila yawned. "You and Mama didn't swim the St. Johns last night. Or tie up a boat under a dock in the rain."

"You should have had a gun. If you'd had a gun—"

Sheila pulled the covers closer under her chin and squeezed her eyes shut. "But I don't. You ought to check on things like that before you count on them."

Teddy flopped over onto her stomach. "Did you check on the bad men comin' here?"

"Ummhmm, sort of. Mostly I put two and two together."

"Which two and two?"

"I can't remember right now. Did your mother send you up here to get me?"

"No," the child admitted honestly. "She said not to wake you up. So I just waited. You know why we had to wake up?" She giggled.

"Why?" Sheila, almost asleep, didn't really care.

"Crispin couldn't get in!" Teddy snickered. "He took a cab back from the hospital but the policeman wouldn't let him in. So he stood out in the driveway and hollered until Mama heard him. He was pretty mad!"

Sheila didn't blame Crispin. Maybe in a day or two she'd get up and sympathize with his indignation.

But Teddy wasn't through. "You know what I did already? I finished the gold horse in the puzzle. Some dumb person had put a piece in upside down. It almost fit, but not quite, so none of the others fit, either. When I turned it right side up—" she turned her palms up, "—it all worked. Then I started workin' on the sky, and ..."

Sheila groaned. Teddy as friend was almost worse than Teddy as enemy. "Give me one more hour," she begged, "then wake me again."

"Okay." Teddy slid off the bed. "Wanna go fishin' later?"

"Ask me in an hour." Sheila buried her face in the pillow.

This time she dreamed she was working a jigsaw puzzle, but a piece was upside down. It almost fit, but not quite. . . .

When she woke, she knew who had killed Daphne L'Arken, Muffy Merriwether, and Eddie Weare. She thought she even knew why.

Suspicion dimmed her spirits as she went downstairs. Brilliant sunshine streamed through a hole where the front door used to be. The hall would not be so cozy once the sun went down.

"Good afternoon!" Crispin called from the puzzle table in the Florida room. Dressed again in his black pantsuit, he had kicked off his Top-Siders and was rubbing his bare feet back and forth on the sisal rug. She joined him and craned to look at the golden horse. Now that all the pieces were in, it looked so simple. The night's terrors had made some other things simpler, too.

"Do I understand you had a bit of trouble getting in this morning?" she asked casually.

He looked up with a glint in his eye. "Are you sure you want to wear those jeans? Seems to me like every time you put them on, you get an urge to swim in the river. One more question like that, and I'll be delighted to help you out."

"I've had my swim for the day," she reminded him, "*and* torn my best blouse to shreds. Knowing you is hard on my wardrobe." Their eyes held, and his lips twitched, remembering. The second time they'd met, they'd escaped down a tree together and she'd ruined her best black silk. Their accident before Christmas had destroyed her new black velvet gown.

"I bought you another silk dress," he pointed out, "but I'm not going to keep on replacing your clothes unless you make me legally responsible for doing so."

"By suing you?" She bent and kissed the top of his head.

He reached out and pulled her onto his lap. "That's one way. There's another that's more pleasant."

After a while, she drew back. "Where is everybody?"

He reached around her to press a piece of tree in place. "Helen's napping again. Teddy's gone over to Charho's. Justin and Hayden got back from downtown a little while ago and since they can't get a carpenter on Sunday or New Year's, they've taken the front door over to Hayden's workshop. They think they can fix it enough to be secure until a carpenter can get here. Sparrow's down with Jack, and from what Helen said, everybody else—and I do mean everybody—is coming for supper. They want to hear all about last night."

She slid off his lap and took the chair across from him. "Crispin, I think I know who murdered Daphne. Muffy, too. And probably Eddie."

He looked up, startled. "Are you sure?

"No, just almost. But I don't know how to prove any of it."

"Who is it?"

She told him.

At first he didn't believe her either. When she finally convinced him, he sat and chewed one knuckle, thinking. At last, he nodded. "You're right that you'll never get proof. I doubt there is any."

She nodded. "They're close to perfect crimes."

"Is a crime perfect merely because it's undetectable? Seems to me like there ought to be some grace, some cleverness to it. This sounds merely ruthless."

"The kind of ruthlessness that can become a habit, if it's not stopped. The problem is, I'm not sure how to stop it."

"Since we're scheduled to leave tomorrow, tonight would seem to be your only chance. And it looks like the first thing you have to do is call Tom." He yawned. "Maybe that's not clever, either, but it's the best I can do on very little sleep."

"Sounds right to me." She returned in a few minutes to report. "I left Tom a message. If he doesn't get it or doesn't come, we'll just play it by ear."

"Speaking of ears—" Crispin said, cupping one of his.

Justin was calling from the porch, "Come and admire! Not beautiful, but it'll do."

They went to the front porch. Hayden expertly tapped in the last hinge, then stood back to look critically at a large piece of plywood where the glass used to be.

Justin clapped him on the shoulder. "Thanks, brother. How about a beer?"

"Or coffee." Helen joined them wearing a calf-length denim dress. She'd brushed her hair and put blusher on cheeks that had lost a good bit of color this past week. "And look who's here!"

Martha's white New Yorker pulled up the drive just ahead of Charho's blue Buick. Libba's red Toyota was right behind. They lined up so that the family could still get out—or Tom Goren in, Sheila noted.

Libba wore a khaki skirt and red checked shirt with sweater trimmed to match, Martha a silky blue pantsuit, and Charho a two-piece green jersey suit. Sheila, feeling greatly underdressed, wished again that she'd known to bring cooler clothes. Only Laura Grace was dressed more casually. She wore a scarlet caftan. Sheila doubted that she had on a stitch underneath.

Nobody else seemed to care how anybody was dressed. Martha hurried up the steps. "You've done a lovely job, boys! And just in time. It's gettin' chilly out here!"

"You're always chilly," Laura Grace complained, following Martha up the steps. "I'm *hot*!"

Charho waved two plastic bags. "Just a little salad stuff," she replied to her daughter's questioning look. "Nothin' much."

Teddy stopped and considered the door nearsightedly. "Uncle Hayden must have done most of it. It fits."

"Hey!" Justin admonished her. "I supervised!"

Sheila greeted them all fondly and followed them in. She was tempted to just enjoy this evening and go home tomorrow, leaving Tom Goren to puzzle out his case. He would probably come to the same conclusions she had, eventually—if hers were right. She still had a niggling little doubt, a piece not quite in the right place.

When Justin closed the patched front door, the downstairs seemed gloomy. Justin, Helen, and Libba went to fetch drinks while Charho circled the living room, switching on lamps.

"Go light a fire, Helen," they heard Justin say from the kitchen, "and I'll call Bono's and order barbeque for dinner. Then Sheila will have tasted every one of our family's favorite meals."

Helen returned to her guests with a rueful smile. "Our children go out to eat and think it tastes like home cooking."

"It does," called Teddy from the puzzle table.

Justin carried in a tray of beers and Libba followed with coffee.

"Are you all right after last night?" she asked, handing Sheila a cup. Pressed by all who had not heard the story, Sheila told about the river chase—assisted by Teddy, who provided a few details Sheila chose to omit:

"I saw Jack shot, but Sheila wouldn't believe me."

"The waves just swept over our boat!"

And, "She jumped in the river in nothing but her underwear!"

"Very wise." Laura Grace nodded approvingly. She held out the top of her caftan and blew down it.

"Sit over here," Helen suggested to the old woman, opening a window a crack and pulling a straight chair by it.

Laura Grace moved the chair nearer the window, sat, then asked, "Was the person who shot Jack the same one who shot my gull?"

"I don't think so," Sheila told her.

"But they fired right at us. Twice!" Teddy added.

Helen gasped. Sheila frowned. "Well, Teddy, between us, I believe they've gotten the whole story."

Teddy scrambled to her feet. "I don't want to just sit here and talk. Can I go watch television until supper?"

"Sure, honey," Helen agreed. "Jack's TV got broken. Use the one in our room. And don't sit too close!"

"How else can I see?" Teddy demanded reasonably.

When she'd disappeared upstairs, Laura Grace swatted at something buzzing near her head. "I declare, a fly. In January!"

"We haven't had enough cold to kill them," Charho mused from a big wing chair. "My granddaddy used to say this kind of winter fills the cemeteries—not cold enough to kill the germs."

"People get killed, too," Laura Grace announced in her deep voice. "Lots of people." Her sharp black eyes turned balefully toward Sheila. "Since *you* got here."

"Oh!" Martha set her cup down in dismay. "I nearly

forgot to tell you. I got a call from Barb Merriwether this morning—Muffy's aunt," she added for Sheila's benefit. "Muffy's funeral is Tuesday at two, at Ortega Methodist."

"Ortega Methodist?" Libba's soft voice was puzzled. "Muffy didn't go there."

"Muffy didn't go period, precious," Charho said drily, "but she has to be buried out of somewhere. That's Barb's church. She even sings in the choir." She made it sound scandalous, as if Muffy's aunt sang in her slip. An aunt of Muffy's, Sheila reflected, might do just that.

The doorbell rang. Sheila waited with both hope and dread for Tom's heavy tread, but instead Rob Wilmer said anxiously from the door, "I wanted to see how everybody is after last night—and whether Tom's had any luck in tracing Treye, Teddy, and . . ." He caught sight of Libba and his face brightened. "You're here, Libba! That's wonderful! Are the others—"

Hayden started to interrupt, but Justin spoke first, from the kitchen door. "Tom's just turnin' in the drive."

Rob turned to Sheila. "Have you solved our mystery before Tom can, Mrs. Travis?"

She shrugged. "Which mystery, Mr. Wilmer?"

Tom charged into the living room like a rhinocerous, huge and belligerent. "I got your message, Mrs. Travis, but like I said, I don't like amateurs messin' in my cases. Tell me what you think you've got, then let me handle it from here!"

Sheila wished she knew how to bat her lashes like Aunt Mary. That little woman would have gazed at the detective with wide brown eyes, exclaiming something like, "I'll bet you've got everything all figured out anyway, and I don't expect I have much to tell you, but you might as well come in and make yourself comfortable while you listen."

She could at least try the last sentence. "I don't have a whole lot to tell you, Tom, but you might as well be comfortable while you listen."

Either he saw some logic in what she said, or her lashes batted better than she thought. In either case, he was soon sitting beside Rob on the couch with a glass of tea in his massive fist.

"Well, Mrs. Travis?" he asked.

Standing by the arch into the hall, Sheila looked around the room. Rob and Tom were on opposite ends of the sofa. Crispin, lounging in the door to the kitchen, gave her a high sign. She gave him a quick smile and let her eyes pass to Libba, on one side of the fireplace. In the glow, her face was flushed and pretty, but her eyes were as anxious as usual—this time, worried about Hayden, who stared into the fire and took long pulls on his beer. Helen and Justin shared a loveseat, her hand in his. He looked curious, she worried. Charho leaned over and gave her a little comforting pat. Martha sat near Laura Grace, who was squirming in her caftan. Any minute now she might get hot!

Rob's murky eyes still regarded Sheila, waiting. "Well," he urged, "are you ready to tell us all who done it?"

"Rob," she flared, "all week now, you've needled me to solve the mystery. Why?"

He shrugged. "I believed you could. I hear you've done a terrific job several times in Atlanta—"

"Maybe. Or did you want to use me like a mosquito—hoping I'd keep Tom so busy swatting he wouldn't have time for anything else."

"Now why would I do that?" His eyes held hers.

She gave him a sour smile but said nothing. His filthy secrets were safe.

Goren's curiosity, however, was aroused. "Rob? What's she talkin' about?"

Wilmer spoke softly. "May I speak to you in private, Tom?"

"Anything you have to say, say in front of everybody," Crispin said from his doorway.

Wilmer sighed. "You don't want to hear it, but okay.

Mrs. Travis came snooping around my place late the other night, and caught me watching a—well, an adult movie. Sorry, ladies." He lifted his palms and shrugged. "But I would point out I *was* in the privacy of my own home, and she had to peer through a window to see me. Nevertheless, the lady didn't approve. I guess she wants to publicly chastise me."

The room was utterly quiet. Sheila could imagine what the others were thinking about her, but she kept her eyes fixed on his. "No. What I want to do is convince Detective Goren that you and Muffy were running drugs through Ortega, using Treye and his boat."

Over the babble of protest, Rob laughed merrily. "What an imagination! But even though she's dead wrong, Tom, you're going to have to investigate me. Sorry, pal. I guess you're right about amateurs. They keep the police doing busywork when they ought to be out solving cases." He shook his head at Sheila in rebuke. "I'd expected more from you than that, Mrs. Travis."

Tom turned to Sheila, baffled. "Whatever gave you that damnfool idea?"

Instead of answering, she asked a question herself. "Did you know that Detective Goren got Treye, Mr. Wilmer?"

The smaller man rounded on his friend in admiration. "Good work! Did you catch the kidnappers, too?"

Tom shook his head. "No, Treye wasn't kidnapped. Mrs. Travis had called from the hospital and warned Teddy to hide everybody until we got here."

Wilmer gave Sheila an appraising look. "Well, you guessed one right, anyway. That was a smart move."

Sheila regarded him levelly. "No smarter than someone else calling the goons from the hospital to say Treye was here."

His eyes widened and he grew very still, but said nothing.

Tom, however, rubbed his short copper hair in continuing bewilderment. "What do you mean?"

She shrugged. "How else would they have known? *Nobody* knew, except those of us in Jack's hospital room. Rob's got a car phone, and he insisted you ride with him instead of calling for a squad car. Phone records may show that he called from the parking garage."

"And out of a possible phone call, you put all the rest together?" Goren demanded.

"No," Sheila told him. "The phone call was just the piece that made all the others fall into place. Ask yourself, Tom: Why has Rob been so present in this case? After all, he's an amateur, too."

"Yeah, but he found Lance floating by his dock."

"Possibly after putting him there. He's laughing at you, just like he's been laughing at me. I think if you ask Treye why he went to Cafe Carmon Thursday evening to 'accidentally' run into Crispin and me, he'll tell you Rob suggested he go there—after overhearing Crispin tell me where we were going. Rob was certainly here waiting to see if we got home alive after our drive-by shooting."

"He came to bring roses," Helen protested, darting a quick look at Rob.

"At ten o'clock at night." Justin's voice was thoughtful, and he had a wary eye on his old schoolmate. "And when Jack said last night that he didn't recognize the face of the other man on the dock Tuesday night, maybe he recognized his build." He looked at Rob's crooked shoulder.

Rob met his gaze steadily.

Sheila turned. "Laura Grace, you've talked a lot about pirates this week. Did you see any pirates?"

The old woman nodded. "On the dock. Christmas Eve, and again the night of the party. I used Jack's binoculars and watched them. I saw them all right." She turned back to the window.

Rob lifted his hands and implored, "Surely you all aren't going to take her word—"

Sheila interrupted him. "Then, Detective Goren, investigate his bank account. Did you know that the same man did his and Muffy's books?"

"You know why I had my man do her books," Rob protested. "Muffy found out about the girlie flicks!"

Sheila persisted. "Compare Rob's books with Muffy's to see if his withdrawals match her deposits, and if they occur around the same time that Treye's man received or delivered goods."

"We can look into it," Tom said. "But *if* Rob was involved—and mind you, I'm not sayin' you are, Rob—but if you've been doing what she claims, I doubt we'll ever be able to prove a thing."

She sighed. "At least, before you go, Tom, look behind the tarp in Justin's garage and take the box that's there. It's one of the ones Jack took from the *Jack Three*, and the thugs this morning missed it. Maybe there are prints on it. There's certainly a return address. The company in France might be able to tell you to whom they shipped the boxes—like Rob Wilmer."

Rob jumped to his feet. "I don't have to listen to any more of this conjecture, innuendo, and slander! You'll hear from my lawyer, Mrs. Travis! Call me, Tom, if you ever get through with this ridiculous investigation, and we'll have lunch."

He strode swiftly out.

"I'm hot," Laura Grace piped up into the silence that followed his exit. She fanned herself with her caftan.

"I need a drink of water." Crispin headed for the kitchen.

Tom Goren shook his head. "I think you're way off base, Mrs. Travis. Even if Rob weren't somebody I've known most of my life, he's got a good reputation around this town. I'll check him, certainly, but—"

A shout rang out. They heard running feet, a door slam, a pause, another slam, a medley of shouts.

Tom dashed to the porch and everyone crowded around the doorway.

Clutching something to his chest, Rob Wilmer darted away from the BMW and sprinted up the drive.

"Halt!" Tom ran after him, drawing his gun. "Halt!"

Rob continued running and disappeared through the gate.

As if by unspoken agreement, Hayden and Justin scrambled down the steps and into Justin's black Mercedes. With a screech Justin backed, turned, and braked near Tom, now halfway up the drive. "Get in!" Tom scrambled into the back seat as the Mercedes roared away.

Crispin helped Treye up from the garage floor. "Rob came for it, love," he said cheerfully, "like a homing pigeon—to which Treye and I both can testify. He tossed Treye like a marshmallow—"

"Not a marshmallow!" Treye protested, rubbing his arm. "He's tougher than he looks!"

"Like a rock," Crispin amended. "Then he carried the box to his car and tried to escape. Happily, Treye had reordered a few wires."

"Good work," Sheila told them. They all strained to listen, but heard nothing.

"We might as well go back in to wait," Helen suggested, rubbing her hands together until they were red.

"How did you get here?" Libba asked Treye.

"Dad bailed me out this mornin'," he replied ruefully. "Mrs. Travis asked me not to show myself around until— you know." He wiped the seat of his pants. "I think I'd better go lookin' for the others. Somebody could get hurt."

Crispin nodded. "I'm coming with you. Sheila, call 911. We may need reinforcements." They hurried toward Jack's red Jeep.

Charho headed back to the living room. "Well, we can't do a blessed thing standing we can't do sitting."

Everyone sat except Laura Grace, who backed to the open window, hitched up her caftan, and asked, "Did that man shoot my gull?"

Sheila, returning from the phone, shook her head sadly. "No, Laura Grace, that was Libba."

Helen and Charho both uttered small, sharp protests.

Libba, seated near the fire, looked up with startled eyes. "What did you say?"

Sheila stood looking down at the small blond woman in the big chair. "Before they come back, Libba," she said urgently, "why did you kill Daphne, Muffy, and Eddie—and shoot at Laura Grace and me in Memorial Park?"

Libba started to rise, then she sank back into the cushions. "Why would you say that? Kill them? They were my friends!"

Sheila nodded. "But they betrayed you, didn't they? Eddie left you for Daphne."

"A lot of good it did him," Libba said bitterly. "She made a drunk out of him. He used to be—" She pressed her lips together. In the firelight, Sheila saw tears glisten in her eyes.

Helen left the love seat to sit on the arm of Libba's chair and circle her with one arm. "Don't, Sheila! Libba couldn't kill anybody, could you, sweetie?"

Ignoring her, Libba continued to speak to Sheila. "Eddie was sweet, handsome, kind—" She stopped, buried her face in her hands, and sobbed. Sheila reached for the box of tissues Helen had put out earlier in the week, and Helen put one in Libba's hand. She swabbed her eyes and blew her nose angrily. "All I ever wanted was to grow up and marry Eddie. Since fifth grade!" She sniffed and pulled out another tissue. When she'd wiped her nose, she continued bitterly, "Then Daphne asked him to be her Homecoming escort. After that, all he ever thought about was Daphne."

"Daphne couldn't help that," Charho remonstrated from across the room. "She couldn't make Eddie love you, honey."

Libba's voice trembled. "Eddie did love me, Charho, until Daphne asked him to Homecoming!"

"She asked you if she could," Helen reminded her gently. "As Queen, Daphne wanted a handsome escort, but she asked you for permission first. Why did you say she could?"

Libba's shoulders heaved. "I trusted him. You have to trust somebody if you love them!"

Sheila remembered what Crispin had said Friday night. *Around dynamite, I need all the protection I can get.* How different life might have been, if Libba had known to protect Eddie instead of sending him toward the explosives!

"Tell us what happened at Tuesday's party," she suggested, perching on the chair across the hearth where Hayden had sat earlier. Thank goodness he wasn't here to hear this.

Libba swallowed convulsively. "When I first saw Eddie at Daphne's, it broke my heart. His daddy was an alcoholic, but Eddie had been so strong in high school about never taking even one drink. He was terrified he'd wind up like his daddy—" her voice deepened in unconscious imitation, "—'a stinkin', stumblin' drunk.' That's exactly what he'd become!" She turned her head and wept into the chair's fat wing.

When her sobs subsided, Sheila prodded, "Then you heard Daphne and Muffy talking about making him drink."

"Braggin' about it!" Libba blazed. Now her voice was Muffy's. " 'Daphne shouldn't have made you drink, sweetie. Wasn't good for you.' Not good for him?" Fiercely she swiped a tear from her cheek. "And then Daphne—'Oh, Libba, that was years ago.' When she'd *ruined* him!" Her eyes were drenched, but they flashed. "Nothing ever mattered to Daphne but Daphne, but she won't ever ruin anybody else!" She held her frosted head high.

Charho put out an imploring hand. "But what on earth did you do, precious?"

"I gave her pills. Daddy's pills. They were still in my evenin' purse from a Navy party we went to right before he died." She interrupted herself with a forced little laugh. "You were right the other afternoon, Sheila. I never throw anything out."

"Me neither," Sheila agreed. "So what did you do?"

Libba hesitated, reached for another tissue, and dabbed her eyes. "First, I cried in the powder room. They made me so mad! Then, when I started to powder my nose, I saw Daddy's pills." She held out her hand, as if still holding them. "I poured them out and looked at them for a long time—or maybe it only seemed like a long time. I decided to wait for her to set down her drink. She always did. Then I would fill it with pills and take it to her."

"You cannot tell me you meant to kill Daphne," Charho interrupted firmly. "You just wanted to make her real sick."

"No, Charho," Libba said—as sweet and patient as if declining a second cup of tea. "I knew exactly what I was doing, and why. I knew how many pills it would take to kill somebody. The doctor had warned me, in case Mama got in them. I didn't want to make Daphne sick. I wanted her to die. Her life for Eddie's—and mine. An eye for an eye. Isn't that what the Bible says?"

"Among other things," Sheila replied, "like 'forgive your enemies.' So you just dropped the pills in the drink."

Simple. And utterly practical. Who would have noticed? Everyone was used to Libba fiddling with things on the table. She would have been nearly invisible.

Helen's arm tightened around Libba's shoulders. "Honey—"

"No!" Libba flung her away. "It didn't work like that! The pills wouldn't dissolve!" She leaned back in the chair and her eyes were wide, remembering. "They wouldn't dissolve!"

"So?" Sheila asked, as matter-of-factly as she could.

"I poured her drink into another glass and put water in her glass, then I took it in the kitchen and ran it through the blender." She gave a high little laugh. "I told Clarinda I was mixin' myself a special drink. 'You sure need it,' she told me, and I said, 'Yes, Clarinda, I most certainly do.' Then I took the drink back to the dining room. I told myself if Daphne's glass wasn't still there, I'd pour that poisoned drink down the toilet." She gave a helpless little shrug. "But it *was* there, just waiting. I poured the extra water on the carpet. Daphne wouldn't ever know."

Libba's eyes met Sheila's. "How did *you* know it was me?"

"A piece that didn't fit the puzzle. You are always so helpful, but when Helen asked you to take the drink to Daphne, you left it for Hayden or Muffy to do. I began to wonder why."

Libba pressed a wadded tissue to her lips; her hand trembled. "I couldn't take it to her. I *thought* I could walk right up and hand her the drink, but when it came time, I couldn't even stand to be there to watch her drink it!"

"But you could dawdle calling nine-one-one, to give the pills more time to work," Sheila remembered. "You suggested paramedics as soon as I said 'Daphne's sick.' She could have needed an aspirin."

Libba shook her head. "Aspirin wouldn't have helped."

Helen touched her arm in puzzlement. "But why did you put some of the pills in Laura Grace's bottle?"

Libba sighed. "I had 'way too many of Daddy's pills in my hand. I'd seen Miss Hayden's bottle under the magnolia leaves earlier, so I stuck my extras in there until I could get them after the party. I thought Miss Hayden had gone off and forgotten her pills."

"I never forget anything," Laura Grace objected loudly. "Why did you shoot my gull?"

Libba looked at her in some confusion. "Your gull? Oh, in the park?" Laura Grace nodded. "I didn't mean to. It scared me." She gave Sheila a quick look. "I was just trying to scare you, too."

Laura Grace's black eyes snapped. "You scare me now. I'm tired of being scared. I'm going up to watch television with Teddy." Laura Grace stomped upstairs, caftan hiked to her blue-veined thighs.

Charho's voice was soothing. "Why you weren't thinkin' clearly, precious! You were temporarily insane!"

Libba flinched. Sheila knew from the way her eyes flickered that she was no longer mesmerized by the flow of the story and the soft voices of her friends. She no longer felt safe.

The next questions were risky. "What about Muffy? Did she know what you'd done? And try to blackmail you? Did you walk her outside and kill her, then pack a bag to make it look like she'd left?"

Libba rose. She walked toward the door and said in a flat voice, "I don't want to talk about this anymore." She slung her purse over one shoulder. Then she turned and looked back. Her blue eyes lingered regretfully on Helen and Charho.

Sheila hadn't really needed an answer. Who was it who had said "Our lives shape our ends?" That was certainly true of Muffy Merriwether.

But two more questions needed to be resolved. "Libba? What about the doubloon necklace? Did you take it when you went upstairs to collect glasses?" It was the only possibility left.

Libba seemed to have genuinely forgotten. "Why, yes, I did. Tell Hayden it's in the chimney in granddaddy's den. Pull on the third brick from the bottom on the right side. Mama used to talk about that hiding place. It's where Granddaddy kept his bourbon. I don't know why I took the old thing." She reached for the doorknob.

"What about Eddie?"

Libba's hand clenched into a fist. Her voice was little more than a whisper. "I saw him out on Helen's dock. I ran out of Hayden's for a minute—Clarinda didn't even know I'd been gone. I wanted to ask Eddie ... I don't know what it was now, but he wouldn't talk to me. He backed away. and then, he ... he fell. He was drunk, and he fell."

"But he couldn't swim. You didn't try to help him?"

Her lower lip trembled. "What kind of a life was he going to have? Tell me that!"

Charho rose like an avenging angel. "Oh, Libba! We'll never know what Eddie might have become. You took away all his choices, honey!"

Libba's blue eyes filled with tears. "You'll never know what I could have become, either, Charho! *Nobody* will ever know!"

She jerked open the door. "Don't try to follow me! I've got Daddy's gun in the car!" She dashed down the steps into the dusk.

"Libba!" Helen hurried to the door. Sheila got there almost as quickly as she did, Martha and Charho an instant later. They were all in time to see her get in the Toyota. But before she could even slam the door, Justin's big black Mercedes growled to a stop behind her.

Justin climbed out of the driver's seat. Tom Goren climbed out of the back—holding a gun. "Steady, now," they heard Tom say softly. "Steady. Walk toward the house."

Sheila thought he was speaking to Libba. Instead, to her amazement, Justin put his hands on top of his head and walked. Both men passed Libba without noticing her. "You don't know what you're doin', Tom. You'll never get away with this," Justin declared.

"Just tell Helen to bring me the keys, Justin. Nice and easy."

Helen went to the edge of the porch. "Justin?" she called. "What's goin' on? Where's Hayden?"

"Hayden's in the car, honey," Justin replied. "Hurt. And Tom wants the *Jack Three*. Would you get him the keys?" He could have been asking for a yard rake, but Sheila could see the expression on his face. Where were Crispin and Treye? And the police reinforcements?

"Where's Rob Wilmer?" she called as Helen ran into the house. "Were you working with him, Tom?"

Tom's big belly shook as he chuckled. "Lordy, Mrs. Travis, you sure got that one bassackwards! If you see old

Rob again, you give him my regards. Tell him I won't be unloadin' any more drugs *or* girlie flicks in Jacksonville. He's welcome to that box you saved."

In a tree, a night bird called. It was like the final, perfect note of a symphony—or the last piece of a puzzle sliding into place.

Helen turned on the porch light as she came out, dangling a key ring from one finger. "Here they are, Tom. Shall I throw them?"

"Bring them, Helen," he said, beckoning. She decended the steps and approached him carefully. When she got near, he reached toward her. "You and I are going for a ride," Tom told her. "That's the only way I know to keep Justin from comin' after me."

"No!" Libba cried behind him.

Tom turned, saw the gun she held. "Drop it, Libba!" he warned, shifting his own gun.

They fired at the same instant. She staggered and lay still, eyes wide in surprise. The big policeman fell forward, clutching his gut and moaning.

Justin seized Tom's gun. "Get help!" he yelled. "Get help quick or so help me, I'm gonna finish the bastard!" Tears streamed down his face.

When the ambulance had wailed away with Tom, and the forensic team (who certainly knew the address) had departed, the family gathered in the kitchen. Treye and Crispin had fetched barbeque, Charho had made her salad, and Sheila had made coffee. Nobody was eating.

Charho and Laura Grace consoled Teddy, who was still big-eyed and weepy about her Aunt Libba getting shot by the bad policeman. The women were all weepy, too, and the men's eyes red with unshed tears. Martha kept reaching out to touch Hayden, as if to reassure herself that he was all right. "I just have a bump on the head," he told her testily. "I'm going to be fine."

He would probably recover far sooner than Helen. She sat like a zombie, repeating, "It's like a war. You don't lose this many people unless there's a war." Justin clasped her hand, giving it little pats from time to time.

Crispin heated up Sheila's coffee and nodded toward one unexpected guest. "Have you asked adequate forgiveness, honey?"

Sheila gave the guest a rueful smile. "I don't know. Have I, Rob?"

Rob Wilmer shrugged. "Hey, Sheila, you got everything right except the name. That's not bad for a stranger in town. How were you to know I'd been working with the police to figure out how a steady stream of pornography flicks and paraphernalia have been coming in? I think Tom was behind that, too. I'm just sorry you stumbled into a bit of my research. Let me assure you, it made feel as sick as you looked." He smiled sourly.

"What happened after you high-tailed it up the drive this afternoon?" Charho asked.

"Yeah," Justin seconded her. "Where'd you go?"

Rob chuckled. "Into the bushes outside the gate. Then when you all roared down Ortega Boulevard, I went over to Hayden's, let myself in, and called some *honest* cops."

Hayden shook his head in disbelief. "And we were riding all over Ortega with a crooked one, lookin' for you! Finally I caught on to somethin' funny—he wouldn't let me use Justin's cellular phone to call for help." He patted the back of his head gingerly. "That's when he hit me and took Justin back home."

Justin sighed. "You think Muffy was in with Tom, and Daphne found out about it somehow?"

The women exchanged glances, and came to a silent consensus. None of them said a word.

Rob shook his head. "I guess we'll never know. But I do know that Tom could have killed Lance. There was nearly an hour at Hayden's party when I couldn't find him. He could easily have gone for a boat ride and come back. He must have laughed himself sick thinking about leaving poor Lance's body at my dock. No wonder you thought I was guilty!"

"And it was Tom, not you, who called the goons from the hospital." Sheila said thoughtfully.

Rob nodded. "You were smart to pick up on the method, though. Tom told me he'd had to stop by the john. He must have stopped to call the goons, instead. When you accused me is when *I* first suspected Tom was our current smuggler. That's why I had to get to that box of evidence before he did."

Sheila leaned forward. "Justin, one thing still puzzles me. You had a snapshot of Eddie on a sailboat, but he hated the water."

Justin nodded. "Yeah. Daphne . . . Daphne wanted a picture of him in his bathing suit. He posed on the bow of my sailboat, but he wouldn't let me take it away from the dock."

"Speaking of taking things away," Charho remembered, "I have one piece of good news." She gave the other women a quick look. "Hayden, Libba put away your necklace for safekeeping, in the chimney of her granddaddy's den. Do you know where that is?"

"She did? I never thought to ask *her*. She must have meant the storeroom behind the kitchen. In the chimney, huh?"

"Pull the third brick from the bottom, right side," Sheila quoted.

"Well." He stood, obviously eager for some kind of action. "Who wants to have a look?"

"Me! Me!" Teddy slid off her stool and jumped up and down.

"I'll go, too," Rob offered. "I love hidden places."

Helen sighed. "I don't know what's gonna happen to Sparrow. She and Jack are so young, and I'm not sure they're really anything except good friends. And Libba can't have left her much."

Laura Grace looked across the table at Sheila. "There's a moon tonight. Let's go get the treasure." She wriggled down off her stool. "Justin, you got a shovel?"

He was ready for a diversion, "Sure, Ellgie. How big
a shovel? A little trowel, or are you plannin' to do some serious diggin'?"

"Serious enough." She pursed her lips and looked
from Justin to Crispin. "Justin, you're not banged up.
Maybe you'd better come, too."

With a shrug, he rose. "Come on, Sheila. Let's go see
what she wants."

Carrying a shovel big enough for serious digging, they
crossed the lawn between the two houses. Laura Grace
came to a stop beneath Hayden's kneeling oak. "Let me
see now." She peered toward Justin's house, shifted a bit,
peered again, and nodded. "Yep, dig here."

Justin flexed his muscles and stuck the shovel's nose
into the soil. "Ellgie, you do know that there haven't been
any real pirates in Ortega for nearly two hundred years,
don't you?"

She bent at the waist, staring at the ground as if to lift
a treasure by personal magnetism. If anyone could do it,
Sheila thought, this old woman could.

Justin sighed. "Okay, here goes. Do you know how far
I have to dig?"

The hole was less than two feet deep when the shovel
struck metal.

This time, the mood around the kitchen island was con-
siderably lighter. In the center gleamed the doubloon
necklace from its chimney hiding place. Around it lay
pearls, rubies, diamonds, and the black box they'd lain in
for who knew how long. Teddy held a ruby to the light
like a tiny kaleidoscope. Charho reached for the box and
headed for the pantry. In a moment she returned and held
it up so they could see one small gleam. "Silver! Dreadfully tarnished, of course—"

"Looks like you're a rich man, brother," Justin told
Hayden as he washed his hands at the sink. "I'll be asking
you for a contribution to my campaign fund."

Laura Grace's fist came down on the island top. "No!"

They all looked at her, astonished. "They're not yours!" She dragged the pile of gems toward her and cradled her hand around them. "He buried them to keep them safe. For the family."

"Whose family?" Crispin demanded. "Do pirates have families?"

"Not a pirate," Laura Grace told him sharply. "The judge. He buried them by moonlight. Then—" She clutched her heart and collapsed forward.

"Ellgie!" Teddy cried in horror.

The old woman opened one eye. "I'm not dead, Teddy. I'm showing you. He buried the treasure, then he died. Don't trust banks, he told me the week before."

Martha was better at translating Laura Grace than the rest of them. "You mean old Judge Covington, dear? He put all his money into jewels back in 1929? And buried them the night of his heart attack?"

"Of course, Martha. I saw him digging. Went to bed. Didn't see him fall." She smiled and held up a diamond, admiring its sparkle. "It's all for Sparrow. I like sparrows." Laura Grace wriggled her shoulders in her caftan. "I'm getting hot, Martha. We need to get home. These clothes are smotherin' me."

Before they all went up to bed, Crispin stopped Justin. "Clear up one more thing for me, buddy. Teddy said at lunch the other day she'd heard you say you'd do absolutely anything you had to to get elected. Did that mean up to, or including, murder?"

Justin looked puzzled, then threw back his head and laughed heartily. "Neither. Hayden and I were talking about the health care issue, and he asked what I'd do about the insurance company if there was a conflict of interest. I told him I'd give it to the kids, put it in a trust, do anything I had to to get elected."

Crispin put an arm around his shoulders. "Well, that's certainly a load off my mind."

Monday,
January 1

~~~~~~~~~~~~~~~~~~~~~~~~~

The next morning, Laura Grace refused to come out when Sheila and Crispin stopped by the Park Lane to say good-bye. "The gulls said sadness today," she called through her closed door. "I don't like sadness, so I'm not having any."

It seemed sensible enough, but Sheila was sorry to miss seeing her. Who knew if Laura Grace would be around next time?

After kissing Martha and promising to return, she went with Teddy down to the park to give Crispin a few minutes alone with his aunt.

"I wonder who the winged statue really is," she said as they approached it.

"Just a dumb old war memorial. There's a plaque." Teddy danced around the fountain wall to show her.

Sheila read:

SPIRITUALIZED LIFE SYMBOLIZED BY THE
WINGED FIGURE OF YOUTH RISES
TRIUMPHANT FROM THE SWIRL OF WAR'S
CHAOS WHICH ENGULFS HUMANITY AND
FACES THE FUTURE COURAGEOUSLY.

Sheila couldn't help thinking about Sparrow, and Treye. Their young lives had been engulfed by chaos

which, as Helen said, was a kind of war. Would they—
would their generation—make anything better of the
world than their parents had? Why did each generation expect its youth to be able to accomplish that which it had
not been willing to achieve itself?

"Ellgie!" Teddy cried in delight as a gruff voice spoke
at Sheila's elbow.

"I forgot there was also hope. You can stand sadness
when there's hope." The black eyes looked far too young
for the wrinkled face, a map of nearly ninety years. She
wore the same black sweater and orchid skirt she'd worn
once before.

Sheila smiled, and pointed to the plaque. "I was just
reading about you—and Teddy. Spiritualized life, rising
triumphant out of chaos, facing the future courageously."

Laura Grace peered at the plaque and grimaced. "Yep.
That's us, all right." She put a sweatered arm around them
both. "All of us."

To the fisherman down the sidewalk, they must look
like stair steps, Sheila thought fondly. So they were. Stair
steps through history.

"Ready, honey?" Crispin called. Oh, but he looked
great in that blue-and-gold warm-up suit, the wind ruffling
his black hair and the sun glinting off his mirrored sunglasses.

"Don't go! I'm gonna miss you!" Teddy cried wildly,
flinging her arms around Sheila and nearly squeezing the
breath out of her.

"I'll miss you, too," Sheila promised, amazed to dis-
cover it was true.

When Teddy stepped back, Laura Grace reached out
her arms and wrapped them around Sheila's midsection,
laying her cheek against Sheila's breast. "You come back,
now. You hear me?"

Then without waiting for a reply, the old woman
dropped her arms and trudged stolidly toward the Park
Lane. Teddy hesitated, then danced after her with a small
wave.

Sheila could have sworn she saw, above both their shoulders, the shadow of wings.

Then she headed down the sidewalk to face her own future.

Courageously.

About the Author

PATRICIA SPRINKLE lives in Miami, Florida, with her husband and two sons. She is the author of *Murder at Markham, Murder in the Charleston Manor, Murder on Peachtree Street, Somebody's Dead in Snellville, Death of a Dunwoody Matron*, and *A Mystery Bred in Buckhead. Deadly Secrets on the St. Johns* is her seventh Sheila Travis mystery.

SOUTHERN MYSTERIES
FROM
PATRICIA SPRINKLE

Death of A Dunwoody Matron
LIFESTYLES OF THE RICH AND FATAL

Dunwoody is the kind of place where opulent homes and luxury cars are the measure of a person's worth . . . where the veneer of suburban serenity and gracious hospitality is rarely shaken. But behind the tennis dates and teas, the cocktail parties and mixers, whispers of scandal—and murder—run as rampant as in any dry, dusty Southern town.   ___29887-9 $4.99/$5.99 Canada

A Mystery Bred in Buckhead
SOUTHERN HOSPITALITY AND COLD-BLOODED MURDER

In genteel Atlanta society there are worse crimes than murder—such as missing Rippen Delacourt's annual Christmas party. As amateur sleuth Shelia Travis joins her family and cherished friends at Rip's gala, she never suspects that before the end of the evening, a long-missing, priceless manuscript will turn up in the hands of a disgruntled servant . . . and dislodge enough closeted skeletons to fill Rip's guest list.   ___56897-3 $4.99/$5.99

Ask for these books at your local bookstore or use this page to order.

Please send me the books I have checked above. I am enclosing $____ (add $2.50 to cover postage and handling). Send check or money order, no cash or C.O.D.'s, please.

Name _____

Address _____

City/State/Zip _____

Send order to: Bantam Books, Dept. MC 5, 2451 S. Wolf Rd., Des Plaines, IL 60018
Allow four to six weeks for delivery.
Prices and availability subject to change without notice.   MC 5 9/95

BANTAM MYSTERY COLLECTION